Helen Evans lives and works in Stratford-upon-Avon. She has a Master's degree from the Shakespeare Institute and has always loved Shakespeare.

H M Evans

THE SHAKESPEARE SILENCE

'Truth Will Come to Light, *Murder* Cannot be Hid Long*'*

H M EVANS

ISBN 978-0-9935844-0-4

Published by H M Evans
First published in 2016

Cover: lime walk, Stratford-upon-Avon

To Stephen,
Elliott and Madeleine

PROLOGUE

Eight o'clock on the night of Wednesday the
20th of April, 1864

Missing the heady scent of hops that pervaded the town during
the brewing season, the air in Ely Court, Stratford-upon-Avon
sat motionless, weighed down by the stench of soot and boiled
mutton. Despite its best efforts, the fresh April breeze found it
impossible to penetrate the long, dank passageway.

Two figures entered the murky darkness. One staggered,
clearly inebriated and the other followed closely behind. Was
he now supporting the drunkard or was he holding him in
place against the wall? Grasping the intoxicated man's head, he
smashed it backwards before this unfair fight descended to the
mud-soaked depths of the alley. As the victim gasped for air,
the attacker, eyes closed, clasped his hands around the throat
and squeezed until the Adam's apple ceased to rise and fall, the
hissing rasp of air had stopped and a small pool of blood had
started to form.

Working man's hat pulled down, shoulders hunched, the
attacker followed his well-rehearsed route, weaving through

the town's dingy back alleys until he emerged onto the clean pavements of Henley Street where gas lamps threw a warm light onto a polished version of Shakespeare's Birthplace. Scrubbed to within an inch of its life, all trace of the ordinary grime of three centuries of daily grind had been removed from the building solely to please the thousands of visitors who made the pilgrimage to its door. To the young man, who had just claimed the life of one with whom he had grown up, the sixteenth-century house offered some small comfort. Its most famous occupant had provided him not only with his livelihood, but also an opportunity to win acclaim for his portrayal of Romeo at the town's Festival to celebrate the three hundredth anniversary of Shakespeare's birth. Tonight, he had to play another role though: not penned by Shakespeare this time, but one that he had written himself.

Standing a stone's throw from Shakespeare's Birthplace, the familiarity of the White Lion Hotel allowed the attacker's shoulders to drop and his back to straighten. Discarding his hat, he ran up the stairs to face his audience of five. His father, who was seated by the window with Mr Patrick Drew, Mayor of Stratford-upon-Avon and Dr Edmund Clemens, had not noticed him, neither had their close friend, Mr Archibald Gastrell. His son, Mr Robert Gastrell, however, gesticulated to him, gathering him into their intimate circle, entirely oblivious of what had just occurred a matter of yards away.

*

Meanwhile, in the alley, a small pair of sharp blue eyes knew that they would never forget the face of the young man who, moments ago, had pulled his woollen hat down in an attempt to cover the escaping wisps of curly yellow hair.

CHAPTER 1

'Welcome to Stratford-upon-Avon, Mr Gastrell, Mrs Gastrell.'

Christopher Gastrell offered his first name before Mrs Chase had a chance to repeat the surname that she'd addressed to his parents. Thomas and Bridget did likewise, but Mrs Chase remained steadfastly, Mrs Chase.

As the owner of what had looked from the outside to be a townhouse, but which once inside revealed itself to be three purpose-built flats, Mrs Chase was eager to show off the attractions of the accommodation to her three new visitors to the town.

'It's a beautiful flat,' Christopher heard his mother agree.

'The apartment,' Mrs Chase corrected, 'was re-appointed last year. As you can see, we gave it a complete make-over.'

And so she continued on and on, but all Christopher could think of was the email. It had come out of the blue last night and although he knew every word by heart, he had to see the actual words again and for that he needed to be on his own.

It wasn't how he'd planned the last day of his thirties – thinking about Monica. When his mother had suggested the family birthday trip a year ago, he'd jumped at the chance to spend time with his parents. He hated that they were surprised when he phoned – pleasantly surprised, but surprised all the same. And London had become a smaller place. His friends had moved to the suburbs to start families, but he'd held onto the life he knew; loving the all-night parties, film nights and shared meals, he'd happily crashed on any available sofa. He'd blinked and somehow a decade had passed and his new friends were all a lot younger than him. Not quite belonging with either the old or the new friends, a sense of loneliness had crept into his life.

'Let me offer you this leaflet,' he heard Mrs Chase say as she thrust a small pamphlet into his hand. 'It gives the history of this site. You wouldn't believe it, but Ely Court used to be the worst slum in Stratford and now it's one of the most sought-after areas!' she announced with a wave of her hand that suggested she might have cleared the slum single-handedly herself. 'It was demolished in 1864 when the street was widened and new tenements were built as part of a major improvement plan in the town. These were replaced by apartment blocks in the nineteen-sixties. Five years ago, they were taken down and we bought off-plan when we saw the architect's drawings for these attractive townhouses.'

'I'll fetch the cases,' Christopher offered, thinking it would give him a moment on his own, but his father wanted to help so it would have to wait.

Keeping a few paces back from his father, who'd insisted on taking the largest case, Christopher touched the moustache of holiday stubble that had already started to make an appearance and watched uncomfortably as his father struggled to control the small wheels on the uneven paving slabs. A painful-looking bump against his ankle stopped him in his tracks and had Christopher reaching forwards.

'Thanks, son. I don't know what your mother's got in here.'

Although now encumbered by two cases, Christopher had to slow his pace to a crawl to match his father's. At six foot four, he'd inherited his height from his father's side of the family, but these days he seemed to tower over him. He couldn't put his finger on exactly when he'd noticed that his father could no longer be described as tall. It had just happened and it made him want to make the most of his time with them both, but first he needed to read the email.

Five minutes later, Christopher was preparing to leave the apartment. He'd told his parents that he wanted to take some photographs for his portfolio, but he was also going to put together an album as a 'thank you' to them for going ahead with the trip in spite of what had happened to them all three months ago.

The overcast April afternoon would suit his particular style of photography; the low contrast in the weather conditions would bring out the grey tones of his black and white pallet. He eased the camera rucksack between his shoulder blades and relaxed into the familiar pressure that it exerted on the small of his back, remembering just in time, as he turned the corner of Ely Court, to wave to his mother who was standing in the doorway to catch the last sight of him as if he'd be gone for ages. But of course, it was only to be expected after what they'd all been through.

It was happening again. Rapid, shallow breaths and an accelerated heart beat. It was as if his breathing and the beating of his heart were no longer automatic. As if he couldn't take it for granted that they'd continue. As if his brain had forgotten how to keep him alive. He'd do what he'd learnt to do over these last difficult months. Simplify. Photography would calm him. Then he'd reread the email. And then what? Well, it was a start.

With a camera in your hand, nobody questioned what you were doing. He could spend as much time as he wanted in front of Shakespeare's Birthplace and no one would bat an eyelid. Shutting his eyes for a moment, he focused on drawing the fresh air into his nostrils and steadily out through his parted lips. Having calmed his breathing, he unclipped the straps of the sling containing his tripod. Steadying it in an upright position as a parent supports a toddler on the cusp of walking, he secured the camera, squeezed the quick-release lever and tilted it ever so slightly upwards. Squinting through the eyepiece, he pulled the zoom to frame the final image of Shakespeare's first home. The moment had arrived.

Reluctantly relinquishing his physical connection to the camera to avoid any disturbance of the image, Christopher locked the cable release pin in place and pushed the remote control button. The green light of the camera was answered by a pulse of red followed by two clicks, at which point the image flashed onto the live view screen for five seconds before it disappeared to be replaced by his peering reflection. In the last few months, he'd noticed that when his face was at rest, he looked as if he was scowling and it made him look old – maybe not old, but certainly not youthful. For so many years, he'd played on his looks and where had it got him? A big fat nowhere! He was determined that this holiday was going to be brilliant – he'd re-establish the relationship that he'd enjoyed with his parents up until his mid-twenties when he'd gone to London and they'd be a family again.

Now he was ready.

I should have contacted you sooner. I need you to know. You have a son. If you want to know more email me. Your choice. Monica.

Three years ago, Monica had abruptly finished their relationship and removed herself from his life. It had taken him a long time to get over her, but now he almost never thought of her – until yesterday. Within the space of three months, he'd gone from second son to only son and now to father. No wonder he kept having these damn panic attacks.

After the initial shock yesterday, he'd been so angry at her that he'd almost fired off a reply where every other word was an expletive, but he'd stopped himself pressing send just in time. In the small sleep-deprived hours of last night, he'd remembered how much his parents had liked Monica and he'd decided to talk his reply through with them first. They'd been going on for years about having a grandchild and after all the crap that had happened lately, they'd be so pleased and he'd be able to send a reply that didn't totally cock his chances up of ever seeing his child.

His first opportunity to tell his parents had been earlier that morning when he'd arrived at their house to pick them up, but their cases were in the hall and his father had opened the door in his coat – there hadn't been time. There'd be less pressure on the journey, he'd told himself. They wouldn't be face to face so it'd be less intense. Perfect. He'd keep to the speed limit to avoid having to concentrate on slowing down for speed cameras and police cars and he'd just come out with it – easy as that. On his first attempt, he'd formed the words and thought he'd said them out loud, but neither his father nor mother had responded. It was like one of those dreams where you shout for help at the top of your voice but no one can hear you.

Shit! It was such a big thing to suddenly launch into. How do you start? 'By the way, Mum and Dad, you've got a grandchild.' After all, he didn't want to give them a heart attack! Then he'd remembered the game he and David used to play in the car on long journeys – when the next blue car passes, you have to go through with a dare. The first time a blue car obliged, he'd turned his face a little so that he could see his father's profile, only to find that he'd closed his eyes.

As soon as his father had woken, he'd glanced in the mirror to check that his mother hadn't now fallen asleep, but only the top of her head had been visible and he couldn't quite tell. At a red light, he'd turned to see that she was engrossed in a book, smiling to herself. It was the first time he'd seen her smile since the funeral and there was no way on earth he'd disturb her with his news. It did his heart good to see her so happy and he'd kept watching, enjoying her enjoyment until the horn of the car behind forced his attention from her. How did she manage to read in the car? On the very few occasions when he'd tried it, it'd made him instantly nauseous. He supposed that there would always be things that separated you from your parents: some inconsequential like reading in the car, but some so enormous you wonder how you can possibly be related. He thanked his lucky stars he'd not left it too late to rebuild the relationship.

But here he was – in Stratford-upon-Avon and he still hadn't managed to find the right words or the right moment to tell them. But he would. Having taken a little longer photographing than he'd meant to, he hurried back to Ely Court.

*

'How did you get on photographing this afternoon, love?' Thomas heard his wife ask the minute their son set foot in the apartment.

'It was great, Mum. The dull weather was perfect for me, but I thought there'd be fewer tourists. They were everywhere!'

'Well, I for one am glad it's brightening up a bit now. It'll look lovely as the sun goes down over the river. I can't wait to get on board. We wanted to book something really special for you.'

Thomas had thought that Bridget would want to celebrate Christopher's birthday quietly in the circumstances, but when he'd told her that he would cancel the booking in Stratford-upon-Avon, she'd said no, she wanted to go ahead with it. He'd been taken aback at her decision, but he admired her determination to carry on as if nothing had happened. But the problem was, everything had changed. Up until January, he'd been happy in the knowledge that his elder son would carry on the family's architect's practice and would settle down with Teresa and have a family. Sooner rather than later, his son had said. And they'd all laughed when he'd joked that finally he'd get those grandchildren to continue the Gastrell name. How wrong could you be?

A couple of hours later, Thomas found himself facing several steep wooden steps leading into the restaurant boat. Gesturing to Bridget and Christopher to go in front of him so that he could climb down without holding them up, Thomas edged gingerly along, certain that he looked older than his years. Time seemed to have caught up with him recently, but Christopher hardly looked his age. He was a good-looking lad. The damp evening air had even brought a slight curl to the ends of Christopher's hair, reminding Thomas of when Christopher was little, having a water fight with his older brother. Inseparable they were – always looking out for one another.

He'd better get a move on or they'd be wondering why he was taking so long, but he needn't have worried. By the time he reached the boat's narrow carpeted aisle, Bridget and Christopher were seated opposite one another by the window, laughing and pointing at something or other. Although there were only four years between them, Thomas knew that Bridget looked younger than seventy-two and he was proud when they were out walking and he could see people looking at her. Somehow, her hair had retained some of its black and the rest was a dark grey, not white like his. Her bird's nest, as she called it, made her look a good ten years younger than him and he told himself what a lucky devil he was. He really must find the time to tell her how good she looked and sooner rather than later.

Whilst the boat's location, level with the pavement, afforded his wife and son a view of the Royal Shakespeare Theatre, Thomas's worm's eye view allowed only a close-up of the arriving diners' shoes: a strange mixture of practical footwear and stiletto heels. And even this view was obscured a moment later when a shadow passed over their table and a man walked along the narrowest of ledges that clung to the side of the boat. The unexpected intrusion was accompanied by a deep revving of the engine as the boat edged forward to enter the lock chamber, causing him to feel a little light-headed. A slight sideward movement accompanied their descent into semi-darkness and despite now feeling nauseous, he smiled at Bridget and Christopher who were chatting away nineteen to the dozen – glass half full they both were and he loved them for it.

They'd hardly left the confines of the canal to enter the wider expanse of the River Avon when Bridget announced, 'we have something to give you, darling.'

'I thought we were going to wait until after the meal,' Thomas whispered.

'Well I can't wait!'

'It sounds mysterious, Mum. In fact, I've got something I wanted to...'

'What is it, love?'

'Erm...nothing, Mum. Let's order first. I can't imagine what you have for me. It's not even my birthday yet.'

The waitress stood next to Bridget, but Thomas noticed she couldn't keep her eyes off Christopher. They all waited. This was one of those minute shifts in their relationship. Up until three months ago, he would have given the waitress his order and Bridget's, but recently she'd started to give her own. When she said nothing, Thomas looked at her. Perhaps she'd changed her mind and wanted him to order, but no, she was opening the menu again and scanning it hurriedly. There were only two choices for the starter and two for the main, so why wasn't she saying anything to the waitress?

'This is the mystery, Christopher. Open it,' Bridget urged, thrusting a large rolled-up piece of paper across the table when she'd finally made her selection.

'I'll just order, Mum.'

'Oh...oh, of course, sorry, I hadn't noticed,' she said,

retrieving the offering.

'Okay, I'm all yours now. What's this mysterious gift?'

When Bridget looked completely bemused by their son's question, Thomas said, nodding at the paper balancing on his wife's lap, 'you know, love, the present.'

'Yes, yes, here it is.'

As Thomas watched his son pull the ends of the ribbon, the over-sized, thick white paper released from its bond, sprang open to reveal passport-sized photographs: black and white in the top half that gradually gave way to colour. The very first one showed an old man, but some pictured younger adults and there was Bridget's beautifully neat handwriting underneath each picture. Christopher eased the roll of paper open with his right hand until it had completely unravelled down to the last entry. The last entry. Almost as soon as he'd registered the fifth of January, that unforgettable date, Thomas saw Christopher's eyes dart back up amongst the comfort of the black and white photographs, just as his own had done when Bridget had written their elder son's name.

'It's your family tree, Dad. I didn't know you were interested in family history.'

'Your family tree too. We started researching over a year ago and then we asked a genealogist to help us. We've got all the certificates at home, but there are some intriguing gaps.'

'It's fascinating, thank you both,' Christopher said, rolling it up as they all watched his brother's photograph disappear into its papery cocoon.

Thomas placed his hand on the paper so that he could point to one name towards the top of the sheet.

'It only goes back to the very late seventeen hundreds so far, but we want to go further. Look at the entry for the 8th of

November, 1830.'

Thomas watched as Christopher peered at a passport-sized black and white photograph of a Victorian gentleman.

'Read the name,' Bridget encouraged. 'I think he looks a lot like you. He's certainly got your height and black hair.'

'Robert Archibald Gastrell.'

'It's a clue to your main present, darling.'

'I can't begin to guess. What relation is Robert Gastrell?'

'He's your great-great-great-great-grandfather. We know some details about him, but there's a lot we don't know. We've got a copy of his baptism record but not his death certificate. It's strange, but it's quite the opposite with regards to his son. We have a death certificate but no birth certificate for him and there's no record that Robert ever had a wife!' Thomas replied.

'I suppose you could say that the whole trip is a clue,' Bridget said, returning the conversation to the birthday present.

'Stratford-upon-Avon, 1830 and my great-great-great-great-granddad, Robert Gastrell,' Christopher said, shaking his head.

'Try to guess. What comes to mind?'

'Well, Shakespeare as it's Stratford-upon-Avon.'

'Yes, that's another clue.'

'I've no idea. You're going to have to tell me.'

'Well, you'll have to wait until tomorrow morning when all will be revealed,' Bridget said, gleefully.

Looking out as the banks of the River Avon glided by, Thomas considered how little he knew about Christopher's life compared to his elder brother's. After his degree in architecture, he'd taken up photography and had become very successful, but whenever he'd asked Christopher about his work, he hadn't wanted to talk about himself, always preferring to turn the conversation back to architecture. When he'd asked him if he had a business card, he'd read ABIPP, ARPS after his name. Impressed by the qualifications, Thomas had asked what they represented, only to have Christopher reply that they didn't say anything about his quality as a photographer – they simply helped him to secure clients. Thomas regretted that he'd missed his opportunity back then to say how proud he was that Christopher had made his own way in the world. But, he'd make it up to him this holiday and when they gave him his birthday present tomorrow, he'd find out what Christopher's plans were for the future. And then he'd have to decide whether or not to tell his wife and son about Sylvia.

*

In stark contrast to the daytime, there were few people around Stratford-upon-Avon on this Monday evening as the restaurant cruiser docked after their meal. A tourist town out of hours looked a little sinister, Bridget decided.

As soon as they entered the apartment, Christopher excused himself saying that he wanted to pop out and take some night shots. He looked as if he hadn't slept well and she was convinced that he'd been about to tell them something on the boat, but had decided against it. She was sure he wanted to talk about his brother and she would've been happy to listen, but he'd stopped himself – probably to spare them. He should talk if he wanted to. They all should.

Thomas said he wanted a shower, so Bridget picked up the leaflet that Mrs Chase had left on the coffee table. Looking at the first black and white photograph, she saw four small, ragged children standing in front of a dingy house. She could just about make out that the smallest, who was leaning on a stick, had over-sized boots, but that the others seemed to have bare feet. The caption didn't offer much information.

'Ely Court, an alley off Ely Street, 1864, photographer: Paul Brook.'

Poor things, not much hope of any sort of a life for them, she thought as she moved onto the black and white tenement photograph of 1865. They certainly got a move on with the improvement plan that Mrs Chase had mentioned – it must have made an enormous difference to their young lives. A colour image of the nineteen-sixties' apartment block complete with white boards and an expanse of glass took her back to her first home as a married woman and the last one brought the site up to date with the brick townhouse in which she was sitting.

The black and white photographs reminded her of Christopher's photography. She'd taken an interest in it right from the start, but he never liked to say much about it. When his black and white architectural photographs had appeared alongside the colourful landscapes that she liked to look at in the Sunday magazines, she couldn't believe it. He hadn't said a word! She'd phoned up straight away to congratulate him and the next call had been to David to make sure he bought a copy too. David. Goodness, she wished she wasn't sitting here on her own. It gave her too much time to think. Where was that book she'd started on the journey?

Eight children were born over a period of twenty-two years from 1558 to 1580. The first two died in infancy but the third was William Shakespeare. At his death in 1616 he left two married daughters and one granddaughter.

> *However, within fifty-four years of his death Shakespeare's direct family line had completely died out.*

She'd really gone off this book with all its negative talk of legacy. Not to worry, she'd brought several others with her in case she couldn't sleep. She did so love to read. And since they'd got the computer, she'd become obsessed with history – there was no stopping her.

'And as for William Shakespeare, he couldn't have left a better legacy,' she said out loud as if the writer would hear her.

Thomas's shower seemed to be taking forever and she needed him to take her mind off the visit to Christopher's birthday present tomorrow. Excitement was getting the better of her and she was convinced she'd give something away. When Christopher had agreed immediately to the birthday trip last year, she'd almost cried. It was such fun having him around and in his company today, she'd had fewer of those irritating little memory lapses that had started earlier this year. It took her brain a while to catch up, that was all, but when it did, it was perfectly good and she now liked to think of her brain as almost separate to herself – giving it time to think, as she would give her legs time to rest if they were aching.

She really ought to go to bed. Tomorrow was going to be busy. Thomas's brother, Charles would be joining them in the flat above, together with his daughter, Joanne and her children, Peter and Madeleine. It was such a shame that David's widow, Teresa, who had initially agreed to join them with her sister, had telephoned in tears three days ago unable to come, but she understood. The top flat would remain untouched for the duration of their stay. She remembered how, when she'd found the townhouse converted into three flats, she'd said to Thomas what a perfect fit it was for them all and that it was too good to be true. And so it had proved. But, she wasn't going to dwell on it. Nothing was going to spoil this trip.

Getting up from the sofa, she was about to go into the bedroom to get one of her other books when the door opened. Thomas's luxurious white hair was slicked to the side, still damp and lying unnaturally tight to the scalp looking as if he'd attempted to copy the male models' waxed hairstyles in the magazines and she thought of their younger days and how it'd been love at first sight for them both.

'Do you know what time they arrive tomorrow?' she asked.

'I think they're coming about three, but it'll depend on the traffic.'

'It will be good to see Joanne and the children. I hope there'll be enough for them to do.'

'They'll be bound to have brought all their electronic gizmos.'

'I was thinking of the theatre trip, but Charles said they were looking forward to it.'

She thought she saw her husband wince at the mention of his elder brother, but he must have had some soap in his eye.

'Hi,' Christopher called as he entered the room, weighed down by photography bags.

'One minute I'm on my own and the next, I've got both of you,' she said, smiling. 'How lucky am I!'

'You've not been out long. Is everything all right?' Thomas asked.

'It started raining, but I managed to get several shots of

Shakespeare's Birthplace. At night, you could almost imagine what it looked like four hundred years ago.'

'We thought of all sorts of places to book. And then the house...erm...and then Stratford-upon-Avon came up,' Bridget said, wishing she'd gone to bed earlier.

But neither Thomas nor Christopher had noticed her slip-up. Tomorrow would be perfect.

CHAPTER 2

Present day: Tuesday 20 April 10.30am

They were in the kitchen the next morning, toasting Christopher's fortieth birthday with champagne and smoked salmon rather than the breakfast of coffee that his head was telling him he needed. For the first time in ages, even his contact lenses seemed to be rebelling. He'd seen two o'clock before he'd turned his phone to mute, staring at the email until the letters appeared to change places and he'd woken up abruptly at six. He'd been about to tell them on the boat yesterday, but then his mother had said she had an early birthday present and he couldn't ruin her moment.

'This is the second clue to your main present, darling,' she said offering him a package wrapped in tissue paper.

Standing out against the raised bands of dark green and red leather on the book's spine, he could see the gold lettering of the word *Journal*.

'Whose is it?'

'Open it. She wrote her name, or should I say names,

inside.'

Looking at the first two mottled pages, he wondered why on earth his parents would think that an old diary would be of any interest to him. A glance at their faces, however, persuaded him to continue. The dark cream paper of the first handwritten entry showed hardly any damage, but the strokes of brown ink had bled into the paper making some of the words a little difficult to read.

'*Anne Dawson, 1st August 1860, my nineteenth year* and underneath it says, *Mrs Anne Drew, 10th April 1861.*'

'She writes about Robert Gastrell,' his father announced.

'How did you come to have her diary?'

'It was in a box in your grandfather's loft and when he died we moved it into ours and, to be honest, forgot about it until your mother decided we needed to put our things in order when...you know.'

To cover the awkward moment, when even his mother seemed to be stumped as to what to say next, Christopher threw out some questions.

'Why would Anne Drew write about Robert Gastrell? Who was she? A relative?'

'No, Anne Drew was nobody important. She lived in Stratford that's all and wrote about the celebrations of the three hundredth anniversary of Shakespeare's birth in 1864 and about Robert Gastrell because he built the temporary theatre for the occasion.'

'We haven't got time to discuss the diary now, Thomas, we'll be setting out in a moment,' Bridget said. 'Christopher, we're going to visit your birthday present this morning. Here's a photograph of it.'

Inside the envelope that his mother had placed in front of him, Christopher saw a snapshot of a detached red-brick house, probably Victorian in age. The house was obviously a clue, but he had no idea where to begin. Looking from the photograph to his mother, then his father, he hoped that their faces might help, but they just stared back as if it was all perfectly clear.

'I give up. I don't know what the clue is.'

'It's not another clue, it's a photograph of your present,' laughed his mother.

'This house is my present?'

'Yes! We've bought the house...'

'We're buying the house,' corrected Thomas, 'and all being well we'll exchange contracts and complete the purchase in three weeks' time.'

'You've bought a house...for me? What are you talking about?' Christopher said, as if they'd just told him that they'd – he couldn't think what exactly, but that they'd done something really awful.

In a split-second, Christopher realised that of course they hadn't bought a house for him, they'd bought a house for *them, for their two sons*. And what a lovely, generous idea. They'd obviously thought it would get him and David back together again as they'd been when they were younger.

'We're going to see it at eleven! It was built in the eighteen-sixties by Robert Gastrell. When I found out that Robert and his father, Archibald had both been architects, I couldn't believe the coincidence, so I asked a researcher to find out which buildings they'd designed. Unfortunately, he couldn't trace any remaining buildings that Archibald had designed, but he came across the house that Robert designed. When we wrote to the owner, her son, Nicholas Chambers replied that if his mother were ever to sell the house he'd let us know. As good as his word, he gave us first refusal.'

'Nicholas will show us around, but the best bit is, there's an American student called Nancy who house-sits for him and she'll transcribe the diary for us so we can find out more about Robert Gastrell's involvement with the 1864 Festival,' Bridget added.

'So, Nicholas doesn't live in the house?'

'No, when his mother died he offered it to Nancy while he sorted through everything.'

'You said Nancy is a student. Where does she study?'

'At the Shakespeare Institute here in Stratford where Nicholas used to be a lecturer and she's been researching the 1864 Festival. It's one of the most significant events the town has ever hosted.'

'Here's a better photograph of Robert Gastrell.'

Christopher had seen the tiny image on the family tree, but he couldn't make out any details. This photograph, about A5 in size, however, clearly showed a Victorian gentleman formally dressed in a dark overcoat with a light-coloured, highly patterned waistcoat and an incredibly tall, even comically tall, top hat. The instant that Christopher thought he recognised his own thick black hair and eyebrows in the photograph, an image of a child with his hair sprang into his mind: a boy with an oversized mop of adult hair. He'd never thought much about family resemblance before, but now there was a three-year-old child running around who might look a lot like him.

Detached houses, individually designed but modern, lined the street and Christopher wondered how a Victorian house had managed to stand its ground when faced with such an onslaught. But here it was, set back from the busy road surrounded by gardens, looking for all the world as if it wanted nothing to do with its neighbours.

The taxi drew up on an enormous tarmac drive that had seen better days. In the shade of a mature sequoia, moss carpeted the crumbling crust and a battalion of dandelions forced their way through its shattered surface. Getting out, Christopher offered his hand to his mother, but she shook her head and gestured towards the house, intimating that he should approach it on his own.

Standing in front of the porch that was swathed in so much suffocating uPVC that it had caused condensation to obscure any view inside, he waited for his parents to join him. Feeling foolish, he looked around to check that they weren't far behind as if he were a schoolboy sent ahead to apologise for kicking his ball over the fence, but they remained resolutely where the now departed taxi had been. The doorbell, so liberally splashed with paint that it looked like a hasty workman had thrown it at the house, took a few seconds to find, but the moment it rang, a tall, thin man with an angular face appeared as if he'd been there all along.

'You must be Christopher Gastrell. Welcome to your house! I'm Nicholas Chambers. Please come in.'

Reddening at the effusive greeting, Christopher mumbled a reply and turned to see his mother approaching, an expression of pure delight covering her face. She greeted Nicholas like an old friend, but of course, they must have been in contact for months. They must have viewed the house and met him on at least one occasion. How much had been going on behind his back? Had David known what they were up to?

'My parents bought the house in 1966. I live in Alveston, a village ten minutes out of Stratford, have done for twenty years and I didn't want to move in myself, so Nancy keeps an eye on the place for me.'

The impressive entrance hall had ceilings that must have been around eight metres in height, Christopher estimated. Although still outlined in mouldings, he could see that they'd lost almost all detail under years of inattentive painting. The wood panelling that remained on the lower part of the walls was similarly deadened beneath goodness knows how many layers of paint and the ubiquitous woodchip wallpaper, constant companion of his rented accommodation in London and a nightmare to remove, he'd heard, had invaded every other part of the walls. A forlorn stair-lift sat at the bottom of the central staircase like a faithful dog that had refused to leave its owner's graveside.

As Christopher traced the path of the silver rail that coiled its way around the chipped newel post and slithered up the side of the balustrade, Nicholas said quietly, 'I haven't got around to taking it out. It seems so final. If I were living in the house, I would have, of course. It goes without saying – it will be gone when you move in.'

'You don't have to explain, Nicholas. It's difficult when a parent dies,' Bridget offered.

He showed them into the lounge, inviting them to sit on a sofa that looked as if it would give, but which proved to be unexpectedly firm as if a piece of wood had been inserted underneath the seat cushions to prevent them sagging. Christopher sat uncomfortably upright next to his mother and tried to concentrate on her conversation with Nicholas, but found himself unable to ignore the room's dilapidated state. A brown water stain at the top corner of the bay window had bubbled the paint and discoloured the plastic frame and an unevenness to the ceiling where the rose should have been, added to the feel of faded grandeur. There was, however, the odd unexpected touch of modernity in the room. Tea-lights in multi-coloured glasses were dotted around – something Monica too had loved.

'May I offer my congratulations on your birthday,' Nicholas said, scattering the thoughts piling into Christopher's head at the sudden reminder of Monica.

'It's...it's been quite a day.'

'Did you keep the house secret until this morning, as you'd hoped?'

'Yes, we did manage to, just about,' Bridget replied.

'May I offer you tea or coffee?'

'No thank you, we've just had breakfast,' Christopher heard his mother answer for them all – he, for one, was gagging for some caffeine.

'Then let me begin the tour of your house. And, I almost forgot, you must meet Nancy.'

Nicholas knocked somewhat apologetically, Christopher thought, at the only door that was closed and didn't open it until they all heard a strident, 'come on in.' At a large desk covered in a tablecloth of papers scattered at odd angles, sat a gorgeous woman of around thirty. She pushed her two plaits behind her ears, but her bubbly chestnut hair seemed intent on escaping, giving her the look of a dishevelled schoolgirl. Beaming at them, she got up immediately to walk around the table with her hand outstretched.

'Nancy, this is the Gastrell family. Thomas, Bridget and Christopher.'

CHAPTER 3

The morning of Monday the 5th of January 1864

The moment he heard his father's carriage announce its arrival on the gravel drive, frozen by a harsh January frost, Robert Gastrell turned down the photograph, removing it from its position of pride in the centre of the mantelpiece where it had stood for all of three hours. He drew his hand through his heavily oiled, thick black hair and then carefully across his eyebrows to confirm that not a strand was out of place. His eyes watered a little and he could not decide whether it was due to his proximity to the fire or to his father's imminent approach. In all of his thirty years, he was certain that he had never before experienced such anxiety.

Although the photograph showed him in formal dress, something of which his father would approve, he did not wish to watch his father's face transform to one of disapproval when he had to admit that it had been taken by Mrs Anne Drew. Pleased as he was to have had his photograph taken by Anne Drew, Robert was not quite ready to inform his father of the decision. Despite the precision with which she had caught the contrast between the darkness of his overcoat and his new, fashionably-patterned waistcoat and the sagacity of her advice to wear, rather than hold his stovepipe hat, his father would never accept that a woman should take a photograph of a man, let alone one who was not a relative. And Anne Drew would never accept that she should not take certain photographs.

Hastening out of the drawing room before his housekeeper, Mrs Sellers, had time to appear, Robert threw open the impressive double doors of the entrance hall to present himself to the person whom in all the world he most desired to impress.

'Welcome father, my very first visitor.'

'Robert, you really should not answer your own front door even if you are the architect,' Archibald replied as he descended from the double Brougham.

'I offer my assurances that I shall never again contemplate such an unforgiveable action,' Robert smiled.

Taking his father's arm in order to delay his entrance into the house, Robert could not resist the question.

'Well father, what do you think?'

Rather than praise his son's careful choice of the simple but effective modern geometric pattern of the two stained glass windows set into the impressive front doors, the older man muttered.

'What I think is that it is too cold to be standing around outside. I should like to see what you have achieved inside that has warranted such secrecy.'

For fear of losing control of the detail of his design, Robert had fabricated elaborate reasons to prevent his father's entry into this, the first home that he had designed on his own, but now he sought more than anything else, his respect as an architect.

'Of course father, I shall be pleased to hear your opinion.'

In the hope that, of all the features in the house, his father would not be able to help but admire the entrance hall, Robert stopped at the foot of the generously proportioned mahogany staircase. As if he were a conductor at The Crystal Palace, he swept his arm from left to right in his eagerness to please, then up towards the three generously proportioned windows from which light cascaded onto each brass rod that held the dark red Venetian carpet in its place, before dropping his hand unceremoniously to his side under his father's unremitting frown. It was true that he had deliberately steered clear of the intricately carved acanthus plant whose heavily serrated leaves adorned his parents' staircase, but Robert had hoped that his father would appreciate that a sparsity of carving could enhance the inherent beauty of the wood. Adornment throughout his house would be simple but worked to perfection allowing the natural elements to shine through according to the new aesthetic: suitability of use and quality of workmanship.

Robert took a sideways glance at his father's face, desperate to catch a glimmer of pride, but it remained unmoved. He would have to keep to himself that, somewhat to the annoyance of his builder, he had even visited the wood-turner to ensure that the banister would be made exactly to his specifications: wide enough to require a man to spread his hand out a little more than was usual so that his attention would be drawn to the quality of the wood-grain beneath his fingers. Disappointingly, he would not now be able to share with his father his strict instructions that the oak wainscoting was not to be clogged with the usual varnish which, once lacquered, could never change its hue, but was rather to be enhanced with oil and wax which would darken naturally with age and give pleasure long after Robert's own demise.

Just as he was about to usher his father out of the hall, he noticed that he was still wearing his hat, coat and gloves. Mrs Sellers, who had retreated to a respectful distance due to her employer's seeming unwillingness to allow his father to proceed past the hall, eventually received a nod of the head to come forward and accept the outdoor accoutrements of Mr Archibald Gastrell. His father's determination to maintain his silence left Robert with no option but to move out of the hall.

'Come into the drawing room, father. Let us hope that the new year of 1864 is not starting as it means to go on. Stratford-upon-Avon can ill afford to endure the continuance of this weather into April.'

'Well, it is impossible to keep winter out entirely, especially with such stark decoration,' his father said, eyeing the absence of festooned curtaining at the doorways.

Positioning himself to the right of the marble mantelpiece, Robert placed his hand over the prostrate photograph and stood stiffly as if to attention whilst awaiting his father's pronouncement on the decoration of this room whose simple lines and dark colours represented such a stark contrast to popular taste. Unlike the green fern-leaves tied up with knots of white satin ribbon that dominated his father's drawing room carpet, Robert had chosen a Persian rug with a reddish-brown central medallion surrounded by dark blue geometric lines. Where his father's floral draperies fought against the multifarious colours of the trellis-work on the wall-coverings, Robert's striped curtains picked out the blue of the simple lozenge-pattern on the paper. His father would detest it.

Having completed his walk around the room, Archibald kept his hands firmly clasped behind his back before joining his son in front of the fireplace. Had he wished to offer his congratulations, Robert knew that his father would have shaken him warmly with both hands. Instead, they stood in silence gazing at the grate and fender, again fashioned in the simplest form that he had been able to persuade the builder to incorporate in a house of such generous proportions. To Robert's eyes, extravagant decoration was utterly destructive of effect to the furniture it was supposed to enhance, but to his father's sensibilities, it was almost as if his son had chosen the cheapest of designs. Would he be able to bring himself to praise any of the house: to praise any of his son's work?

'How did you find your first night as master of your own home?'

'I hardly slept, I was so...' excited, he was about to say, before being interrupted by his father who pounced on his words.

'Well, you cannot blame anyone but yourself. It was your own design after all. It is a very masculine style of decoration. Perhaps you should have listened to your mother's suggestion of the large floral wall-paper and the carpet with the trailing roses.' After a moment's pause as both contemplated the proposed spectacle, he continued, 'however, in spite of the decoration, with this substantial property to your name you must now be one of the most eligible bachelors in town. You will be in demand more than ever from the mothers with daughters of marriageable age.'

Robert knew that his father's words were selected to raise the dreaded subject of his unmarried status: so unacceptable at his thirty years. These days, it seemed that Archibald could shoehorn his concerns in that direction into almost any conversation with his son. Looking to their favourite distraction, Robert guided his father out of the room, past the substantial sash windows that graced the square-fronted bay, another feature which he had hoped would elicit favourable comment, but which drew not a single word and along the hallway towards the one room that would surely meet with his father's approval.

Not wishing to taint the drawing room with even the hint of the smell of tobacco, an aroma he knew to be distasteful to the ladies who would be joining him on the occasion of his first dinner party the following evening, father and son would partake of this particular pleasure surrounded by the deep burgundy walls and dark wood panelling of the study. Feeling more at ease in this room that was traditionally apparelled, his father shook his son's hand and even touched his back by way of silent congratulation before putting on his smoking-cap: a highly decorated affair that gave him an exotic appearance of which, had he realised, he would have severely disapproved. Not for the first time, Robert wondered if his father was the very last man in England who still indulged in this practice.

'Now, to return to our earlier conversation,' Archibald announced in complete ignorance of the fact that it had been entirely one-sided, 'you are in a strong position to marry. I shall not go to my maker without the knowledge that I have a grandson to carry on the Gastrell name. There is nothing greater than the birth of a son,' he stated, signalling the end of his speech by taking his meerschaum pipe out of its leather case. Both knew that not a word would be expected to pass their lips now until the air in the study had attained a moderately greyish hue.

Caressing the bowl of the meerschaum, ripened over the years from its original creamy-white to a rich nut-brown, Archibald commenced his smoking ritual. Running his fingers over the points of the carved eagle's claws that encircled the pipe bowl before reaching down along the ridges of the bird's foot, he finished by stroking the glass-smooth amber mouthpiece whose coolness he would soon press against his tongue.

Over the years, Archibald and his meerschaum had adapted to accommodate one another's needs. The pipe, saturated with years of moisture and tar absorbed from the tobacco and his own saliva, felt satisfyingly heavy, almost as if it were a living being that was feeding off him. For Archibald's part, notches in his upper and lower front teeth, worn down over the decades by the stem, allowed it to lie comfortably these days between his lips without any need to remove it from his mouth even when speaking.

Robert, who now favoured the sturdier briar-root pipe when not in his father's company, brought out his meerschaum whose pale colour betrayed its lack of use. Following the three-stage process of filling his pipe exactly as he had been taught by his father, he was acutely aware under his father's gaze that he now needed to prove that he had not completely abandoned the meerschaum. Loosely dropping a generous pinch of tobacco into the bowl, he patted it gently with his finger before pushing a second down a little more firmly and then a third with even more force so that each layer compressed those beneath, enabling an even packing of the tobacco. After the last pack, Robert turned his pipe over to give it a gentle tap to release any that was loose, before placing his thumb over the top of the bowl and rotating the stem six times so that the tobacco would become entangled and there could be no air pockets. This process, his father had instructed him that very first time, would ensure that he should not need to draw constantly on the pipe in order to prevent it from going out.

Striking the match and puffing until the tobacco lit, Robert shut his eyes in anticipation of the most pleasurable part of the ritual: drawing slowly, he held the smoke in his mouth for a moment before blowing it out, repeating the action until the pipe was warm. When he had first started smoking he could taste nothing, but with careful instruction he had learnt to sip and not to suck on the pipe, to pay attention to the smoke's journey as he took it to the back of his throat, rolled it over his tongue and let it trickle out of his mouth. He had also found that the flavours were more intense if he blew a little smoke through his nose. Smoking a pipe was not to be hurried: it accompanied an hour of calm and soothing conversation, diluting his father's attention from the subject of matrimony.

A tentative knock at the study door startled Robert out of his reverie.

'You really must work harder to convince yourself to appear more at home in your new house or the servants will take advantage,' Archibald observed.

'Excuse me for troubling you, Mr Gastrell. Mr Drew has sent a note that requires an immediate reply,' announced Mrs Sellers.

My dear Robert

I shall depart on the 4 o'clock train to London this afternoon regarding an urgent request from my great friend Mr Charles Dickens. I trust that it will be agreeable to you to take my part as Chairman of the Committee this evening. As you know my Deputy is unable to attend due to illness.

I regret most heartily that I shall therefore be unable to attend your dinner party tomorrow. I wish you every success with the evening. I shall write immediately to extend my apologies to your guests.

Regards

Patrick Drew

Robert blinked and admitted to himself that he could not postpone for much longer his acquisition of spectacles. He handed the note to his father who retrieved his pince-nez from his pocket and who, for once, kept a diplomatic silence. Aware that his every move was being observed not only by his father, but by Mrs Sellers, Robert crossed the room slowly to take his seat at the desk and allowed himself a moment of contemplation to construct this awkward reply. Smoothing the green leather that covered the desk, he traced his right index finger along the blind tooling and remembered the pleasure he had taken from choosing the pattern and visiting the workshop in order to watch the heated embossing wheel roll around the edge of the dampened leather. His only regret was his decision to gild three of the borders: he relished touching the quality of the work, but knew that he would have to avoid forming a habit of running his fingers over the indentations of the pattern or he would lose all of the gold and the impression would be permanently worn down on the right hand side of the desk.

He had almost forgotten what he was supposed to be

doing when his father cleared his throat in too obvious a manner to be ignored. Reaching for his favourite Mother of Pearl pen, Robert realised that it was the first time he had written a letter at his desk; it was an important letter, but not the one he had hoped would be his first. Dipping the nib of the pen carefully into the inkpot, he set down his reply, but under the watchful eye of his father he blotted the note and much to his annoyance had to write another.

Robert could not believe his ill fortune. He had expected Patrick Drew, Mayor of Stratford-upon-Avon to chair the meeting that night to enable him to concentrate on the two speeches that he had to deliver: the first, his progress report on the building of the pavilion, the temporary theatre for the Tercentenary Festival of Shakespeare's birth would be well received, but the second, a proposal from Mrs Anne Drew to photograph the members of the Festival Committee would be troublesome. His presence in the chair tonight would weaken the power of both speeches.

But even that was not Robert's main anxiety. Patrick Drew's absence at his party the next evening troubled Robert even more because his guest of honour, Philip Wimlett, the manager of the prestigious Princess's Theatre in London had been invited principally because of his friendship with Patrick. Robert had heard only the merest outline, but he gathered that Philip Wimlett, his wife, Amelia and their two sons George and Percy were staying in Stratford-upon-Avon as guests of Patrick and Rachel Drew in order to remove their sons from the temptations of London where a sweetheart had caused division between the brothers.

Despite living in London, Stratford-upon-Avon's only rival in the bid to host the national Festival to commemorate the three hundredth anniversary of Shakespeare's birth,

Philip Wimlett had been wholly supportive of Patrick Drew's idea to hold the celebration in the town of Shakespeare's birth and death. For a period of nearly three years, it had absorbed the two friends' time and attention and letters had flown back and forth between Stratford-upon-Avon and London. Very few outside the committee could form an idea of the labours which Patrick and Philip had undertaken together and how close they had once again become. As for himself, Robert had met Philip on only two prior occasions: the wedding of Patrick's son, Harold to Anne Dawson just over two and a half years ago and Harold's funeral a mere seven months after the wedding. Now, he would have to lead the evening's conversation in the company of Philip Wimlett, a man whom he barely knew.

It was widely known that Patrick Drew and Philip Wimlett could trace their families back three generations in Stratford-upon-Avon and that Philip had been the first of either family to leave for London. It had been a shock for both families when Philip had departed in 1832 before the railways opened up travel to the metropolis. But when Patrick and Rachel Drew had been blessed with the arrival of Harold and two months later, Philip and Amelia Wimlett with the birth of George, they had again become close. Two years later, Percy had completed the Wimlett's family, but Patrick and Rachel Drew had had to wait a further twelve years before Benjamin's arrival.

Archibald waited until the door closed behind his son's new female servant whose name he had already forgotten.

'Patrick has conferred a great honour upon you in asking you to act as Chairman. Your speech regarding the progress on the building of the pavilion will carry more authority.'

'Father, did you say something to Patrick? Did you

suggest he should ask me to chair the meeting rather than you?'

'It is the right decision. To be seen in a position of authority, even in a temporary capacity, will stand you in good stead when the corporation chooses an architect to design a permanent theatre for Stratford.'

'I do not think everyone will be as happy as you, father, to see me leading a meeting of my superiors.'

'Our family's connection to the Drew family is as close as that of many cousins.'

'Father, I did not mean to denigrate the strength of the relationship between our family and the Drews, I meant only that I do not wish my legacy to rely solely upon the significance of my family name. My legacy must be a theatre which offers the audience the best acoustics and sight-lines and attracts the most accomplished actors.'

'You cannot afford to dismiss the importance of asking for support from the people with whom your family has forged connections: the world turns upon whom you know. Look at how influential Mr Dickens was in our campaign to buy Shakespeare's Birthplace. Without his persuasive prowess we would never have raised the three thousand pounds required to purchase the house in 1847 and who knows what would have happened to the building. Without saving the Birthplace for the nation we would not even be discussing a theatre in Stratford-upon-Avon, whether temporary or permanent.'

Robert was not blind to the fact that his father's reputation in the town had secured him the contract to design and build the temporary theatre, but a permanent theatre would be another matter. Somewhat chastened, however, he seized the opportunity to take up the subject of Mr Dickens, a discussion that was guaranteed to unite father and son as it had done so many times before: it was impossible not to be interested in Mr Dickens.

'I wonder why Mr Dickens needs to speak to Patrick with such urgency.'

'I hope it is a literary and not a medical crisis.'

At Robert's concerned look, Archibald smiled.

'You remember last October, when Mr Dickens wrote to tell Patrick that he had settled upon the title, *Our Mutual Friend*, but was exhausted by the year-long struggle to write the book? Well, Patrick took it upon himself to take the next train to London in the belief that he might have been able to assist Mr Dickens and I expect he has received another such letter and has taken it as his invitation to offer his thoughts on the progress that has been made.'

Everyone wanted to be associated with Mr Dickens and his work no matter how tenuous the link. Robert, for his part, had never met him but was happy to listen to stories surrounding the great man until noon heralded the arrival of Archibald's carriage and an end to their discussions. Although he would have preferred to walk to the committee meeting through the newly paved streets, Robert agreed to be conveyed to the Town Hall at a quarter to eight in his father's carriage; Archibald had reasoned that it would be inappropriate for the acting Chairman to arrive on foot. Robert had to acknowledge that he still had much to learn from his father before he could fully engage in the life of the town's higher echelons.

CHAPTER 4

The evening of Monday the 5th of January 1864

Robert pulled back the blue damask curtain of his father's Brougham as they clattered past the site of the pavilion. Although work on the temporary theatre that he had designed had only started on the twenty-eighth of November the previous year and there was nothing to see in the darkness, he could not pass the spot without looking towards the foundations which were already well under way. The completion date of the main structure set for the beginning of March and of the interior decoration expected to be around the first of April, three weeks before the Shakespeare Festival, would present a challenge, but he must not lose heart just as he was about to take the Chair of the Shakespeare Tercentenary Committee for the first time.

Settling himself deeply into the leather seats, Robert closed his eyes as the most carefully tended carriage in Stratford-upon-Avon rattled over the paving stones; kept in a dry, well-ventilated coach-house, every particle of mud was removed daily and both the exterior varnish and the leather were polished with a little sweet oil. The well-matched pair of Cleveland bays and the smartly dressed coachman and, unusually for a carriage containing only men, a groom, presented an impressive display as the Brougham's iron-shod wheels clattered over the cobbles at the approach to the Town Hall. Despite the arrangement of the doors that would enable even a lady to let herself out from the inside if she so wished, Archibald had insisted that his groom must at all times accompany the coachman in order to open the door of the carriage.

The gas showed only a little light over the entrance to this substantial stone building and Robert had to peer up through the thick darkness to make out any features of the life-size statue of Shakespeare that kept watch over the men who gathered, almost one hundred years after the statue had been erected, to honour his memory. Like too much of the town, to Robert's irritation, the statue's surface had been obscured and made to look like something other than its true nature: its lead had been painted to simulate the stone of the statue in Poet's Corner on which it was based. The statue had been presented to the Corporation by Mr David Garrick to commemorate the famous 1769 Shakespeare Festival in Stratford-upon-Avon. It depicted the poet leaning against various volumes placed on a pedestal and pointing to a scroll containing lines from a *Midsummer Night's Dream*.

> *The poet's eye, in a fine frenzy rolling,*
> *Doth glance from heaven to earth, from earth to heaven;*
> *And as imagination bodies forth*
> *The form of things unknown, the poet's pen*
> *Turns them to shapes and gives to airy nothing*

A local habitation and a name.

In need of some of those fine words himself shortly, Robert descended the carriage, half-shutting his eyes as swirls of fine snowflakes appeared from nowhere, catching the breeze and turning on him like an angry swarm of insects. He bowed his head, but gathering in a cloud they moved furiously sticking first to his black cloak and then to his stove-pipe hat; one tiny white pest landed on his eyelid and gave him a frosty bite. The sudden rush of light and warmth from the reception hall prickled Robert's eyes and he blotted the corner of his left eye with his handkerchief as father and son handed damp cloaks and hats, with gloves placed inside, to the clerks. Amongst the top hats, just four bowler hats, belonging to the only tradesmen on the Committee, would be handed in this evening.

Knowing that his father deplored his choice of a wide, dark-coloured cravat which had in his day been suitable only for day-wear, Robert looked out of the corner of his eye to confirm that his father was, as usual, wearing his traditional white cravat and double-breasted waistcoat. It was a style that he had first encountered in the eighteen-forties and declined to relinquish despite his expanding waistline which would have sat far more elegantly in the fashionable single-breasted, longer-length waistcoat favoured by his son, but he would not be told.

Once hats were removed, the average age of early sixties became more apparent in the receding, white-grey hair on display. Save for his friend, Dr Edmund Clemens, and the second Master at the Grammar School, all were nearer his father's age than his. Robert's closely trimmed thick side-whiskers and short black hair were so unlike his father's bushy whiskers and long hair, once luxurious but which now hung as straggly rats' tails, that they hardly resembled one another.

Having shaken hands and enquired after one another's families, committee members took their seats at long, narrow tables around three sides of the oak-panelled room. Standing at the lectern, Robert had to remind himself to look the members in the eye; his habit of avoiding looking directly at people, as if something more interesting were happening elsewhere was, his father had told him on numerous occasions, off-putting if not downright discourteous. Tonight, in his position as Chairman he would also have to forgo his habitual practice of taking his own notes and would have to content himself with the official minutes. Patrick's absence was a damned nuisance.

'Welcome to all, at this, the first Shakespeare Tercentenary Committee Meeting of 1864.'

Cheers, some of which quickly turned to coughs, especially from those furthest from the large stone fireplace, greeted his announcement.

'The building of the pavilion on Mr Patrick Drew's land in Southern Lane has commenced. The laying of the foundations will be completed by the end of this month. As you all know, the pavilion is modelled on the wooden amphitheatre that Garrick used for his Festival in our town in 1769. For those who may have missed the previous meeting due to the inclement weather, it will take the form of a duodecagon one hundred and fifty-two feet in diameter and will be constructed of timber. A strong wrought iron band will be placed around the circumference of the upright timbers to resist thrust and in total, twenty thousand cubic feet of timber, twelve tons of wrought iron and upwards of four tons of nails will be used.'

Robert paused briefly hoping that the architect in him had not taken over from his responsibility as Chairman, but there was hardly a sound in the room and not a stifled yawn in sight. All eyes were upon him.

'The stage will be seventy-four feet by fifty-six feet deep with nine dressing rooms and a green room. The pit is to be one hundred feet in diameter. Five hundred and thirty performers will be accommodated. There will be two tiers of boxes, refreshment rooms, cloakrooms and stalls for opera glasses. We are now ready to discuss the interior decoration of the pavilion. I propose that we allocate three hundred pounds.'

The first of Robert's speeches, concluded in something of a rush, he had to admit, was followed by a suitable pause for more cheers and acceptance of the proposal before he was able to deliver the Chairman's address. Confirming that Patrick was booked to address public meetings in, amongst others, Manchester, Edinburgh and Glasgow to put the case in favour of Stratford-upon-Avon over London as host of the national Shakespeare Festival, he added that Mr Parker, who would be proceeding to the south of England on professional business, had been authorised to promote the town in Southampton, Portsmouth and Brighton.

Again he paused, but all were attentive.

'I may tonight report that after the blunder of the London Tercentenary Shakespeare Committee in excluding Mr William Makepeace Thackeray from the office of Vice-president and his untimely death on Christmas Eve last year, we have heard that the London Committee is now denounced in the press for mismanagement. As the London Committee declines in public confidence, our Committee should rise in popularity and strengthen our case to hold the national Shakespeare Tercentenary Festival in Stratford-upon-Avon.'

Low sounds of disapproval that had rumbled around the committee room at the reference to the despicable treatment by the London Committee of Mr Thackeray who, until his death, had been second only in literary significance to Mr Dickens, were replaced by further cheers as Robert went on to remind everyone of the correspondence that Patrick had sent to *The Times* in December.

'The letter set out the difficulty in which Stratford-upon-Avon found itself. No sooner had Stratford-upon-Avon formed a Committee than a Committee was formed in London, not to assist us but to cut our celebration to pieces. We accepted our altered circumstances and set to work upon a smaller, more local celebration but the provincial towns offered to aid us if we would hold a national celebration. We have nothing against a London Committee but we find that a number of eminent men have joined that Committee in ignorance that we at Stratford-upon-Avon are engaged in a similar work. As you know I appealed to *The Times* as the leader of the press to give publicity to our design. We require all men: men of rank, men of wealth, men of letters, men of influence, in any class who think that Stratford-upon-Avon is the more appropriate location for a national celebration of the tercentenary of Shakespeare's birth to speak out in our name.'

Cheers and clapping erupted from the committee. Like a group of small boys who had outwitted a gang of bigger boys, the members enlivened by Robert's last words slapped one another on the back, shook hands vigorously and waved a defiant hand at those who sat too far away for them to reach. Delighted faces shook away the years as each congratulatory gesture built upon the last and Robert abandoned his solitary position to join in the merriment. A glance from his father, however, brought him back to the lectern.

'Thank you, gentlemen, but we must not get ahead of ourselves. There is much work still to be done. We have resolved to open lists at the various banks in Stratford-upon-Avon to receive subscriptions to support a monument fund, a scholarship fund at the local grammar school and the Tercentenary Festival Fund. In London we have opened a central ticket office at number two Exeter Hall where information might be obtained and contributions paid.'

Robert invited Mr Johnson of the Entertainments Committee to speak about the two principal actors engaged to take part in the plays to be staged in the pavilion. Mr Phelps, to whom they first wrote, immediately placed his services at the disposal of the Committee. Mr Fechter, to whom they then wrote, had stated in November that he would be unable to attend because he would not be able to close the Lyceum Theatre of which he was manager. However, in the middle of December, Mr Johnson reported, it was discovered that Mr Fechter might be obtained and so the Entertainments Committee had instantly invited him to play Hamlet due to the unprecedented run which his performance of the part at the Princess's Theatre had enjoyed. A surprised delight showed on the faces of the members to whom this was news. Mr Fechter was an actor of international reputation and his attendance would be a huge vote of confidence in favour of the Stratford-upon-Avon Festival's right to claim its national significance over London.

It was now time for Robert to deliver his second speech: a proposal he had merely to read out to the Committee but which had caused him more anguish than he cared to admit. Taking a deep breath, he looked up at an oil painting of the former mayor, whose brother had positioned himself disconcertingly beneath the portrait, and started to deliver the widow's proposal.

Mrs Anne Drew wished to photograph each committee member for a commemorative photograph album that would be kept in the Town Hall as a record of Shakespeare's Tercentenary, an event that all hoped would become one of the most significant moments ever recorded in the town's history.

CHAPTER 5

The morning of Tuesday the 6th of January 1864

In the last hour, Anne Drew had been rewarded with three minutes of pure joy. She was on the cusp of enjoying her fourth when a knock at the locked door followed by a commanding voice delivered the message that Mr Robert Gastrell had arrived. As always, the door remained resolutely closed.

At twenty-two years of age, Anne was clear about her priorities: since her darling Harold had passed away a little over two years ago after only seven months of marriage, photography had become her true love. For the first few months, her fair hair had remained undressed and her white skin had become dry and irritated from weeping. Her mother-in-law, Rachel had become anxious about her absence at the dinner table and had commented that her tall, slight figure could not bear the loss of any more weight. Photography had given her life purpose.

Determined not to lose her hard-earned moments of pleasure, Anne forced herself to dismiss thoughts of those terrible times in order to focus on the small plate of glass that she was holding tentatively by the fingertips of her left hand. With her right hand, she poured developer onto the upper edge of the inclined glass, tilting it until the liquid had run to all four corners to cover the whole plate. The moment had arrived. Holding her breath to counter her rising excitement, she watched the image of Benjamin, Patrick and Rachel Drew's ten-year old son and her own dear brother-in-law, begin to show itself and grow steadily in strength much like the subject himself.

When Anne had married Harold Drew, his brother Benjamin at only seven years of age had not been an important part of her life, but when her beloved husband had died, she had sought out the company of her young brother-in-law. Her eyes darted as different parts of the photograph became visible from Benjamin's hair to his hands and lastly to his eyes. Her mother-in-law would be delighted with this image of her young son. The glass plate had received just the right amount of exposure: the picture had not come out reluctantly nor had it flashed out suddenly.

To maintain the developer's even spread, Anne inclined the plate, ensuring that she kept it in a state of constant motion. Although it had taken only a minute for the image to develop, she elongated the time by once again examining each detail of Benjamin's form in turn. Satisfied, she poured the excess developer from one corner back into the jar and washed the glass with cold water to stop the development process. The developed plate could now be taken back into the work room where, thankfully, natural light flowed unimpeded.

Blinking at the sudden brightness, she placed the precious picture in a bath of cyanide to fix the image and remove any unexposed silver salts. Setting the tap running, she washed off the cyanide taking care not to splash any of the harsh chemical onto her clothes. She would have liked to see the process through to its conclusion when she would varnish Benjamin's likeness, but time was pressing due to her visitor's appearance and so she sought her assistant, Paul Brook.

Paul was the nineteen-year old son of one of Rachel's cousins. His father had been a photographer in charge of his own studio but had died when Paul was fifteen. Rachel, with her husband's and her son, Harold's agreement, had offered Anne the chance to take on Paul as her photography assistant upon her return from honeymoon. Anne had been pleased beyond measure because it proved that, not only her husband, but also her father-in-law, Patrick was supportive of her interest and she had been careful to make it clear that she would always be in charge of taking and developing the photographs. Since Harold's death, photography had, more than anything else, preserved her sanity.

Trying not to make her eye any more watery than it already was, Anne rubbed her eyelid gently. It always happened when she used the cyanide. She made sure that she did not work for too many hours on any one day because it was impossible not to breathe in the noxious chemical fumes, but whatever she did, her left eye would always weep a little. Today of all days, she did not want to appear as if she were flustered or, worse still, had been crying when she greeted Robert Gastrell.

'I have been telling Robert about the photographs you have taken of Benjamin today,' Rachel said as she welcomed her daughter-in-law into the bright drawing room of her spacious house.

Rachel was wearing a crinoline as bright as the very room in which she sat: the new mauve colour was set off to perfection with purple embroidery and a deep plum frill that trimmed the hem of the skirt. Excepting the two sad years of mourning, Anne always knew what the latest fashion was because it would be worn by her mother-in-law before anyone else had even heard of it. At forty-three, Rachel was determined not to acknowledge her age, even if it meant on occasion the embrace of a style or colour that did not quite show her to her best advantage.

'Anne takes four photographs of Benjamin every three months.' At Robert's look of surprise, Rachel added, 'children change so much in that time, unlike adults. One could probably keep a perfectly good record of an adult life with one photograph every few years.'

But Anne knew that embedded in her mother-in-law's words was the regret that she had only one photograph of her elder son, Harold: his wedding photograph. Rachel's need to record Benjamin's life so frequently was borne of a fear that she might lose her second son as she had lost her first-born.

'I believe you have come to speak to me on the subject of photography.'

Anne did like to get to the heart of a matter. She had seen Robert's discomfort as she entered the room and hoped it would alleviate his anticipation of causing her distress if he were able to offer his news quickly. This way, she hoped they would move on to talk in a more positive vein and when the time came for his departure, it would not be with the upsetting news ringing freshly in their ears: for she was sure that it was bad news.

'It was decided last night to appoint Burton and Sons to

be the official photographers of the committee. I am most dreadfully sorry. I was fully in favour of your proposition to photograph the committee members but the majority voted against, I am afraid.'

And Robert had the sneaking suspicion that both his father, Archibald and his closest friend, Edmund were included in that majority. He had delivered the unfortunate news without emotion and had looked her calmly in the face as he had practised at home in front of the glass but it did not take long to say and he was left attempting a half-smile so as not to sound quite so blunt.

'Thank you for coming to tell me in person. It is not a surprise, only a regret, that I have not been chosen. I do appreciate the time you took to read my proposal to the committee.'

That was what she said but what she should have done was deliver the proposal herself, although, of course, as it was an all-male committee that was impossible and she would not even have got past the entrance hall. Although she had known in her heart of hearts that the response of the committee would be negative, it still somehow came as a shock to hear it spoken out loud. Suddenly aware of an ache in her neck that had hitherto remained unnoticed, she was glad to have a physical rather than a mental pain on which to concentrate.

'I admire photography. One feels that a photograph may be trusted whereas a painting may not be as honest a representation,' Robert ventured.

'I believe it too,' Anne added, keen not to let the irritating news dominate their conversation. 'Portraits are painted to flatter, whereas I believe it is possible for a photograph to reveal the true nature of the individual.'

'Anne has photographed some of our well-connected guests. She spoke to Mr Henry Fox Talbot and to Mr Charles Dodgson regarding the photographic process,' Rachel boasted of her daughter-in-law, despite having not the least idea as to the content of their discussions at one of her many dinner parties.

Anne's mother-in-law was delighted that, instead of the usual banal comment in her visitors' book, she now had a photographic record of the prominent visitors to the town and more importantly, to her house.

'I would, however, like to photograph people other than my family and your friends,' Anne could not help saying.

'Who would you photograph? Celebrated actors or writers?' Robert offered.

'No, I want to photograph people in the street in their ordinary clothes, not just in their Sunday best. I do not want people to think that they must adopt a certain posture, put on a show for me as soon as I set up my camera.'

Anne's words hung around the ornate drawing room like irritating flies. She watched Rachel's eyebrows rise ever so slightly as she said a little bit more than she should have said. She really must work harder to govern her thoughts: commit them to her journal rather than speak them out loud.

Robert excused himself, citing preparations to be made for that evening's dinner party and looked forward to receiving at least one of these two ladies.

CHAPTER 6

The evening of Tuesday the 6th of January 1864

Whilst her younger sisters, Dorothy and Mary, shook off their velvet mantles, laughing at one another in nervous agitation, Anne undid the ribbon of her midnight-blue cape in silent contemplation.

The novelty of wearing a heavy silk evening gown, its bronze-coloured bodice and crimson skirt panels chosen to shine in candlelight, rather than the long sleeved, high-necked matt mourning dresses of the last two years, delighted her more than she cared to admit. The black had dulled her senses, almost convincing her that she was much older than her twenty-two years. Her clothes had swamped her thoughts but now she felt a desire to dress as she pleased, convention always permitting of course.

The lady's maid hired for the occasion of Robert Gastrell's first dinner party was helping Rachel out of her elaborate cloak and heavy, pinned shawl and Dorothy and Mary were still giggling over nothing. She would have to contain her own excitement for it would be many more minutes before either her mother-in-law or her sisters would be ready for presentation to the other guests. Smoothing down the fashionable outline of her skirt so that it displayed its modern flatter front and sides to their best advantage, its fullness reserved solely for the back, Anne looked over to Rachel, who was still receiving the maid's attention. Her full-skirted crinoline, a style that she had worn all of the twenty-five years of her adult life, left Anne wishing that her mother-in-law would not wear such elaborate dresses that seemed to take an age to put in order. After making a final check in the glass to ensure that her sleeves were resting just off her shoulders as she had rehearsed at home, she attempted to quieten her sisters, but to no avail.

In order to pass the time that appeared to be lengthening like a shadow at sunset, she rubbed in the hand lotion, as instructed by Rachel, to keep her skin soft and white before wiping a tincture of benzoin across her lips to prevent dryness in this cold January weather. Although her mother-in-law had told her in no uncertain terms that any other decoration of the face would be frowned upon, Anne had noticed that recently Rachel had taken to putting a tint of rouge on her cheeks and a fine powder over her face.

Followed closely by Dorothy and Mary, Rachel and Anne finally entered Robert's drawing room. It was a room that had none of the expected fancy adornment and was an echo of the entrance hall; dressed with simple solid dark-wood furniture, there was not a single frill, fringe or braid to be seen on any of the fabrics. The only concession to the usual arrangement was the large palms planted in square brass holders which were situated on pedestals reaching above head-height to frame the square bay. As the antithesis of Rachel's elegantly fashionable drawing room, whose decoration changed almost as frequently as its owner's clothes, Robert's room seemed to Anne as if it would remain the same forever.

Anne watched Robert attend politely to Rachel before he turned in her direction, bowing with a broad smile. Her sisters giggled and she almost wished that they had not been invited, but they would provide a perfect match to the two young gentlemen, George and Percy Wimlett, who were accompanying their parents, Philip and Amelia. The Wimlett family had been invited because they were staying as guests of Rachel and Patrick due to a problem between the brothers regarding a sweetheart in London, Anne had been told.

Philip Wimlett, who must have been aged in his late fifth decade, was a stout man whose pleasant face was dominated by freckles and whose faded sandy hair stood out from all other men of his years for having retained a modicum of its natural colour. And it was as if Percy, the younger son at twenty-two, had inherited his father's build but in a much more attractive form. His well-built stature and his vibrant red hair must catch the eye of many a young lady, Anne thought. George, the elder by two years, more resembled his mother, Amelia in that his build was slight and his fair hair formed delightful, natural-looking waves. Anne could not blame Amelia, a petite, bird-like woman, for whole-heartedly embracing all things feminine in her appearance, surrounded as she was by her husband and two sons; Anne's own father too had made strenuous efforts to maintain a sense of masculinity in his own all-female household, but, in his case, to no avail.

From her all too brief seven months as mistress of the marital home, Anne understood the significance of tonight for Robert: as host, it was his responsibility to ensure that the evening was a success. But, she felt a certain anxiety for Robert. Her father-in-law's absence from this evening's party, due to a letter from Mr Charles Dickens requesting his presence in London, would mean that Robert would have to entertain the Wimlett family without Patrick's assistance. And yet it was because of Patrick that the Wimlett family had been invited; the Drew and Wimlett families went a long way back. She could only hope that Robert's father, Archibald, would support his son on this most important of evenings.

After having received appropriate compliments regarding his new home, it was Robert's duty to direct attention towards Philip Wimlett. As the manager of the Princess's Theatre, whose company had just finished a highly successful season of *Romeo and Juliet*, Philip Wimlett was Robert's most prestigious guest.

'I only wish I had been able to attend the play. The newspapers reported that George and Percy played Romeo and Tybalt to great acclaim.'

'You are too kind. Our sons did us proud,' Philip Wimlett beamed, turning to his wife, Amelia, who reflected his smile.

'George and Percy, are you hoping to follow in your father's footsteps as famous actor-managers?' Robert added.

Anne wondered if Robert too had been asked to include the young men in the conversation whenever possible and to welcome them into Stratford-upon-Avon's society so that they did not beat a hasty retreat to London where the problem with the sweetheart could be reignited. So mismatched in size and hair colour, the brothers barely resembled one another and as for character, from what she could gather, they were similarly at odds: Percy's manly proportions disguised a shy nature and George's slight build revealed great confidence.

Both handsome, but in very different ways, she could understand how Percy's masculine figure and George's fair features could become the talk of the town.

'I should be honoured to achieve as much success as my father but at present I am content to act in my father's theatre and I am, of course, delighted to be taking part in the Tercentenary Festival in Stratford-upon-Avon,' George replied as if the question had been directed solely at him.

A pleased murmur of gratitude at the mention of the Festival filtered through the room.

'And Percy, are you committed to the life of an actor?' Anne was pleased to hear Robert's father, Archibald ask.

'I should like to continue to build my acting career in London and then to establish myself abroad as an actor.'

Amelia let out a cry at her son's words, before covering her mouth with her gloved hand. Robert's mother, Constance moved to her side, whilst Philip gestured open-palmed as if to appeal to his son, his face flushing a similar colour to his hair, his freckles all but gone.

'Percy, in London we have the finest theatres in the world and I know that...that a bright future awaits you.'

'I am grateful to you both, mother and father for your moral and financial support, but George and I should separate our lives so that we never have to compete with one another for the great stage roles,' Percy replied quietly and reasonably, Anne thought, especially if there were a personal difficulty between the brothers.

George's immediate concurrence with Percy's words was interrupted by the arrival of the last guest. Dr Edmund Clemens extended a bow to the assembled company. His prematurely lined forehead and receding hairline belied his thirty-four years, but his ability to speak and behave exactly

as one would expect, worked hugely in his favour with the
great majority of people. Since his recent inheritance of his
father's practice, his short, wiry figure was often to be seen at
social gatherings amongst the mature elite of the town.

'Edmund, thank you for joining our party tonight,' Robert
said a little louder than was usual, as if he were more grateful
than he could express at his friend's customary lateness.

Anne knew that Robert's closest friend had been asked
to replace Patrick so that, according to a tradition to which
his father held steadfastly, there would be an even number
of gentlemen and ladies at the table. Edmund, for his part,
appeared delighted to reacquaint himself with her sister,
Dorothy, but Anne thought that she detected a fleeting look
of irritation when he acknowledged her own presence.
What had he thought of his friend's decision to put her
photography proposal before the Festival Committee the
previous evening? Would he consider it an embarrassing
misjudgement?

A master in the art of conversation, Edmund put almost
everyone at their ease and by the time that dinner was
announced it appeared that the uncomfortable moment
caused by Percy's revelation had been consigned to history.
For the first time since Harold's death, Anne waited in turn
to take the arm of a gentleman who was not a relative. As
befitted the host, Robert offered his arm to Amelia Wimlett,
the most honoured lady in the company. Bending over at
an awkward-looking angle to accommodate Amelia's small
stature, he lead the way slowly into the dining room. They
were followed by Philip Wimlett and Robert's mother,
Constance and then Robert's father, Archibald and Anne's
own dear mother-in-law, Rachel. Determined that there
would not be a hint of awkwardness upon her acceptance of

Edmund as her escort, Anne allowed a smile to cross her lips. George and Percy, the most junior gentlemen amongst their party accompanied Dorothy and Mary to the table.

Grace was offered by Archibald before the meal served 'à la Russe' commenced. It had taken some time to become accustomed to eating separate courses as opposed to having all of one's food presented on the table at the same time and Anne knew from Rachel that Archibald still preferred the old 'à la Française' service. Making it clear at every gathering that he thought it was wasteful of food and meant that many more servants were required to deliver and clear away after each course, he had stuck to the French style as long as he could, but after fierce rivalry between the two styles in the town, he had had to give way to his wife Constance's remonstrations. She had confided in Rachel that she was fed up with being the talk of each dinner party for not moving with the times and this had immediately been relayed to Anne.

Having taken off her kid gloves at the table, Anne was thankful that the blue veins still showed in her white hands: photography had not yet left its physical mark upon her person. Her mother's early death had resulted in a succession of governesses from whom she had learnt basic skills, but it was not until she had met Harold Drew that her social education had begun in earnest. Rachel had taught her how to act her part at the table as much as any actor on a stage and from the several etiquette books that Rachel had given her over the years, Anne knew what was required of her; following her mother-in-law's lead tonight, she would keep her elbows off the table so as not to roughen them and would not consume any wine due to its well-known capacity to flush the cheeks, leaving them hot and uncomfortable. As a woman's complexion was thought by some to be an indication of inner character, it would not become her status, even temporarily, to allow anything to mark her countenance, her mother-in-law had told her in those early days.

Looking around the table, she saw that Dorothy and Edmund were conversing closely whilst Mary and Percy were pretending not to look at one another, but she should not worry: it was to be expected since their young lives had been so dominated by mourning, first their mother and then their brother-in-law, Harold. Death had prevented ordinary social interaction with anyone but their close family. As for George, he was paying close attention to his brother's words. It was heart-warming to see such deep fraternal love, so pleasing that they appeared to have put their differences regarding the sweetheart behind them.

After three hours, Amelia Wimlett rose from the table signalling that the ladies should leave. Anne pulled on her gloves, chosen because they preserved their shape better than silk and tried not to draw attention to Rachel who, in her attempt to create an appearance of smaller hands, was struggling to pull on gloves that were a little too tight. Since her son's death, Rachel took increasingly extreme measures to preserve the appearance of youth.

Amelia spoke first when the ladies had settled themselves into Robert's drawing room.

'Rachel, I am delighted that we are staying as your guests. As the dinner progressed, I noticed that George and Percy were becoming more comfortable with one another. It was so generous of you to invite us all to stay again like we used to when the children were younger. Being away from London is like a breath of fresh air and I see that the boys are renewing their childhood acquaintance with Dorothy and Mary.'

The two young women, who were out of earshot, received the smiles of the other ladies. Anne could imagine the discussions her sisters would be conducting with regard to George and Percy: how many tones of yellow could be seen in the waves of the former's hair and the tall, well-built stature of the latter. She would have so much more to write in her journal now that her official period of mourning was over and she was again able to engage in social events. The words sounded harsh, but they did not mean that she had forgotten her darling Harold, merely that she no longer displayed her loss to the world.

*

In the dining room, Robert missed the ladies' company, or perhaps just one lady's company. He spent the majority of his time accompanied by men and relished the ownership of his first house because it meant that he could host parties in mixed company. Unlike the gatherings hosted by his father during which the men sat at the dinner table for over an hour before rejoining the ladies, Robert preferred the more modern approach of joining the ladies soon after their departure.

Until that moment arrived, however, he would engage George and Percy in conversation. His father had apprised him of the reason behind the Wimletts' visit: to sweeten relations between the two brothers and it seemed to be working. At first, it had appeared that their personalities were entirely irreconcilable, but George now appeared to have lessened his compulsion to answer everything for them both and he looked at Percy when he was speaking instead of staring directly ahead, as he had on arrival. Percy, for his part, had softened his blunt-speaking, never impolite as such but enough to stop the easy flow of conversation. He said the unexpected, which in company was most unusual.

The time had come. For once, Robert did not have to wait for his father to stand up before he could return to the ladies. As he pushed back his chair, the young men immediately followed his lead and stood up, whilst his father seemed to be taking longer than was necessary. Whether it was because he had drunk more alcohol than was usual or because he was irritated at the break with tradition, Robert could not quite decide. He watched his father and Philip rejoin their wives; he watched George and Percy stand together at a distance from the more senior members of the party, but within easy earshot of Dorothy and Mary and he watched Edmund take his place next to Rachel. It had worked out beautifully. Robert would be delighted to make up a four with the latter group, positioning himself at Anne's side. They talked of the forthcoming festivities in the town until they became aware of an animated conversation emanating from his father's direction.

'That was a frightening dream, Amelia,' Robert heard his mother say with much sympathy in her voice.

'It has convinced me that something awful is going to happen to either George or Percy,' Amelia replied.

'She cried out three times in the night. What do you think, Archibald? You have a son who has just left the family home. Have you had any nightmares about his safety?' Philip asked.

'Of course I have not experienced any nightmares. I rarely remember my dreams and I would never act upon one,' Archibald replied abruptly.

'But Archibald, could dreams warn you about the future?' Philip pursued.

'Only in Shakespeare's *Julius Caesar*, but not in ordinary life. Philip, I do not know how you can even ask me such a question. How can something that happens to you when you are unconscious be of any relation to your conscious life?'

'I suppose you are right,' Philip replied, sounding unconvinced.

'Why would I have such a dream?' Amelia said, refusing to loosen her grip on her anxiety.

'My dear, let us take Archibald's advice and forget all about the dream. Nothing is going to happen to our sons. Look at them now, pretending that they are deep in conversation when actually they are casting glances at the Dawson girls.'

The four laughed and Robert considered that his first dinner party had been a success.

CHAPTER 7

The morning of Wednesday the 7th of January 1864

'Let us stop the carriage and walk.'

'Anne, you really are determined to be contrary to every advice book. You know how harmful the cold air is to your complexion. You wait until you attain the age of twenty-five, then the red veins will start to show, especially if you insist on photographing outdoors,' Rachel replied.

'Well, I shall not take any photographs today. I intend to stroll around the town with my mother-in-law. After two years of virtual confinement, I desire to be out of doors as often as I may.'

'I do understand. It has been a difficult time for us all.'

Not for the first time, Anne had to acknowledge her own lack of consideration towards Rachel who, after all, had lost her elder son. Placing her fingers on her mother-in-law's gloved hand, she mouthed a word of apology.

'If we descend here, we may walk up Bridge Street and along High Street. I am sure that the activity will do us both good.'

Anne enjoyed walking along Bridge Street made broad by the gradual demolition, over a period of thirty years, of a row of houses that had run down its middle. She remembered the fanfare in the town when the last house had been demolished six years ago making its scale more suggestive of a city than a provincial street. As they passed The Red Horse, the principal hotel of the town, she hoped that Rachel had forgotten about the important American gentlemen associated with the brewing industry, who had snubbed the invitation to stay with her in preference to spending the night at the hostelry. But no, she had most definitely not and it did not help that Mr Lowry, who kept The Red Horse, repeated the story to anyone who would listen. The American visitor had decided to stay at the hotel because, some forty years previously, Washington Irving had written in such a complimentary manner of it in his illustrated 'Sketch Book'. Being one of the very few visitors of any note not to avail themselves of Rachel's generosity, the story it seemed would never be consigned to history.

'Is this where the Shakespeare monument will stand?' Anne asked her mother-in-law, in an attempt to steer her mind away from the oft-repeated insult.

'Yes, Patrick told me that it was chosen because it is where the five streets converge and will be seen by all who reside in, or visit the town.'

'I have always found it surprising that Stratford does not have a monument of its most famous son,' Anne replied as they reached the top of Bridge Street and turned left into High Street, the main business thoroughfare of the town and the greatest marketplace for all things Shakespearean.

Despite the town's best efforts, the pavements were

splashed with mud from the vehicles that crowded the narrow street. A bustle of shopkeepers and customers made progress a little slow and Anne hoped that Rachel would not mind, for she loved the vitality of the street. They made their way past the Shakespearean bookbinding and printing establishment, which was opposite Mr Adams's Shakespearean book and print warehouse and the endless businesses bearing the same name, before stopping a few yards further ahead in front of an Elizabethan house that bore the date of 1597. Anne liked the idea that this house with its fine old carved oaken front, now in the possession of Mr Williams the glover, would have been a familiar building to William Shakespeare the glover. It was only a shame that the building next door, The Garrick Inn, detracted somewhat from its neighbour's beauty with its non-descript rendered walls.

They had somehow come upon Mrs James's on the corner of Ely Street more quickly than she had expected. Holding a number of Shakespearean relics and the autographs of distinguished visitors to the Birthplace, it was where she and Harold had laughed together at the enormous number of items that Mr William Shakespeare must have possessed in his lifetime. The sudden remembrance stung her eyes so swiftly that she had to put a handkerchief to her face. Pretending that dust had been kicked up by the crossing boy at the junction with Sheep Street, she turned to see that Rachel was doing exactly the same. The child, who was clearing a path across the street by sweeping it clean of the horse dung and debris from the over-laden carts that frequented the thoroughfare, tipped his over-sized cap to Anne and she dropped a coin into it. How she wished she could photograph just such a scene.

Slowing her pace as they passed the Town Hall from

which the Shakespeare Festival would commence in just over three months' time, mother- and daughter-in-law approached the Shakespeare Hotel; the venue of so many delightful mornings spent in the private coffee room named, 'As You Like It' in the company of their husbands, they had not ventured inside since Harold's death. It felt as if an age had passed since then and Anne realised for the first time that she missed her visits to this ancient hostelry whose every room was named after a Shakespearean play. She closed her eyes as an unbidden image leapt into her mind of the antique clock enclosed in a double glass case to preserve it from, 'decay's effacing fingers'. Its label boldly announced that it had once belonged to Shakespeare, 'as does everything else in the town,' she and Harold had said in unison, causing much laughter.

Upon opening her eyes, she saw Robert rush out of the hotel in a rather undignified manner.

'Ladies, how fortunate that we should chance to meet. I wish to extend my gratitude to you for your charming company yesterday evening,' he said a little breathlessly.

'It was our pleasure. Are you in town on business?' Rachel enquired.

'I have just concluded my business and felt in need of some fresh air.'

'Our very idea. I decided last night at your dinner party that we should take a walk through the town today,' Rachel answered, not quite honestly as it had been all Anne's idea.

'I wonder, ladies, if I may join you for a short while.'

'Of course, it would be a pleasure,' Rachel agreed for them both.

At the corner of Chapel Street and Chapel Lane, they stopped so that they could take a moment to decide upon their route.

'Thank goodness for those individuals, such as Patrick,' and here Robert nodded to Rachel, 'who realised that the site of New Place needed to be saved for the town.'

'It is such a shame that Shakespeare's house was destroyed...Forgive me. I meant no offence, I was not thinking,' Rachel said, her voice trailing off.

'None taken,' Robert replied quickly before continuing. 'I never think of sharing the same surname as the man who was driven out of Stratford for destroying Shakespeare's last home. After all, it was not even the house that belonged to Shakespeare that the Reverend Gastrell pulled down; Shakespeare's house had already been demolished and rebuilt in the early seventeen hundreds.'

Although Anne knew that Rachel was well aware of the history of the site in front of which they were standing, she heard her mother-in-law say, 'remind me of the story,' and realised that Rachel was enjoying this most unusual chance meeting and for his part, Robert appeared to be in no hurry to leave.

'In 1756, the Reverend Gastrell uprooted the mulberry tree that Shakespeare had planted in the garden because he wished to lessen the taxable value of the building. The mulberry tree, as you know, was the first point of interest to Shakespearean tourists before any of the buildings associated with him became significant. Without the tree, the Reverend Gastrell thought that the building's value would be reduced, but instead the corporation increased the parochial rate and in 1759 he demolished the property and was hounded out of the town.'

'Did your father ever experience any prejudicial remarks with regard to his surname when he first arrived in Stratford-upon-Avon?' Anne ventured.

'Although there was no familial link between our family and the Reverend Gastrell, my father did suffer at first from the stain upon our shared name, but Patrick,' and here Robert bowed slightly to Rachel, 'welcomed my father and due to his impeccable connections, our family name's reputation was transformed.'

'Patrick told me that as soon as your father qualified in architecture, he moved to Stratford-upon-Avon,' Rachel said, eager, it appeared, not to allow a silence to develop during which Robert would have an opportunity to suggest that they should part.

'Yes, his family had made a tour of the area when he was about ten years of age, stopping first in Leamington Spa and then in Stratford-upon-Avon and his father had remarked how much the latter could be improved if it were modelled on the architecture of its neighbour. It was at that moment, my father says, that he decided to move to the town and make it, in his words, more fashionable.'

'And Robert, do you wish to remain in Stratford-upon-Avon? Is there enough work in the town for an architect in these modern times?' Rachel asked.

'Yes to both questions, but much hinges on the success of the pavilion,' he replied, looking a touch uncomfortable.

'Patrick told me that the town is fortunate to have been able to purchase the site of New Place two years ago,' Anne said, returning their conversation to what she deemed was a slightly less controversial subject.

'Yes, it is true and we must not forget that without Mr Halliwell's enthusiasm, the site might well have been lost.'

'Mr Halliwell stayed as our guest last July,' Rachel observed. 'What would the town be without such famous supporters?'

'We must also not forget that it was the general subscription that actually secured the site. Without the public's willingness to give their money it most definitely would have been lost to the nation,' Anne pointed out.

'It is truly a great acquisition for us all,' Robert agreed. 'The boundaries of Shakespeare's garden have been ascertained and the foundation stones of his house can now be seen. His well, still in good order, has been discovered in the grounds and portions of his rooms, believed to be his offices and kitchen, have been uncovered. It is proposed that these excavations should be preserved and the garden should be put in order.'

'Would you mind if we walk down Chapel Lane and look at the site of the pavilion? I have not seen it since the first stone was laid. There must have been much progress since then and you could explain exactly what we can see,' Anne asked, pleased to prolong a walk that was becoming more and more enjoyable.

'Yes, there has been steady progress. The foundations will be finished in a week's time, but there is not much to see, I am afraid.'

'I should be pleased to see whatever is visible of what will be a truly memorable structure in our town,' Anne replied, smiling.

As they were about to turn the corner into Chapel Lane, Anne caught sight of George and Percy several yards ahead in Church Street. No distinct word could be heard, but raised voices were evident and their postures suggested that they were close to a heated physical exchange. Robert stepped in front of Anne, obscuring her view from this unseemly behaviour in the public street, but not before she had noted

George's right hand on Percy's collar. Perhaps they had not, after all, resolved their disagreement over the sweetheart in London. Despite Robert's immediate engagement in conversation regarding the use of the building in New Place's garden as a police-barracks during the Festival, Anne, usually so attentive, wished he would have the decency to be quiet and stop ushering them so briskly down Chapel Lane.

Robert must have walked too quickly because a moment later, when she turned to look at him, he appeared transformed; his cheeks and ears were flushing with colour and he kept touching the right side of his face as if to shield himself from the sight of the two young men. When he looked at Anne, she was saddened to see that his smile did not extend to his eyes, but remained stubbornly suppressed upon his lips and by the time they had arrived at the site of the pavilion, he hastily offered his apologies for having forgotten a pressing appointment and rushed back towards Church Street.

'It is such a disappointment that Robert had to leave us so soon. I should like to return home now Anne, but we shall meet this evening at Mrs Wilson's for supper.'

Anne did not mind a premature return for it would afford her time to write about the incident in her journal and to prepare her words of warning to Dorothy and Mary against any intimacy with George and Percy, given their ungentlemanly behaviour in full view of every passing stranger. And at the very least, it would add a modicum of interest to the tedium of these all-female gatherings, for her sisters could be counted upon to rail against such advice. She was convinced that the majority of the other ladies must share her dislike of this endless round of parties, but were kept in check, as she acknowledged she was herself, by the conventions of polite intercourse and for particular ladies, and they all knew who they were despite never breathing a word of it out loud, by the combination of morphine and ether that steadied their nerves and enhanced their wit.

Anne was certain that the gentlemen must pass a more enjoyable and stimulating time at their evening clubs and committees. How she wished to know what it was that they discussed when not in female company. Even the ornamentation of the ladies' drawing-rooms, all decorated in a similar manner, added to the monotony. It was so refreshing yesterday evening to find that Robert's drawing room defied convention and remained stoutly masculine. She would look forward to the next occasion when she would be certain to be in his company again: her friend Ellen's wedding the following month.

CHAPTER 8

Present day: Tuesday 20 April 11.10am

'Hey, I'm Nancy. It's so good to meet with you all. Happy Birthday!'

Christopher was so taken aback at the second effusive greeting that he'd received in the house that he stood rooted to the spot, staring at the woman. Her eyes reflected the exuberant smile that had taken over her whole face and before he knew it, he found his hand being warmly shaken by their owner.

'We've brought Anne Drew's diary with us,' his father said, as if it were still in his possession and he hadn't just that morning given it to Christopher.

'I can't wait to check it out. I'm guessing you've already read it,' Nancy said, turning back towards Thomas.

'Not exactly. When we cleared out the loft we found boxes from my mother's house that we hadn't gone through at the time. I tried to read it back then but I found it impossible to understand the handwriting and, to be honest, we just put it back again. When Nicholas mentioned that he knew of a student who was an expert in the eighteen-sixties,' and here, to Christopher's surprise, his father echoed the woman's broad smile, 'we thought it might be of interest to you. I'm delighted you will be able to interpret it for us.'

'I'll pull some all-nighters to transcribe it for you if you'll permit me to cite it in my thesis.'

'Yes of course,' Thomas replied, without hesitation.

'I'll be pleased to credit you as the owners of the diary.'

'That would give me great pleasure,' Thomas acknowledged with a nod that almost became a bow.

His father was smiling at this woman. It had never crossed Christopher's mind that his father might be attracted to other women. That he could even look at another woman. This birthday was a revelation. First, they'd announced that they'd bought a house and now, to top it all, his father was flirting with a woman half his age!

'I believe you're a doctoral student at the Shakespeare Institute here in Stratford,' Christopher said, wishing to divert her attention away from his father.

Nancy looked at him. She was one of those people who looked you straight in the eye and kept looking, not in a harsh way, more as if she was listening intently to something fascinating that you were saying. As he tried to decide if her eyes were green or hazel, he realised he'd completely forgotten what he was going to say next, but it didn't matter because she'd already launched into an enthusiastic explanation of her studies.

'So, although the Shakespeare Institute is a part of the University of Birmingham, you spend most of your time in Stratford?' Thomas asked when she'd finished.

'Sure, my thesis supervisor is based in Stratford and

there's a great reference library and I'm never out of the town archives in Henley Street. Everything's only a five minute cycle-ride from here.'

'It sounds like this house has been the perfect place for you to study,' Thomas observed to Christopher's embarrassment, since they were about to throw her out of her home.

'Yeah, I've never been so happy writing. It must be the house,' Nancy laughed, twirling a rogue strand of hair around her finger.

Having never experienced the slightest emotional attachment to any of his rented flats in London – after all they'd been no more than practical places to put his stuff – Christopher had to admit that when he'd stood at the front door of the house, all that had crossed his mind was the value of the property in the rental market. At first sight, it'd been no more than a money-making venture. But if she could write in it, perhaps he could do something with it.

'I also have a part-time job digitising the archive for the Shakespeare Birthplace Trust so that more original sources can be found on-line. In fact, anything to do with the Tercentenary Festival in Stratford in 1864.'

'It must be difficult to work with such delicate items,' Thomas responded before Christopher had chance to speak.

'We scan thin items including slim volumes as long as it won't cause damage to the spine. A digital camera is used for everything else. And it's my job to interpret any handwriting in these primary sources. It's why I was so made up when you emailed Nicholas to say that you'd found the diary. You said you have it with you?' Nancy prompted.

Christopher held out the diary to Nancy, but she backed away saying she must wash her hands first, leaving him wishing he'd left it in the tissue paper. She returned with, of all things, a pillow and accepted the book in silence. Cradling it in the palm of her left hand for a moment, she slowed her movements and her breathing almost as if in meditation before placing it carefully on the pillow. But she still didn't open the diary. Instead, she tilted her head to look at its spine and the gold lettering on the front cover. It was almost as if she didn't want to discover its contents, he thought. Finally, she turned the hardback cover, supporting it with her thumb until it lay at ninety degrees on the pillow. It wasn't what Christopher had expected. From her animated talk about her studies, he'd thought she'd plunge into the diary, flick through its pages and exclaim how significant it was, not hold each page apart with her fingertips in complete silence. He watched her run her front teeth over her lower lip making it redden to a deep pink. Only once did her concentrated frown turn into a half-smile. It was as if she was on her own.

'Perhaps you could look at the diary while I show Christopher the rest of the house?' suggested Nicholas, much to Christopher's irritation as he could've stood there all day watching Nancy. 'If that's all right with you,' Nicholas added, looking from Thomas to Christopher, unsure as to who was the rightful owner.

When both father and son nodded their agreement, Nancy spoke as if she'd been in a trance, 'Uh...uh, sorry, it's just I can't believe I've got it in my hands. Do you mind if I photograph it so I can look at it in my own time? I won't sleep tonight.'

Christopher didn't mind what she did. The diary meant next to nothing to him – that is, it hadn't meant anything until she'd showed such an interest in it.

Following Nicholas reluctantly into the dining room, Christopher felt as if he'd walked onto a stage set. A dark brown carpet criss-crossed with checks of various colours housed a mixture of furniture. A display cabinet on top of a drawer unit was full to bursting of tiny crystal glasses and at least three decanters. Above it, a shelf placed where the picture rail would once have been surely contained every Toby jug ever made. Vases, plates, glass dishes, prints, old Reader's Digests were stuffed onto every other shelf. One of the many small tables, a delicate oval sitting on spindly, turned legs that splayed out like a baby gazelle's, was covered in doilies displaying a collection of china knick-knacks. Even the grand piano was not permitted to stand unadorned; a set of brown leather Dickens's novels sat in a solid row across the back while a number of framed black and white photos of a child, presumably Nicholas, and a colour one of him in academic robes, scattered themselves over the rest of its surface. The kitchen, similarly, looked set in a time-warp, but perhaps the bedrooms would be more modern, he thought – especially Nancy's room.

The large handrail of the staircase fitted him so well that it was as if it had been made to size for him, but he couldn't understand why there wasn't any intricate carving on the staircase to such a large house; even the prominent newel post was topped by a simple unadorned finial. Accompanying them upstairs, old family photographs gazed out showing the stages of Nicholas's mother's life: black and white photographs of a child in a christening robe, a plump little boy and girl, a wedding group, then colour snapshots of people at the beach, a meal and finally a family grouped around a very old lady.

'Again, you'll have to excuse the decor. As you can see, it was my mother's bedroom. I haven't quite found the time to clear it out yet, I...' Nicholas gestured helplessly.

On top of his mother's dressing table, laid out on an oval embroidered mat, were a hairbrush, hand mirror and long-handled comb, making it look as if she'd just stepped out of the room for a moment. The double bed, made with a white candlewick bedspread covered in tufted orange and pink flowers complete with a lavender bag still on the pillow, left Christopher feeling as if he was in her bedroom without her permission. As if he was a voyeur. Trying to focus on the less personal aspects of the bedroom, he took in the generous size of the room that would be his if he was to move in. The square bay, a replica of the one in the room directly below, enlarged the room, but the en-suite carved out of one corner had destroyed the original Victorian moulding.

If he was to move in! Where the hell had that come from?

The other bedrooms passed in a daze of piles of clothes and dustbin sacks that looked as if someone had been half-heartedly sorting through them before giving up, until he came to the last room. Despite being decorated in the same old-fashioned manner, the room had more of the modern touches that he'd noticed downstairs; dresses hung from the picture rail as if they were works of art; fairy-lights were draped around the door; a pile of textured cushions seemingly in every shade of purple covered the bed and a Kindle and an iPod sat on the bedside table. Stuck to the back of the door, he could see a Royal Shakespeare Company poster advertising *Romeo and Juliet*, the production that his parents had booked and he wondered if Nancy had connections to the theatre. Leaning against the wardrobe, piles of books were stacked in a haphazard manner resembling a giant version of Jenga that looked about to topple and photographs of groups of friends, all of mixed company, covered the wardrobe doors and Christopher couldn't help looking to see if any might be of a boyfriend.

Returning downstairs, they found that Nancy had cleared a rough space in the centre of her desk, pushing everything to the sides like one of those arcade machines where, if a coin is dropped in the slot at the right time, it will shove the others over the edge – but which invariably stops just short. Propped on its pillow, the diary looked as if it were some sort of relic to be worshipped and when they entered the room to signal the end of her time with the precious object, Nancy didn't speed up her last turn of the page, but closed it slowly with great care.

'I'll put it in acid-free tissue and then bubble-wrap to protect it. I've got some spare for you to use,' she offered.

Having thanked her for her care of the diary, both father and son held out their hands to receive it and she laughed.

'I'm made up! Just what I need for my thesis. An original source that no one else has ever studied. I've a load of questions to figure out though. I'll start right now transcribing the pages I've just photographed,' Nancy enthused.

'I know we're busy this evening with my uncle and his family, but why don't we meet tomorrow morning and you can show me how you're getting on? That's...That's if Mum, you haven't got any plans for me then,' Christopher asked, aware of an almost imperceptible intake of breath from his mother.

'No, no I've nothing planned for the morning,' Bridget replied quietly.

'It's decided then! 10.30 okay?' Nancy confirmed.

CHAPTER 9

Present day: Tuesday 20 April 12.30pm

In the taxi on the way back to the apartment, Christopher couldn't believe what he'd done. He'd actually asked a woman out on a date in front of his parents for goodness' sake. What'd got into him? Was it the house? The email? Or David? Perhaps it was just what happened when you got to forty!

And his child, his son. He was that close to telling his parents last night on the restaurant boat, but then they'd put so much thought into the evening – into the whole trip. He really was enjoying it and they seemed to be too. He had to choose his moment so that they didn't both keel over with the shock. He'd say something general. Test the water first.

As Christopher looked into the kitchen, his mother shooed him away, but not before he caught a glimpse of a large white cake surrounded by numerous smaller boxes. No one had made any reference on the journey to the box that had sat next to his mother, knowing that it would be a fruit cake and that she'd have moulded each of the decorations as she'd done every year up until he was twenty-one. Somehow, she'd managed to think of a completely different theme each year.

'It feels a bit early to be going to the pub,' his father observed looking at his watch. 'Bridget, are you sure you won't come?'

'You two go ahead. I've things to do.'

'They'll think we're alcoholics!'

'They'll get a lot of tourists, I think your reputation's safe,' Christopher reassured his father.

He planned to approach The Garrick Inn from the opposite side of the street so that he could guide his father to the exact spot from which he'd photographed it yesterday afternoon. In the past, he had to admit, he'd never felt the need to talk about photography or any other part of his life for that matter, but since David's death, he wanted to show what it was that he did with his time – what was important to him.

Ten minutes later, he and his father were over the road looking at The Garrick. It was squeezed between Harvard House, a beautiful Elizabethan building that was the former home of Catherine Rogers, mother of John Harvard the founder of the American university, and to its left, a baguette bar, a reminder of the practical needs of the town's tourists. As Christopher explained exactly how he'd zoomed in on the inn's highly decorated walls until just one of the panels of curved wooden tracery was in view so that he could take his signature photograph – the close-up, he noticed that his father was hanging on his every word. And at that precise moment, he couldn't have been happier.

'I'd like to see the photograph when you've got a

minute,' Thomas said, as they started to cross High Street and Christopher almost forgot to show his father the plaque giving the inn's history, he was smiling so much.

'Just a minute, Dad. It says The Garrick is the oldest pub in Stratford. There's been an inn on this site since 1718. It's been The Reindeer, The Greyhound, briefly, The New Inn and then it became The Garrick Inn around 1795 in honour of the actor David Garrick who organised a jubilee in celebration of Shakespeare's two hundredth birthday.'

'I wonder if that was the first Shakespeare Birthday Parade.'

'I'll ask Mum. She's bound to know, what with all the research she's done.'

'And to think it's still going strong now and we'll be watching it in four days' time,' Thomas added, walking into the pub whose substantial front door was propped wide open in a gesture of welcome.

The entrance to the snug, however, to its immediate right was closed as if a password were required to proceed into this intimate room and when Thomas pushed on the door, it didn't budge at all. To Christopher's surprise, it resisted his initial touch too, so he put his shoulder to the door and pushed heavily down on the latch and the door suddenly gave way, resulting in an embarrassingly rushed entrance into the middle of the tiny space.

The dark room had a square bar carved out of one corner. Two men who were sitting on stools at the bar looked from him to one another and Christopher imagined they were thinking, 'tourist'. While his father sat at the only table next to the window that had chairs rather than stools, Christopher stood at the bar avoiding the locals' eyes. Only one hand-pumped ale, the rather unimaginatively named Drew's IPA, was visible amongst the gas-pumped lagers, but craning his neck he could see that the bar extended into a larger room on the other side.

'What other ales do you have?'

'Greene King IPA, Abbot, Garrick Shakesbeer. You are welcome to try any sir, but the Drew's IPA is our best-seller,' the barman replied as he placed a small shot-size glass in front of Christopher.

'Dad, would you like to try any of the ales?'

'I'll have whatever you're having, thanks.'

'In that case, we'll start with two pints of the Drews IPA please.'

After the barman had waited for the head to settle a little so that he could top each glass up to the rim, Christopher took a sip of the golden ale, then two more. Licking away any trace of its thin, foamy white head from his upper lip, he manoeuvred with some difficulty, trying in vain not to spill any of his father's pint in front of the watchful eyes. As he sat down, he told himself that this was the right moment to broach the subject of children, but a dark shadow fell across their table and his father shuffled his chair closer so that his face was only an arm's length from Christopher's and he closed his lips.

The men responsible for the shadow continued vaping outside. Sheltering under the overhang of the inn's upper storey and leaning against the window, they obscured much of the daylight into the snug. Not yet able to trust that the words would come out how he wanted, Christopher peered out seeking some natural light through the only small, clear pane of leaded glass that he could reach amongst a sea of green panes. But, the bubbled glass dissected his view of the street and distorted the double yellow lines, giving an impression of rippling movement so unlike the featureless glass of any modern building that he had to look away. It gave the illusion that people were walking past the window a little too briskly, made them seem a little too close to him despite the presence of thick glass acting as a buffer between them. He felt hemmed in.

The smokers moved on and there was a moment of light that was almost immediately displaced by a group who gawped at the inn, then a couple looked at the blackboards outside and a red tourist coach picked its way slowly along the street, obscuring all but the very tops of the buildings opposite and the room seemed as if it was getting smaller by the minute. The oak beams and low ceilings of the bar, that at any other time would have relaxed him, now stifled and confined him as he cursed his decision to tell his father about his child in a public space. He'd thought that the pleasant environment would mitigate his anxiety, not to mention the alcohol, but it was having the opposite effect.

Sucking in a deep mouthful of beer from the pint glass, Christopher swilled it around in his mouth for a moment, savouring the bitter taste of the hops before the biscuity flavour of the malt developed in the very back of his throat. After several more gulps, he realised that he'd almost finished his pint and his father had barely started his and it was only a little after one. It was now or never.

'Mum's glad I'm out of the way, isn't she?'

'She's enjoying this birthday trip very much.'

'I really appreciate what you've both organised. It's made me realise that it's quite a landmark age. It's not old but it's not young either – a bit of an in-between age. It's made me think that I'd like to have a family sometime. I'm sure you'd like a grandson…grandchild.'

Once Christopher started speaking, his words tumbled out like a child running downhill unable to stop. He'd expected his father to be surprised that his son had initiated the conversation about wanting a child, but not as much as he seemed to be. As Thomas spluttered into his glass, Christopher scratched the stubble around his chin and wished he hadn't said quite so much all in one go.

'You all right, Dad? Went down the wrong way did it?'

'All right,' Thomas said, clearing his throat several times. 'I'm glad you're considering your future.'

'You know that forty is the new thirty, don't you, Dad,' Christopher added, trying to inject some humour into the awkward situation that was all his own creation.

'Do you really mean that you would like to get married and have a family?'

'You don't have to get married to have a child these days, Dad and most children aren't planned anyway. In fact, by the time many are born, the parents are no longer together or even in contact. A bit different from your day, I suppose.'

Exaggerating his words to incorporate his own situation, Christopher had kept his eyes on his diminished pint, but when he looked up, he was startled by his father's appearance. In front of Christopher's eyes, blotchy red patches tinged with purple had appeared on his father's face and sweat had started to break out along his hairline, sticking small white hairs to his forehead as if he'd come out without combing his hair, something of which he'd have severely disapproved, had he known.

'In an ideal world, I'd like to meet someone and have children but it doesn't always work out like you want, does it?' Christopher said softly, trying to lessen the shock a little.

'If you met someone now, would you get married sooner

rather than later?' Thomas asked quietly.

'I don't know. You never know what's around the corner do you? I've been working on a photography book and it's not left me much time.'

'A book?'

'I've got about half way,' he replied, relieved that his father's face was returning to a near-normal colour.

Until now, he hadn't realised how little pressure there'd been on him before David's death. David had always been so happy to share his life with others.

'Talking of photography, have you noticed the black and white photographs of The Garrick Inn?' his father said, pointing to the far wall.

'There are more photographs along the corridor if you're interested in the history of the building, sir,' the barman advised as he cleared Christopher's glass.

'You go ahead, son. I'm quite happy sitting here.'

Photography. Ever the useful excuse when he needed a bit of breathing space. That hadn't gone as he'd expected. If his father was that shocked at him raising the subject in a general context, how would he react to an actual grandchild?

Scrutinizing the photographs in the dark corridor, Christopher recognised the name and date on an image that claimed to show Harvard House and The Garrick Inn. The former hadn't changed, but the latter, from what he could make out, looked nothing like the building in which he was standing; all trace of its exposed timbers had disappeared beneath a rough render, depriving it of any connection to its heritage. The photographer, Paul Brook, had taken it in 1864. It was the same name as the one on Mrs Chase's leaflet that was taken of Ely Court in the same year. For a man who would've had to lug heavy equipment and chemicals around whenever he wanted to photograph anything outdoors, he certainly got about, Christopher thought.

*

As soon as Christopher was out of sight looking at the photographs, Thomas let out a huge sigh of relief. He couldn't believe that Christopher had spoken about having a family. It was so utterly unexpected. When Christopher had said, 'a bit different from your day,' it had taken him back over fifty years to when Sylvia had entered his life. With only two years between them, Thomas had got on well with his brother, Charles. In 1952, Charles and Sylvia had married and then he, Thomas, had made the biggest mistake of his life. He didn't even know why it had happened. He loved his brother.

He'd become friendly with Sylvia when Charles had had to go away for a few weeks for work and they'd had a very brief affair. Joanne was born and then he'd met Bridget and they'd married within six months. Two years ago, Sylvia had confirmed on her deathbed that Joanne was his. She hadn't told Charles up to that point, but was unsure whether or not to tell him the truth before she died. She'd passed away before Thomas had been able to see her on her own again. Did Charles know that Joanne was his niece, not his daughter? Since January, Thomas had been tortured by a deep feeling that he must confess to Joanne. 'You never know what's around the corner.' Christopher's words rang in his ears and surely Joanne deserved to know the identity of her biological father. But, Bridget, Charles, Christopher, Peter and Madeleine – what would it do to them? And the necklace he'd given to Sylvia – had she passed it on to Joanne?

CHAPTER 10

The birthday morning had been everything Bridget had hoped for and more and it was good to finally meet Nancy. Nicholas had sung her praises in the recent flurry of emails about the house and her infectious enthusiasm for the diary had made Bridget want to see what it was that this young woman was getting so excited about. Settling herself on a wooden lounger in the townhouse's garden, she unwrapped the diary, mimicking Nancy's care and attention. It would be difficult to read the spidery handwriting of a hundred and fifty years ago, but she wouldn't be put off. She estimated that she'd got a couple of hours to herself before Thomas and Christopher got back from the pub and Charles, Joanne, Peter and Madeleine arrived.

She could just about make out that on the 1st of August 1860 the writer, Anne Dawson, had been given a camera for her nineteenth birthday. A few pages further on, an illustrated poem caught her eye and then a heavily embellished date,

Wednesday the tenth of April 1861 and *My Wedding Day*, with her married name, *Anne Drew*, written several times. Skipping over the pages of fancy handwriting, one simple phrase stood alone.

The worst day of my life.

The worst day of my life. It was her phrase when David had died. What on earth had happened to this woman?

Before she could begin to answer this question, she was startled by a loud, rustling noise directly behind her. But, turning around, she could see that it was only a large pigeon flapping on a branch, bowing it down like David and Christopher used to do in the baby bouncer that Thomas had set up in the doorway between the lounge and the dining room all those years ago. David. The brightness of the sun's rays suddenly blanched the diary's pages, stinging her eyes so that she could no longer focus on the words. Shafts of sunlight pierced the garden, illuminating a world of swarming gnats hovering at her eye-line. The insect column reached as far into the sky as her eye could see, reminding her of a TV programme in which the deep sea was illuminated by a diver's light showing up a thick stew teeming with too much life. The chaotic movement in the congested air pressed down on her chest as if the flying masses would attack her and stop her from taking her next breath. Since David's death, her brain had this ability to transform something enjoyable, without any warning, into a sudden overwhelming assault, but she'd learnt what to do – focus on just one thing to the exclusion of everything else.

A speckled white butterfly obliged by landing on the leaf of a plant whose name was on the tip of her tongue.

The butterfly, despite another's insistence on a resumption of their earlier dance, flattened its wings to reveal orange tips eager to catch the early warmth of the sun, and Bridget imagined herself to be that butterfly, relaxing into the sun's heat. As the butterflies took to the air over the yellow flowers of the golden dead nettles, she realised that the name had sprung automatically to mind. Her memory was definitely better when she relaxed. And she was relaxed – the first time since David's death. She was ready to give the diary another look.

The worst day of my life.

My darling Harold is lost.

Here was a woman, almost a quarter of her age, who'd lived a hundred and fifty years ago, writing her exact words. She almost felt as if she knew this woman. As if they could have been friends. The next few sentences spoke of Anne's love for her husband, Harold and her grief at his loss and Bridget wished with all her heart that she could reach back through the years that separated them and help Anne.

Voices entered the periphery of Bridget's hearing and for a second, she didn't know who it could possibly be. Rising a little stiffly, she combed her fingers as best she could through her bird's nest hair and listened.

'It was stationary as we approached the roundabout because of the narrow bridge. It's that old one with the view of the theatre,' said a man's voice.

Not her husband's or son's. Whose voice could it be? Of course, how stupid of her, who else could it be, but Charles? Goodness, the time had passed quickly.

'It's the Clopton Bridge. Would you believe it was built in the fourteen hundreds? Bridget's been reading up about the history of Stratford.'

'Thomas, I wouldn't expect anything less,' Charles replied before, much to Bridget's annoyance, lighting up a cigarette.

In generation order, the brothers were followed by Joanne and Christopher, then Peter and Madeleine. Peter was eyeing his granddad's cigarette as if he hadn't tried it yet for himself. How quickly attitudes had changed. At his age, she'd been smoking for a good two years, unfortunately.

'Bridget, how lovely to see you,' Charles grinned as he embraced his sister-in-law.

He'd got new glasses. They were mid-brown with a silver metallic strip down the arms. A bit flashy for my liking, she thought as she looked over at the unobtrusive pair that Thomas had kept for too many years. She was sure that her husband would remain unchanged forever and she loved him for it.

'Hello Auntie Bridget,' Joanne said, giving her a peck on the cheek before nodding to her children to approach.

Madeleine ran forwards and wrapped her arms around her great-auntie's waist, but Peter held back. She couldn't blame him – he was fifteen, after all. A tall, lanky boy, who slouched forwards with his hands thrust deep into his pockets, he looked as if he'd elongated overnight and hadn't quite got used to his new height. She liked his hair though – longish with ends that curled up. A memory of Thomas's hair sprang to mind. When they'd first met, his had curled in exactly that way when he was due a haircut or when the weather was damp. Come to think of it, Christopher's hair did exactly the same.

'I'm so looking forward to your birthday meal tonight.

How has your birthday been so far?' she heard Joanne ask Christopher.

'Surprising!'

'Have you had your present yet?'

Bridget watched Christopher mumble that he had.

'I was sworn to secrecy. Not that we're in touch.'

For the first time, Bridget wondered how Christopher felt, knowing that Joanne had been told about the house.

'How was your journey?' she asked Joanne, attempting to change the conversation.

'Congested as we entered Stratford, but we got a great view of the church and the theatre. I can't wait 'til Saturday. I've seen the occasional play but I've never seen anything here. Have you seen much Shakespeare?' she said, turning to Christopher.

'I've seen a few at the National and *Henry the Fifth* at the Globe.'

'I have to admit I tend to choose the cinema rather than the theatre and there's not a lot of Shakespeare on offer there. I find it easier to suspend disbelief in a film,' Joanne added. 'It's a controlled medium and I can relax into the film and just let it happen. You know that what you see is what you're expected to see.'

'I'm the opposite,' Christopher said. 'I love it that something unplanned could happen. In fact, anything could happen.'

CHAPTER 11

Present day: Tuesday 20 April 6pm

Christopher looked out of the taxi's window as a mixture of brick-fronted and timber-framed seventeenth-century townhouses flashed by. Although the early dinner had been booked mainly to suit Madeleine, Joanne had been quick to assure everyone that she would take herself off to a quiet corner to watch a film on her tablet so they could stay as long as they liked.

'Before we go in, there's something I want to tell you,' Christopher heard his mother say to Madeleine. 'We're going to eat at Lamb's restaurant in Sheep Street!'

To his mother's obvious delight, the puzzled look on Madeleine's face turned to a broad grin.

'That's wicked!'

'Look at the window above the coach entrance,' she pointed out to her great-niece. 'That's our private dining room. It's called the Hayloft.'

'Is it just for us?' Madeleine wanted to check.

Having received an enthusiastic nod of the head, Madeleine insisted on being the first to enter the restaurant, looking from side to side at the rows of closely-packed tables as if she were the owner, Christopher thought. His cousin, Joanne took Madeleine's hand to help her negotiate the steep, narrow staircase while his mother, father and Uncle Charles pulled heavily on the banister, pausing half way up. Gesturing to Peter to go before him, Christopher saw the young man jog up the first few steps, his long legs easily catching up with his granddad before he'd reached the top. Last to enter the room set aside for their party, Christopher ducked just in time to avoid a low, heavily padded beam that led into the area that had formerly been used to store hay. Its sloping roof and exposed beams were set off beautifully by the gentle wall lighting and candles on the table and he wished he'd brought his tripod.

He watched as Madeleine decided where they should all sit, his mother only stepping in to tell her that the birthday boy must be placed at the head of the table. As Madeleine dissolved into giggles at the thought of someone so very old being described as a boy, Joanne mouthed a word of apology to him. Turning to Peter, she brushed a curl aside and whispered something – whatever it was, he took his earphones out, wrapped them carefully around his mobile and eased the latter into his pocket.

Hardly had Christopher taken his seat, when he heard his father take up the subject of Robert Gastrell again.

'Was he a famous actor?' Madeleine asked.

'No, Robert Gastrell was an architect who lived in Stratford a long time ago. He designed a theatre here.'

'Oh,' she sounded disappointed.

'He's a relative of ours. He's your great-great-great-great-

great-grandfather,' Thomas added.

'That's a lot of greats! But why wasn't he an actor?' Madeleine pursued.

'Not everyone in Stratford is an actor.'

'It's my fault, Uncle,' Joanne explained. 'I told Madeleine that David Tennant had acted in the theatre in Stratford, so she thinks that everyone in the town is an actor.'

'David Tennant?'

'He played Doctor Who for about five years, so all the children know him. We got the box set for Peter but Madeleine's become a fan recently. We have to watch it together, though, as some of it's a bit scary,' Joanne said, smiling at her daughter who shook her head vigorously, put her hands on her hips and scowled for a second before she broke into yet another fit of giggles.

Christopher looked at Madeleine. She was only four years older than his child. She looked at you with her head on one side and didn't look away until you'd answered her question, and then she asked more, each reply sparking another, 'but why?' Looking from mother to daughter, witnessing their easy teasing brought his own situation into sharp relief. His child would soon be asking who his father was and where he was, if he hadn't already. What would he say to his son? If only he could see him from a distance first, observe him without anyone else knowing. Shit, he sounded like a stalker.

'Christopher, have you any idea what you will do with the child?' his Uncle Charles asked.

He must have said something out loud. Shoving his hand over his mouth, as if to grab back the words, Christopher stared at his uncle.

'What do you intend to do with the house?' Charles

repeated, touching the side of his glasses, as if not quite used to them.

Removing the suddenly redundant hand in slow-motion, Christopher scratched the stubble around his jaw, stopping only when he saw his uncle's perplexed look.

'The lease on my flat in London is up in six weeks. I could...well, I thought I might give the house a go...I mean, move in and see how I get on. I'm not tied to any one location and I can travel whenever I need to.'

He'd actually told the whole family! Now he'd have to do it, or at least try it. He'd been so relieved that he'd misheard what his uncle had said, that the words had come out of his mouth before he knew what he was saying.

'Won't you miss London?'

'Well, I've only been in Stratford for one day and I've already taken lots of photos, so perhaps it will do me good to get away from London for a while,' he answered flippantly.

'You could set it up as a photographers' retreat,' Joanne offered, tongue firmly in cheek. 'I'd definitely come, if only for the peace and quiet away from these two. I couldn't promise that I'd take any photographs though!'

Madeleine adopted an exaggerated frown, but Peter kept his head down, his hair obscuring his face, apparently oblivious to their conversation – or at least pretending to be. All Christopher could think was thank goodness he hadn't found out about his child when he was a teenager. How the hell would he talk to someone who was always on his phone? Come to think of it, he had precious little to offer a child of any age. The house might help, though. After all, his unwillingness to consider buying a place was one of the things that had split him and Monica up – that and his refusal to commit to having children.

Surprised to see that he wasn't the only one paying more than usual attention to the children, he watched his father look from his Uncle Charles to Joanne and to Peter. As soon as one of them looked his way though, his father turned his head, seeming to want to watch them rather than to engage with them. What on earth was he up to?

Looking from his father to his mother, Christopher saw the latter nod to a waitress, who swiftly disappeared through a swing-door to return carrying a silver-coloured cake board supporting a magnificent cake. Decorated as if it were a parcel with blue icing covered in silver stars and tied with a navy-coloured icing ribbon in a perfect bow, it looked from a distance as if he could actually unwrap it. As he bent towards the cake, the heat from the forty candles made him recoil and the candlelight pierced his eyes making them water a little. People would think he was crying and that was definitely not the case.

His mobile bleeped and he looked with relief at the message.

'Hey! How's your meal going? I've got to talk with you. Found something odd happening in the stuff I photographed from the diary this morning. Can't wait to see you tomorrow at 10.30! Nancyx'

A kiss! Was it a mistake? Was Nancy trying to be friendly or did it signify nothing more than, 'from' on a card? He'd never put an 'x' on a text to a woman other than his girlfriend, and even then he wouldn't bother if it was only a short message to make an arrangement. With or without a kiss? How could one letter cause so much trouble?

CHAPTER 12

Present day: Wednesday 21 April 10:30am

Cradling his black coffee whilst Nancy scooped the top off her cappuccino, Christopher wondered why she'd chosen such an unfashionable place to meet, and as if she'd read his thoughts – a very disturbing premise – he heard her say.

'It's dead in here 'til lunchtime. No one will bother us. You can sit with one drink for ages. So, how'd it go last night?'

'Good. Mum made an amazing cake and they all sang 'Happy Birthday' to me. I haven't seen my uncle and my cousin and her kids since...well, in a while anyway.'

Stopping himself just in time, Christopher realised that he'd become so used to everyone knowing about his brother's death it'd hardly registered that Nancy knew nothing of the family tragedy. It was refreshing to be in the company of someone who didn't feel pity every time they looked at him. But she seemed to be avoiding eye contact this morning. When she looked up briefly from her coffee, he could see that her eyes were covered in red veins. Blinking frequently, she opened her laptop.

'I hardly got any sleep and when I finally dropped off, I dreamed about being a photographer. Excuse me, I'm so wired from all the caffeine I downed during the night, I hardly know what I'm saying. I'm pretty sure it was all that stuff that Anne writes in the diary about the photographic process – the lighting, location, all those noxious chemicals, how the equipment was set up, the exact image she sees upside-down in the camera. Right from the get-go she gives such precise details of each photograph she takes, it's like an instruction manual. I guess it meant everything to her.'

'She was a photographer in the eighteen-sixties?'

'Sure, as far as I've transcribed, but she only photographs relatives and female friends, oh and some landscapes. Anyways, I wanted to run this dream by you.'

'O...kay,' he said a little too hesitantly to be convincing, but she didn't seem to notice.

'Get this. I had a Victorian camera, the type that Anne uses in the eighteen-sixties. Here's the thing – I was at a wedding, but by the time I'd gone through all the rigmarole of getting the camera set up and the black cloth, everyone had moved on and I was alone. I don't remember any more but, you know, it was one of those dreams where you wake up, but you're not sure if you're still in the dream and just dreaming that you've woken up. It freaked me out. I've never been so glad to veg in front of the TV. Don't get me wrong though, I'm made up you're letting me have access to Anne's diary. It's the sort of primary source people would murder for.'

'Well, you don't need to dream about it or kill anyone,' Christopher said, pleased to take ownership of the diary without his father's presence.

Peeling aside the layers of bubble-wrap and tissue paper as if it were a museum piece, she folded them over to form a cushion.

'I had to work on a chapter for my supervisor last night before I looked at the diary and it was around two when I started the transcription. It took me time to get my eye in. Some of the flourishes in the handwriting are almost illegible.'

Taking her right index finger, she touched the far corner of her eye before pressing gently on her eyelid and blinking several times.

'I'm beat. Excuse me, I'll just pop to the restroom.'

He watched her as she left the table. Her bubbly chestnut hair, set free from its plaits, would have looked scruffy but for the sheer volume which detracted from its untidiness. Pushing the restaurant door open, she turned and, much to his embarrassment, caught him staring at her. His instant half-smile felt more like a grimace and he buried his head in the diary as if he'd been mulling over something that he'd just read and simply happened to be resting his eyes in her direction.

When his parents had given him the diary, he'd thought it was the sort of present you'd give someone much older than forty and he wasn't ready for the pipe and slippers just yet. He'd opened it and all he could think was – is that how they see me? Not as a young guy, but as a middle-aged man who might like to sit of an evening and look at some old diary his father had shoved in his attic and forgotten about. But since Nancy's interest in the diary, like a child who'd seen another child enjoying a toy he'd previously dismissed, he was going to try his level best to read the damned difficult handwriting.

1ˢᵗ August 1860

My nineteenth year! Rose early, 6 o'clock. The morning very bright. Had many pretty presents - a brooch from dear papa, a locket from Dorothy and a red-leather... from Mary. Soon after 10 o'clock had visit from dear Harold and his parents, Patrick and Rachel Drew. He looked very well and was in good spirits. He remained some time talking with me during which he made it known that he had taken note of my interest in photography. I can talk so confidently and openly to him. He made me a present of a <u>camera</u>! This has been a most surprising day.

'How much have you managed to read?' Nancy asked as soon as she returned.

'Part of the first entry about Anne's birthday, but there's one bit I can't quite make out. What did Mary give her?'

'A red-leather photo album. You don't, by any chance, have that as well, do you?'

'No, not as far as I know. I can ask my parents though.'

'Thanks. I only got as far as January 7ᵗʰ 1864, but boy does she take her photography seriously. I looked her up on the net but she doesn't have any entries. It's a shame. I wonder what happened to her. Would you like me to email you the pages I've transcribed so far or shall I wait until I'm done with the whole diary? It's your call. I'm a bit slow 'cos I've got my thesis supervisor breathing down my neck. He's chasing me for my next chapter so I've been juggling the two.'

'If you could send the pages as you transcribe them, that'd be great. Thanks. You said in your text that there was something going on. What have you found?'

'Anne wrote on January 6ᵗʰ about attending a party at Robert Gastrell's new house – your house! She says tons about what great pains Robert took to ensure that all of his guests were happy including two brothers, George and Percy Wimlett. In the next entry, Anne says that she was walking in the street with Robert and her mother-in-law, Rachel when they saw George and Percy talking in violent tones. Robert looked *alarmed and concerned* and because they were all too embarrassed to speak further, Anne remained at quite a loss to know what was the matter between the brothers. She knew that there'd been a problem with a sweetheart, but couldn't imagine that they'd display their grievances in this manner.'

'Normal sibling rivalry?'

'They were Victorian gentlemen and to be seen arguing in the street would never have happened. It must've been some serious problem,' she said, starting to photograph the diary.

'I wonder if she explains the incident later in the diary.'

'I only wish I could transcribe it as quickly as I can photograph it. Her handwriting is quite small and narrow, which was appropriate for a woman of the time, but combined with the flourishes it's quite difficult to read, but I'm no quitter.'

As Nancy moved from side to side photographing each page, she offered a running commentary on the diary. Thank goodness there were so few other customers and the self-service restaurant area was at the other end, he thought, or they'd be chucked out.

'The punctuation isn't consistent either, which is again typical of a diary of the time. She uses a load of hyphens, dashes, exclamation marks and long spaces. She maxed out on the description of the photography process though, which can be a bit tedious. Sorry! But, at other times she writes emotionally, almost poetically, underlining significant words or phrases two or even three times.'

'How will you present the diary in your thesis?'

'I wanted to run it by you first. If you agree, I'll put in photographs of significant pages alongside the transcriptions exactly as they appear with grammatical errors intact. But, in the transcription I do for you and your family, I was thinking of putting in periods – I mean full stops – and correcting misspelling and punctuation so it's more readable. It's your call.'

'Whatever you think's best. I don't mind.'

'Great.'

'I've brought our family tree for you to have a look at, if you think it could be any use to your studies. It has some weird gaps though. There's no reference to Robert after 1864 or even a death certificate, but in the 1911 census, a man named Francis Robert Gastrell was living at my house. Sorry, I mean, your house with his wife and son. It's got to be Robert's son as we have a family tradition that the first-born son takes his father's name as his middle name. Francis died in Stratford-upon-Avon, but they couldn't find any record of a birth certificate for Francis. Strange, don't you think?'

'Not really, there's so much missing in history. Sometimes I think I'd love to know every tiny detail about people's lives, but maybe it's for the best that we don't. None of us would live up to too much scrutiny would we? Your folks have done a killer job on this family tree. I wish mine were more like yours,' she said, pausing briefly before she continued to photograph.

Mention of his parents reminded him that he should have met them ten minutes ago for lunch. Too embarrassed to stop her photographing straightaway, he let her carry on before apologising for his awful timing. When she invited him to join her at Holy Trinity Church later if he had a spare hour so that she could show him some of the Gastrell graves, he almost choked. But of course, he hadn't told her about David.

CHAPTER 13

Present day: Wednesday 21 April 4pm

As soon as they reached the end of Waterside and entered Southern Lane, the traffic noise disappeared to be replaced by the distinctive cooing of pigeons and all sorts of other birds Nancy didn't recognise. It was sweet finding someone who was more of a tourist than her. Playing guide to Christopher would be fun.

Once the narrow red-brick terraces had given way to the grey stone wall enclosing Holy Trinity Church, an expanse of mature trees opened up in front of them. The tops of the gravestones, yellowed by a hazy sun added to the feeling of time slowing down that she always got in this part of town. A faint breath of wind lifted the budding leaves of the limes and caught her hair, but didn't cause so much as a hint of movement in the conifers that stood stock still – as if their lives depended upon maintaining their guard of the church that was so significant to the Shakespeare story, she liked to think.

'I'll just set up my camera and tripod.'

'It looks professional.'

'Yes, I'm a freelance photographer.'

'No way! That reminds me, I've got a photo to show you on my cell that I found in the archives. It's of a wedding that happened here at Holy Trinity Church in early 1864. There's Robert Gastrell and his parents Archibald and Constance. Anne Drew is there. You can see she's quite tall by the standards of her day and very pretty. She's standing with her father, the Reverend Walter and her two sisters, Dorothy and Mary. Oh, and George and Percy Wimlett, you know, the two young men Anne wrote about having the argument over a sweetheart are there too.'

'How d'you know who's who?'

'Their names were written on the back of the photo!'

They laughed.

'Check out how the women are dressed. It's almost impossible to tell which one's the bride. It originates from Roman law when they thought that jealous evil spirits would cause disharmony between the happy couple and so to confuse them the bridesmaids dressed the same as the bride, even down to identical veils and bouquets. The detail of the dresses is picked out well, but the men's dark suits have lost all of their shading. They look like cardboard cut-outs,' Nancy observed, unable to hide the same disappointment that she'd felt when she'd first found it in the archives.

'The Victorian black and white developing process didn't cope very well with tonal subtlety. Anything dark can often look flat, unless the photographer was highly skilled, especially when there was so much white to focus on,' Christopher explained. 'You can see that one of the young bridesmaids and a boy of maybe nine or ten must've moved because their faces look deformed, almost as if they're wearing masks.'

'There's another thing that's bugged me right from when I first saw this photo – the composition. What I can't understand is why one man is standing in front of another so that you can only see the other's eyes and top hat. Surely, even back in the day, a professional photographer wouldn't have stood for that.'

'You're right. No adult would have dared move a muscle until they'd been given the signal that it was okay to do so. And the photographer would never have placed one man in front of another. The man must have deliberately moved to obscure the other man.'

'I love old photos don't you? They tell you so much and yet pose so many more questions than they answer.'

Nancy wondered if photography hadn't done a huge disservice to the early and mid-Victorians because it made them all seem much more alike than they could ever have looked in real life. Prior to photography, painting had displayed the great variety of colour and tone in clothing, skin, eyes and hair, but in these early photos there wasn't a single blond or red-head in evidence. In this photo and in most from this era, everyone appeared to have the same dark hair and it was all down to the early photographic process.

Standing close to Christopher's shoulder, the wind whipped up her hair weaving a tangle of long chestnut curls and thick black strands as she watched him touch the screen of her cell with his thumb and forefinger. Having gently moved them apart to enlarge the face of Robert until it blurred a little, Christopher released his finger and thumb so that the photograph reverted to a slightly smaller image but clear enough to see the individual features of his ancestor on the small screen.

'I reckon he's about your height. How tall are you?'

'Six foot four.'

'You look a lot like him,' she said when he continued to scrutinise the image.

'Sorry, it's a bit sentimental isn't it? It must be because of his house.'

'I figure the desire to resemble somebody else is one of the most powerful forces there is. To unconditionally belong to a group, a group to which you have a connection without having to officially join or fulfil any criteria, is what most people crave when it comes down to it. You belong simply by being born, even if you don't get along with your family, even if you detest them,' Nancy finished, an image of her own folks crossing her mind.

'Do people really care that much about their blood relations these days?'

'Yeah, sure. Look at all the DNA testing that's done and there still seems to be a basic human need to know that you look like someone else. I caught a TV programme once where two women were reunited as adults. When one of them saw a photo of her half-sister, the first thing she did was show it to her husband and ask him, 'do you think she looks like me?' It really burned me up because he answered, 'yes' very quickly although they looked nothing like one another.'

Christopher was gazing at the ground as if she wasn't there.

'You okay?'

'Yeah, sorry, carry on.'

'It happened to one of my friends who had a very happy childhood with her adopted family, but when she got to eighteen, she went out on a limb to look for her biological parents saying that she needed to find someone else in the world who looked like her. Straight up!'

Despite a thin smile and a nod, he turned his back on her to resume his photography.

'I'll just take a walk,' she said to the top of his head, receiving only a wave of his hand in acknowledgement. What was his bag?

A few minutes later, he came back and stood at her side.

'Sorry, Nancy, thanks for waiting. The light was perfect back there and I couldn't resist it. Sorry, you were going to show me something.'

Taking her lead from his renewed enthusiasm, she guided him along the path lined with ancient headstones. Set at odd angles and differing heights, they looked like the, 'before' publicity shots at her dentists' office: the teeth all worn away and blackened. Stepping gingerly onto the graveyard's close-cropped grass and taking care not to walk too close to the headstones, she made her way slowly towards the monument that she wanted to show him.

Standing with her hands clasped, head a little inclined as if at a new grave, the student in her longed to tell him that the cross on top of the marble headstone was a Latin cross because its upright was longer than its horizontal bar, and that the three steps of the plinth symbolised the virtues of Faith, Hope and Charity, but instead she kept respectfully silent. Something had touched a nerve with him. It had started so well, but after she'd spoken to him about the DNA, it was almost as if she'd done something wrong. What the hell had she done?

Looking at him out of the corner of her eye, she saw his gaze drop from the cross to the headstone whose inscription looked so clear it could have been carved that day.

IN LOVING
MEMORY OF
A DEAR HUSBAND
AND FATHER
ARCHIBALD GEORGE GASTRELL
DIED 31 MARCH 1865 AGED 69 YEARS
"HE LIVED FOR THOSE HE LOVED
AND THOSE HE LOVED REMEMBER"
CONSTANCE FRANCES GASTRELL
A LOVING MOTHER
DIED 23 DEC 1882 AGED 73 YEARS
"TOGETHER AGAIN"

As Christopher moved forwards, Nancy took a step back as if they were performing a dance in slow-motion. Waiting until he turned towards her, she spoke in a whisper.

'It's almost as if they passed recently isn't it?

Ignoring her comment, 'is Robert Gastrell buried in this churchyard?' was all he wanted to know.

'I'm really sorry, but I couldn't find a headstone for him and since there isn't a death certificate, it's unlikely he'd be buried here. There's nobody with the name of Robert buried here at all. Francis Robert Gastrell and his wife are buried in the cemetery that was opened in Stratford in 1881 on the Evesham Road, though.'

'Have you traced any of your ancestors?'

Christopher's question wrong-footed Nancy. She was prepared to talk about Victorian funerary rituals and other people's families, but not her own.

'I...I've never really thought about it. I couldn't wait to

leave home. My dad left when I was two and mom drinks. You're so lucky to have folks you can hang with, you know, the birthday and all.'

She hadn't meant to tell Christopher about her family, but she felt bad for him that Robert Gastrell wasn't buried in Holy Trinity's graveyard and it had just sort of come out.

'Look, I'm sorry. I didn't mean to pry. Did you find any other headstones of people who appear in Anne's diary?'

'I know it's not your family, but I did find the surname of Dawson – Anne's parents.'

Treading carefully on the spongy spring grass before pausing in front of another headstone, Nancy was more comfortable this time, knowing that she didn't need to spare his feelings. After all, the Dawsons weren't his family.

'If you look at the border, you can see it's decorated with ivy. Its three-pointed leaves represent the Trinity and it's the symbol of undying affection.'

The moment it left her mouth, she wished she hadn't said anything. Suddenly, it seemed inappropriate to make an academic point at the graveside of the parents of Anne Drew, the young woman whose diary she'd had in her hands just this morning.

Sacred
To the Memory of
The Reverend Walter Dawson
Late vicar of this parish
who died January 2nd 1885
aged 84 years
also

May Laura Dawson

wife of the above

who died July 6th 1857

aged 32 years

'Is Anne buried here?'

'There's no mention of her, but of course she probably married again and changed her surname of Drew. She was widowed so very young after all. Only twenty.'

'Is there anyone at all with the first name of Anne of around the right date?'

'No. I've not found anything to suggest that Anne is buried here, I'm afraid. I've searched the cemetery records but there's nothing there either.'

'That's a shame.'

'There's another monument I'd like to show you, if that's okay. It's over here. If you read this side first and then move around clockwise it will make more sense. It's quite poignant as Anne writes about it as being, 'the worst day of my life'.'

Nancy watched Christopher read the first inscription on the enormous white obelisk that, at a height of about eight feet, was easily the grandest monument in the entire churchyard.

Sacred

To the memory of

HAROLD DREW

who departed this Life

November 11th 1861

Aged 22 Years

This time, she would keep her mouth shut until he spoke. Walking slowly around the obelisk, reading the dedications to Harold's parents, Patrick and Rachel Drew, he returned to stand in front of the young man's name for a few minutes more before telling her that he'd had enough of looking at graves.

'Would you like to go look inside the church?'

'I'll give it a miss today unless you want to,' he replied quickly.

Walking towards the exit of the churchyard along the avenue of fiercely lopped lime trees that had taken on a sinister look since the sun's disappearance, they followed the curve of the pavement past a small wooden gate that led to an expanse of grass and mature trees. She pointed out the sign that announced the Royal Shakespeare Company Gardens, but he hardly looked. The distant siren of an ambulance or perhaps a police car, barely audible a moment ago, increased in volume as they walked along Mill Lane and she thought she saw Christopher shudder, but she might have imagined it. It had been a mistake to take him to the graveyard, but she couldn't get why.

The uneasy silence sat heavily between them, but for the life of her she couldn't think of a word to say to him and when she saw the cascading purple flowers of the wisteria, she almost broke into a run, thankful for any distraction. How she loved this beautiful reminder of home, whose exotic-looking flowers grew in some eastern states as invasively as a weed where the climate matched that of their native China. It was strange that they also somehow perfectly suited this corner of Warwickshire. Unobscured by any significant leaves, a profusion of pendant sweet-pea-like buds had opened up to reveal bluey-purple flowers that dripped from the bare branches. Although she knew its very sweetest fragrance was released at night, she closed her eyes, and eased one of the racemes towards her nose, pushing it deep into the petals to force the scent into her nostrils.

Feeling slightly heady, she withdrew from the plant, wondering what on earth Christopher would make of her leaving him standing in the street on his own to shove her face in a plant growing up the wall of somebody else's house. Ready for a sarcastic comment, she glanced at him, but he came forwards and asked her to hold one of the tiny mauve florets so that he could photograph it close up.

'Would wisterias have been around in Stratford four hundred years ago?' he asked.

'I don't think so, but they could well have been here in Victorian times, so Robert Gastrell may have seen one somewhere in Stratford. Actually, I think there might be one in his garden. It's an unusual year though. Ordinarily the wisteria is out in Stratford around the first two weeks in May, but this year the blooms will be fully open for the Shakespeare Birthday Parade.'

'How long have you been in Stratford?'

'Two and a half years and I was hoping to finish my PhD next year but now I've got the diary, well, I was wondering... if you'd give me permission, you never know, perhaps there's even a book in it.'

'Absolutely. That'd be great! And you'd stay in Stratford longer?'

Nancy hadn't meant to mention her idea of a book but his enthusiastic reaction got her thinking that maybe it wasn't so crazy after all.

'I guess I would, yeah. I almost forgot, there's some more from the diary that I want to run by you about George and Percy Wimlett. Hang on, I've made notes on my cell,' she said flicking through the screens, 'Here we go. On April 19th, Anne witnesses a rehearsal of *Romeo and Juliet* at the temporary pavilion that Robert Gastrell designed. George is playing Romeo and Percy is Tybalt, but there's an incident during a sword fight when George catches Percy's leg. There's a lot of blood and Anne wonders if it was accidental or deliberate.'

'It sounds like they had a real problem,' he agreed, but she noticed he checked his cell. 'I've just remembered. I've got to get back to my parents to eat something, somewhere. Sorry, it's all I ever seem to do.'

'Hang on, there's something else. I touched on the diary at the end of my visit yesterday with my supervisor. I didn't plan to mention it, but he looked as if he was losing interest in my thesis because I've got a bit behind. He was very interested in the diary though. He said something about friends of his whose relatives were around in Stratford at the time of the Festival. He was having dinner with their son who's working in Stratford for a few months and he was sure he'd be interested as well. We didn't have time to discuss it as another student was due, but we will later today. I hope that's okay with you.'

CHAPTER 14

The morning of Wednesday the 17th of February 1864

Monday for health, Tuesday for wealth, Wednesday best of all,
Thursday for losses, Friday for crosses, Saturday for no luck at all

She had survived the marriage ceremony, but only just. Although Anne would be eternally grateful to her friend, Ellen Cushman and her new husband, Bernard Howard, that they had waited until her two years of mourning had ended, the sound of the bells of The Church of the Holy Trinity had threatened to overwhelm her. Trying as best she might to keep her sentiments in check, she had allowed herself only a sideways glance at the enormous white obelisk that Patrick and Rachel had erected by which to remember their son. The space they had insisted upon leaving for her own name, if she were to die before marrying again, beckoned to her as if fate had decreed that she would not escape its clutches for long.

The white kid gloves, the handkerchief embellished with the initials of her maiden name and the diamond necklace that she had worn on that special day, a gift from her darling Harold, she had kept, but she had not been able to bear to preserve the wedding dress. How important it had all seemed: the tightness of the bodice giving her the smallest of waists, the full skirt held out by hoops and petticoats and the softness of the embroidered silk stockings. Most of the time it felt as if it had happened to someone else and that she had created the whole day in a dream.

But, today there could be no escape from remembrance: it was the same day of the week that she had chosen, the same church, same broad flagstone path, same lime branches entwined overhead and the four grey horses and carriage came to a standstill precisely where hers had stopped. Excusing herself from the cluster of family and friends, she wondered if her need to be solitary at times of high emotion had been exacerbated by the long period of mourning. Had it assisted her recovery or had it resulted in quite the opposite effect? It had been such a close repetition of her own service that, as she had stood in the church, it was as if she were somehow being forced to watch her own wedding from the periphery and she wished with all her heart that she could have advised her younger self to throw caution to the wind, liberate herself from convention and squeeze every last drop of enjoyment from those precious seven months.

> Married when the year is new, he'll be loving, kind and true,
> When February birds do mate, You wed nor dread your fate.
> If you wed when March winds blow, joy and sorrow both
> you'll know.
> Marry in April when you can, Joy for Maiden and for Man.
> Marry in the month of May, and you'll surely rue the day.
> Marry when June roses grow, over land and sea you'll go.

> *Those who in July do wed, must labour for their daily bread.*
> *Whoever wed in August be, many a change is sure to see*
> *Marry in September's shrine, your living will be rich and fine.*
> *If in October you do marry, love will come but riches tarry.*
> *If you wed in bleak November, only joys will come, remember.*
> *When December snows fall fast, marry and true love will last.*

As was the bride's prerogative, Anne had chosen the month of April and the rhyme had rung true until that terrible November morning in 1861 when Harold had passed away and she joined Queen Victoria in mourning the death of a beloved husband. Anne was not even sure if she had been truly superstitious at the time or had been blindly following tradition in allowing the rhymes to affect her choices. She remembered copying the words into her diary, but could not believe how differently she now felt. The girl who had written those words had vanished the day her husband had died. Photography had reinforced her interest in science and superstition had no place in her life.

Breathing a deep sigh of relief as the carriage arrived at Ellen's father's house, Anne made a promise to herself that she would, for her friend's sake and her own sanity, join in the merriment. She looked around to see if Robert was present, but a tone of voice that was not only out of keeping at a wedding, but was a clear breach of etiquette stopped her in her tracks.

'I have just received a letter from Mr Phelps to say that he will not now take any part in our Festival in Stratford.'

'Why on earth should he say that? Mr Phelps is our foremost British actor and upon receipt of our invitation immediately agreed to perform.'

'Mr Phelps states that he has recently received word that Mr Fechter has agreed to play Hamlet.'

'There was no intention of insulting Mr Phelps,' countered the speaker defensively.

'Mr Phelps writes that in the committee's second letter in December thanking him for his agreement to take part in the Festival, it was mentioned that the programme of events had not been decided, except that *Hamlet* would be on the twenty-sixth of April,' continued the other man.

'Mr Phelps was not directly offered the part of Hamlet though was he?'

'No, but he expected to be offered any part that he wished since he had been approached first and his choice would naturally have been that of Hamlet.'

Moving a little closer in order to confirm her suspicion of their identities, Anne saw her father-in-law, Patrick Drew talking to Robert's father, Archibald Gastrell. Patrick was waving his spectacles in his right hand whilst they talked animatedly. His thick, brown eyebrows, that had miraculously preserved their original colour, were moving up and down at an alarming rate and he kept pulling the fingers of his left hand through his beard as if he might pluck those hairs to make his chin resemble his bald head.

What could possibly have led these prominent men to air their grievances in public, and at a marriage of all places? It reminded her of George and Percy's argument in the public street a few weeks ago. What was happening to gentlemen's manners these days?

'Certain of the public and a number of British actors will feel indignant at the news that Mr Fechter, a Frenchman, has been selected to play Hamlet at such a great national celebration, rather than the English, Mr Phelps,' Archibald said.

'Yes, but it was as Hamlet that Mr Fechter excelled. It was because of his unprecedented run in London that he was asked to play the part in Stratford. We must not forget that it was the British public in the main who went to see him play the Danish prince,' Patrick replied.

'I don't dispute that particular success, but at such a showcase for our country I do think that Mr Phelps would have been a more suitable choice.'

'I have to admit I was most concerned when Mr Johnson called to see me last night to tell me the news. His position as Chairman of the Entertainments Committee seems to have gone to his head. As you know, I did not authorise him to offer the part of Hamlet to Mr Fechter, but since he has taken it upon himself, I do not believe that we are in all conscience able to withdraw the offer.'

'What has been done cannot be undone and after the complete endorsement of *The Times* of Stratford's right to hold the national Festival, I am confident that everyone will eventually come round to Mr Fechter's appointment as Hamlet.'

'I have to agree that it was most heart-warming to read in *The Times* that either the London Committee or the Stratford Committee must be extinguished altogether or become auxiliary to the other and that their sympathy lies wholly with Stratford.'

'It was better than I should ever have hoped, particularly the conclusion that the world thinks of Shakespeare, not in connection with London, but with Stratford and that London should seek to assist our small country town.'

'Well, let us hope that every newspaper in the land will take our side. Mr Phelps is to have all correspondence regarding the committee's request that he take part in the

Festival published in the morning papers. We shall wait and see which of them condemn and which support us.'

'At least we may rest easy in the knowledge that Charles Dickens will write in favour of Stratford,' Archibald said.

'Your words remind me that I received a letter from Charles this morning to say that he will return to England on the third of February. He travels so frequently to France. I do wonder what attraction that country could possibly hold for him over his native land,' Patrick mused.

Anne heard no more as she was gathered up by the crowd of wedding guests surging towards the rear of Ellen's father's magnificent house. The February light allowed for far clearer images outdoors than indoors and when there was a large party to be photographed, it was the only option, but Anne disputed the decision to use the French windows as a background. She would have chosen a more natural setting to display the dresses to their best advantage, but she had heard that the photographer had bowed to Mr Cushman's insistence that his grand residence should take pride of place.

Positioning the bride and bridegroom on the top step, Ellen's father to his daughter's left and Bernard's father between his son and the groomsman, the photographer asked Ellen's three sisters to take the next step down in front of the young couple. Anne had been so engrossed in the spectacle before her that she had not noticed that Robert was now standing by her side until he cleared his throat a little too deliberately. As she turned towards him, the photographer asked them to take their places and they shared a moment of frustration that they had been parted before they had even spoken a word.

None of the adults dared to move. It was a different matter for the children, though. Standing on the ground directly in front of the happy couple, the two child bridesmaids, who were wearing their dresses short but clothed in the same veils and flowers as the bride, fussed and fidgeted as did the four young nephews, two of whom had settled for sitting cross-legged and two who had decided that this was not comfortable enough and sat with legs out to one side. Benjamin Drew, alone of the children, maintained a rigid pose.

In common with other ladies of their age, Anne and Ellen had both been inspired in their choice of wedding attire by Princess Victoria's wedding, an occasion widely illustrated in the newspapers six years earlier. Ellen and her five adult bridesmaids wore creamy-white silk gowns trimmed in handmade lace displaying a fine network of floral motifs and each wore a coronet of orange blossom and myrtle as symbols of purity, love and domestic happiness. A lace-trimmed veil attached to the crown covered each lady's face and a matching floral bouquet completed their armoury of protection against the Devil. Superstitious nonsense. It certainly had not worked for her. If she were ever to marry again, the ceremony would be so very different from her first.

How she wished that Ellen had allowed her to suggest to Mr Cushman that she should take the marriage photograph, but her friend did not want to irritate or embarrass her father and Anne could not really blame her: a woman wedding photographer would make him the laughing stock.

The insistence of Ellen's father that all of the guests should be included in the photograph, left Anne to ponder what could possibly be the outcome; a group of this magnitude almost always resulted in the failure of at least two people to remain still, spoiling the image for the couple and their families. But, over and above the difficulties of keeping a large group of people motionless for several minutes, was the mismatched exposure that the combination of hair colour and complexion would require. Anne knew that her own clear white skin and fair hair and that of her sisters would impress its image rapidly onto the film, but that Robert's thick black hair would take much longer to develop. As for Percy's red hair, it would require more accurately timed exposure or the details of the hair would not fully come out and they would all look as if they had the same dark hair.

Of course, it was Ellen upon whom the photographer would judge the exposure. Her fair hair, skin and white dress would mean that the dark-haired guests and the darkly-clad gentlemen would lose detail in the final image unless the photographer was highly skilled. A collodion containing up to one half bromide to deal with such variation would be employed, but in order to counter the likelihood of a harsh picture due to the excess of contrast, Anne knew that a strong developer would be favoured to allow for a more equal deposit of silver. However, even after taking all of this into consideration, she had to acknowledge to herself that it would still be difficult to obtain texture from the abundance of white material. A slow, careful development would be required so that the faint shadows, which gave life and form to the white dresses, would not be overwhelmed by a rapid deposit of the silver. In the end it was all about the silver.

The photographer asked George to move to the side so that Percy's face could be seen more clearly, but the moment he lifted the black cloth attached to the camera, Anne noticed that George moved back in front of his brother so that only the latter's eyes would be seen. One of the little bridesmaids sneezed and Benjamin moved his head to look at her, reminding them that it was still only February after all.

CHAPTER 15

The morning of Wednesday the 2nd of March 1864

Robert could not believe that they were having to travel to London at this late stage: the second of March for goodness' sake! With the Festival just fifty-three days away, Patrick had received a letter from their principal actor Mr Fechter, friend and business associate of Charles Dickens and Philip Wimlett, informing the committee that he would not now be able to play Hamlet in Stratford-upon-Avon, despite having agreed to perform the part.

Mr Fechter had come to believe that the general public was turning against him because they did not want a Frenchman to play the leading role in celebrating England's greatest playwright. It could not be denied that Mr Phelps's letters to *The Times* in January had convinced some of its readers that the Stratford-upon-Avon Committee must be condemned for having cast Hamlet to Mr Fechter: indeed, for soliciting any foreigner to play before a British audience on an occasion of such national pride. It was of course impossible to find a suitable actor to replace him at such short notice so they would not now be able to offer this great play at all, but would have to suggest a performance worthy of taking its place or the Festival and Stratford-upon-Avon would lose face.

Patrick had sent immediate word to Philip requesting his assistance in the matter and Philip had welcomed the opportunity to repay the generosity of the Drews in opening up their home to his sons, George and Percy, especially as, a full two months later, they were still living there. Philip did what he practised daily as a theatre manager in London; from the sudden indisposition of a principal actor to a failing piece of stage machinery, he found solutions to seemingly unsolvable problems at very short notice. *Leave it to me. It is all in a day's work!* he had scrawled in flamboyant style at the end of his reply inviting them to visit him in London and discuss the details of the performances that he could offer.

As he guided his father through the throng of people gathered at Stratford-upon-Avon's railway station, Robert scoured the crowd until he could see Patrick, George and Percy. Glancing up at the large station clock to confirm the time, he knocked his knuckles against the cast iron of the freshly painted green pillars supporting the canopy over the platform and cursed under his breath. Much of the town seemed to have been offered a similar treatment and it grieved him, not only because it reminded him of the close proximity of the Festival but also because there were many hidden areas of the town that had received no such attention.

Pulling open the wooden door of the railway carriage, Robert waited for the two elder men to seat themselves before he took his position next to his father. Patrick excused himself from inclusion in any conversation, saying that the recent Festival difficulties had sapped his vitality and, taking off his spectacles, let his eyes close. Robert could not wait to change trains at Leamington Spa when both men would fall asleep on the long journey to London so that he could take off his hat. His father always insisted upon keeping his top hat firmly upon his head, no matter what, and he expected his son to follow suit. After they had settled into the London train, his father, true to form, stroked his eyebrows and Robert watched as his eyelids drooped and he forced them open once, twice, but not a third time. As his father rested his head against the back of the seat, he tipped his hat over his eyes presenting a comical picture of which, had he known, he would have seriously disapproved.

Rail travel excited Robert, but only when he travelled alone and could look out of the window at his leisure as the fast-moving countryside hurried by. He loved the bumping and jolting of the train that created a disrupted view of multiple visual impressions, reminding him that he was rushing from open fields to the crowded metropolis to join a jostling stream of people and vehicles. Today, however, he would make an effort to engage George and Percy in talk of London and the theatre. Since his father and Patrick were both asleep, he was the next most senior gentleman in their party and as such it was his duty to entertain them, but it would be hard work. Lately, the young men had stopped talking as easily with one another as they had earlier in the year and after several lapses into awkward silences, Robert was glad to have taken Edmund's advice to bring a newspaper: a signal to his two young fellow travellers that he too would no longer partake in the conversation.

As they descended the train a few hours later, steam snorted heavily into Robert's nostrils causing him to sneeze, but it was not for himself that he had cause for concern; he knew that the dense London fog would soon begin to irritate his father's asthma, resulting in unsuccessful clearings of his throat whenever he attempted speech. The smell of smoke clung to their heavy layers of clothing like a distressed child and Robert watched his father's face succumb to angry patches of red, tinged with purple. Archibald's left eye looked as if it had been subjected to an assault; leaking tears which he blotted with his great cotton handkerchief, he presented an unwarranted image of provincial simplicity amongst the hurly burly of the capital city.

A porter arrived with their luggage set upon a truck which he wheeled through the station gate to Philip's carriage. As the station bell rang, cabs dashed up driving hard so as not to lose the train and Robert smiled as the confusion of the city gathered them into its gigantic arms. He could not decide whether its strength would embrace or crush the members of their party; he, for one, could not wait to greet the vitality of the metropolis, but he feared the chaos of the traffic-choked streets might overwhelm his father who winced every time that the carriage turned and juddered across the blue-grey granite setts of the road that contrasted so harshly to the rounded rose-coloured cobbles of his home town.

Pulling the curtain to one side, Robert pressed his face against the carriage window. The new plate-glass of the elegant shop-fronts sparkled in the main thoroughfare, but his eye could not penetrate the many dingy narrow streets leading off towards...towards...he realised he had no idea where they went. Advancing towards the West End, on the other hand, the rows of goldsmiths' shops displayed tableware and jewellery sets of all kinds suggesting transportation to an unbelievably beautiful other world as if Robert had dreamed up the gloomy alleyways.

Taking a sharp right turn, they now entered a straight, broad avenue studded with more gas lamps than the whole of Stratford-upon-Avon put together. Each house was identical in outward appearance from its black cast iron railings to its imposing stairs leading up to the grand front door and its meaner steps leading down to the cellar. The order of such streets pleased Archibald, but Robert was eager to experience the ancient lanes that he had seen in many a watercolour, in which deep bays and overhanging eaves seemed almost to touch one another and the cobbled street cut a precarious pathway between them. Successive plans to demolish these alleyways had been rejected because they were seen as a monument to Elizabethan London. Robert thought it was better to preserve some of the past rather than sweep it all away in the name of progress, but believed that the city must change to satisfy the needs of its poorest communities.

As soon as the carriages stopped in front of the Wimlett family house, George and Percy hurried out in great excitement. Philip shook hands with Archibald, Patrick and then Robert before patting his sons on the back, suggesting that they go upstairs immediately to find their mother, who had been looking forward so much to their return that it had brought on a slight headache.

'Gentlemen,' Philip announced, 'it is with great pleasure that I welcome you to my home and receive news of the tercentenary arrangements first-hand. Do not worry about the replacement for *Hamlet* because I have the solution. I shall place my own theatre company at your disposal. The Princess's Theatre will offer *The Comedy of Errors* followed by *Romeo and Juliet*. George will play Romeo and Percy will play

Tybalt. I shall come to Stratford on the nineteenth of April and assist with the preparations myself. What do you think, my friends?'

'It is such a relief. I cannot thank you enough, Philip. We shall forever be indebted to you for your generosity,' Patrick replied, placing a hand on Philip's shoulder.

The latter's face flushed with colour until his freckles almost disappeared.

'I suggest that you take out announcements in the newspapers in order to offer people a choice of a refund of their ticket money for *Hamlet* or a replacement ticket for both *The Comedy of Errors* and *Romeo and Juliet*.'

Although they had slept for most of the journey, his father and Patrick both looked worn out and expressed a desire to rest until the hour of dinner. Robert was surprised at his father's fatigue and wondered if his usual energy at home was a result of rest and routine and that this journey had revealed his true frailty. Philip, however, appeared glad of the opportunity to talk to Robert out of the earshot of the elder men.

'I trust my sons have been conducting themselves in an appropriate manner,' he said in a light tone belying his desperate need to know the truth.

Robert was content to talk generally about George and Percy but skirted around any direct comment.

'They are a breath of fresh air in our town. They had hardly been in Stratford for two days before they received invitations to dine. Hearing their stories of the Princess's Theatre makes me long for a permanent theatre in Stratford. We hope that if the pavilion is a success, the people of Stratford will gather behind us to support a permanent home outside London in which Shakespeare's plays may be performed.'

'I am certain that the pavilion will succeed and that Stratford will indeed have its own theatre in the very near future. Now, I shall leave you to rest for an hour so that you will be fresh for our dinner appointment with Charles at the Athenaeum this evening.'

As the clock chimed a quarter to eight, Philip Wimlett ushered Archibald, Patrick and Robert between the paired columns of the portico that announced the entrance to the Athenaeum Club. The impressive vaulted ceiling of the hall looked over a knot of gentlemen gathered around a figure whose back was presented to them. Beaming and shaking his head indulgently whilst he circled the crowd, Philip found a space behind a gentleman whose height was even shorter than his own, and Robert, who had a distinct advantage over the rest of his party, managed to catch the moment when the man at the centre of this attention caught sight of Philip.

'My dear, dear friend, how wonderful it is to see you.'

Mr Charles Dickens strode through the pathway that had opened up before him and embraced Philip. Heartily shaking the proffered hand of each guest with both of his, he did not let go for several moments longer than was customary, Robert noticed.

'Let me welcome you all to this great institution,' he announced.

As the crowd dissipated in the realisation that Mr Dickens was entertaining guests, the contours of the marble-columned hall revealed themselves, throwing shadows onto the gleaming mosaic floor and looking for all-the-world like a stage set from one of his many theatricals. Mr Dickens and Philip embraced one another and Robert stole a look at the great man. His grey beard and moustache, bald head with side hair brushed fiercely forward looked out of keeping with the flamboyantly ruffled shirt-front and bright red flower in his button-hole and gave him the appearance of an ordinary man dressed in someone else's fancy clothing. When Mr Dickens's eyes rested not on the more senior men in the party but on him, Robert could not help thinking that somehow he had read his thoughts in the expression on his face. Everyone knew that his character observations were nothing short of miraculous.

'It was here shortly before Christmas at the bottom of this staircase that I saw Mr William Thackeray for the very last time,' he announced. 'You know we had avoided one another for twelve years due to an artistic difference of opinion? Well, I was so shocked to see the great difficulty with which he was descending that I waited to speak to him and shivering violently, he told me that he had been in bed for three days,' and here he paused before adding in a softer tone. 'Those were the last words that we ever spoke to one another, so mundane, but thank goodness we made our peace before the awful news on Christmas Eve. It is hard to believe, but he was my exact age, only fifty-two and his mother still alive. So unnatural when the parent outlives the child.'

Robert could not think of a suitable response to this most unexpected of revelations, but his father, who no doubt already knew the story and whose rest appeared to have revitalised him, found the words.

'At least he achieved his last wish to be interred in the simplest manner at Kensal Green Cemetery and not at Westminster Abbey as many others thought befitting of a man of such stature.'

'That is true. I too have stipulated in my will that I am

to be buried in an unostentatious manner with a simple inscription and no public announcement. I favour a small local churchyard but I have not yet decided which. All I know for certain is that I, like Mr Thackeray, do not wish to be buried in Westminster Abbey. Now, gentlemen, before we entertain dinner, I insist upon showing you the famous south library.'

Floor-to-ceiling bookcases hugged each wall, shelves extended over the doorways and a wrought-iron spiral staircase led up to a gallery to reach the highest books which, Robert estimated, must have been over twelve feet in the air. The dizzying array of spines allowed the eye no resting place. Most were held rigidly upright but occasionally a row leaned slightly, due to the smallest of gaps and he had to resist the urge to ease them back into position. Charles suffered no such qualms and took a book off a lower shelf.

'Look, it is Thackeray's last book and he has even written a dedication to the Athenaeum,' he said, with the hint of a catch in his throat as he ran his fingertips over the black ink.

Replacing the book with great care, Charles led them solemnly out of the library, passing to the north of the hall and through the morning room before he entered the dining room. A lull in the chatter of voices and clinking of cutlery and glasses accompanied his arrival, to be followed by a rippled return to the myriad of conversations as he passed each table. As soon as they were nestled in the far corner, he lost no time in offering his proposal for the evening's entertainment.

'Gentlemen, would you believe that I have been mulling over my latest novel, *Our Mutual Friend* on and off for sixteen long years? Frankly, it is exhausting me. My publication date is almost upon me and I thought last evening of my younger years when I found inspiration during my nightly walks on the London streets. Since this leg started troubling me, I have had to forgo that pleasure and my writing has suffered, but I am pleased to report that my health is better than it has been in months and so, my dear friends,' and here he paused, 'I should like to invite you to accompany me this very evening.'

'When is the first instalment due?' Patrick enquired, making no attempt at a response to the invitation.

'May! I've made a return to monthly issues rather than weekly but it has worn me to death, with all the travelling to see...with all the travelling I do.'

Charles's momentary correction of his words puzzled Robert. Who was he about to say he travelled to see and why would this man whose conversation was known for its openness and honesty, suddenly prevent himself from completing the sentence in their company?

'How many instalments will there be in total?' Philip asked so quickly that Robert had no time to consider possible solutions to his questions.

'Twenty. I always try to stay a few months ahead when writing each issue in case any difficulties arise. I have been writing in instalments since 1836 and I have never experienced a problem before but I have to admit that this one...' and here he nodded ruefully, 'has almost beaten me.'

Seeing their concern, Charles's face broke into a generous grin as he filled their silence with a question of his own.

'Gentlemen, may I ask you something? Would you prefer a happy or a sad ending to *Our Mutual Friend*? I have written the first three instalments but I have not yet decided. Would my readers prefer to be left with a smile on their lips or tears in their eyes?'

As the three older men made no attempt to respond

to the question, Robert assumed that it must have been rhetorical. To offer an opinion would make him look naively foolish, he decided and so he took his opportunity to turn the conversation back to their plans for the evening. He could not wait to experience a side of London about which he had only ever read or seen depicted in paintings and in Charles he would surely have the best possible companion.

'Mr Dickens, if you do not mind, I should like to talk about the night walk. I for one would not miss it for the world.'

'Young man, I should delight in your company, but only if you use my Christian name. What do you say, Philip, Patrick, Archibald?'

Robert could see his father shift with some discomfort in the plush velvet seat and look at Philip whose lips moved soundlessly as if he were trying to conjure an excuse from the air around him.

'My dear friends,' Charles said laughing, 'I shall of course take no offence if you would prefer to rest this evening. Archibald and Patrick, you must both be tired after your journey and Philip, you will naturally want to spend time with your sons.'

The combination of Charles's talent for putting people at their ease and Robert's enthusiasm appeared to dispel any discomfort that the three older gentlemen may have experienced. They excused themselves from the night walk leaving the way clear for Robert, much to his delight, to be the sole beneficiary of the invitation.

At eleven o'clock that evening, Charles's carriage pulled up outside 57, Gloucester Place, Hyde Park Gardens. Robert hastened to follow his host who had, without so much as a word, rushed into his house, thrown his hat on the hall table and, still in his cloak, run up the stairs as if he had quite forgotten his age. Calling his name, Robert found Charles in a room on the first floor furnished with several tall chests of drawers, two hat stands and a long glass.

'You may choose whichever clothes you wish from here', he said breathlessly. 'They are clothes that my acting company used to wear in our amateur theatricals,' and after another pause. 'I would like you to keep the ones that you select. You may be able to put them to good use in Stratford-upon-Avon and see for yourself what is really going on in your town.'

Replacing his white tie and tails with the rough materials of old trousers, shirt, jacket and a coarse great-coat belted with a large brass buckle, Robert put his silk stovepipe hat carefully to one side and selected a working man's cloth cap.

'Are you ready, Robert?' Charles said, wheezing a little.

'Yes, it is quite a change,' Robert replied, viewing his reflection with some trepidation.

'The idea of disguising myself on my night walks came from my friend Mr Charles Field, or Inspector Field as he likes to be known. He joined the Metropolitan Police on its establishment in 1829 and retired in 1852 as Chief of its Detective Branch, but ever since he has been working as a private detective. He is fifty-nine now and is about to retire and fortunately his last working days have coincided with my own return to health.'

Charles's carriage rattled through the darkness throwing its two occupants from side to side and on one occasion it pitched Robert forwards almost bumping his companion's head. Thankful that it had finally come to a halt, as he did not wish to be the person responsible for injuring England's foremost living writer, Robert alighted in time to see Charles greet the outline of a portly figure who was standing in the dim light cast by a solitary gas lamp.

'Inspector Field, how good of you to meet us. May I present Mr Robert Gastrell.'

'Mr Gastrell, it's a pleasure to reinstate my night walks with my great friend Charles in my last working year. I used to act as a guide to him during my time as Chief and he, as I'm sure you know, wrote about our exploits.'

'I have indeed read and hugely enjoyed *On duty with Inspector Field* and count myself most fortunate to be able to accompany you on your next adventure,' Robert replied, the word slipping out before he could prevent it.

The naivety of the word, 'adventure', that was more suggestive of a young boy's speech than a grown man's, circled the three men, refusing to move and Robert could have kicked himself; it was a provincial reminder of the distance between him and these men who had made their own successful way in the world.

'Keep close, Mr Gastrell. I have my contacts but you never know what may happen. Drink is the main problem, but you can't blame 'em. What else do they have to look forward to, made to live like animals in hovels?'

On the street, Robert was surprised to see how aged Charles looked. He must have been drawing upon his considerable acting skills at the Athenaeum because the features and voice that had commanded the attention of all now seemed to have shrunk into those of a man much older than his years. His shoulders slumped forwards and his rounded back betrayed exhaustion and Robert could imagine that, when on his own without any audience,

Charles would resemble a very tired old man indeed. It was his face that particularly displayed the conflicts and anxieties of his life. Certainly, the separation from his wife six years ago had caused him untold misery and the announcement just last month of the death of his son, Walter, in India had profoundly shocked him, but there seemed to be something else that was on his mind; something that caused him to stumble across his words from time to time; something to which no one else was party.

Brought on a keen gust of wind, a sickening stench alerted the three men to the proximity of their destination; blackened slum-houses spewed out charcoal rags which dwarfed their occupants for whom desperation appeared to have overcome fear. Robert, who had wrongly assumed that the heaps of haunted faces filling the alley would melt into the shadows at the approach of a former policeman, tried in vain to take control of his erratic breathing as more and more spectres spilled out of the filthy gloom as if it were an enormous machine churning out an endless supply of bedraggled people. By way of reassurance, Inspector Field told him that they came because they saw a face that they had grown to know over the years. But it was not only his words that this audience craved, it was his generosity.

A call rang out with increasing urgency, but Robert could not quite catch the name. A man of middle years emerged from his lodging-house and shook the proffered hands of Charles and Inspector Field before Robert realised that he was in turn expected to take this wretched being's hand. Never before had he felt unsure about the manner in which to shake a man's hand; the filthy, fragile fingers looked as if they would be crushed to dust by the customary firm handshake and, despite wearing gloves, he could not help imagining that the dirt would penetrate the smallest holes where the silk stitching had pierced the fabric and would seep through the soft lining to touch his skin. Ashamed, he ended up unsatisfactorily cradling the collection of bones, making it horribly obvious that he had never before been confronted by such a social situation.

Lamp at the ready, Inspector Field followed the man down slimy steps into a damp cellar in which a dozen men, all smoking clay pipes, were gathered on benches at a long table littered with pots of bitter beer and playing cards. The man took up the pot at the head of the table and thumped it hard upon the wood, scattering the chaos of raised voices which immediately gathered themselves into one chorus of, 'Inspector Field, Inspector Field.' Grinning as if they were chanting his own name, the man raised his beer to toast the former policeman while holding up his other hand and to Robert's astonishment the peculiar choir instantly terminated its rendition. It was only then that Inspector Field motioned to his companions to step forward and join him. Charles strode purposefully to take his place at the inspector's side but Robert could only shuffle a couple of paces to stand behind the two men.

Watching as Charles handed the man a bag of coins, which the latter received with a broad grin before bowing deeply from his waist, Robert's gaze was drawn to a clattering on the stairs and animated voices followed by loud hushes and a gathering of eyes. It was as if the money had an aroma that had alerted more and more wretched residents, but the moment the man clapped his hands and pointed to the top of the steps, the eyes grew legs and scurried away. Leading his three visitors back up into the alley that was now hardly any less confined than the cellar due to the vast crowd that had amassed at the top of the stairs, the man was forced to put up his skinny arm as an inadequate barrier. Fast behind him, Inspector Field held out his own muscular great-coated arm and Charles and Robert squeezed through the mass of misery. A church clock struck half-past twelve and Inspector Field's vast form, made larger with truncheon and handcuffs bulging in his pockets, led the way to another cellar where another man gratefully accepted a similar monetary gift.

Casting an eye over his gentlemanly followers, one of them so very out of place in these surroundings even though dressed in Charles's theatrical costume, Inspector Field declared, 'Charles, we are both fatigued. I know that you desire to continue these nightly visits to confirm the common humanity that you share with the poor, but I strongly suggest that you forgo these walks. We are neither of us in the first flush of youth and I wish to return you to your home.'

Although Inspector Field looked not in the least tired, Charles agreed without hesitation and blew away a great breath as if blowing out three church candles at once.

'Remember Robert, you must keep the clothes because you may be able to wear them on your return to Stratford-upon-Avon and observe the parts of the town into which you have never ventured,' Charles suggested, with some little provocation his younger companion felt.

'But surely there are not areas in Stratford-upon-Avon as poorly served as these in London?' Robert replied defensively.

'Maybe not quite as deprived as those in our metropolis, but I am afraid you may be sorely disappointed at what exists in your town only a stone's throw from your own front door.'

'How will I find out what conditions exist. I do not possess your connections?' Robert could not help saying as he eyed Inspector Field's reassuring bulk.

'Put on the clothes and adopt the posture of the people around you and then simply walk. We used to cover miles and miles in our younger days, but now I have...I have other ties on my time. We must have seen a great proportion of the city back then,' Charles explained as if, Robert thought, an excuse or apology were required.

But none was due. Charles knew the sprawling metropolis better than he knew his own small town.

CHAPTER 16

The morning of Thursday the 3rd of March 1864

The next morning, an exhausted Robert joined his father, Patrick and the Wimlett family at Paddington Station for a journey on the Metropolitan Underground Railway to Farringdon Street. The world's first underground railway, Philip had announced with pride, despite the knowledge that all of his party were well aware of this fact.

'Although it has only been open for just over a year, its popularity has already led to a decision to expand the network of underground tracks,' George added, nodding to his father who smiled expansively at his son.

'It will not happen a moment too soon. There is no greater irritation than arriving at speed by railway only to have to join the congested London streets and take longer to travel a quarter of a mile than one has taken to cover fifty,' Philip continued in his usual mix of exuberance and exaggeration.

'I remember reading in the newspapers that there would be deaths from noxious fumes and that the capital would collapse into the tunnels!' Robert ventured, looking towards George and Percy, whom he had not seen since leaving for dinner the previous evening.

Philip cast a benevolent eye in the direction of Robert's smile and beamed at his two sons.

'The newspapers love to scaremonger, but the only incident they managed to find on that busy first day was that a porter was hospitalised due to the vitiated atmosphere, as they insisted on calling it. It was probably because they had to put on more trains than was expected and he was tired, or he might already have been ill, for all we know,' Patrick said, glad to support Philip's delight at this engineering feat: after all, the success of his brewery relied on scientific invention every bit as much as the railway.

Robert kept to himself the report that had found that underground train drivers who had complained of pains in the head due to choke-damp, a condition from which miners suffered when confined in an area where there was a build-up of sulphurous fumes, had been allowed to grow beards in order to filter out the worst of the smog. He did not want to dampen the high spirits of Philip to whom they would be eternally grateful for his generosity towards Stratford-upon-Avon.

As they descended the steps into the cavernous underground station, an exhalation of steam and smoke announced the train's arrival and as if it too had been deprived of air, it screeched to a panting halt in front of them. Although it smelled as if someone had thrown chemicals onto a bonfire and his breathing pinched in the suffocating atmosphere, Robert did not dare show any discomfort for fear of causing offence to the Wimlett men. Philip and George appeared as proud of the underground system as if they had designed it themselves, but Percy, he noticed, remained silent.

Waiting until he was able to see clearly through the odorous steam to confirm that the lettering denoted first-class, Robert reached for the handle to help Amelia and then the three older men into the carriage, followed closely by Percy and George. Inside the compartment, the commodious maroon leathered seats offered the visitors a comfortable welcome worthy of a gentlemen's club, complete with a carpeted floor, highly lacquered, gleaming wood and even mirrors to enable passengers to check their appearance. The generously padded chair arms ensured that the entire first-class carriage would accommodate no more than sixty passengers whilst the second and third class carriages would seat at least eighty travellers and frequently more if required, Philip had remarked.

Expecting to feel oppressed by the realisation that he was many yards, he could not bear to think how many, below the very London streets upon which he had earlier travelled, Robert was much surprised at the brightness of the light that was dissipated by the novel introduction of gas into the carriages. All sense of being underground was dispelled. The brilliance of this carriage was most unlike the ordinary oil-lighted railway carriage in which he had ridden the previous day from Stratford-upon-Avon; there was none of the haunted semi-obscurity into which they had all been plunged during their transit through each and every tunnel.

'It is so much pleasanter to have gas lighting than oil in the carriage,' Archibald observed, 'but how do they supply gas to a train?'

'The gas is carried in long India-rubber bags in the wooden boxes you can see overhead and the jets in the carriage are supplied by a gas pipe from these bags,' Philip replied.

'The gas shines brightly enough for a newspaper to be read with facility,' returned George, much to the pleasure of his father; Percy uttered not a word.

Again, Robert dared not repeat the newspapers' reports that it was indeed possible to read when the train was stationary, but that when in motion the draft through the aperture of the lamps created so much flickering as to render reading exceedingly difficult and downright unpleasant. A whistle sounded and the train, like a mole, started to burrow its way through the earth.

A mere three minutes later, however, they passed through an open cutting allowing daylight to intrude upon the blaze of gas illumination, a reminder to Robert that they were indeed moving far below the streets of London.

'Although we were lucky enough to travel on the underground train when it first opened last year,' Amelia said, 'I feel as excited and anxious as I did on that initial journey.'

'I must confess, I never fail to become swept up with enthusiasm,' Philip said to his wife, offering her small hand a comforting pat. 'We must not forget that the journey that would have taken us half a day through the London streets will take only around a quarter of an hour underground,' he continued, hardly pausing to take a breath in his haste to convey its magnificence.

It was as if he had to tell them all there was to say about the underground whilst they were travelling inside it: that once they had disembarked and returned to the open air, his observations would somehow no longer be valid and his audience uninterested.

'Conventional steam engines are used, but pipes

condense the exhaust steam into side tanks on the train as if it were holding its breath whilst in the underground tunnel and as soon as it enters an open-air cutting it exhales through a chimney,' Philip continued, his passion unstoppable.

'These tanks contain one thousand gallons of cold water,' George added as if reading a prompt written by his father.

There was an expectation, due to the father and son's confident appraisal of the underground system, that no steam or smoke would be experienced during the journey and when white wisps wafted in through the open window of the compartment, not a single comment was made. Only one part of the line remained in which the foul air caused more than a small amount of discomfort to Robert and which he knew would distress his father greatly. Engaging the Wimletts in discussion at this point, he gave his father time to clear his throat behind his handkerchief in a vain attempt to hide his breathlessness. Although the total underground journey had lasted a mere thirty-three minutes, Robert could see that his father was in need of repose. Taken out of his familiar surroundings, he was an old man like any other; he was not possessed of the extraordinary vitality that Robert had managed to persuade himself to believe over the last couple of years.

'I think we should retire to our house for luncheon and a rest or we risk being too exhausted to meet Charles later this afternoon,' Philip announced, as if reading his mind.

The early March breeze had picked up to a keen wind as they entered the Wimletts' front door and, much to Robert's relief, his father announced his intention to forgo their afternoon arrangement so that he could take his leisure before their visit to Philip's theatre that evening.

It was a little after three o'clock when Robert and Patrick, together with the three Wimlett men, shook Charles's hand. With scant regard for the presence of the two more senior gentlemen in the party, Robert set aside his usual reticence in such company to engage the writer's attention. Last night had shown him a world far beyond anything he had seen before and he meant to make the most of the opportunity to broaden his outlook.

'I lay awake for hours unable to sleep last night. I have never walked such streets after darkness, not even in my own town. I sometimes walk a little during the day but at night I always take a carriage.'

'But why, my dear fellow, why?'

'I can offer no reasonable response. It is something I have always done, I suppose.'

'I cannot recommend it highly enough. It cures almost all ills,' Charles replied with a small but significant emphasis on the word 'almost', Robert thought.

'Gentlemen, I have brought you to this spot so that you may witness for yourselves the commencement of the construction of the Victoria Embankment on the north bank of the river,' Philip declared, gesturing with pride towards the seething water of the Thames.

Marshland was being reclaimed in an attempt to tame the Thames. That wild beast, who trampled over the land leaving a muddy trail of faecal matter beneath its feet, growled and spluttered as it raged backwards and forwards. Robert had read that nothing less than a wall of iron, concrete and brick faced in granite would pen in this wild water. Massive foundations would penetrate fourteen feet below low-water mark to keep it from threatening the life of the city and maintain this unruly being's subservience forever more. The city's determination to impose order on nature and control its disobedient behaviour was unstoppable. This renewing, rebuilding and recreating of the metropolis presented such a stark contrast to the previous night that Robert could almost persuade himself that the slums had disappeared, but of course they were still there, hidden away, segregated from the so-called civilised society.

'Not only will the river be channelled, but underneath the embankment there will be a sewer and eventually part of the underground railway,' Philip added, smiling at Charles, who remained courteously quiet so that his friend could continue to impress his guests.

Robert had closely followed the course of the working life of Joseph Bazalgette, Chief Engineer of the Board of Metropolitan Works since he had produced a plan in 1852 demonstrating that sewer water did not need to continue to flow directly into the Thames. Frustratingly, finances had not been put in place until the humiliating Great Stink of the summer of 1858 had forced Parliament to hasten the decision to build the embankments and sewers. The outbreaks of cholera that had plagued this century would soon be a thing of the past. The river would become easily navigable and unusable dangerous land would be reclaimed. The Thames would be transformed and London would be redefined, he had read, but at what cost?

The methods used by the gas, water, electric telegraph and especially the railway companies sat uneasily with Robert; the appropriation of common land, the purchase mainly of cheap lodging houses and tenements by compulsion, the diverting of roads, drains and watercourses had affected the poor so much more than the well-off that he was convinced that the numbers quoted in the newspapers regarding the expected displacement of people were severely underestimated because they did not include the unregistered under-class. Even the dead seemed to have more rights than the very poor: there had been months of heated discussions in the papers regarding the disturbance of closed cemeteries and the removal of thousands of human remains. There was always a cost. Whether or not it was worth the cost was a moot point.

But, whatever he thought about the contradictions of London, tonight he would be at Philip's theatre amongst the well-to-do decked out in all their finery. He would not speak out of turn in the company of the man who had saved the Stratford-upon-Avon Committee and thereby the whole town from great embarrassment. Robert would make certain that he would find delight in all that was placed before him.

At a quarter past seven that evening, he entered the Princess's Theatre in Oxford Street to watch *The Comedy of Errors*, one of the two plays that Philip had offered to the Festival. Guiding them towards the three tiers of expensive boxes that lined the horseshoe-shaped auditorium, Philip showed them to the seats that faced directly onto the stage, as far from the gallery of cheaper seats as was possible: 'the best seats in the house,' their host had declared. As if they were actors on their own stage, all eyes looked their way as they took their seats in the company of the manager of this prestigious London theatre.

It was here in Philip's theatre that Mr Fechter had performed his celebrated Hamlet two years before, applying French techniques that displayed a subtle, natural interpretation of a meditative Danish prince. The Shakespeare performances at the Princess's Theatre had since continued to great acclaim, but none had quite repeated the success of

Mr Fechter's Hamlet. Robert could not imagine the depth of Philip's embarrassment at the breakdown in the relationship between the Stratford-upon-Avon Tercentenary Committee and Mr Fechter. It was his recommendation that had led to their invitation to the famous French actor in the first place and must certainly have contributed to Philip's generous offer of *Romeo and Juliet* and *The Comedy of Errors*.

'My honoured guests, I welcome you all to my theatre and hope that you enjoy the entertainment of my company,' Philip announced with an extravagant gesture of his hand that almost upstaged the entrance of the actors.

Mr Vining and Mr Nelson, who played the Antipholus brothers, were a good match for twins; their identical long waved wigs, embroidered pointed caps, gathered skirts that reached down to the floor each covered with an apron and orange cloak draped in precisely the same manner over the left shoulder, all helped to persuade the audience of their similarity. But, it was Messrs Charles and Henry Webb, natural brothers playing the Dromio twins who rendered the audience helpless. Everyone roared with laughter for several minutes before the actors were able to utter a single line. Wearing short tunics pulled in at the waist to emphasize their bulky physical presences and white ruffs and ribbons to pull their hair into comical contortions, they were a joy to behold.

From his seat at the end of the box, Robert took the opportunity to look towards George and Percy. Whilst the rest of the theatre wiped its eyes, they were pushing their shoulders against one another, elbows out, as if they were naughty children. Although Robert could barely see Percy's features, George's face was slightly angled towards him. A sheen of perspiration bubbled in the middle of the young man's forehead and his jaw pushed forward compressing his lips into a thin arc, bulging out the skin between his nose and mouth. It occurred to Robert that the prominent v-shaped indentation under his eye suggested a young man who had not slept well for weeks, if not months. It was perhaps a good idea that George and Percy were to stay in London with their parents if their argument in the street was anything to go by. The young men would not return to Stratford-upon-Avon until the week before the Festival. Robert, for his part, could not wait to return home where he would try out Charles's theatrical clothes. He had to know more about his town.

CHAPTER 17

The morning of Friday the 4th of March 1864

The early March air in Stratford-upon-Avon tugged at the
hem of Anne's skirt, pulling at the blanket that she had
wrapped around her legs and those of her mother-in-law,
Rachel. Wishing for the hundredth time that she had sold
the landau, better suited to the spring and summer when the
low shell of the carriage allowed for maximum visibility of
the occupants, Anne tried not to think of that first summer
before the worst day of her life.

Bought by Patrick and Rachel as a wedding gift, complete
with two horses and a groom, it had suited the newly-
married Anne and Harold, but since becoming a widow she
had no desire to be put on show. On the very few occasions
on which she had used the carriage during her two summers
of mourning, she had kept the hood closed, causing heads
to turn because hers was the only one to present itself in
such a manner in the warm weather. Nowadays, she would
prefer to ride in the smaller and more practical landaulet,

but had not yet plucked up the courage to broach the subject of selling the landau with her father-in-law. Since she was officially out of mourning she really must find the right time to approach him.

The frosted pavements glistened, but Southern Lane, which had already been churned up by delivery carts, was its usual muddy self. Guiding the landau as closely to the elevated platform as possible, the groom, Frank Adams drew up on the right-hand side. After quietening the horses, he turned them slightly to the left, spreading the carriage wheels on the side facing the platform in order to give Anne and Rachel the best opportunity to disembark without soiling their dresses on the wheels. Rachel manoeuvred her full crinoline skirt with difficulty and Anne had to admit that even her dress, which possessed only a frame at the back, had to be moved with great care.

As soon as she had heard that her father-in-law would be visiting London, Anne knew what she had to do. She would photograph in the public street commencing with the pavilion. Although she knew that it would displease Patrick, she knew equally well that Rachel would not tell him. Since Harold's death, her mother-in-law had come to view Anne almost as if she were her own flesh and blood and at the age of forty-three, there would be no more confinements for Rachel. She did not share Patrick's belief that a lady should photograph only her family and close friends in a domestic setting and she would be happy to support her daughter-in-law's endeavours even if it meant risking her husband's wrath. Anyway, since he was away in London, it was unlikely that he would ever hear of the contravention of his wishes, Anne had reassured her.

Thankfully, the weather, neither too bright nor too dull,

would provide excellent lighting conditions for this most significant of photographs. Starting two hours earlier, Anne had measured and mixed the chemicals before supervising their packing into wooden boxes that her assistant, Paul Brook, had put into the cart. He had placed the most precious one containing the camera and the glass plates beside him on the bench seat, putting the chemicals at his feet. The largest box, containing her Carbutt's darkroom tent, he had heaved behind him, together with the tripod and three gallons of water. She wished she could have helped unload the boxes and erect the tent, but it would not have been seemly for a lady to behave in such a manner in public and word would be certain to have reached Patrick, so she had arranged for Paul to set off an hour before her.

As they joined Paul at the encampment, Anne could not help noticing the line of mud that had appeared on the hem of Rachel's skirt. It was not an auspicious start to her first foray into public photography but it would not dampen her enthusiasm. When she saw the sturdy wooden tripod set up next to the darkroom tent and the camera perched on a tall, square-topped stool that looked, for all the world in its folded-up state, like an ancient tome full of secrets, pleasure flushed through her fingertips. The moment signalled her transformation from widow to photographer and when she unhooked the metal fastening at the top of the camera, she would start in motion the camera's own transformation. Guiding the hinged runner down to its horizontal position, she wound the handle to extend the leather bellows and watched the slow separation of the wooden frame that housed the lens from the back of the camera into which she would slot the precious glass plate. Once she had lifted the camera onto the tripod, she attached the heavy black cloth that would shield the glass plate from the ravages of daylight and both camera and photographer were ready.

A hive of sawing, hammering, shouting and hurrying backwards and forwards greeted Anne and Rachel. The pavilion's exterior was complete, but work was continuing on the interior woodwork and she would have to choose her moment with care so that she did not blur the photograph with a moving figure. Built on one of Patrick and Rachel's paddocks in Southern Lane, the vast wooden amphitheatre dominated the provincial landscape and was larger than any theatre in London. It was a strange-looking building to Anne's photographer's eye, not at all what she had expected. She had imagined everything would be contained within the twelve-sided shape, but there were so many add-ons that she thought the lopsided building almost ugly. Designed so that, upon disembarkation from the carriage, the outside air would barely breathe upon the theatre audience let alone ruffle a strand of hair or caress a magnificent dress, the exterior covered walkways protruded from the dodecagon like unwieldy tentacles.

The pavilion's low roof and large diameter demanded that she set up her camera at a distance far greater than she would ordinarily have chosen. With only a few small windows and little contrast in the materials used, namely wood, she knew that it would be difficult to bring out the detail in her photograph, but she would not worry; she doubted whether anyone other than Paul would ever see the finished image. Having seen many a photograph that had been taken with a lens of too short a focal length, giving the buildings a tilted appearance as if they were about to fall forward, she had chosen a Zentmayer's lens. The large angle allowed the image to continue clear to a great distance from the centre and the focal length of twelve inches would keep the perspective of this complex structure, sharp and true. Her only regret was that she would not be able to photograph inside the pavilion due to the lack of natural light. No doubt the newspapers would send artists to produce their own interpretations of the interior decoration.

After edging each leg of the tripod to the right ever so slightly until the upside-down image of the pavilion was positioned centrally, she put the magnifier to her eye and examined the scene. Satisfied that the camera was ready, Anne took off her kid gloves, aware for the first time that her fingertips were throbbing with the bitter cold. With great difficulty, she eased on her protective gloves. Although they limited manipulation, they were essential as she would now be dealing with potent chemicals and, no less important a reason Rachel had observed, they would protect her hands from the dark brown stain that male photographers often wore but which, on a lady's hands, would be wholly unacceptable. If she desired to pursue photography, it must leave no mark upon either her person or her character.

Blinded for a moment as she entered the darkroom tent whose dim yellow light cast only the faintest glow on the operating table and racks of bottles, she knew that her physical transformation would now be complete. The lady who had disembarked from the carriage now sported an inelegant red nose, chafed lips and watering eyes. How had Rachel managed to remain impervious to the cold's effects? Her mother-in-law's elaborate bonnet decorated with lace trimmings, curled ostrich plumes and wide ribbon ties, all designed to set off her pale hair, was positioned exactly where her lady's maid had pinned it earlier this morning, whereas Anne's simple hairnet covered in green velvet had somehow worked its way slightly to the side of her head, allowing pale yellow strands to escape and giving her, she was certain, a somewhat down-at-heel appearance.

Having meticulously cleaned the glass on which the image would be formed, she dried it repeatedly on blotting-paper before drawing her soft camel's-hair brush across its smooth surface. She turned the labels of the bottles of acid and varnish to face her in order to prevent any danger of mixing them up in the haste that this photographic process necessitated and something of which she had read far too often in the newspapers. Supporting the glass in a horizontal position on the tips of her fingers, she steadied it by lightly pressing her thumb onto its edge where it would not cause any damage to the image.

A prickling of her eyelids, as if fragments of glass had been trapped inside them, seeped down to sit just below her lower eyelashes. Unable to relieve the sensation by rubbing her eyes, she had to content herself with a tightly squeezed blink and much willpower since there was no room for any loss of concentration. She poured the collodion, her own homemade mixture that included amongst others, sulphuric acid, nitrate of potash, ether and bromine, onto the glass plate. When it had half covered the glass, she inclined it, extending the liquid to each corner in turn without letting it run off too fast which would leave too thin a film; her full attention was critical now or the mixture would form unsightly lines. Since the collodion coating would set within a minute at this time of year, she could not stop, even for a moment, from rocking the plate until it became tacky. With the tip of her finger, she touched the corner last covered and the slight depression left on the collodion surface confirmed that it was indeed ready for immersion in the silver nitrate solution that would sensitise the glass to light.

Steeling herself to concentrate despite the numbing cold, Anne placed the glass plate into a porcelain holding frame before she took off the lid of the container that held the corrosive silver nitrate, responsible for many a severe burn and again reported in the newspapers that seemed to take great delight in such incidents. It was imperative that she maintain a steady uninterrupted motion as she lowered the glass plate vertically into its silver nitrate bath; if she were to pause for any fraction of time there would be a line between the part that was submerged and the part that was yet to be bathed. The small surface area of this narrow container helped preserve the silver solution by keeping out dust and light, the photographer's enemies and responsible for that irritating white fogging on images that was all too often apparent. Watching as the hand completed two rounds of the face of her pendant watch, she removed the glass plate to the protective holder that would maintain its upright position and provide a barrier against its destructive nemesis: daylight.

Leaving the darkroom tent to return to the camera, the glass plate dripping the silver nitrate through the holder, Anne bowed her head and lifted the black cloth, letting it fall down to her waist, but not for a second losing sight of the proximity of the dangerous solution. This was the crucial moment when all could be lost. Taking the light protection holder off the glass plate, she placed it into the camera and stepped out from underneath the cloth to remove the lens cap. Based on the calculation that she had made on arrival due to the moderate light conditions, she timed the exposure to exactly four minutes before replacing the cap.

She returned under the cloth to put the protective cover

back onto the precious glass plate before hastening back to the tent to pour the developer onto its surface where it would mix with the silver solution and provoke the image into life. Waving her hand in Rachel's direction, she hoped that the gesture would in some way pacify her mother-in-law, who was looking decidedly unimpressed at having to wait for so long. Meanwhile, Paul carried the tripod and camera to a point she had earlier identified so that she could ready herself for her next photograph. Under the pretence of capturing a close-up of the building, she planned to take a photograph of the workmen.

Having positioned and focused the camera, Anne asked Paul to ascertain whether or not the two carpenters would allow a photograph to be taken. Securing the next glass plate, she could hear the gasps of the obliging workmen as she, not he, dived under the black cloth. On her return to the camera, her third prepared plate in hand, she noticed four boys in Sheep Street who were watching her. If they came back in a quarter of an hour, stood exactly where they were and kept stock still, they would be paid. It was an unexpected bonus: street children at the pavilion a day ahead of what she had decided to undertake tomorrow. Her only problem now was how to convince Rachel to accompany her.

CHAPTER 18

The morning of Saturday the 5th of March 1864

The landau wheels waded through the mud-encrusted lane. In a few moments, they would arrive at the alley in Ely Court. Yesterday, Anne had thought that she would have trouble in persuading her mother-in-law to accompany her to photograph the children, but Rachel had agreed immediately because she was furious. Whilst Anne had been photographing the four boys in Sheep Street, Rachel had recognised the sharp blue eyes of one of them. His parents had told Rachel's schoolmaster, Mr Gardner, that their son was required to work on Fridays and would therefore be unable to attend her school, yet there he was yesterday, loitering on the street corner. Rachel had said that she had a good mind to go to the boy's house that very minute and ask his parents how her school could be expected to have any impact on his moral wellbeing when they were so happy to lie. But that was yesterday.

Anne had spent a disturbed night. Although the presence

of Frank, her groom, and her photographic assistant, Paul, would add credence to her plan and, in Patrick's absence in London, there was no one to forbid her action, she could not help voicing her misgivings to Rachel as they left the cobbles outside the most comfortable house in Stratford-upon-Avon, heading for the warren of alleyways leading where, she did not rightly know.

'I do wonder how their parents will react to my presence in their streets.'

'Most of the men work in our brewery. If there is any trouble I shall threaten them with the loss of their livelihood. Anyway, surely when they are not working they are too drunk to notice what is going on under their noses.'

Saddened as she was at Rachel's dismissal of the working men of the town who were her husband's employees, now was not the time to argue; without her chaperone she would not be permitted to continue. The photographic evidence from these streets would both enable Anne to show to those of her class the manner in which fellow residents of the town were forced to live and also enable her to confront the notion that a lady was incapable of taking images of anything more than picturesque landscapes and portraits of family and friends.

'It is almost impossible to believe how they first came to my school. Do you remember? Some were shoeless and dressed in ragged clothes and they all had weather-beaten faces and matted hair.'

'It is a sight that I shall take it to the grave,' Anne replied sadly, recalling how, two and a half years ago at the opening of her school, Rachel had persuaded her to photograph each boy when he first arrived in a dishevelled state.

What Anne had not realised at the time was that these

photographs would be used as a comparison to subsequent images showing smartly dressed children with faces scrubbed and hair brushed to within an inch of its life as a permanent record of the influence of Rachel's benevolence. Although Rachel had hoped that children would be admitted by personal application, in every case, Rachel's teachers and beneficiaries had sought their pupils out: most often these children were reported by members of the community who invariably described them as pests. These children did not come easily to school and their parents had to be convinced that it would assist the family. Some, Anne had heard, were bribed to come with gifts of baked potatoes.

The carriage lurched without warning into a deep rut in the alley, juddering to a complete standstill and they hitched up their skirts as they did when playing croquet, an image so incongruous to their present situation that Anne could not resist a smile. Her amusement did not last long, however, when she saw Rachel's determined face; she was on a mission to convert these children and their parents to her belief that poverty was no excuse for letting moral standards slip. Taking Frank's proffered hand, Rachel positioned one delicate boot onto the alley, but as it sank beneath her, she reversed the process without a moment's hesitation and took her place back in the carriage.

'I shall watch from the landau. My boots are so small that they sink instantly and I find myself unable to walk. Your boots are so much more suited to the conditions.'

The same four boys sat on the front step of a dingy house. The one with the piercing blue eyes stood up immediately and pressed his back into the wall as if he would become one of its bricks if that were possible, his long-sleeved smock flapping loosely around his filthy bare feet, that on first glance, Anne had assumed were boots. Two smaller boys performed precisely the same manoeuvre, but the fourth wriggled to the edge of the step and levered himself up with the aid of a stick onto his one oversized boot, his right trouser leg hanging limply. He was the only child to be wearing clothes that even moderately fitted the season.

As she took a tentative step forward, Anne noticed more children crouched in a circle. They must have become immune to the stench emanating from the gutter in the middle of the alley, she decided, as she looked back at Rachel who, despite being in the comfort of the carriage, was holding her handkerchief to her nose and was reaching for her smelling salts. Desperately fighting the need to follow suit, Anne determined that she would not allow herself to show these children that until this very moment she had never before entertained the thought that such levels of deprivation existed in her own town. As soon as the first child in the circle had spotted the unusual visitors, a domino of nudges alerted the whole group to the intruders. Edging towards the wall as if they were one body, this crab-like creature scuttled behind a rotting heap of, she knew not what. It was only when she and Paul stopped, that the crab advanced slowly sideways. Like its stalked eyes, the tallest boys stood in front with two fierce-looking boys right behind them as if they were the pincers ready to snap at any aggressor. The rest formed the legs of this ubiquitous creature.

The darkroom tent rendered unusable due to the confinement of the alley, Anne had brought the only viable alternative: the developing box. Apart from the yellow glass let into the front to protect the precious glass plate, it resembled a modest travelling case. It was only when she attached the sleeves, provided with India-rubber rings through which she would pass her arms to manipulate the chemicals and the silver nitrate bath, that its true nature was revealed. It was far from ideal because of the danger of spilling the hyposulphite and exposing the delicate photographic operations to the effects of its dust, but it was all that was available in the cramped conditions.

Having set up the camera and the developing box, curiosity began to triumph over the survival instinct of the crustaceous creature as it deconstructed itself back into a swarm of ragged spectators. Like an audience member who knows the plot and feels he has to announce the fact in an overly loud voice to a friend during a performance, Anne heard the tallest boy authoritatively tell the other children that the man was going to photograph them and that he would pay good money. The boy with the sharp blue eyes shot a look from the speaker to the man but then to the lady in the brown dress. He had never before been photographed by the man, but the lady had photographed him just yesterday.

As the children had gained in confidence, so Rachel had somehow managed to negotiate the mud to join Anne.

'Rachel, the boy you recognised yesterday is over there. Did you find his name in the school's record book?'

'His name is Samuel Brown. Patrick has employed his father as a labourer since he was a boy, loading and unloading casks onto the drays and his older siblings for short seasonal tasks such as kiln-pricking in the summer when it is too hot to brew.'

Anne was reminded of the meticulous records kept at the school that detailed each family's involvement with the brewery as if it existed for the sole purpose of supporting Patrick Drew's business.

'There was a terrible incident a couple of years ago when

Samuel's mother almost strangled his father!'

As Rachel told the story of Samuel's parents, Anne wondered if any part of the Brown family's life was kept private from Patrick.

'Do the other Brown children attend your school?' she asked to distract her mother-in-law from her ever-increasing delight in the chaotic nature of the family's difficulties.

'Mr Brown would not permit us to take any of his other children because they all work: the younger ones in the fields and the brickyard.'

'Why ever did they allow Samuel to enter the school?'

'They had little choice in the matter. He got into trouble in the town and when he was caught stealing for the second time, the corporation considered a punishment of one month's hard labour and five years at the Reformatory School. Patrick suggested that, as Mr Brown worked for the brewery, Samuel should attend my 'poor school' and his progress would be carefully monitored to see if my experiment in education as reform would work. If it were not a success, Patrick would defer to the committee and the boy would indeed undertake the punishment initially prescribed.'

'Is he thriving at the school?'

'Mr Gardner notes that his wits are as sharp as his eyes. He will be able to earn some money by becoming a pupil assistant to the teacher and then in time he may become a teacher, although it would not support his whole family.'

'Since I photographed him successfully yesterday and his is the only name in my possession, I shall address him first.'

'Samuel Brown, would you and your friends please move back and stand by the wall so that I may photograph you all. I shall of course pay you for the privilege.'

'A la-di-da lady is gonna tek our pitcher? Was wrong wi' th' fella?'

Samuel Brown uttered not a word, but a ripple of snorts accompanied the older boy's remarks. Anne had assumed that because Samuel had accepted her as the photographer yesterday, the same would occur today but this reaction had taken her by surprise: not at their lack of respect for her station, but at her pitiable ignorance. She had expected to cause a stir amongst her own class if word were to leak out that she had been photographing in public, but not amongst these children.

Rather than attempt to tell the children to reposition themselves, Anne tried to edge the camera a little to the left, but it wobbled precariously on the uneven surface. Her quiet determination to prove that she was capable of taking charge of the camera despite the continued jeering was in jeopardy. There was only one option. She pulled off her scarf and hat, pushed them under the tripod's leg and all the time noisily shook the coins in her purse.

CHAPTER 19

Present day: Wednesday 21 April 7pm

'Went badly with supervisor!' Nancy's text read.

What had gone badly? Christopher wondered. Nancy's next chapter? He knew that, when she'd told her supervisor about the diary's existence at their last meeting, he'd been very interested. And today, she'd been talking in more detail about it with him. So, surely the diary couldn't be the problem.

'What went badly?' he texted back.

'He wanted a copy of the whole diary. I refused and he got angry!'

'I could meet after the meal tonight.'

'No, I'm not letting him put me off. Will work into night transcribing. Thanks!xxx'

Three kisses this time. An uninvited memory of Monica's anger at him not texting back the same number bubbled to the surface. And then Uncle Charles stood up and looked at him as if he was about to propose a toast. Christopher couldn't believe it. His birthday was yesterday, he'd thought that at least today he could rest a little easy, stay out of the limelight.

'Here's to Christopher,' Charles said, smiling broadly as he looked around the table and then the whole room, as if to incorporate every one of the diners in the Shakespeare Hotel's restaurant. 'It's good to have this time together.'

Clinking glasses first with his uncle, Christopher continued around the table from Joanne to his mum, Madeleine and Peter before he came to an abrupt halt at his father's glass which remained glued to the table almost as though he'd forgotten where he was. As Christopher took a long, slow mouthful of wine, he noticed that his father remained quieter than usual, but his silence was lost amongst the talk of future family get-togethers in the house and renting rooms to famous actors. Then, out of the blue, his father asked if he'd consider settling down permanently in the house and raising a family in Stratford-upon-Avon. It was a giant leap of a question that sat uncomfortably with their fanciful talk, but of course he shouldn't have been too surprised. After all, it was he who, only yesterday at the Garrick Inn, had raised the subject of children with his father.

'Steady on Dad, I said I'd try the house out, but as for spending the rest of my life here in Stratford, I...I don't know. I could definitely run my photography business from the house, though and it's not a million miles from London.'

'Peter,' Joanne said. 'Look it up for us. How far is it from Stratford-upon-Avon to London?'

Surprised, Peter took his Smartphone off his lap where he'd been messaging his friends, thinking none of the old people had even clocked his presence.

'It's a hundred and ten miles. It takes one hour and

forty-eight minutes but in current traffic one hour fifty-six minutes.'

'So you think that if you could make your business work from the house you'd consider making it your permanent home?' Thomas pursued.

'Anything's possible, Dad, but I would like children, so I'd better get a move on!'

The statement caught them all unawares, not least of all Christopher. What the hell did he think he was doing?

'I might get those grandchildren after all,' Bridget beamed.

Christopher watched his father's face echo his mother's.

'It's the one blessing of old age,' Charles added, looking from Peter to Madeleine.

'Do you have a moment, Charles?' Thomas asked. 'I've got something I'd like to check with you.'

Stretching out their backs and shaking their legs in exactly the same manner, as if keeping time to music only they could hear, his father and his uncle started to make their way out of the restaurant. As they aged, they were starting to look more alike. Christopher saw his Uncle Charles brush the back of his father's arm and he could've sworn that his father twitched, almost as if he didn't want to be touched by his brother, but Christopher couldn't quite be sure because his mobile vibrated for the second time and all he could think of was reading the message. He didn't usually feel the need to look at his texts as soon as they came through when he was in company, but for some reason at the moment he couldn't wait until a suitable time arose. It must be because he wasn't used to being with his family for such an extended time, he reasoned. Who was he kidding? It was Nancy. Excusing himself, he looked at his phone as soon as he was out of sight of the family.

'I've read the strangest thing about Robert on April 21!xxx'

What did that mean? Did Nancy want to see him or was she simply sharing the discovery? He didn't want to read too much into the message. Monica's accusatory refrain, 'you're overthinking it again,' rang in his ears.

'It sounds intriguing! I can't wait to hear what you've found!xxx'

'Will keep transcribing. Going to archives tomorrow. See you at 5.xxx'

As Christopher pressed send, he remembered that they were going to Mary Arden's Farm for the day and he'd no idea what time they'd get back. In London, since he'd split up with Monica, he made few social plans ahead, preferring instead to text on the day, sometimes just an hour before he went out. Sending a general message asking what people were up to, he'd arrive at the pub when it suited him and leave when he chose, keeping no fixed timetable.

'What are you trying to say, Thomas?' his uncle's voice interrupted his thoughts.

'I told you, I merely wished to know if Sylvia said anything to you,' he heard his father reply.

'It was just things you say when you're nearing the end, I suppose,' Charles answered softly.

'Think, Charles, did she say anything about Joanne?'

'I don't know what you're getting at, Thomas. If you've something to say, maybe you'd better just say it.'

Christopher strained to hear his uncle's increasingly quiet voice.

'Is there something wrong with Joanne that I don't know about?'

'No, of course not.'

'Then why are you going on about my daughter?' Charles asked.

'Sorry, old man. I was thinking of you, Sylvia and Joanne and wondered if Sylvia had asked you to leave anything in particular for Joanne to inherit.'

'Not that I recall.'

'I hope this isn't awkward for you. You know, us giving the house to Christopher.'

'Of course not. We discussed it at the time. You're the architect, not me! The house means a lot to you, but it just doesn't hold the same meaning for me. Don't get me wrong, though. I think it's great you've given it to Christopher. It's a fantastic legacy.'

Christopher didn't hear any more and when he returned to the table, his father and his uncle were chatting away. What on earth his father's interest in Joanne was, he had no idea.

CHAPTER 20

Present day: Wednesday 21 April midnight

Pressing her fingertips against her eyelids, almost enjoying the pain that it sent behind her eyes, Nancy reached for the cooling mask and tightened the straps, forcing the soft material to press heavily against her skin. Her body sank into the worn leather armchair for the cat nap that she'd promised herself, but the oppressive darkness was populated with patterns of ever-changing light and if she wasn't careful she'd trigger a migraine.

Four hours of transcription had left Nancy unable to focus clearly. She knew she ought to concentrate on writing her thesis about the lasting effect that the Tercentenary Festival of 1864 had left on Stratford-upon-Avon, but now that she'd texted Christopher to tell him that something had happened to Robert Gastrell on April 21st, he'd have questions about what was going on with his ancestor. If she didn't carry on with the transcription, she wouldn't be able to provide a single answer and she hated that. She wasn't somebody who could pass something by on the other side of the street, she just had to cross right over and sort it out.

Running the diary entry for Thursday April 21st 1864 through in her head, she recalled Anne's words. Rachel had arrived early at Anne's house, *flushed with excitement saying that poor Percy's life was most precarious*. He'd experienced breathing difficulties the night before and Edmund had attended him. Patrick had booked a whole carriage and Philip, George and Edmund had taken Percy back to London that morning on the first train. Rachel was more agitated, however, that her husband had left *hot tempered and boiling up with rage* very early that morning to attend a meeting about the Festival and she had no idea why. She could understand Patrick's sadness at Percy's sudden illness but not his anger.

How did it go? Taking the eye mask off, Nancy blinked slowly several times before allowing the light to fully penetrate her eyes. Squinting a little to reduce the glare of her laptop screen, she traced back to Anne and Rachel's arrival at the pavilion where the former set up her camera. Anne had then gone on to describe how she'd given up on Robert ever turning up and had started photographing the pavilion. When finally he'd shown his face, he looked *as if suffering some inward conflict*. He excused his *slightly shabby-looking appearance*, putting it down to his distress at Percy's illness. But, *what weighs most heavily on my mind*, Anne had written, *was the unexpected appearance of Samuel Brown*, the boy she'd photographed in the street. *It was as if the boy had followed Robert's carriage for he arrived out of breath a minute after Robert's appearance. The boy fixed his eye on Robert until the latter inclined his head towards Samuel who, cap in hand, took off with much haste. What possessed a man of Robert's importance to acknowledge the presence of Samuel Brown under any circumstances, let alone in the public street?* Anne had queried with three under-linings.

To understand Robert Gastrell, Nancy knew that she'd have to understand his relationship to Samuel Brown. Never one to leave a mystery unresolved, it was this that she loved most about research: making sense of the past and more importantly, bringing people back to life – as far as possible anyways. Recalling that it was the name of Samuel Brown that Anne had written several times in the margin of her diary, Nancy started to search back through her screens with increasing excitement. She'd transcribed Anne's scribbled margin note at the time, but the name Samuel Brown had meant nothing until Anne had photographed the boy and Rachel had given her his name, but even then there was no great significance to his name. Now though, Robert Gastrell had nodded to Samuel Brown in public and the boy had taken off in response. What was going on? She wasn't going to let go 'til she knew.

Clicking on Anne's first margin note of Samuel Brown's name on Monday November 23rd 1863, Nancy read that it was the start of the building of the pavilion and the end of Anne's two-year period of mourning. One sentence stood out. *This is a new beginning for me.* Anne had taken photographs of the new children at Rachel Drew's school and had written at least two pages about this day, but at the time of writing the entry, she hadn't actually named Samuel Brown. The margin note of his name was written in a different ink that had developed a distinctive brown halo.

Rushing forwards through the screens to return to the entry on Thursday April 21st 1864, Nancy could see that it was the same ink. The distinctive brown halo around the words was identical. Each iron gall ink reacted slightly differently to paper over time due to the varying proportions of the four ingredients: crushed oak galls, the small growths on oak trees; tannins; iron sulphate and gum Arabic, a resin from the Acacia tree. She scanned her photos of the diary but could find no other trace of this particular ink apart from the entry on April 21st and the margin notes of Samuel Brown's name. Thank goodness there was none of the consistency of modern ink. She could trace Anne's own investigation of the relationship between Robert Gastrell and Samuel Brown through the ink.

As far as Nancy could surmise, the meeting that Anne had witnessed between Robert and Samuel on April 21st 1864 had so shocked her that she'd retraced her steps through her diary and written Samuel Brown's name in the margin where previously she'd simply written of him as one of a group of unnamed children. It was certainly unprecedented for an upper-class gentleman to have nodded his head to a poor child and it made Samuel Brown significant to Robert Gastrell. Anne Drew had made a point of recording the event and if it was important to her, it was important to Nancy.

She re-read the first time that Anne had found out Samuel Brown's name from Rachel on Saturday March 5th 1864.

> *I took photographs of the children again. As always, Rachel accompanied me, for which I am truly grateful, but I long to take photographs unaccompanied. I recognised a boy from Rachel's school. She told me that his name is Samuel Brown and a terrible story about his mother. Mrs Brown, who was suffering from delirium tremens due to excessive consummation of alcohol, had been seen to grab her husband's neck-handkerchief and push him to the ground, twisting it so that she was on the point of strangling him. He could barely make any noise and*

had become black in the face when his neighbour took a knife to cut the handkerchief and set him free. Mr Brown was left with permanent marks around the neck. Behind each wretched child is a whole family of misery and living conditions the like of which I have never before seen with my own eyes. I believed that these conditions existed only in London, but I was much mistaken. I knew nothing of this other life in my home town. I am ashamed.

Nancy continued to look for all mentions of Samuel prior to April 21st to gauge the involvement of this young boy with Robert. On Monday April 18th, Anne had spent the day photographing the Festival actors.

As I left the Town Hall I saw Samuel Brown. No wonder he does well at school, he is always watching. It must be that I notice him now that I have taken photographs of him and am able to put a name to his face. If one does not look for these children, one does not see them. It is as if they are not there.

On Tuesday April 19th 1864, Anne had written of Robert's enthusiasm for her photographs of the Festival actors. So encouraged had she been that she'd shown him two of the street scene photographs that she'd taken at the beginning of March. He was surprised and scrutinised them, asking where exactly in Stratford they'd been taken and she'd told him about the Brown family and her desire to photograph more such scenes. Her last entry that day had stayed with Nancy. *Strange to say, I saw that very boy, Samuel Brown, as I left the pavilion. He is everywhere.*

Texting Christopher, Nancy was annoyed when he didn't

reply immediately until she checked the time and realised it was two in the morning. She'd dived into the transcript to forget what had happened during her meeting with her thesis supervisor, Dr Martin Morrell, and it had worked. Arriving excited for the meeting, brimming with confidence because she had access to the diary, a primary source never before seen by any academic, she knew that it would mitigate Dr Morrell's annoyance at her slowness in getting her latest chapter to him. So, she'd wasted no time in starting to tell him more about the diary, but as soon as she mentioned some of the names of the people involved, his tone had changed and he seemed shocked. He'd asked her to continue telling him about the diary, but he'd really got her back up and had made her feel uncomfortable. She'd said she hadn't had time to look at any more of it.

Her assurances that she had access to the diary didn't appease Dr Morrell and he'd asked her to bring the actual diary to him as soon as possible, explaining that he'd be better able to support her use of the diary in her thesis if he handled the original. When she'd told Dr Morrell that the diary had been given as a birthday present and that she could only see it when she met up with the owner, Dr Morrell had asked her to email him the photos that she'd taken so far. She'd lied and said that the family had made her promise that she would be the only person to have the diary stored on her computer. There was no way she was going to share it with an academic who almost seemed to want the diary for himself. She'd shown Dr Morrell the first page and that was all. But, she wished she hadn't mentioned that the owner's surname was Gastrell.

Christopher would think she was an obsessive maniac when he looked at his cell, but she had to text him again.

She couldn't sleep without letting him know that if by any miracle he were contacted by Dr Morrell, who now, thanks to her, knew Christopher's last name, he must under no circumstances allow him to see or copy the diary. God, she needed some sleep.

CHAPTER 21

Present day: Thursday 22 April 10am

'Of course I won't let Dr Morrell see the diary if that's what you want. We are out for the day at Mary Arden's Farm but will see you at 5.xxx,' Christopher had texted.

'On my way to the archives. Loads more to tell you!xxx,' Nancy had replied straight away.

And that would usually have been it. He'd been accused by Monica of being emotionally stunted when he'd told her that he thought it was pointless to reply to a text unless a direct question was being asked, but now it was different.

He was different.

'Can't wait!xxx,' he'd added just before his father called over to him.

'Christopher, I forgot to tell you. Charles asked if he, Joanne and the children could have a look at the house. Nicholas said we could visit this morning if that's all right with you?'

'Er...yes okay, Dad.'

'If we set off at ten, it should give us enough time to catch the 12.26 train to Mary Arden's. We can have lunch and spend the whole afternoon there.'

Bugger. The visit to the house meant they'd be arriving later than expected at Mary Arden's, so he'd probably have to come back on an earlier train to meet Nancy. Now, he'd have to tell the family about his arrangement to see her again, unless he asked her to meet him later. She seemed so keen to see him, even if it was only because of the diary, and he didn't want to push his luck. She was like no one he'd ever met before. He'd see how the day went. Whatever happened, he wouldn't let Nancy down.

'Hello again. Welcome to you all. Please come in.'

Nicholas Chambers greeted them with his usual enthusiasm.

'This is my brother, Charles, Joanne...his daughter, and her children, Peter and Madeleine.'

It was at that point Christopher realised he'd forgotten to text Nancy to say he'd be at the house. Shit! Looking up from his mobile, he saw the door to her study room being opened. Not wanting to be in her room without her knowledge, he remained on the threshold, but couldn't help noticing the desk. Cleared, except for an untidy stack of papers gathered in the middle, it now appeared careworn and more like a junk shop find than the antique piece of furniture that Nicholas had said it was. Its edges had splintered and chipped; the cracked green leather had split apart across the top left corner and the three gold borders had smudged and in some places were missing altogether, but the indented border was perfect, except for a little wearing to the right of Nancy's chair. It looked as if somebody had nervously run their fingers backwards and forwards over that spot, perhaps while trying to compose their letters. He hadn't noticed any of these details the first time. It was as if he was in an entirely different house, but all that had changed was that Nancy wasn't at home.

When they went upstairs, Christopher stayed in the hall, telling them that he wanted to check out the staircase, but in truth he couldn't bear to intrude on the privacy of Nancy's bedroom without the invitation of its occupant. Between his first visit to the house on his birthday and today's visit, he'd gone from wondering how much he could rent it for, to telling his whole family that he'd live in it, at least on a temporary basis. He certainly couldn't be accused of over-thinking that one!

The taxi arrived and he dashed upstairs to tell them all. They were in a room that was connected to the master bedroom that he hadn't even noticed the first time. It was a large dressing room full of wardrobes with sliding doors that Nicholas was showing to Joanne.

'I could do with this at home,' she said.

Embarrassed at the vast amount of space that was so soon to be his and not wanting any such comments to be directed his way, Christopher called out that he'd go down to let the taxi know they were on their way.

Within ten minutes, they were drawing up outside the small Stratford-upon-Avon station, a single storey red-brick ticket office that was decked out with an array of hanging baskets. Although Christopher said he'd queue for the tickets so that the rest of the family could move through to the platform, they all stayed with him, filling the confined space and forcing an elderly lady to announce in a loud voice that if people didn't get a wriggle on, she'd miss the train. But, when they moved through there wasn't a train in sight and the place looked deserted. Thomas, Charles and Bridget settled themselves on a bench while Joanne and Madeleine went to the small shop to buy a bottle of water. Peter distanced himself from the family group. Plugged into his phone, hands stuffed into the pockets of his low-slung jeans making them drag on the floor as if they were at least a size too large, he pretended not to notice three young teenage girls who were giggling and nudging one another.

'Charles, since our conversations about Robert Gastrell's house over the last year or so,' Christopher heard his father say, 'I've become more acutely aware of the importance of legacy, more especially since January, since...well, you know. I asked you yesterday if there was anything in particular that Sylvia gave to Joanne or that she wanted Joanne to inherit and you said, not that you recalled. Well, surely Sylvia left her jewellery to Joanne.'

He wished his father would stop going on at his Uncle Charles about the importance of leaving a legacy to Joanne. This was the second time already and they'd been together for less than forty-eight hours. He'd noticed his uncle kept touching the side of his glasses as if he had a nervous tic and when he wasn't doing that, he was smoothing down his already perfect hair.

'I thought you meant something substantial, but of course Sylvia left Joanne her engagement and wedding rings and the pearl necklace I gave her on our wedding day. There was another necklace, but I didn't recognise it and Joanne said she'd never seen her mother wearing it.'

'What was it like?' Thomas asked.

'Joanne, what was Mum's necklace like? You know, the

one she left that we didn't recognise,' Charles called over as his daughter and granddaughter came out of the shop. 'Thomas would like to know.'

Christopher watched Joanne turn to his father.

'It's not difficult to describe because I'm wearing it today. You can see for yourself, Uncle Thomas. It's really beautiful.'

Joanne pulled the neck of her jumper down slightly and eased the chain up until her fingertips closed around the pendant. From a cluster of diamonds arranged in a heart shape, tassels of silver dangled, each with another diamond at its end. Christopher didn't know anything about jewellery, but this necklace looked incredibly expensive if the gems were real. As if she'd read his mind, Joanne confirmed that indeed they were.

His father stood up to speak to Joanne, but Christopher couldn't quite hear what they were saying. Looking over towards the rest of the family, he heard Madeleine ask his mother how long it would take to get to Mary Arden's Farm.

'It's two very short stops on the train and it only takes seven minutes.'

'Can we see the pigs first, Mummy? Have they got any piglets?'

'I've printed a leaflet off the internet. It's here somewhere,' Bridget said, rifling in her handbag. 'There will probably be some baby animals, I'd think, it's spring after all. I bet they've got sheep, cows and goats,' she added, giving up on her search for the leaflet.

Looking a little flustered, she hurried off saying that she'd pop to the loo while they were waiting for the train. Christopher watched his father, who was still talking to Joanne, and moved behind them, curious as to what kept them a little apart from everyone else.

'Mum told me that it had been given to her years ago by a friend to celebrate my birth.'

'Did she give you any idea of their identity?' his father pursued.

'No, but they must have been very close for her to have kept the necklace to give to me. It's very special.'

'Yes...very special.'

'I would have loved to know who gave Mum the necklace. Dad quizzed me over it at the time but I didn't have a clue, then or now. I wish I knew its significance to Mum. Of course, I have Mum's engagement and wedding rings which I treasure, but they're way too small for me and I don't want to have them altered. This and the pearl necklace are the only pieces of Mum's jewellery I can actually wear.'

'It's beautiful. May I have a closer look at the pendant?'

She cradled it in her open palm and Thomas examined the necklace, chosen with care forty-one years ago.

When Madeleine shouted that she could see the train, Christopher looked up in surprise. He'd been so engrossed in his father's interest in Joanne's necklace that he'd almost forgotten why they were there. Unlike the sudden surge at the large London stations whenever a train was announced, there were very few passengers and they didn't seem in any rush. His mother was the only person hurrying along the platform from the direction of the waiting room, waving the leaflet.

CHAPTER 22

Present day: Thursday 22 April 1pm

Entering the Shakespeare Centre, Nancy signed the visitors' book. Opened in 1964, the square, red-brick building housed the town's archives and the many collections associated with William Shakespeare's life and works and was one of her favourite places. Following the well-trodden path up the narrow stairs into the compact reception area of the archives' reading room, she produced her library card and stowed her rucksack in the locker, taking only her laptop, pencil and notebook. She enjoyed the no-pen rule. When her eyes got too tired making notes on her laptop, she took up her pencil with pleasure, finding that she pressed less heavily than with a pen and adopted a more relaxed writing position.

As she set up her laptop at the large research table on the far wall, one of the archive assistants brought in a trolley containing the letters that she'd ordered on-line. Anne Drew's friend, Ellen, who was travelling throughout Europe with her new husband after their wedding in February 1864, had corresponded with many family members and friends in Stratford-upon-Avon. Ellen's husband had invested well in the railways and their family papers had been kept by their eldest daughter whose descendants had given them to the town. For two and a half hours, Nancy trawled through Ellen's documents before she found it. A single letter from Anne Drew.

Hardly daring to read the letter in case her hopes that Anne had written about the Festival were unfounded, Nancy first examined the quality of the paper. Taking it between her thumb and index finger, she felt the slightly rough texture that appeared almost warm to the touch and spoke of high quality, so utterly unlike printer paper whose cold smoothness gave nothing away. She wouldn't rush. Anne had taken time over this letter and she would too. Placing her left hand on the paper as Anne might have done, Nancy traced the words as if she were the writer, always keeping her pencil a few millimetres above the paper.

Tuesday, 19th April 1864

My dearest Ellen

I beg you to accept my best thanks for your kind letter. How I miss our conversations!

By the urging of my heart, I must tell you about Robert Gastrell. You will not believe what you are about to read. Even in my dreams I never imagined I should find another who could possess every quality that my dearest Harold embraced – being straightforward, amiable and unaffected. On top of that, he has the most pleasing and delightful appearance.

His expression of interest in my photographs of the actors filled me with such confidence that I showed him some photographs that I had taken of the street children. He admired them and asked if I would like to photograph the pavilion in two days' time. I shall write again the moment I return home after my meeting with Robert.

I beg you to take care of your health and I trust all will go on prosperously for you and for Bernard.

Your most affectionate friend

Anne

This lively letter, written on Tuesday April 19th, showed how an excited, happy Anne had seen a possible future with Robert, but by her diary entry of Thursday 21st everything had changed. Robert had been distracted, agitated and dishevelled, as if he'd had a complete personality change and to top it all, Anne had witnessed Robert nodding to Samuel Brown. Anne's happiness had changed to anxiety and her diary had become full of questions regarding Robert. And it all seemed to have started after Percy Wimlett had become dangerously ill. Although Nancy was disappointed at the content which, in making not a single reference to the Tercentenary Festival, would be unusable in her thesis, she knew that at least she'd be able to tell the Gastrell family about it. It was a crying shame that no other letters had been found, but it did confirm that Anne had harboured hopes of a relationship with Robert.

She'd photograph the letter of course, but while she had the original in front of her, she'd assess the ink's appearance on the paper to see if it gave anything away about Anne's state of mind. Having taken time to elaborate the initial letter, Anne had shown little restraint in the rest of her writing. Unlike the self-contained crossing of a typed letter 't', Anne's handwritten horizontal stroke extended through to the end of the word. The tail of the letter 'y', in Anne's hand, looped low touching the words in the line below and ended with a flourish and certain words were linked showing that the pen had not been taken off the paper. It certainly looked as if Anne had been so desperate to get her thoughts onto paper once she'd started that she'd disregarded convention.

At the Shakespeare Institute, Nancy had used a dip pen to experience writing in the mid-eighteen-sixties. Despite becoming proficient in the use of the pen, she'd found herself thinking much more carefully about the content, not only because she didn't want to make a mistake and have to start from scratch, but because it took time to physically form the letters and she relished the control that she could impose over the ink. It flowed more strongly when she pressed down on the paper. By splitting the nib apart minutely, she could leave a slightly wider, raised line, but as she released the pressure, the nib would come back together, restricting the ink to a thin, flat stroke.

She could see in Anne's writing that she'd started slowly and considered each word. Dipping her pen often, she'd pressed down evenly on the paper, but as soon as she'd mentioned Robert Gastrell, less ink had been used. As the ink ran low out of the pen, it produced a thin, scratchy line showing that Anne's train of thought had remained uninterrupted. When she'd written Robert Gastrell's name, it looked as if she hadn't wanted to take her pen off the paper, perhaps carried away with excitement at the prospect of future happiness. But, within two days it had all vanished.

Whereas typescript gave nothing away, marks made by hand would always convey more than the simple meaning of the words. Nowadays, the ability to delete meant that the great majority of letter writing happened with little forethought and both sender and recipient knew this was the case and it all meant very little. And Nancy wondered if there would be anything much to interest future generations.

Reluctantly, Nancy released Anne's letter and returned to her thesis until her stomach grumbled so loudly that she thought she'd disturb the other researchers. Leaving the reading room, she entered Henley Street, taking care not to walk directly in front of Shakespeare's Birthplace in order to avoid appearing in every tourist's photograph of Stratford's most famous building. As she approached Christopher's house, she stopped and took a long look at it. Living and writing here suited her down to the ground, but she knew that any day soon she'd have to find somewhere else to live. She couldn't imagine writing anywhere else now that she'd found it and she wondered if she should tell Christopher how she felt or keep quiet.

Anyways, she didn't have time to worry about the house right now. Torn between working on her thesis to gain her doctorate and transcribing the diary which she'd started to think could possibly lead to a book, Nancy couldn't help herself. She had to look at the next diary entry of Friday April 22nd 1864 to see if Anne found out what Robert's problem was. It was one of the briefest but most unexpected of entries. Anne had visited Rachel, only to find out that her mother-in-law hadn't seen Patrick since Thursday morning and even that had been for only a few moments from the bedroom window. He'd left a message with the housekeeper to say he'd be in meetings again all day Friday as well. Anne's last entry from that day read.

> *I cried myself to sleep. I view Rachel as my second mother. The death of Harold brought me even closer to her. I cannot bear it if there is a problem between Rachel and Patrick.*

There was no mention of Robert, but Patrick too seemed to have been caught up in something he wouldn't discuss with his wife. What was wrong with these men?

CHAPTER 23

Present day: Thursday 22 April 6pm

'I've got so much to tell you. You remember I texted you about Samuel Brown? Well, I hadn't taken much notice of his name before, I was so preoccupied with George, Percy and Robert, but when I looked back over the diary, Anne keeps coming across him. It's so odd.'

Nancy and Christopher had arranged to meet at a coffee shop in the High Street. It was one of the few that stayed open after the shops had closed and the town centre was eerily quiet, as if everyone had gone to a party to which they'd not been invited. He'd hardly sat down before she'd started to speak, giving him no time to apologise again for having to push the time back by an hour.

'Samuel Brown?'

'He's a street child Anne photographs, just one of a crowd of kids. Nothing special until Thursday April 21st. It's the strangest thing. Anne sees Robert nodding to Samuel in the street. It just wouldn't have happened. An upper-class man would never have acknowledged a street kid.'

'So why did he?'

'I don't know yet. There's more. It made such an impression on Anne that she went back through her diary to identify Samuel from every single one of her previous entries. There's nothing referring to Samuel the next day, Friday 22nd, but Anne writes stacks on Saturday April 23rd, the day of the Shakespeare Festival, so I'm hoping she mentions him again. It's the most so far that she's written on any one day. I've got to the end of the banquet at around seven o'clock, but I thought we could look at Patrick and Rachel Drew's evening party together.'

'Okay, but I'm not sure how I can help.'

'It would just be good to share it, I guess. Anyhows, so far on Saturday, April 23rd, Anne spends two pages writing about how great the town looked and how busy it was. At two, she watches Patrick and some other bigwigs arrive to view an exhibition of Shakespeare paintings at the Town Hall. He is closely followed by Robert and his father, Archibald and then Robert's best mate, Edmund, rushes in at the last minute. At three, they arrive at the pavilion for the banquet and are joined by Philip Wimlett and his son, George.'

I avoided Robert's gaze as best I could, but he kept looking over towards me. Once only, did he catch my eye and then he nodded to me and I am convinced that I did not imagine his face light up, the anxiety of Thursday dismissed like an insolent servant. But, almost as soon as I formed the thought, his face took on an impassive, cold manner as he looked at George. George nodded to Robert but Robert did not return the courtesy as if he bears the young man a personal grievance. I cannot for the life of me begin to guess what this may be. George, who had up until that point been an enjoyable and lively companion, suddenly clenched his hand and brought it down on the table, making the china rattle. Philip, usually so flamboyant and generous-spirited, whispered, 'think on it' to his son in what I may only describe as a bullying tone. He may have thought that he spoke under his breath but it came out as would a stage whisper. From that moment onwards, George was never free from his father's constant attention and talked little with anyone else.

'So, there wasn't just a problem between George and Percy, but between George and his father, Philip. Anne also seems concerned about Robert's relationship with George,' Nancy observed before continuing:

Something disagreeable has passed between Robert and George to which I am not party. I took my chance to observe Robert whilst he was engaged in conversation with his father and the tired, drawn appearance had returned to ravage his features. He appears to have developed a nervous habit of placing his hand upon his throat as if to constrict his breath. I mean to get to the bottom of the difficulties between Robert and George.

'You think there was a connection between Percy's illness and Robert?' Christopher asked.

'Yeah. I think so. Anne notes that during the banquet, Philip looked from Robert to Archibald and then to Robert's mother, Constance, becoming more and more angry. I can't for the life of me figure out what Philip has against Robert and his parents and it's really bugging me,' Nancy acknowledged.

'And what about Samuel Brown? Surely he didn't appear at the posh banquet?' Christopher joked, trying to lighten the moment.

'It's funny you should say that. Anne writes that she steps outside to get some air and sees Samuel!'

'That boy gets everywhere. How strange that he appears so often in the diary of a lady.'

'Look, I'm going to get another coffee. My brain needs a shot of caffeine.'

'I'll get them,' he said, eyeing the queue.

It was a good ten minutes before he rejoined Nancy and this time she didn't even wait for him to sit down. She stood up as he approached the table and walked towards him, almost barring his way.

'Are you okay? You look like you've seen a ghost.'

'I need to tell you something, but you mustn't look round. Okay?'

'Okay. But let's sit down first...Nancy? Are you all right?'

'It's okay, I'm just being stupid.'

At a loss for what to say next, Christopher said the first thing that sprang to mind.

'I meant to tell you, something a bit strange happened to me just before we met. I left the family at Mary Arden's around five and called in at the flat to get the diary. I could swear there was a man hanging around watching the door. But, as soon as he saw me, he ran off. What do you think?'

'What?'

The harshness of her tone and the sudden accusatory look in her eyes so surprised Christopher that he completely forgot what he'd just said.

'What did he look like?' Nancy said, frowning.

'Who?'

'The man outside your apartment!'

'I only saw him from the back. Curly blond hair. Short,

slim build, young – early twenties perhaps,' he added when she said nothing.

The silence that ensued, so unusual in her company, oppressed him into telling her something he'd not given a second thought to until that moment.

'That reminds me, my mum told me that at the station this morning, a young man engaged her in conversation about accommodation in the town. She was in a rush because the train was due at any time, but he was very pleasant, she said, but quite insistent, so she mentioned the flat that we're renting. He said it sounded perfect and asked for the exact address, including our flat number, so that when he contacted the owner he could ask for that particular flat.'

Christopher had simply hoped to fill the void, but his words served only to add to Nancy's irritation.

'What did he look like?'

'I don't know. I didn't ask Mum. I've only just thought of it,' Christopher said, embarrassed, feeling like someone who'd told a joke only to forget the punch-line.

'Look, I'm going to have to go.'

'What's up?'

'Don't look, but the guy over in the corner is Dr Morrell,' she whispered, her head so close that her hair brushed against his forehead. 'I said, don't look!'

'Sorry. Your supervisor? The one you texted about?'

'Yeah. When I woke up this morning, I felt stupid worrying about his interest in the diary. As if he might steal the diary from me! But now you've told me about a man asking for your address and another one, or perhaps the same one, hanging around your apartment, I'm not sure it is so ridiculous. What do you think?'

'I think we should keep a close eye on the diary and your

Dr Morrell,' Christopher replied, glad that they seemed to be on the same side again.

Leaving the coffee shop without a backward glance, Christopher noticed that as they passed by the window outside, Nancy looked in and shrank back.

'He looked straight at me. He's standing up as if he's about to leave and yet he only arrived five minutes ago. I know how mad it sounds, but I feel as if he's following me. I wish I hadn't told him your name and that you're staying in Stratford. Now, he knows what you look like too!' she said, starting to run down the one-way road to the side of the coffee shop.

Christopher, too astonished to question her, followed silently. He had no idea where they were going until he recognised the house.

'Damn it! Nancy, look, I'm really sorry. I have to leave. We're going out for another bloody meal tonight!'

'I'll be okay. But tell me one thing before you go. Do you think I'm being paranoid about Dr Morrell?'

'I really don't know,' Christopher answered, immediately regretting his honesty.

'Promise me you'll keep the diary with you. Don't leave it in the apartment.'

She turned her face away from him and he let her run up the steps and enter the house, wishing all the time that he'd had the courage to stop her and tell her that, yes he was worried about Dr Morrell's attitude to the diary and maybe he was actually following them. And the young man? What the hell was going on? He hadn't expected a family holiday in Stratford-upon-Avon to turn out like this.

CHAPTER 24

The morning of Monday the 18th of April 1864

Anne could not believe that it had been over a month
since she had photographed the street children. Keeping
the images secret had been easier than she had expected
though, as Rachel seemed to have forgotten all about their
outings, as she called them. Patrick had returned from
London so full of enthusiasm for *The Comedy of Errors* and
Romeo and Juliet that all thoughts had naturally turned to
the Tercentenary Festival. Now, a mere five days before
the Festival, Anne found herself taking photographs of the
actors to provide a record for posterity, courtesy of Robert's
successful persuasion of Patrick. She had no idea why, but
Robert seemed to have risen greatly in Patrick's estimation
since their visit to the metropolis: a connection of some sort
to Charles Dickens, her mother-in-law had gleaned.

As Anne replaced the lens cap, Mr Buckstone, costumed
as Antipholus of Syracuse and the last actor from the cast of
The Comedy of Errors, moved stiffly from the ivy-clad pillar

against which he had been leaning stock-still for several minutes and broke into a broad grin of relief. The only facial expression that he had been able to hold for the requisite time made him look serious, even a little sinister. He had a horror, he had explained to her, of a twitch of his eye at the wrong moment or an itch that would cause him to move involuntarily as he had done during his very first sitting. It had happened during a group photograph when he had sneezed, resulting in a photograph in which he looked as if he were wearing a mask, his face swollen to twice its size and so dark that no features were visible. Everyone else in the group was not only recognisable, but sharply defined.

Having set up her studio in the only room on the first floor of the Town Hall that contained large enough windows to allow sufficient daylight to illuminate the actors, Anne worked as if in a small factory. After taking each photograph, she would pass it to Paul in the portable darkroom that they had set up in the room next door and under her instruction he would set up the chemical process which she would complete. The chatter of the actors for whom refreshments had been provided downstairs wafted up on the air with the smoke from several pipes. Despite having undergone extensive enlargement and redecoration in honour of the Shakespeare Tercentenary, the Town Hall, at that moment, resembled a carnival.

It was now the turn of the actors in *Romeo and Juliet*. In her flowing white dress drawn tightly in at the waist, fine delicate hands and hair curled in tresses that were pulled back by an ivory comb, Juliet resembled a princess. The backdrop that had made Mr Buckstone feel awkward, complemented her appearance and when Juliet was joined by her handsome Romeo, George Wimlett, whose curly fair hair had been smoothed and flattened, the fairytale should have been complete. But, her simple attire jarred somewhat with his highly embellished blue-green tunic and its close-fitting nature served only to emphasize his rather unmanly slight build and thin legs.

Pleased to have finished photographing Mercutio, Friar Lawrence and the Nurse, Anne was looking forward to capturing the image of her next actor. Percy Wimlett stood before her, not as handsome as his brother, but with a tall and well-built stature that would be shown to its best advantage dressed all in black as Tybalt; the short pleated skirt of his velvet tunic displayed his muscular legs and the tightness of the sleeves hugged the contours of his arms. He would photograph beautifully.

Although she had discussed at length beforehand the colours that would photograph well and those that would appear bland, she had found herself faced with a procession of vibrant reds, oranges and warm yellows, all of which would appear as a block of matt black. The costumes had, of course, been chosen according to their appearance at the theatre, but the magnificent red dress that would command the stage, Anne had warned, would look surprisingly dowdy in the photograph. Ironically, it was black that photographed best of all, but they would not be told.

Anne had even heard of people who could barely recognise their own images, who were angry and disappointed because they had gone to extraordinary lengths to look their best, especially ladies, who had dressed their hair with ribbons and gems for a photograph. As fair and red hair both showed up as a dull black, she knew that George and Percy's oiled hair would make them resemble one another more in the photograph than in actual life; a point that would no doubt please the brothers whom Rachel had told her had become much more amenable of late. Anne could not help wondering what the future would think of them all: a dour lot who always wore black and never smiled?

As usual, Anne had dressed as unobtrusively as possible, which in the present company was not difficult. The actors looked at the camera and hardly noticed her and they did not even appear to consider her as important enough to stop their banter. Quite the opposite was true the moment Rachel arrived, dressed immaculately almost as if to outdo the performers: the actors moderated both their speech and their behaviour. Anne, for her part, preferred the freedom of her anonymity.

Having partaken of some refreshment, she entered the committee room to look at the oil paintings of previous mayors, vowing that one day she would see her photographs hanging on that very wall. As she turned to leave, she heard raised voices coming from the next room.

'You ass. I would never do such a thing.'

'She was my sweetheart.'

'She is *still* your sweetheart.'

Labouring to listen at the door, Anne moved to the adjoining wall and closed her eyes to focus on the sound of the voices and, despite the loud beating of her heart, was able to distinguish those of George and Percy, but not which brother was which. One hissed under his breath, but the venom in his words added volume and the other defended himself vigorously, almost as if they were rehearsing a part.

'You have disgraced our family name.'

'That is a false accusation.'

'You piece of filth. You pressed your blasted affections upon my sweetheart!'

'I did no such thing.'

'You be hanged! I shall never forgive your shameful conduct.'

And with that, a door slammed and Anne waited to hear the remaining brother's footsteps on the stairs before she would venture forth. Goodness, if it were not for Robert's interest in viewing her photographs tomorrow, she would think that the exertions of the day had not been worth the trouble.

CHAPTER 25

The afternoon of Tuesday the 19th of April 1864

Samuel Brown's sharp blue eyes scrutinised the pavilion that he'd been told was to become a theatre where all the important people of the town would watch famous actors. Carpenters and painters hurried past his small figure, but it wasn't these workmen who'd captured his attention. It was the gentleman whom he'd been following. Rooted to the spot, he'd decided that he'd stay to catch a glimpse of Mr Robert Gastrell when he left the pavilion, but so far all he'd seen was an actor dressed in peculiar garb with a door-knocker of a beard, who'd paced backwards and forwards on his own like a caged lion, calling out to the surrounding trees. But, this looked more entertaining.

Two young men circled one another before lashing out with their swords. Drinking in their fast movements like the quart of small beer that he'd supped when his mother wasn't looking, Samuel became light-headed in the expectation that one would surely kill the other. The instant they stopped, however, they looked ridiculous standing there by the River Avon dressed in fancy, garish clothes. No, only the one with the curly yellow hair wore a fantastical costume, the other, the one with the red hair, was dressed all in black like he imagined a knight of old. Tiring of watching these young men who were now speaking at the air and throwing their arms around at nothing, Samuel scoured the entrances of the pavilion. He waited to see Mr Gastrell who, on countless occasions during the month of March, had visited the street where he lived under the cover of darkness. He hadn't realised that these wealthy men could adopt different clothes and become other people, but here, today, they all seemed to be doing it.

His first sight of the stranger, whom he later found out was Mr Gastrell, was just over a month ago. Samuel had assumed he was a poor man from a neighbouring town. With his rough, misshapen great coat and cap that he pulled down over his forehead, he'd looked half-rats like every other man on the streets. But, now and again he'd seen the man glance around to make sure that no one was looking his way before he'd pull out a pocketbook and write furiously. When he'd tried to follow the man, he'd walked off towards the paved part of town that had been all primped and preened ready for the Festival and Samuel's courage had failed him.

That next evening in March, however, Samuel had determined that he would see where the man went. Sometimes hurrying and looking around as if he were being chased, then at other times, hunched over and unmoving, the man had continued until he'd arrived outside an enormous palace of a house where only the toffs live. Snatching off his cap, the man had brushed his fingers through his thick black hair and had run up the front steps. Samuel had felt frightened in this unfamiliar part of town, far away from the alleyways and the crowds of children with whom he'd grown up and he'd run so fast he could hardly breathe when finally he'd reached Ely Court.

Returning the next day, he'd seen the gentleman, for that is what he now appeared to be, leave the house dressed in a velvet frock coat and stovepipe hat. From that point on, Samuel had kept watch over the man whenever he'd ventured onto his patch. Then the unthinkable had happened: the man had presented himself at the school. It had started as an ordinary morning a couple of weeks ago when Mrs Drew, the school's benefactor, had entered the schoolroom and had introduced Mr Robert Gastrell to the children. Looking up from his slate, he couldn't believe that it was the same man. What was he doing in Mrs Drew's company? Did she know what he did at night-time? But then Samuel remembered that Mrs Drew had kept strange company before; she'd stood by the side of the lady who'd photographed him at the beginning of March outside the pavilion of all things and then, to cap it all, they'd only gone and turned up outside his house the next day. He couldn't for the life of him think why these posh people were so interested in other people's lives when they had such easy lives themselves.

It was then that he'd decided to look for Mr Robert Gastrell around the town. Instead of keeping his head down, Samuel now looked into the faces of the gentlemen, but he found that they were annoyed and shouted at him or looked away. They didn't return his gaze, almost as if they couldn't bear to look at him or as if they had something to hide, he thought. One day, he'd spotted Mr Gastrell getting out of a carriage at the Town Hall and he'd committed every detail of the carriage to memory. He was sure that he needed to keep an eye on the man. Was he a toff pretending to be poor or was he really a low-born man acting like a swell?

Today, he'd again followed Mr Robert Gastrell's carriage to the pavilion and now there was another fancy carriage pulling up, but he couldn't quite see the occupants. The manner in which the groom fussed, however, made it most likely that it contained a lady and one of high status at that.

*

Anne and Rachel, each carrying a slim valise containing the actors' photographs, alighted from the carriage and entered the pavilion's covered vestibule. Spending a frantic afternoon and evening the previous day, Anne had printed the images of the actors. Placing the light-sensitised albumen paper on top of each varnished glass plate, she had carefully exposed it to daylight, ready to pounce like a hawk and arrest the exposure at exactly the right moment.

They passed the pavilion's offices for opera glasses and cloakrooms that would soon be bustling with excited crowds, but which were now filled with scurrying workmen criss-crossing their paths and tipping their caps on each occasion. Watching the actors rehearsing in the costumes that she had photographed the previous day, their vivid outfits shining out from the stage, Anne thought of the colourless offering that she was carrying.

'Thou, wretched boy, that didst consort him here,
    Shalt with him hence.'
'This shall determine that.'

Anne could not take her eyes off George and Percy as they fought in the guise of Romeo and Tybalt. Drawn towards the stage, she was unable to prevent herself from moving closer and even closer, absorbed in the spectacle of the movement between George's freely-moving slight body and Percy's more constrained muscular build. Watching with no consideration for propriety, she felt a sense of threat crackle around the auditorium. The fight appeared horribly unequal as if it were too obvious who would win, despite the knowledge that of course Tybalt and not Romeo must die from this interaction.

Like a barn owl's territorial screech, the shrill clash of swords sent a shriek shivering through the air before slicing apart with a piercing scrape of metal upon metal that erupted into a shower of flinty sparks. Ripping through the harsh air, one sword pinned the other to the ground, edges grating as the defending sword hurled up its attacker and they parted.

'They have learnt from the best. They trained with a fencing master for years and then I taught them the routines of stage combat,' Philip Wimlett announced proudly as he wiped his eye and brushed aside a wisp of sandy hair.

Irritated to be startled out of her reverie by such pedestrian words, Anne let out a heavy sigh, realising for the first time that she had been withdrawing her breath little by little, but she could not tear her eyes away from the Wimlett brothers. She watched as each body sized up its opponent, its shoulders and fists tense, elbows pinned to the torso and chest thrust forward. Circling like buzzards, the swords cut and scratched one another until one body stumbled and retreated only to turn and launch itself at its nemesis. The block jarred the hand of the attacker who side-stepped to avoid retaliation. Aggression spilled from the two bodies, their swords glinting in each other's eyes. A lunge to the right was parried by a sharp thrust that knocked a sword clattering to the ground, sending out an alarm that pierced the air and it was easy to imagine that they were fighting for the hand of the sweetheart in London.

As she slowly turned towards Philip, Anne's attention was again ensnared by the two young men.

'You blasted idiot, you have caught my thigh.'

Percy's words carried easily around the pavilion, insistent on being heard.

'Of course, accidents may happen even to the best of us,' Philip said by way of filling the embarrassing stillness caused by the cessation of the fighting and the strong words.

Juliet ran onto the stage and shouted. Looking around, Philip caught sight of Robert.

'I should be obliged if you would show our two lady guests into the committee room. I wish to confirm that no great harm has come to Percy. I shall be along presently.'

Only then did Anne become aware again of the many workmen moving backwards and forwards across the area behind her. Had they too stopped to watch the fight or had she been too wrapped up in the excitement to notice them? But, she did not have time to contemplate what she had witnessed, as Robert ushered them hurriedly past the stage and along a covered path that led directly into the pavilion's committee room. The calmness of this functional space, so entirely at odds with the vitality of the stage, left Anne struggling for a moment to recall the purpose of her visit.

'I believe you have brought your photographs of the actors. I am sure that Philip will not mind if we do not wait upon his return. I am eager to look at the results of your work,' Robert prompted her.

Anne and Rachel spread the images out upon the table and Robert inspected one after another.

'I do not profess any expertise, but to my mind you

have captured the essence of the character whom they are portraying. I particularly admire Juliet.'

'Thank you, it was most enjoyable and I am honoured to have been offered the opportunity to be part of such an important occasion.'

'Would you like to photograph other significant events if you were given the chance?'

The thrill of the fight still coursing through her brain, she found that she could not help but talk of a different kind of photograph.

'I should like to conduct more outdoor photography rather than studio photography. I have already started to make some studies of Stratford-upon-Avon.'

'I should dearly like to see them in due course. In the meantime, would you like to photograph the pavilion? I shall return here on Thursday and I should like to be present if you have no objection.'

'I shall be pleased to see you on Thursday. As for the photographs of our town, you are in luck. I have brought a couple with me.'

Not daring to catch her mother-in-law's eye, knowing that she had already photographed the pavilion when Robert was in London, Anne retrieved the two street photographs from her valise. Why she had secreted them amongst the photographs of the actors she did not know. How shocked Ellen would be when she wrote of this tonight.

*

Robert's delight at being entrusted with a glimpse into Anne's future aspirations turned instantly to recognition as he viewed the photograph of Sheep Street. In the foreground, to the left hand side, were four figures: one of them had no features at all, two had indistinct features, but one could plainly be seen. The sharp blue eyes of Samuel Brown looked straight at the camera. He had found out the boy's name when he had visited Rachel's school and been introduced to her pupils at the end of March and had recognised him as one of the children about whom he had been writing during his night-time vigils. This child, so quick in his movements and so keen in his observation, must have stood practically motionless for several minutes staring at the camera, hardly daring to breathe.

The second photograph was of Ely Court. It showed a group of children strangely posed and he could not for the life of him understand why Anne had asked the two tallest boys to stand at the front of the photograph whilst all of the other smaller children crowded as an indistinct mass behind them: all except for Samuel who, despite being in the background, must again have stood so still that his eyes shone out at the observer. Although the composition of the image was not perfect, it was clear enough to see the grimy conditions in which these children spent their lives. Anne had captured visually what he had committed to paper during those nightly visits.

Hardly able to contain his excitement, he replied a little too quickly in the affirmative when she asked if he would like to see more of her photographs of the town when they were to meet in two days' time. He could not have wished to be anywhere else in the world. It was time for him to loosen the reins held by the elder men of the town and, as his own father had advised, take up his place in Stratford-upon-Avon. He would find the courage to tell Anne how much he admired her street photography and that he too had captured those very streets, not in images, but in words. Robert hoped that tomorrow night's meeting at the White Lion Hotel with his father, Patrick, Philip and Edmund would not finish too late because he wished to present himself bright and early on Thursday to meet Anne at the pavilion.

CHAPTER 26

A quarter past eight on the evening of Wednesday the 20th of April 1864

Robert looked up as the door to their private room in the White Lion Hotel opened. His father, Patrick and Edmund, who were listening to Philip discuss the timings of his productions of *The Comedy of Errors* and *Romeo and Juliet*, seemed not to have noticed that George Wimlett had entered, so he waved the young man over to their table.

'Good evening George.'

On first sight, Robert had barely registered the condition of the young man, keen as he was to alert Philip to his son's unexpected appearance at this exclusive gathering, but the intruder's inability to perform any of the necessary pleasantries of greeting, obliged Robert to take a second look at him. George was filthy; mud or worse was smeared across his cloak and his gloves were similarly encased in dirt and, heaven knows what else. Robert felt obliged to assist the young man due to his proximity, but he could not for the life of him think how exactly to accomplish this task since George stood as still as a statue. Philip did not move either. As both father and son remained motionless, Robert got up awkwardly, making such a noise of scraping his chair on the floorboards that it was as if he had arisen with annoyance. Walking over to George, he still had no notion of what he would say or do when he reached him. With the other men's eyes boring into his back, Robert wished that he had not made the gesture. He had thought that someone else would follow his lead but still no one stirred: it was as if they were all trapped in a photograph and only he possessed the power of movement.

'George, come and sit with your father. Would you like a drink? We are talking about the Festival programme of events.'

Robert knew that he sounded ridiculous, acting as if there were nothing unusual about the young man's appearance and offering a drink to a man who already smelled strongly of alcohol. Placing his hand in the small of George's back, he found an area that was untouched by mud and gently manoeuvred him towards Philip. Close to, the alcohol rose from his clothing like dew in the morning sunshine, but as George breathed out deeply, Robert could not detect any fumes emanating from his breath. It was clear that George had consumed no alcohol.

'My son, tell me what is wrong. Whatever it is, I shall help you. Speak now,' Philip said with increasing urgency in his voice.

'It...I...Percy. He's hurt...Help.'

George's breath exhausted, he stood open-mouthed.

'Where is Percy?'

Unable to speak, George stumbled out of the door.

'You two run ahead. My old legs... Send word to let us know where you are,' Philip gasped, his face turning a deep red that rendered every freckle invisible.

As Robert and Edmund followed George down the stairs and through the narrow panelled corridor of the White Lion Hotel, Robert saw his friend hook his fingers around an oil lamp and gestured for him to do the same. The blast of cold air was an unwelcome reminder that they had left their outer garments in the hotel and for the first time in his adult life, Robert found himself in the public street without his hat. For a young man who had just witnessed goodness knows what, George was certainly still able to move adroitly, Robert thought, hurrying to keep sight of Edmund's back as he disappeared down a side alley in close pursuit of George.

Leaving behind the gaslights of Henley Street, the blinding darkness of the alley flooded Robert's eyes and his pace slowed to a crawl. He knew that it was best not to look directly at the flame of his lamp or it would render his vision useless when he tried to pierce the corners of the alleys. Instead, he looked around at its dim pool of cast light, absorbing each minute drop as he bent over like an elderly gentleman. Keeping his feet close to the ground, not daring to lift them too high in case he tripped, he had to admit that it was hardly what Philip had in mind when he had asked them to follow his son. Damnation! He had no idea where Edmund and George had gone.

The alley coiled around and he was faced with a choice of paths. Drinking in the drops of light, he turned to the right for no other reason than it widened a little and much to his relief, he came upon Edmund crouching down. George paced backwards and forwards, but as Robert approached, he caught sight of what looked like a smile on the young man's lips.

'Take his arm,' Edmund ordered, gesturing towards George whose face had now crumpled into a perfect picture of distress.

Muttering and throwing his hands out into the darkness, the young man covered his face at Edmund's words. Robert hesitated, but Edmund stood up and roughly reached forward to take George's arm at the elbow as if the young man might escape were he not restrained. Signalling to Robert to take his place as guard, Edmund kneeled in the mud. For a small man, Edmund was surprisingly strong, Robert thought as he struggled to contain George, despite his much taller stature than his friend. The young man quietened for a moment and something caught Robert's attention in the darkest corner of the alley, a dog possibly, but George started to gasp again somewhat in the manner of a melodrama and when Robert looked back it had vanished.

'Two men...head on wall...breathing difficult,' George whimpered.

Edmund took charge of the shape that was Percy. His lamp illuminated a wound to the side of Percy's head that made Robert retch. The young man's blood was pooling, painting the muddy ground with a clean sheen of red. The skin below Percy's eyes was black and blue and a clear fluid streaked with red was draining from his nose. Edmund unbuttoned Percy's clothes in order to place his hands on the chest. Kneeling in the dirt, he moved his cheek towards Percy's mouth, then his nose and back again to the chest. To dispel all visual stimulation, he shut his eyes and brushed once more against Percy's nose with his cheek before sitting back on his heels. Drawing his hand over Percy's eyes, he looked directly at Robert, shaking his head. George dropped to the ground, taking Robert down with him.

'George, what happened?' Edmund's voice pierced the darkness.

'Two men...pushed us...from behind...Percy fell. Hit head on the wall. He...he didn't get up.'

'What did you do?'

'One man stood over him. I ran to fetch help.'

'What happened to the second man?'

'He chased me. I ran for my life. I looked back. I couldn't see him. I ran to the White Lion. To...to...father.'

George pushed the last word out in a gasping breath and then slumped forwards as if to collapse head first into the mud, forcing Robert to haul the young man backwards so that he could take his weight against his chest. Bracing himself to support George whom he believed had lost consciousness, Robert was surprised when the young man stood upright, exhibiting full control of himself with not a sign of shock.

'Percy received a serious blow to the back of his head, but he also has red marks streaked with blood around his neck.'

Edmund spoke as if he were in his surgery and not in a filthy alley viewing the body of a person with whom he was acquainted. Robert tasted an acrid lump deep in his mouth and, pushing George to the right, vomited onto the mud. He was aware of Edmund standing up and moving towards George. When he was able to stand upright, Robert found that his friend had somehow clamped his hands around the young man's upper arms, pinning him against the wall. Edmund was speaking in a low, steady voice.

'George, a terrible thing has happened to you. I am sorry to have to tell you that your brother is dead. We must in all haste return to your father.' With a short pause that was long enough for Robert to nod to his friend that he was able to listen to his next instruction, he continued. 'Robert, would you stay with the...with Percy. I must be the one to speak to Philip.'

As George edged past his brother's body, his foot caught the side of Percy's head and if he did not know better, Robert could have sworn that it was a deliberate act. Moving away from Percy's body, Robert pressed his shoulders hard into the wall, seeking the roughness of the bricks as if to confirm to himself that he was awake and had not just imagined the whole terrible scene. Pushing harder and harder, he moved his head around a sharp edge, concentrating on just that one sensation until he feared he might cause himself serious injury. Missing Edmund's presence and even that of George the moment that they disappeared into the gloom, Robert prayed that Edmund would return before someone discovered him and accused him of Percy's death. How could this have happened a mere two hundred yards from the hotel where a quarter of an hour ago all any of them had to preoccupy their thoughts was the Festival programme?

Out of the corner of his eye, Robert thought he caught a movement again to his right, but he could not be certain. It was as if his sight were not quite joined up; as if he were looking at unconnected individual photographs in an album instead of a continuous stream of vision. There were gaps between the images of which he could make no sense. Since whatever it was that had moved, must now be stock still, he dared to turn his head a little so that he was no longer straining his eyes to the right.

A small figure, whose face was so dirty that he could hardly see if it were animal or human, darted out from under a cover to hide behind a pile of refuse. Edging along the wall, Robert maintained contact with the rough stones and kept his eyes fixed on the site of the movement. Looking over the heap, he saw the matted hair of a child, hands covering his eyes as though that gesture could make him invisible. Squatting down, Robert grabbed its hair. The child overbalanced, his filthy feet flailed in the air and Robert put his hand over its mouth.

'I will not hurt you. Be quiet. Stop kicking. I have money.'

The mention of money seemed to have the desired effect and the child allowed itself to be turned around. Looking into those sharp blue eyes, Robert recognised him as Samuel Brown, the boy that Anne had photographed and that he had watched in the streets when in disguise. It was difficult to determine his exact age. He knew of only one other child and that was Benjamin Drew. This child was much smaller and thinner and looked around seven or eight, but he could not be certain.

'What did you see? Come on now, I have a shilling for you.'

The shilling rolled out of Robert's hand and the boy caught it before it touched the ground. Closing his little fist around it, he kept his mouth clamped shut.

'Tell me what you saw. Did you see two young gentlemen who were attacked?'

Robert was shocked when the boy spoke. He could not possibly be seven or eight. He was sure of himself and of what had happened.

'Dunno if they was gentlemen, but there was two of 'em. Worse for drink they were, like me mother, they were.'

'What happened?'

'One of 'em pushed the other 'un hard against the wall

and throttled him when he was on the ground. Disgustin' it was. Blood 'n' and guts all over his face.'

'What about the other man?'

'He ran off.'

'There were only two men? No other men?'

The boy looked at Robert as if he were simple and spoke slowly, placing particular emphasis on the last three words.

'Told yeh didn't I. Jus' two men.'

With that, he strode off, looking as if he had just conducted a successful business transaction, leaving Robert reeling from the revelation, wishing that he had not questioned the boy. In truth, he had only spoken to the child because it gave him a measure of control over the situation in which he had found himself; he had found someone more vulnerable than himself. He had no interest in what the child had to say, but of course, once Samuel had spoken, there was no turning back. How would he tell Philip that one son had killed the other?

CHAPTER 27

Ten o'clock on the evening of Wednesday the
20th of April 1864

'I agree to keep my silence regarding the death of Percy
Wimlett.'

Robert's memory of the last half an hour was sporadic.
He recalled watching over Percy whilst Edmund cajoled
George back to the hotel. After what seemed an age, he heard
the rattle of the hand cart pulled by Edmund. Desperate to
tell his friend about the boy witness, he had run forwards,
but Patrick had emerged from the gloom, half-carrying the
weeping Philip. He could not tell Edmund the truth in their
presence and within a second of his arrival, Patrick had
issued his orders: Robert was to guide Philip from the alley
to Patrick's brewery where Archibald had been sent ahead
to unlock the gates. So palpable was Philip's distress that
Robert had at first feared touching him in case he would
injure this vulnerable wreck of a man, but one look from
Patrick dispelled any such reticence.

Now, standing in the brewery yard, the six men formed a tight circle around Percy's body. Robert bowed his head as his father, Philip, Edmund and George had done before him. Patrick had asked each man a question and it was Robert's turn to answer.

'I agree to keep my silence regarding the death of Percy Wimlett.'

'I have spoken to Philip about how to proceed,' whispered Patrick, but somehow even his whisper was authoritative. 'Philip's priority is to protect George from unnecessary attention. We know that George and Percy were walking together when two men attacked them and murdered Percy, but what we will tell everyone else outside this circle is that Percy has suddenly become ill and has had to withdraw from the Festival. There will be no mention of any attack.'

An uncontrollable yawn engulfed Robert's face, followed by a sharp, clammy sweat. Taking a deep breath as his vision blurred, he moved backwards, breaking the circle to put his hands on his knees. It had all happened too quickly for him. Turning his back to the group, Robert retched and coughed to cover his revulsion, before moving over to the corner of the yard under the pretence that he was attempting to bring his cough under control. Patrick continued to speak with head bowed, as they all did, with the exception of George whose face, lit by the two oil lamps, appeared a counterfeit of sneering sorrow. Was he seeing what he expected to see, knowing that George was a murderer or did George just shake his head and smile at the grief of his own father? Robert could not believe how stupid he had been. He should have found a way to tell Edmund that Samuel Brown had witnessed George's murder of Percy, but he had kept silent. He had missed his opportunity to speak. If he told the truth now, he would not only be calling George a murderous liar, he would be sending the young man to a public hanging.

'If we acknowledge that a murder has occurred in the town, the police investigation would mean either the termination of the Festival altogether or, at the very least, it would cast a huge pall over the celebrations. Philip has made it clear that we must not risk either the reputation of Stratford-upon-Avon or our own personal reputations,' Patrick continued.

Glancing at the distraught father, whose face had retained its viciously red complexion as if he too had been subjected to an assault, Robert doubted very much that Philip had given a moment's thought to the reputation of the town or anyone else's, for that matter. The words were Patrick's alone.

'Percy shall be taken to London and buried there in a private, respectful ceremony. Meanwhile, we will announce that Percy has fallen ill. George will perform on stage as expected and we will find an actor to replace Percy. After the Festival, Edmund will certify that the death has just occurred.'

Patrick had devised a plan as if he were conducting one of his committee meetings. The only sign that this was not the case was that at each mention of Percy's name, he nodded in the direction of Philip, without, however, stopping to take breath. Adjusting his spectacles, he looked directly into each man's eyes.

'Where shall we say that Percy is recuperating?' Edmund asked.

'We shall say that he has been sent back to London to his mother where a doctor has been engaged. He will receive expert care there.'

Patrick had spoken with such unhesitating authority

that Robert could almost persuade himself that Percy would indeed be sent to London to recover. But then his father started to speak and fear flushed again through Robert's body.

'Patrick has asked me to escort Philip and George back to the White Lion Hotel. Edmund will accompany us in case any medical needs arise. Robert, you will remain with Patrick until he has finished.'

Robert saw his father wince and scratch at his side whiskers as soon as the words came out of his mouth. It would have sounded so much kinder to say, 'until he is ready'. His choice of, 'has finished' emphasized the significance of the next job to be undertaken.

'Robert, open the gate for them,' Patrick ordered.

With those few words of command, Robert opened the left gate just far enough for his father, Philip, George and Edmund to exit, shutting it silently behind them so as not to attract unwarranted attention. As the brewing season had just come to a close because the warmer weather resulted in problems of infection in the brew and ales that were thick and poor, there should be little or no activity in the yard at night.

'Robert, you have nothing to fear. I have everything under control. In the morning, as we do every year in April, the premises will be cleaned from top to toe with water and lime. All walls, ceilings, passages and staircases will be scrubbed and then whitewashed to eliminate dust. Any trace of the body ever having been in the brewery will be eradicated during this process. No one will ever find out that we were here with the body.'

Rather than being issued as a reassurance, Robert understood the tone of Patrick's last sentence to be a reminder that he had vowed to keep his silence.

'Robert, I find I have forgotten to give a message to your father regarding the plan for the body.'

'What would you like me to say?' Robert asked, grateful for any reason to leave the scene.

'I shall go. There are details I need to discuss. I shall be back in a few minutes.'

In Philip's absence, Robert noticed that Patrick did not use Percy's name. He was merely a body that needed to be disposed of. Alone once again with Percy, Robert took a sideways glance at the young man almost as if this did not count as looking. He had seen many dead bodies before, but they had all been laid out respectfully in their coffins for the mourners to view, not lying unceremoniously on a rough cart in a brewery yard.

Now empty of its jumble of heavy horses pulling the wagons, of ostlers, draymen, coopers, carpenters, joiners, labourers, tunners and senior cellarmen directing operations, the enormous brewery yard looked out of scale. The thousands, if not millions, of bricks that had gone into the making of the three malt-houses, each three storeys high housing the huge mash tun, coppers, kilns and coke bore down on Robert. The chimney stack, that pierced the sky like a modern church spire, made his head spin as if it would come crashing down upon him. Cupping both hands over his mouth and nose, he took small comfort from the warmth of his breath, but then his skin became irritated and he scratched and scratched until he feared he would draw blood. An ache in his back that he had not previously noticed, then a shooting pain in his left leg made him feel that his body was under attack and he had to persuade himself that Percy's manner of death was not infectious. George had murdered his brother

Percy and Samuel Brown had witnessed it.

Robert froze. He had allowed himself to become distracted and it was too late to hide. The brewery gate was opening. He stared and Patrick entered. Wordlessly, he pointed to the cart, then to Robert and over to a shed that was nestled amongst older-looking buildings whose cellars stored barrels for the export of the famous Drew pale ale to India. Obeying the older man's silent command without question, despite his complete ignorance as to the reason for the removal of the cart, Robert entered the shed.

There was a large wooden table in the centre and piled against two of the walls were stacks of timber from Cox and Sons. Patrick had a very close relationship with the owner of the large timber yard that stood in a prominent position next to the River Avon. In fact, Patrick had a close relationship with everyone of note in the town. Looking along the far wall where casks had been organised according to their precise state of disrepair, Robert saw neatly hung coopers' woodworking tools that would enable the newly repaired casks to pass the head cooper's silk handkerchief test. He knew that Patrick took this opportunity each year to have the damaged casks repaired and the sacks used to store the barley mended, but why had they brought Percy into this particular shed? His eyes rested on several saws. In the lamplight, he watched Patrick put what looked like a large rubber-treated cloth over the table, before walking around to Percy's head.

'No!'

A fluttering pain in Robert's ear, a ringing deep inside and a burning sensation as if he had been stabbed, made him shriek out. Jerking his neck, he scanned the shed trying to detect the threat before he realised that it was he who had screamed the word. *Patrick was going to cut up Percy's body and put it into a cask.*

'Robert, whatever is the matter with you? Help me to lift the body onto the table so that we may undress it. We all talked about what we were going to do and we all agreed that this was the best course to pursue.'

They had not all talked about what they were going to do, they had simply agreed with Patrick's plan. No one had had the stomach to discuss the arrangement or to offer another solution, so they had stood in silent acquiescence. Wriggling his hands under Percy's knees, as instructed, Robert almost dropped the young man when Patrick hauled him off the cart without warning. Roughly taking off the outerwear of gloves, scarf, shoes and cloak, the clothing that could be traced back to Percy's or rather Philip's tailor would have to be burnt. Patrick would leave nothing to chance. Throwing them onto the floor, he said that the watch and chain would be given to Philip at a later date.

Lifting Percy so that Patrick could remove the semi-fitted dress coat, silk handkerchief and waistcoat, Robert felt the weight of the muscular body and closed his eyes so that he breathed only through his mouth; he could not bear his senses to take in any more of Percy than they already had. Patrick tugged at the ends of the cravat that clung to the stiffly starched standing collar of Percy's shirt, before deciding that it would be quicker to unbutton it, cravat still attached. Undoing the tab, whose job it had been to prevent the pleated linen shirt from riding up, Patrick took off the leather braces and muslin under-shirt. As he pulled off the socks and unbuttoned the trousers, Robert thought, surely this young man will be permitted to keep his under-wear, but no, no indignity was to be spared.

'Take the bucket over there and get some water from the pump in the yard. Whatever is wrong with you?'

All energy had drained from Robert's arms. Hanging limply by his side, the tin bucket bumped against his thigh as he forced his legs to move forward by repeating silently to himself, 'foot, foot, foot' and in this way he progressed like an ancient gentleman nearing the end of his days. His right hand moved the curved cast-iron handle up and down, but he did not have the strength to draw any water. So he pushed with both hands, pumping more and more vigorously as if his life depended upon it until, by some miracle, the bucket was full. Placing the bucket on the stone floor, he took a step back as Patrick squeezed water from a cloth onto Percy's head wounds. Rubbing fiercely backwards and forwards, Patrick had to hold the young man's head as it lolled about. The blood had congealed and matted the hair, so he plunged a scrubbing brush into the water and Robert looked away. Continuing the action until the hair was clean and stuck close to the scalp, Patrick had made Percy look as if he had simply used too much maccassar oil to smooth down his red hair.

'We need to dress him,' Patrick announced.

The sound of a human voice startled Robert after their silent activity and he spoke involuntarily.

'I will fetch some of mine.'

'You may not. You are forgetting yourself, Robert. They will be traced to you. I have some workmen's clothes that will serve the purpose.'

Robert wished with all his heart that he could return home and refuse to participate in Patrick's plan, but, of course, it was impossible. He had no choice but to continue. As mayor and principal employer in the town, Patrick could determine a treacherous individual's fate in a trice.

'Shall I go to the hotel and tell the groom to bring your carriage here?' Robert asked.

'No. Gossip may spark rumour if we were collected from the brewery at this time of night and not from the hotel. It was what I was discussing with your father. We will walk him between us as if he were drunk. It is only around the corner after all.'

With an arm draped over their shoulders, they clasped Percy's body around the waist and dragged him through the brewery entrance and around the corner where they rested for a moment. Entering Henley Street, Robert saw that Patrick's carriage had pulled up outside the hotel, where, as instructed, his father was distracting the groom. Edmund took Patrick's place and with a supreme effort, they lifted Percy into the carriage. As the groom descended, suddenly aware of his master's arrival, Patrick announced in a loud voice that he was most concerned that Percy had not yet revived from his collapse in the street. Philip and George ascended the carriage, followed by Edmund who would administer medication to the father and son as necessary. Archibald, Patrick and Robert were to continue their evening in the White Lion Hotel as if nothing had happened.

CHAPTER 28

The morning of Thursday the 21st of April 1864

At the sound of the crunch of gravel, Anne pulled the curtain to one side to see that Rachel was alighting from her carriage a full hour before their appointed meeting time. She could not for the life of her imagine what had caused this unexpected haste in her mother-in-law.

'Anne, have you heard the news?'

'Well, that depends upon its nature.'

'Percy was taken dangerously ill last night. His very life hangs in the balance, or so Patrick told our housekeeper, Mrs Betteridge. Philip, Edmund and George brought him back to our house in the early hours of the morning and I missed it all. When I awoke, I saw Patrick, hot-tempered and boiling with rage, rushing into the Brougham. It left immediately and when I questioned Mrs Betteridge, she said that he would be in meetings regarding the Festival for the rest of the day.'

'How terrible.'

'Yes it is. They will have to find someone else to play

Tybalt. And at such short notice!'

Anne was unable to respond at first.

'No. I mean, what is wrong with him?'

'Apparently, Percy collapsed last night with severe breathing difficulties. Edmund attended him and it was decided that Philip, George and Edmund should take Percy back to London to receive attention from the best physicians and, of course, the care of his mother.'

'Will they stay with Percy until he is out of danger?'

'No, they would be unable to assist in his recovery and the Wimletts do not wish to disadvantage the Festival any more than Percy's illness already has. They will return on the next train so that they may participate in the Festival as planned.'

'I shall write to Amelia to extend my sympathy. Please would you speak to Philip and George on my behalf.'

'Well, they cannot return a moment too soon. It has placed a lot of extra weight on Patrick's shoulders. Mrs Betteridge said that he looked most unwell this morning, as if he had the world on his shoulders. He throws himself into everything he does. This Festival will be the death of him!'

'Why not ask Patrick if we may share some of that weight. I should relish the opportunity to assist in any way that he deemed appropriate,' Anne replied, displaying more irritation in her tone than she meant to, riled by Rachel's insistence on her husband's indispensability.

'You have plenty to do, if you would only put your mind to it. I have completed my final appointment with my dressmaker and I know that you have only managed to fit in one and have left yours to her own devices. You will regret it when your costume does not show your figure to its best advantage at the ball.'

'The Festival will preserve their names forever whereas ours will be lost, thrown away with our...our dresses. Do you not wonder what Patrick does when he leaves the house? What it would be like to live a man's life outside the domestic sphere?'

'No, I do not. It is not my business. Anne, whatever is the matter with you?'

'Please excuse me, I am fatigued,' she offered lamely.

'Ever since you photographed the street children, you have been troubled. Might I suggest that you return to taking portraits? You were content then.'

'I do not deny that when I first took up photography, I was content with such subjects, but since our darling Harold departed, I have become weary of photographing women dressed up as allegorical and historical figures posed against a whimsical background. They are as fictitious as the old oil paintings in the Town Hall.'

At this point, Anne thought she had better walk to the window so that she did not have to meet Rachel's eyes.

'I have photographed all of the male relatives I ever wish to and although I am most grateful to you for the chance to photograph the men of note whom you and Patrick invite to your house as guests of the town, I believe that I have found a more worthy subject to capture. I have made up my mind to take photographs of the polished streets alongside images of the back streets, the forgotten streets and the people who live in them.'

'But what would you do with photographs of people who do not belong to you, people who live such a different life? Where is the artistic merit?'

'It is not their artistic merit in which I am interested. I wish to show the true nature of how people have to live, even here in a town that has been scrubbed for the public gaze. We are used to seeing illustrations of the conditions in London, but how much more powerful would a photograph be that cannot lie?'

'But, who would want to look at ordinary street scenes and taken by a lady, at that?'

'Perhaps I should make up a nom de plume like Marian Evans or the Bronte sisters. Who shall I pretend to be? Not Anne Drew, but Andrew something?'

'Anne, you are too fanciful. Your name would be discovered and you would be subjected to common talk. You will bring disgrace upon the name of Drew, on Patrick and, as mayor, the reputation of Stratford-upon-Avon. I find myself somewhat to blame for I have indulged your fantasy of photography. I do confess that when Patrick made the visit to London in March, I was a little put out. The Festival has taken so much of his time over the past year that we have not entertained as we used to do and I was pleased that you had asked me to accompany you. I see now that I was over-hasty in my agreement. I hoped merely to use the photographs as evidence to show Patrick that Samuel Brown's parents were guilty of keeping him from attendance at my school, that he was not unwell as they had suggested. I never considered the possibility that you might wish to make your photographs public. You must dismiss such thoughts. Let today's photograph of the pavilion be the last that you take in the public street.'

Rachel's use of her serious voice, of a slower, deeper tone when speaking this last sentence meant only one thing: obedience was expected. When Rachel put it like that, it did seem an impossible task. Had she really suggested to Rachel that she should use a pseudonym? Charles Dickens had guessed that George Eliot was a woman and Anne would be meeting him in two days' time. No, a pseudonym was definitely not one of her brighter ideas. But, would people be able to guess from a photograph, in the same way that they had worked out from a piece of writing, that the photographer was a woman? Would a woman have a different style of photographing than a man if she were permitted to create the same images as him? Better to be honest right from the start and put her own name to the photographs. After all, Robert had reacted positively when he had seen those two photographs on Tuesday and had asked to see the rest today. What surprised her more than anything was that he had asked her to photograph the pavilion. It was as if he wanted her to be seen taking photographs in public and she could not be happier.

Arriving at the pavilion half an hour later, Anne could hardly contain her excitement; she could not wait to show Robert her entire collection of street images, as he had requested. Adjusting the camera's position so that the pavilion would be shown to its best advantage, she glanced around several times. When she had last seen Robert on Tuesday, he had asked if he may be present, but the appointed time had passed and he was nowhere to be seen. She could delay the photograph no longer since Rachel looked as if she might insist upon their departure at any moment. Where was he? Was he simply being polite on Tuesday, saying what she wanted to hear? He had seemed delighted to see the street photographs, but now she felt foolish having taken him at his word. He had obviously had second thoughts. She had brought the street photographs and he had not even had the grace to send a note to say that he had been detained.

It seemed that she was destined to take photographs that would never be seen.

But, here was Robert looking as if he had dressed in a hurry and behind his carriage, Samuel Brown, the boy from Rachel's school. What on earth was Robert doing nodding to this boy in the street?

CHAPTER 29

The afternoon of Friday the 22nd of April 1864

They were back at the brewery, but this time they sat in some comfort in Patrick's office. Patrick, Philip and Archibald kept their pipes in their mouths as they talked, unlike the three younger men, Robert, Edmund and George, who, not as practised in the art, held their pipes in hand whenever they were required to speak, which was not very often. To Robert's surprise, he noticed that Edmund occasionally spoke with his pipe in his mouth. It was as if his closest friend had spent time in the company of the older men of which Robert knew nothing.

'We welcome back Philip and George from London where they buried their beloved son and brother with all due respect and dignity,' Patrick announced. 'We extend our love and gratitude to Amelia for her understanding and we thank Edmund who ministered most attentively to her needs during the service. Now that the matter has been brought to a close, we shall all stand together, shoulder to shoulder with our friends, the Wimletts.'

'The Wimletts,' chorused the four men, toasting Philip and George as if they had achieved a personal success.

Joining in the chorus sickened Robert, but he knew that his words and actions must not stand out from those of the others. He could not, however, bear to look any of them in the eye, not even his father, especially since Patrick kept whispering, 'Archibald,' to his father and drawing him away from the rest of the group to share something to which he was not party. Directing his attention away from their faces, Robert watched the six white trails of smoke advance upwards along their well-worn track towards the ceiling where they rose to augment the thick fog that peered down at them. An unexpected shaft of spring sunlight attempted to pierce the blue-grey veil that had been drawn across Patrick's office, but the territorial fumes stalked this ray of light until it retreated, returning the room to a cave-like gloom. Satisfied, the smoke rubbed its body against the walls, ceiling, floorboards and finally the men's clothing and hair and even their hands and faces, marking them with its stubborn scent.

'If only I had listened to Amelia when she talked of her dream. She was certain that something awful was about to befall our boys and I dismissed it,' Philip repeated for the umpteenth time, glancing in the direction of Archibald.

Robert was most concerned that his father was being blamed by Philip for his dismissal of Amelia's dream, but Patrick cut across Philip's words before Robert was able to challenge him.

'We all agree to recount the following story. Philip, George and Edmund have returned from London where a doctor has been engaged to treat Percy who is slightly recovered. His mother remains at his bedside. This incident will bind us together forever and will always be a part of our shared history. Percy will not be forgotten,' Patrick stated.

Robert winced at the word, 'incident'. How could Patrick describe this tragedy in such bland terms? More like a secret history, was what he wanted to shout out loud, but he kept silent.

'Patrick has suggested a solution to an impossible situation and therefore we shall all agree,' Archibald seconded the proposal.

Robert felt a chill run down his spine at his father's words. He had answered for them all. There was to be no discussion.

'Thank you, Archibald. It is imperative that we close ranks. If one of us falls, we all come tumbling down. Now, it is time to look to the future. It is agreed, gentlemen, that we shall not deviate from the announcement in the Tercentenary programme that George will perform next Monday in *Romeo and Juliet* and will attend the banquet as expected. George's courage is to be commended. He has assured me that he will contain his grief in public and will not in any way provoke speculation that Percy's situation is anything other than what we have said.'

Patrick had spoken as if George were not in the room, but upon his conclusion, he had thrown a broad smile in the young man's direction. As for the rest of the company, he addressed them as if he were the commander of an army; his questions did not require answers but merely acquiescence and his statements all spoke of, 'we' not 'I'. They were all involved, equally culpable and there was no escape. If Robert were to speak now, he would lose everything that he knew and held dear and he would be forced to leave the town and thereby his family; the two were so inextricably linked. Handed from the nursemaid to the governess, to his father's architectural practice and on to the committee, he had been passed from one to another with no requirement to consider himself as a separate entity. He had no connections outside those established by his father and all could be traced back to Patrick Drew. Patrick would be looking for unity. Any sign of difference would be considered an act of defiance or perhaps weakness and Robert could not decide which was worse.

Although he missed his well-used briar root pipe, whose veins streaked through the close-grained root to offer a sweetness to the smoke absent from that of the meerschaum, Robert knew that he must not allow his pipe to set him apart from the others. Curling his hand around the meerschaum's bowl, he attempted to hide the paleness of his pipe against the dark reds and deep browns of the other men's pipes. For the first time, he noticed that even Edmund's meerschaum was showing its age and use, but when out with him he always used the briar-root. It really was beginning to look as if his friend had spent time in the older men's company which he had kept secret.

It was only George who defied the tradition, puffing on an inexpensive clay pipe, the sort that a working man would smoke. It did cross Robert's mind that George would not, and indeed, should not, readily have come into contact with such a pipe. He should have his smoking accoutrements delivered to the house as any gentleman would. Robert thought he could see written on Patrick's face, exactly the same thought and he wondered whether Patrick would have taken such trouble to conceal Percy's death if it had occurred at any time other than at the commencement of Shakespeare's Tercentenary Festival. Was he intent on saving his friend's family and the reputation of the town or was it his own reputation that was uppermost on his mind?

And then George spoke. Robert was startled to hear the young man's voice, but the contents of his speech were infinitely more shocking. George cried out that he could no longer keep his silence about the true nature of Percy's death and Robert held his breath. George condemned Percy as a drunkard who had started the fight on Wednesday evening. Percy had been a madman, raving, George explained. His brother had attacked the two men and they had had to defend themselves. His audience of five sat in stunned silence. Philip buried his face in his hands and Patrick whispered to him. Philip nodded his head in agreement to something no one else had been allowed to hear. Robert sank into his chair, unable to fully comprehend the easy lies that were destroying Percy's reputation. He knew that George was an accomplished actor on the stage, but here in front of him, Robert knew that he had witnessed George's most convincing role.

Growing in stature, the smoke reached down from the ceiling, pawing at the men's nostrils, overpowering their senses and now sitting heavily on their chests. The older men watched one another, but the younger men avoided eye contact, sucking insistently on their pipes, concealing rising coughs. Reaching inside Robert's mouth and down his throat, the smoke cloyed, constricting his airways, but it was not only the fumes that prevented him from breathing freely. He felt as if he had committed the murder himself.

'Gentlemen, friends,' Patrick announced after a brief pause, 'this terrible news has shaken us all,' and here he looked at Philip, 'but, we thank George for his honesty. It could not have been easy for him to tell the truth about his brother's death. But now, we will turn our thoughts to the great day, for which we have been planning these three long years. Tomorrow, the world will celebrate the three hundredth anniversary of the birth of William Shakespeare. Tomorrow, Stratford-upon-Avon will host the first day of the greatest national Festival in honour of the greatest writer that has ever lived. The world's eyes will be upon us.'

CHAPTER 30

Idiot!

As soon as Christopher had returned home from his coffee with Nancy, he'd questioned his mother about the stranger who'd spoken to her at the station and, although her recollection was vague, it seemed to match that of the man whom he'd seen hanging about outside their flat. Perhaps Nancy was right. Someone was after the diary. The image of her retreating back wouldn't leave him. Why the hell hadn't he followed her? He couldn't blame her for not replying to his embarrassingly lame text, 'Are you all right?' Of course she bloody well wasn't! And he'd let her run up the steps without saying a damn thing. Patting his shoulder bag until he'd made contact with all four corners of the diary, he swore that at least he'd keep his promise to her that the diary wouldn't leave his side.

'It's the only building in Stratford to remain thatched,' he heard his mother say.

'Why?' Madeleine asked, using her favourite word.

'There were lots of fires in the town about four hundred years ago and the thatched roofs spread the fire so people were forced to use tiles.'

'But why is this one still thatched?' Madeleine pursued.

'That's a good question. I...I'm...I'm not sure, darling,' Bridget said, looking around at Christopher, who was checking his mobile again almost as if it would prompt Nancy to reply.

For goodness' sake, he was starting to look like Peter – always on his phone!

'It's because, four hundred years ago, this building would have been on the edge of the town and they didn't need to have such strict fire regulations as the buildings in the centre,' Thomas replied.

'Of course, of course, that's what I was about to say. Here we are,' Bridget said hurriedly, nodding towards the heavy wooden door of the Old Thatch Tavern.

Knowing that his mother wouldn't enter the inn before the 'birthday boy', as she still insisted on calling him, Christopher pushed open the door to be greeted by a dark, low-beamed room with a bar running the length of one wall. Negotiating the customers propping up the bar and those clustered on a mixture of sofas and easy chairs around tables in the lounge, he stopped at the far end of the room where a curtain was hooked to one side in a theatrical flourish. A huge central wooden pillar divided the restaurant which, together with the low ceiling of criss-crossed beams, had managed to retain the footprint of the original rooms. His mother had decided in advance where they should each sit and Christopher wasn't surprised to see that she placed him between herself and his father and that she asked Madeleine to sit on her other side at the end of the table. His mother was thoroughly enjoying her great-niece's company.

'I told them it was a very special occasion when I booked,' Bridget said, as the waitress arrived. 'I'll ask for a couple more candles on the table, but don't worry, I remembered to say again that you didn't want balloons or banners.'

'Happy Birthday,' the young woman smiled.

Christopher hoped that his mother hadn't told the pub his age, but of course she would have had to in order to explain the special occasion. Echoing the waitress's smile, he kept silent, not wanting to prolong her questioning gaze in his direction. She was only in her early twenties or perhaps even late teens and he imagined her deciding whether or not he looked his age. She'd be wondering why, at forty, he was out with his parents and not with his own family. To an outsider's eyes though, they'd look like the perfect nuclear family – with Joanne as his wife and Peter and Madeleine, his children, he looked every bit the husband and father. And he was a father, wasn't he? Could you be a father if your child didn't know of your existence? Had he been a father for the previous three years or not? As for his own father, he was drinking far more than Christopher had ever seen before. Thankful that the hearty main course arrived promptly, he thought that it would slow his father's alcohol intake, but instead he took a deep mouthful from his glass.

'So, Joanne, I can't seem to forget about that necklace of yours. Did you say you wear it every day?'

'Not every day, but quite often. When I wear something else, I put it in my handbag. I like to have it with me as a kind of talisman.'

'It sounds as if it's very important to you.'

'When Mum gave it to me, just before...' Joanne glanced

at Madeleine who was paying no attention to the grown-ups, busy as she was closing down the game on her cerise-pink tablet, 'before she died, she asked me to always keep it with me as she'd done since my birth.'

What was it with the necklace? Why was his father banging on about it again? Christopher couldn't decide if it was the necklace or the mention of his Aunt Sylvia that had touched a nerve, but Uncle Charles couldn't get up from the table quickly enough, knocking his knife clattering to the floor, bumping against another diner and looking at them as if it were their fault. Fumbling with the door latch, he tripped up the step while the whole room watched him – all except Madeleine, thank goodness, who, had she seen, would surely have asked why Granddad was in such a tearing hurry. A shiver shuddered across Christopher's shoulder blades and sprinted down to the small of his back as a couple opened a previously unnoticed door to a smoking area. Cold air blasted the table.

What with his dad and his uncle acting as if they were in a soap opera, he'd completely forgotten about the diary. Stretching his left arm until his fingertips made contact with his bag, he eased them to the right until they found the top corner of the diary. Feeling his way along the book's edges, rounded by their leather blanket, he smiled to himself at his paranoia. As he released his left hand, he knocked the candle nearest to him clean off the table and onto his bag – flame first. The damned diary was in more danger from him than from anyone else, he thought as he viewed the waxy snail's trail that had wound its way down the leather.

Nancy!

Not wanting to be seen texting at the table under his mother's attentive gaze, he excused himself, which was easier said than done, what with the bag and the fact that his mother had not only to get out of her seat, but had to move around to the end of the table to let him pass by.

'How are you?'

No reply. Nancy must be seriously pissed off at him. As he looked up from his phone, Christopher saw his Uncle, who now seemed to have recovered, approaching him.

'We really must stop your father from drinking so much. I'm getting quite worried about his health. What do you think?'

'I'm not sure, Uncle.'

'He keeps babbling on about nothing, reminding Joanne of her mother's death,' Charles continued.

'Oh, I'm sorry. I didn't know it had upset Joanne. I'll see what I can do.'

Still no reply from Nancy.

*

Thomas had deliberately drunk too quickly at the table. Thoughts of Sylvia, Charles and Joanne wouldn't stop going round in his head and he wanted to feel the effects of the alcohol sooner rather than later. What he couldn't dismiss from his mind was that Sylvia might have confessed to Charles that he, Thomas, was Joanne's real father and Charles had kept quiet. He'd stop skirting around the subject and ask Charles directly. They'd sit down with Joanne and tell her the truth and then they'd tell Peter, but not Madeleine – not yet. But when to tell Christopher? It would have to be as soon as he'd told Joanne and before Peter. Yes, that's exactly what he'd do – that's what he told himself when he was alone anyway. It was a completely different matter when he was actually with them all.

*

'Okay, Dad?' Christopher said, as he sat back down at the table.

'All right, son?'

'Are you enjoying the meal, Dad?'

'Are you?'

It was like one of those American shows where every question is answered with another question. The inappropriateness of the comparison that sprang to mind caused Christopher to smile which worked instantly on his father for some unknown reason.

'What are you laughing about?'

'Nothing. I think I've had too much to drink. I can see Mum looking a bit concerned.'

'It's your celebration. You may do whatever you like.'

'It'd be best if we stopped. Move onto water.'

'We?'

'Slip of the tongue! See what I mean. Must be the drink. I'll go and ask the waitress for some water.'

From the corner of the bar, Christopher looked over at the table to see his father leaning in towards his uncle as if to prevent him from making an escape. God, he'd forgotten to ask him to stop talking about the necklace. He'd better get back.

'I'm sure I've seen that necklace before. Charles, what have you to say for yourself?'

'Dad, let's go for a walk.'

'No, I want an answer.'

244

'It's fine, Christopher. I don't know who gave the necklace to Sylvia. I'd like to know, but I don't know anything. Sorry old man.'

*

Thomas couldn't believe what a fool he'd been. Charles knew nothing about his affair with Sylvia. Of course she hadn't told Charles – she wouldn't be that cruel. He knew there was nothing to be gained by telling Joanne that he was her father, so why the hell had he felt the need to tell Joanne the truth when all it would do was rip his and Charles's family apart?

'David.'

It was all because of David's death. He'd not spoken his son's name since he'd died. Too painful. It just didn't seem right to be happy so soon – it was as if he needed to stop the happiness, as if he ought not to be happy, as if he should never be happy again. And so he'd thought he should tell Joanne that he was her father and make them all unhappy. But he was happy. There was nothing in the world that made him happier than Bridget, Christopher and his brother, Charles. That was it – he'd never tell Joanne.

*

Bridget knew exactly what was wrong with Thomas and it was all her fault. She'd been selfish. He'd wanted to cancel this birthday trip for Christopher, but she'd insisted on carrying on, and he'd supported her. It wasn't that she wanted to pretend that nothing had happened – it was that she'd made a conscious decision to embrace what she had. And she had so much. Even the memory problems that she'd experienced since January had lessened and, to be honest, they probably weren't ever that bad. She'd dwelt on them, become obsessed by them after David's death. But, she should have cancelled this trip. She should have seen Thomas's pain. They'd talk back at the flat when it was just the two of them. No – she couldn't unless Christopher went off to visit Nancy.

'Christopher, are you seeing Nancy later?'

'I haven't got any plans to see her, but I could do with texting her, if you don't mind. Sorry, she had a problem earlier and I want to see if she's okay.'

'She's a nice girl, you should keep in touch.'

Christopher got up and started texting before she'd even stopped talking, so she turned to her great-niece.

'Madeleine, how are you getting on with your guitar? Your mum said you're enjoying playing it.'

'Mr Jacobs says I'm a very good musician but I have to practise every day.'

'It's a shame you haven't brought it with you.'

'I have brought it! It's in the flat. I'm playing it in our assembly on Tuesday with Jonathan, Reece and Jessica.'

'I'm surprised you haven't heard her, the walls are obviously thicker than they look,' Joanne replied with a grimace.

'Mum, Mum, can we go and get it?'

'No. I know what we'll do. You can play when we get back to the flat after the meal.'

'No. I want to play now.'

'Young lady, that's enough, thank you. It wouldn't be appropriate to play in the restaurant anyway. It would disturb the other guests.'

'I s'pose.'

'You'll be able to play for much longer in the flat and you

can arrange the chairs so we can sit facing you like grown-ups do at a proper concert.'

At her mum's words, the exaggerated frown vanished to be replaced by an equally extravagant smile. The waitress brought paper and pens and Madeleine set to work. One minute she'd been irritated, about to cause a scene, the next, she was excited, making tickets, paper money, programmes and a poster to advertise the concert. How wonderful childhood was. Bridget walked over to Thomas, put her arm around his shoulder and planted a kiss on his cheek.

*

Still no reply from Nancy. He'd blown it. Standing in the corridor outside the restaurant, Christopher could hardly face returning to the table. Who was he kidding, thinking someone like Nancy would be interested in him? It was the diary, pure and simple. *What a fuck up* he mouthed into the mirror.

Back at the table, all seemed to have returned to some semblance of normality. His mother, father, uncle and Joanne were chatting away and laughing, Peter was focused on his screen as if his life depended on it and Madeleine was busy drawing.

When it was time to leave, Christopher offered to carry Madeleine who'd fallen asleep amongst the paper and pens. He was sure she'd wake up when her mother eased her into a sitting position, her little legs dangling like pieces of string, but she'd remained slumped into the chair, head to one side. Kneeling on the floor in front of her, he sort of threw her against his right shoulder. Pausing for a moment to see if she'd wake, he heard a reassuring deep sigh as she nuzzled her sweaty head against his neck. As he adjusted to the unexpected heaviness of this child who was dead to the world, he wobbled on his knee before rising unsteadily, leaning back to take her weight. It was almost as if she pressed into him deliberately, making herself heavier than she really was – not at all fragile as he'd expected. He was a father. He was forty years old and this was the first time he'd ever held a child and it felt right.

CHAPTER 31

Present day: Friday 23 April noon

At a few minutes to twelve, Nancy arrived at the Shakespeare Institute. The former home of Marie Corelli, the best-selling novelist who'd championed the preservation of Stratford-upon-Avon's historic buildings, sported a blue plaque. When Nancy had first seen the plaque, she'd looked Corelli up and had been delighted to find that the novelist, who'd moved to the town in 1898, had campaigned for the annual Shakespeare Festival in Stratford to be developed into a more significant event and also for Stratford to hold Shakespeare conferences. Both of these had been achieved and the Institute, along with venues in London, now hosted the annual Shakespeare World Conference. Nancy was proud to have helped organise the last two. But, how times had changed since Corelli's day. Nancy had read with surprise that the Memorial Theatre, as it was then called, was open less than half the year due to the price of its tickets and that it couldn't attract enough actors who wanted to travel to Stratford.

With a wave to Lucy, the receptionist, Nancy rushed up the oak staircase and knocked on Dr Morrell's study door. Putting her ear to the door in case she'd missed his voice asking her to enter, she shut her eyes, but she couldn't hear a thing. She pushed the door handle in case he hadn't heard her, but it was locked. There was no sign of him. She'd agreed the time of the meeting to coincide with a seminar that her friend, Shari, was attending in the room next door, but that would be over by twelve thirty. Where the hell was he?

Despite asking Lucy and several students she came across in the common room and conservatory, no one could say where Dr Morrell was. She knew he walked to work, so she returned to the reception and sat uncomfortably on a chair as if she were a visitor rather than a student. She didn't dare move in case she missed him. He'd emailed to say he had significant information to add to her thesis and she couldn't afford to ignore it. It was only then that Nancy remembered she'd meant to apologise to Christopher for not replying to his texts last night. She'd become so fixated on what she'd transcribed from the diary that she hadn't even noticed that her cell was dead until she'd woken up late this morning wondering why her alarm hadn't gone off. When she'd plugged it in, the concern in his four texts was obvious, but she was so late that she'd rushed straight out of the door for the meeting with Dr Morrell – who hadn't even bothered to turn up on time!

When the heavy front door creaked open, she abandoned her text to Christopher and gathered her bag. In came Dr Morrell, apologising and rushing up the stairs two at a time, asking her to give him a few minutes and Nancy was left looking at his retreating back. It was twelve twenty-six. She'd give him four minutes tops.

Knocking on the large panelled door for the second time, she entered before waiting for the customary, 'come in.'

'Er hello Nancy, thank you for coming. How are you progressing with the transcription of the diary?'

'Slowly. I'm focusing on the third chapter as you suggested.'

She wanted to know what on earth Dr Morrell could have to add to her thesis without giving anything away about the diary.

'Would you like me to have a look at what you've completed since our meeting yesterday?'

'No, it's okay thanks. You said you had some information that would support my thesis that was not in the public arena?' she said, throwing his exact phrase back at him.

'Well, as I told you before, the family of friends of mine was significant in Stratford at the time of the Festival. I'm sure that if I may have a copy of the diary, I could see if they have any information to add to your thesis. I can promise that the diary would remain your intellectual property.'

On the face of it, it didn't seem unreasonable, except that she was the only one giving. He was not offering anything. There was to be no exchange of information as he'd promised.

'If you give me their email address, I can contact them direct,' she offered.

'No, they would prefer me to deal with you.'

'So you've spoken to them about my research?'

'Not at all, simply that you're researching the 1864 Tercentenary Festival in Stratford-upon-Avon,' Dr Morrell replied with a rising note of annoyance in his voice becoming more obvious.

'I don't feel comfortable sharing the diary with anyone. I'm sorry, I'm sure you understand.'

'Of course I do. If you have a change of heart, let me know,' Dr Morrell answered, looking down at the mess of books on his desk.

So that was it. She was being dismissed like a naughty schoolchild. She doubted if he'd ever had anything for her. It was another ploy to get his hands on the diary.

'Thank you for your time, Dr Morrell.'

As Nancy opened the door, he called out.

'Does the Gastrell family still keep the diary in their possession, or do they let you borrow it?'

'They keep it in their possession. I see it when I'm with Christopher.'

Relieved to be leaving the room, she'd answered before she'd had time to stop herself. It was like one of those old detective re-runs she caught sometimes during her nightly writing sessions. Was it *Columbo*, where the detective turns to leave and casually appears to ask a throw-away question, which in fact turns out to be the key to the solution of the murder? What a waste of time. She'd better let Christopher know she was okay.

CHAPTER 32

Present day: Friday 23 April 1pm

'Sorry not to reply to your texts. My battery was dead. Saw my supervisor. He had another go at persuading me to email him the diary. I didn't mean to, but I told him your name. Sorry! Please keep the diary safe. Where are you?'

Christopher breathed a sigh of relief as he looked at Nancy's text. Contact at last.

'We're in town. Are you ok?'

'Will drop laptop back home then I'm off for a jog. Need fresh air after that!!'

'We're booked to go up the theatre tower at 1.30.'

'I'll jog around the river. Look out for me!' Nancy texted back.

The theatre tower sat beside the theatre, looking for all the world as if it wanted nothing to do with its famous neighbour. To Christopher's eye, its square brick-built walls and arrow slit windows resembled a fire-fighters' training tower. It was as if a fire was expected at any moment – a prospect that was a little unnerving, he thought, since they'd be at the theatre on Saturday night. Whilst the rest of the family took the lift to the observation room at the top, Christopher chose to walk up the stairs because he'd heard that the utilitarian interior of red brick and grey steel was punctuated by large photographs of Shakespearean actors from the past. As he turned the corner, he came face to face with one of the black and white images that he recognised from a transcription that Nancy had sent to him. Anne had described in detail how she'd taken the photograph of George Wimlett as Romeo at the Town Hall a few days before the Festival. Stopping for a moment, his eyes were drawn to the photographer's name: Paul Brook, 1864. Where was Anne's name?

Attempting to shoot his own photographs out of the slit windows made Christopher feel vaguely nauseous; the out of kilter perspective from this odd angle afforded only the narrowest of views of the town and he was quite relieved to reach the observation room. His mother, father and Uncle Charles were laughing with Joanne and Madeleine, who was pointing at something or other and jumping up and down, nodding and giggling uncontrollably. Peter, as usual, was plugged into his phone.

Looking out of the window at the now un-obscured town to get his bearings, Christopher traced the river towards Holy Trinity Church, but could see no sign of Nancy. The adjacent window uncovered a jumble of roofs that belonged to the main theatre and to the left, that of the Swan Theatre, but still no Nancy. He tried to pick out their townhouse for his mother, but it had been swallowed up by its neighbours and he gave it up as a bad job. Again, Christopher searched the path that skirted the river and this time he spotted Nancy. If she hadn't told him that she was going to be jogging past the theatre, he'd never have been able to pick her out – luckily, amongst the sightseers, she was the only jogger. Then she stopped and his phone rang.

'Come down now. I've just been sent a text telling me to stop researching George and Percy Wimlett!'

Christopher ran. Circling round and round, the photographs of the actors whirled past his face in a blur. A sudden tight pain on the outside of his right knee made him lose concentration for a moment. Putting his hand on the brick wall to stop himself falling, he sanded off a layer of skin. As he reached the last step, he found he couldn't stop and practically hurled himself at a young woman dressed in the theatre uniform of black trousers and red t-shirt. A tightening in his chest made it impossible for him to apologise until he'd taken in a gulp of air. The woman's repeated, 'are you all right, sir?' forced him to mouth silently, 'yes,' as he pushed through the gathering crowd of tourists and out of the theatre.

Nancy was standing, hands on her waist and breathing deeply. He threw his bag on the pavement and had a split second image of putting his arms around her, but she looked like she'd sooner punch him than embrace him. Shaking her head so that her plaits flung themselves from one side to the other and sucking in her breath in an inverse whistle, she didn't look like someone who needed any help at all.

'Nancy?'

'Would you believe it? Stop researching George and Percy Wimlett!'

'What?'

'The text I just got.'

'Stop researching George and Percy Wimlett.'

Well I certainly wouldn't stop her doing anything at this precise moment, Christopher thought, feeling completely surplus to requirements. Since he couldn't possibly put his arm around her now, he looked at where he'd flung his bag. It had skidded to a halt against a planter stuffed with conifers, but as he bent to pull it back towards him, the strap resisted and slid through his fingers. The bag was moving away from him. Stamping his foot on the bag – hardly the gentle treatment Nancy had advised but it was all he could think to do – he snatched at his mobile. As a man ran off, Christopher dropped his phone onto the pavement and the screen cracked.

'Screw you,' he shouted out as he swiped the phone and jabbed at the camera icon in time to get a shot of the retreating figure.

About to take up the chase, Christopher felt Nancy's hand touch his.

'Please don't. You don't know what he might do if you catch him.'

'Look, I got a snap of him running off. It's only a shot of his back and I can't quite tell if it's the man I saw hanging around our flat. He's certainly got the same curly, blond hair. I'll check with Mum and see if it's enough for her to tell if it could be the man who spoke to her at the station. Mum and Dad! I hope they didn't see any of this.'

Leaving them without so much as a word, he hadn't given his parents a second thought. As he scrolled through his contacts to his father's number, he remembered that he only brought his mobile when asked to and only turned it on when he knew in advance that he might be texted.

'I'm really sorry, Christopher,' Nancy said, seeing the frustration on his face. 'It's my fault. I told Dr Morrell that your family kept the diary and that I only get to see it when I hang out with you. It can't be a coincidence. He has my cell number and he knew we'd meet at some time. I think the text was used to hasten our meeting so that the diary could be snatched.'

'What could Dr Morrell have against your research on George and Percy Wimlett?'

'It's not his area of research. He's too busy editing the Arden edition of *Romeo and Juliet* at the moment, but he did say that he had friends whose relatives were at the Festival,' Nancy replied. 'It's got me thinking. Last night, I transcribed the weirdest thing and maybe it has something to do with all of this, but it might not be easy for you to hear.'

'Go on.'

'At Patrick and Rachel Drew's party on April 23rd, Anne says that Robert took her aside because he thought that she'd overheard Edmund and him talking about Percy's death. But, she hadn't heard a thing! Robert told her she must never speak to anyone about Percy's death because the family had suffered enough,' Nancy said, not yet able to tell Christopher that Anne had gone on to write that she was frightened of Robert.

'Death? The last I heard of it, Percy was very ill but not dead!'

'You're right. It's only April 23rd. I've got copies of all the newspapers of the time, national and local and they all carry his obituary which reports that he died on May 9th! Anne goes on and on in the diary debating what to do. I just don't get it.'

'Are you saying that Percy actually died sixteen days before his death was officially announced?'

'Yeah, according to Anne. The newspapers reported on

April 22nd that Percy was being replaced as Tybalt due to ill health and carried Percy's obituary stating that he died on May 9th. But, at Patrick and Rachel's party, Anne describes Archibald, Patrick, Robert and Edmund arriving with Dickens and...'

'Dickens! You don't mean Charles Dickens?'

'He came to the Festival and was a special guest of the Drews,' Nancy replied, waving away Christopher's excitement at the mention of the name, but he wasn't going to let something like that go.

'I had no idea someone so famous would come to Stratford. Wouldn't there have been bigger celebrations in London? After all, Shakespeare wrote most of his plays there, didn't he?'

'William Shakespeare was born and educated in Stratford-upon-Avon. His wife and children stayed in the town and he bought New Place in 1597 so that he could return to the town,' she said, as if speaking to a school child. 'He most probably wrote *The Tempest* here. Stratford has as much right to claim Shakespeare as London. Anyways, it was Charles Dickens who galvanised people to contribute to a fund to buy Shakespeare's birthplace, so he saw the value of the town right from the start.'

Rubbing the stubble that would soon be less designer, more lazy shit, Christopher felt as if he'd been told off.

'What else does Anne say in the diary about the 23rd of April?' he asked lamely.

'She writes that Robert and Archibald laugh with Dickens, but look uncomfortable as soon as they're not in his company. Listen to this.

I can hardly bear to write the sentence, but, if I do not, I fear I shall go mad. I cannot talk to anyone about what I have heard and I cannot keep Percy's death to myself, so I will commit it to paper as if I were sharing it with a friend. I have never truly felt the loneliness of my state of widowhood until this day. I grieve for the loss of my husband as if he died yesterday.

'What sentence was she on about?'

It was time he knew about his great-great-great-great-grandfather.

'*I fear Robert Gastrell.*'

'What?'

'She goes on to say, *I fear that Robert Gastrell is in some manner responsible for Percy's death.*'

'What the hell? I didn't see that coming. When can you transcribe more of the diary?'

'I need a break from it today, but I'll start first thing tomorrow.'

'Dr Morrell must be writing something you don't know about and he doesn't want you to tread on his toes,' Christopher offered, adding when he saw Nancy's expression, 'but, it's a bit extreme for an academic!'

'Don't you believe it! There's nothing we're more passionate about than our research.'

And he did believe it.

CHAPTER 33

Present day: Friday 23 April 7pm

Christopher's photo of the man had only caught his profile, but it was enough for his mother to confirm that it was indeed the same man who'd engaged her in conversation at the station. As for the diary, it had survived Christopher's size twelve with only minor damage to the front cover.

It was odd to see Nancy sitting at the table with his family. Apart from their initial meeting at the house, he'd kept the two worlds apart. He'd asked Nancy not to tell his family about the attempt to steal the diary as they hadn't seen anything from the tower and he didn't want his parents to know that the diary, one of his birthday presents, was causing so much trouble. Explaining to his parents that he'd run off because Nancy had sent him a text telling him she was upset over her thesis, he'd invited her to join them for the meal to take her mind off it, telling them that they, in turn, mustn't mention the incident or the thesis. It felt as if he were conducting some huge deceit of his family and of Nancy – as if he were having affairs with two different women and he'd found himself unexpectedly in the company of both.

And he still hadn't told Nancy about David. He'd reached that point where he'd spent too much time with her now to tell her something so significant. If he told her now, she'd know that he'd deliberately kept it from her, almost lied to her. Despite knowing that the longer she remained in ignorance, the worse it would get, he still couldn't bring himself to broach the subject. How do you say, 'by the way, my brother died in January'? He'd put it off by persuading himself that Nicholas could have told her and that she, understandably, hadn't mentioned it. If this were the case, he would never actually need to tell her, he'd reasoned. It would be something he'd know she knew and she'd know he knew and that would be good enough. In time, he'd speak about it, of course, but since he hadn't and he couldn't be certain that Nicholas had mentioned it, at any moment this evening, Nancy might say something inappropriate along the lines of, 'what a lucky family they were to be all together' or some such innocuous pleasantry that had the potential to ruin the evening.

Asking Nancy to join the family had been a throw-away comment, the sort that is more rhetorical, the sort that is said but not taken up, the sort that you say, 'thanks, but I won't if you don't mind'. But Nancy had said 'yes'. At that moment, he'd realised how little he'd said about his family and his own background. He'd mentioned at the churchyard that he'd broken up with Monica and that was about it. What was it Nancy had said about her parents? Her mum or was it her dad was an alcoholic? He wished he'd asked her about her family at the time when she'd brought it up but he'd been too wrapped up in his distant ancestors to give a second thought to her relatives.

Looking at Nancy, he realised he needn't have worried. She was entertaining the family by showing them some of the transcriptions that involved Robert Gastrell, except the bit about him frightening Anne, thank goodness. When she brought out the copy of the photograph that she'd printed of Ellen and Bernard Howard's wedding, showing Robert Gastrell in the back row, Madeleine was fascinated.

'Why do they look so sad at a wedding? What's happened?'

'They're not sad. There are different theories on why people don't smile in Victorian photos, but it's probably because they had to sit for a long time in the same position and it's impossible to hold a smile without your face starting to twitch,' Nancy said, adopting a Cheshire cat grin. 'Or it could be that, because having your photo taken happened so infrequently, people thought they should adopt a serious expression,' she said, mimicking 'The Thinker'.

'You're funny!' Madeleine declared, copying Nancy's pose.

'Let's see how long you can keep a smile,' Nancy challenged.

Collapsing in a fit of giggles after only five seconds, Madeleine insisted on seeing how long everyone else could smile. Pointing her mother's phone close to their faces, she delighted in their exaggerated laughter when they lasted only two or three seconds, bowing out so that she could be declared the winner.

'I think we'll have to delete one or two of these,' Joanne smiled.

'That's another thing about Victorian photos. You have to remember they couldn't delete any. They had to accept whatever they took, even if the photo wasn't that good,' Nancy added.

'What I've never understood is why all Victorians have black hair. Where are all the blonds and red-heads?' Bridget asked Nancy.

'Over to you for that one, Christopher!'

'The Victorian photographic process distorted colour. In very broad terms, it showed all the warm colours, such as yellows, reds and oranges, as black. The cool colours, like blue, showed up as white. So, blond and red hair came out as black. It's only white hair that photographs as light-coloured hair. Our skin tones would look different as well. They would show up at least two tones darker than we'd expect. To correct this, the photographer could over-expose the image but this would then affect the shading of the garment.'

'So, in Victorian photos when everyone seems to be wearing black, they could actually all be wearing bright colours,' Bridget observed, this time looking at Christopher.

'Well, it could be that, or it might be that they really were wearing black. I read on the net that young ladies were advised to wear a black silk dress and older ladies to wear black moiré because the sheen of these fabrics would photograph best. As if sorting out the colour and the material of your clothing wasn't bad enough, the time of day affected the image as well due to the amount of yellow or blue light present. I have to admit, Victorian photography was a much more complex business than what I do today!' he said, putting his camera on the table.

'Take some photos of me, Christopher, please, please,' Madeleine demanded.

She posed firstly with her hands on her hips and a pout, then with both thumbs up and a broad grin until her great-aunt requested a nice smile.

'She's copying the singers she's seen on telly,' Joanne offered.

'Are you coming to Shakespeare's Birthday Party tomorrow?' Madeleine asked Nancy.

'You mean Shakespeare's Birthday Parade,' Joanne explained.

'I'll be walking in the procession, so I'll look out for you all,' Nancy said, looking at Christopher.

'Why are you in the Parade? Are you an important person? Have you been on the television?' Madeleine pursued.

'No, I just love Shakespeare, that's all.'

There was no stopping Madeleine. She loved the attention. Asking Nancy if she could plait her hair, she then questioned her as to why she talked so funny and, all this time, Christopher wondered if Nancy would be the first person he'd tell that he had a son.

CHAPTER 34

The afternoon of Saturday the 23rd of April 1864

Bedecked with ribbons, the open carriage picked its way along High Street where bunting and garlands of laurel joined the flags of the Union Jack, Royal Standard and St George's Cross in celebratory mood: Stratford-upon-Avon was sporting its holiday apparel. Much to the delight of the hotels and lodging houses, the railway company had put on many extra trains, depositing thousands more visitors than the town had ever before welcomed onto its streets. Resplendent in all its finery, the town prepared to enjoy its privileged position as host of the largest Festival in the world to honour the tercentenary of Shakespeare's birth.

Dressed in their official corporation robes, heavy with badges and medals made especially for the Festival, Patrick, Archibald and Edmund were waving so enthusiastically to the crowd that they did not notice Robert's understated offering. Sitting beside his friend with their backs to the horses as their more inferior status deemed appropriate,

Robert was thankful that the crowd's eyes passed hastily over him as they strained to look at the occupants of the next carriage, unable as he was to keep up the smiles that his three companions appeared to be able to embrace with ease.

And then he saw the boy. Samuel Brown was running as if his life depended upon catching up with their carriage. Head held high, he kept his arms out to the side, palms raised, fending off anybody who crossed his path, stumbling on the uneven paving stones, but never stopping and all the time keeping his eyes locked onto Robert's. Wherever he went now, the boy followed. Not waiting for his father and Patrick to descend the carriage as befitted their seniority, Robert stood up without a word and hastened into the Town Hall. Running up to the first floor, he looked out of the window that faced High Street and scoured the crowd for that one face amongst an army of faces, but the seething multitude had swallowed Samuel up.

The jubilant bells of the Church of the Holy Trinity rang out their melodic announcement that it was two o'clock and the official start of the Festival. There was no time to dwell upon the boy. Hurrying to join the back of the line of corporation officials headed by Patrick, whose demeanour suggested that there was nothing in the world other than the Festival to occupy his mind, Robert forced a smile to register upon his lips. To welcome the Earl of Carlisle, Knight of the Garter and his Grace, the Archbishop of Dublin was Patrick's proudest mayoral duty and no one would be allowed to spoil the occasion. His honoured guests alighted from their carriage to the salute of the local Rifle Volunteer Corps. Formed because of the perceived threat of invasion by the much larger French army and fears that Britain might be caught up in a wider European conflict, the Volunteers proudly pointed their rifles skywards. The crowd fell silent.

Patrick regaled the distinguished guests with stories of the town as if he had been solely responsible for the organisation of the Festival and Robert took the opportunity to look out of the nearest window to see that Samuel had manoeuvred into a position directly opposite the entrance hall. Shrinking back as if the boy were an assassin with a rifle of his own, Robert turned to see his father approaching him with a questioning look on his face. A round of applause, however, saved an awkward explanation of his behaviour in the carriage, as Professor Leitner, from the association that had purchased Goethe's house in Frankfurt, handed a beautifully illuminated gold and blue medallion of Shakespeare to the Tercentenary Committee, an acknowledgement of the warm relations between the German and the English nations.

Walking slowly down the staircase, Robert wished with all his heart that he did not have to leave the Town Hall. They had all prayed that it would not rain, but now as the sun streamed into the entrance hall, Robert longed to reverse that prayer: if it had threatened rain, they would have travelled in a closed carriage and the boy would not have had the opportunity to approach him in such a public manner. The newspapers' illustrations of William Hamilton, who had shot at Queen Victoria when she was travelling in her open carriage, flashed into his head. But he was not a monarch and the boy was not even ten years of age. How ridiculous he was to fear such a child when it was George who posed the actual threat.

Nevertheless, Robert held back in the shadow of the stone arch and regarded the two policemen who were keeping the people at some little distance from the carriages awaiting their occupants. Satisfied that the crush of the crowd combined with the presence of the policemen would ensure that the boy would not be able to reach him, Robert started down the steps. A harsh noise rang out. Robert threw himself onto the pavement. The pistol shot had narrowly missed him, but why was he the only one lying face down on the ground? His right arm was being pulled upwards in a none-too-gentlemanly fashion.

'Robert, whatever is the matter? Did you trip on the steps? Are you hurt?'

Edmund's breath hissed over Robert's face like a gas leak.

'I...I...the boy...I...'

'You are making a spectacle of yourself in the public street.'

With that, Edmund pushed Robert's top hat into his gloved hands, now scuffed with dirt from the pavement, and bundled him into the carriage where an irritated Patrick and a concerned Archibald had been kept waiting for what seemed like an age whilst the mob laughed and pointed at the gentleman who must already have taken too much alcohol.

'What condition would he be in after the banquet?' the crowd joked.

As the carriage picked its way along Chapel Lane, Patrick waved to the cheering crowds who had no idea that one of the toffs had fallen outside the Town Hall, yards from them, but who would very soon know every detail by heart and more, due to the elaboration that would build as the story was passed from mouth to mouth. And all Patrick could think was that the newspapers would have to be paid off or it would taint their reports of the Festival and jeopardise the town's reputation and thereby his own.

*

If the distinguished party had not been so thoroughly engaged in waving to the crowd, they might have detected the reason for Robert's misunderstanding. One small figure was not cheering. He was standing stock still and staring. Samuel Brown couldn't take his eyes off Mr Robert Gastrell who, three days ago, had given him more money than he'd ever before seen in his life, let alone held in his own two hands.

Turning the coin over and over between his thumb, forefinger and middle finger in imitation of the street magician who performed with a pack of cards, he was mesmerised by his power to transform the cold touch of the coin to an almost burning heat. That first evening of ownership of this precious metal had brought its own anxieties though. He hadn't dared to take it inside his house where he shared a bed with his three brothers as it would surely have been lost or worse still, discovered. So, hollowing out a shallow hole in a crack in the wall by his house, he'd carefully placed the coin inside before covering it with scraps of brick dust and dirt. As if he were giving the coin an honourable burial, he'd stood before the wall with his hands clasped, but it was for a much more practical reason that he'd taken his time: he was committing to memory the exact location of the coin so that he could prise it from the wall whenever the opportunity presented itself, noting that the nearest brick, crumbled and blasted by successive frosts, had taken on the vague resemblance of a rat.

But, what he couldn't fathom was why he'd been given so much money. Occasionally, he might be given a farthing for rushing a note to a shopkeeper or hanging around waiting for a lady to beckon him to sweep the road in front of her, but he'd never been given money for doing nothing. Since he hadn't earned it, he'd told neither his parents nor brothers and sisters. It was his guilty secret.

Samuel watched Mr Gastrell get into an open carriage with the other nobs before he squirmed his way out of the smelly huddle of children, his small stature enabling him to break free of the well-behaved crowds who were proud to be in the company, albeit from a carefully controlled distance, of such honourable gentlemen. Keeping Mr Gastrell in sight, he bumped and scraped against the people who momentarily forgot their manners and cursed him, pushing him away in disgust. Mutterings about how he'd no right to be there in the presence of such great men, rang in Samuel's ears.

As Mr Gastrell's carriage pulled up in Southern Lane and the military band struck up, 'Ye Warwickshire Lads and ye Lasses,' to which the crowd answered as one, 'For the Lad of all lads, was a Warwickshire Lad,' Mr Gastrell had looked him straight in the eye and inclined his head before he disappeared into the pavilion. Alone now, Samuel was left to the mercy of the surging tide of people who propelled the insignificant figure backwards and forwards with no hope of escape.

CHAPTER 35

Mid-afternoon on Saturday the 23rd of April 1864

Robert was so immeasurably relieved to enter the pavilion without further incident that he sank into his seat before realising that the Earl of Carlisle had not yet taken his. Repeated cheers and applause greeted the Earl as he took his place at the head of the table, allowing Patrick and Rachel, Archibald and Constance, Robert and Edmund to follow suit, a signal to the remaining guests that they too were now permitted to sit. Gasps and joyous voices rang around the pavilion as the non-committee members marvelled at the grandeur of the decoration. A generous three hundred pounds had ensured that the Elizabethan style had been carried throughout and that every conceivable opportunity to make reference to Shakespeare had been grasped. The magnificent drop-scene featured medallions representing Comedy and Tragedy on either side of a life-size statue of Shakespeare and a beautiful bronze memorial bust of Shakespeare stood in the centre of the stage attended on either side by the figures of

Genius and Immortality.

After the Reverend Dawson had offered Grace, he added, 'may good digestion wait on appetite and health on both,' to which the guests cheered anew. Each type of nourishment on the bill of fare, that had taken Mr Mountford of Worcester a week to put together, was accompanied by a quotation from Shakespeare; from the boar's head, fowl and lobster, to the cakes, jellies and creams and copious quantities of ale, champagne, hock, claret, port and sherry, all was to be consumed in the name of the sweet Swan of Avon. Robert, who had hardly touched his food since Wednesday night, felt a rising sense of disgust at the gross extravagance presented before him, but knew he would not be permitted to refuse anything.

Everything had been arranged to set the top table apart from the rest; its curved semi-circle of scarlet seats positioned on the raised platform, where the orchestra would play for the musical concerts and the grand fancy dress ball later in the Festival, afforded a spectacular view of the other guests and more significantly, Patrick had reminded them, allowed them to be seen by all. Every gesture would be observed and every morsel consumed or alcohol imbibed would be commented upon. To be in the company of such distinguished gentlemen was an honour for every one of the people who were in attendance at the banquet to end all banquets, Robert had been told time and time again.

The majority of the seven hundred and fifty invitees sat at nine rows of tables set at right angles to the top table, with the exception of three rows of tables that were arranged on the stage to keep the actors separate from the other guests. Anne, her father and sisters had been positioned at the central table as close to the top table as was possible, permitting Robert a clear view of its occupants. It was the first time that he had seen Anne since Thursday morning when he had arrived disastrously late to meet her at the pavilion. Despite having partaken of several beverages, he had not slept a wink on that short Wednesday night and, feeling as if he had a grain of sand lodged under each eyelid, he had found that he could not meet her gaze. Having taken only the most cursory of glances at her photographs of the town's streets, he had made his excuses to leave and now here they were, in sight of one another, but unable to utter a single word.

Worse, much worse, was the company at Anne's table. Anne was sitting opposite George. She was sitting opposite a murderer. She was looking at the face of a murderer and she was talking to a murderer and she knew nothing about it because he, Robert Gastrell, had kept his silence when he should have found the courage to tell the truth. Although he knew that she would be cautious in her speech towards Philip and George, due to her belief that Percy was seriously ill, Robert feared that an innocent observation might at any moment spark a passion in the son. Having witnessed George's manipulation of events first-hand the previous day, Robert desperately wished to warn Anne of her proximity to the murderer, but under Patrick's watchful eye, he had no choice in the matter. It was an intolerable situation that was all of his own making.

*

For her part, Anne was content that she was not seated in the presence of Robert Gastrell. He had shown scant regard for the images she had taken of the town's people, had even appeared to have had second thoughts about the validity of her photography when last they had met. That Thursday night, as she had pondered the various reasons for his volte-face in the morning, she had realised that he had not once looked her in the face. It was obvious that he lacked the courage to tell her directly that he had made a grave error in adding his support to her endeavours. She was a lady photographer who had overstepped the bounds of convention in portraying the reality of life in Stratford-upon-Avon.

Persuading herself that her interest had lain not in him, but rather in his representation of the world outside the domestic sphere, she had decided to resume her photography at the first opportunity after the Festival. With hindsight, she now wondered if Robert had indeed presented her proposal to photograph the committee members as a serious consideration or if he had merely paid lip service to it. Perhaps he had not even read a single word of it to the committee. Who knows what really happened at these all-male meetings? She would make the most of the agreeable company at her table. Ignoring Robert would be no hardship for her. Taking her lead from George, who was making a commendable effort to enjoy the occasion despite Percy's terrible illness, she was happy to return the young man's smiles and conversation.

'George, we must drink a toast to you. It is St George's Day after all,' her father announced.

George, who looked delighted to accept the compliment, stood up to acknowledge the applause of his table before drinking deeply of his wine. He was a particularly accomplished actor, Anne thought, as she watched him laugh outrageously at one of Dorothy's remarks much to the consternation of his father and her own. A stranger would have no notion of the acute grief that George was suffering at his brother's illness. She was certain that George was about to reply to her sister when Philip whispered to his son and George glanced towards the top table. Robert was looking directly at him, but he did not acknowledge George's nod of the head as he should. Instead, Robert looked away and George brought his fist down on the table making the china rattle. At this, Philip brought his lips so close that they brushed George's ear and the young man lifted up his head with some effort as if he had been transformed into an automaton. From then on, he offered only the merest hint of a tight-lipped smile. Why on earth had Robert not acknowledged George with the usual courtesy and what had Philip said to effect such a marked change in his son's temperament in a hair's breadth of a moment?

'What a lovely idea it was to decorate the tables with all of the flowers that are mentioned by Shakespeare,' she observed in an attempt to return to the jollity of a few moments ago, but a nod was the only response that her comment now elicited from the father and son.

She remarked upon the bronze statuettes of Hamlet and of Ophelia distributing flowers for, 'thoughts and remembrances' and she admired the intricate wooden carvings of Romeo and Juliet, both embellished with rainbow-coloured jewels, but it was hardly the sparkling conversation that they had formerly entertained. Looking around for inspiration, she glanced at the upper galleries where spectators, whose tickets had been issued on the strict say-so of a patron, vicariously enjoyed the pleasure of those they watched. Finding it impossible to reconcile herself to the knowledge that these people, who had not been invited to the banquet, were happy to pay to derive enjoyment from observing those who had, Anne felt a tightening of her throat. She simply must escape from the room.

As she stepped outside the pavilion for a breath of air, the first person upon whom her eyes rested was Samuel Brown. Sitting in the gutter, the boy was bent double, staring intently at something which unexpectedly moved away from him. Pouncing upon it, he danced around waving his hand in the air. How happy he looked, this child in whom nobody showed the slightest interest and who found delight in next to nothing.

*

Having excused himself from the top table, Robert headed towards the same exit through which he had watched Anne depart a couple of minutes ago. This was precisely the opportunity that he had been longing for: a chance to apologise properly for his lack of interest in her street photographs on Thursday morning. He would beg her forgiveness, explain that he had become overcome by fatigue and would ask if he may see them again. Frustratingly slowed down by several ladies in bulbous crinolines, he could not help looking up at the quotation from *The Tempest* that was inscribed around the pavilion.

> 'The cloud-capt towers, the gorgeous palaces,
> The solemn temples, the great globe itself,
> Yea, all which it inherit, shall dissolve,
> And like this unsubstantial pageant faded,
> Leave not a wreck behind.'

In the space of a few weeks, this temporary theatre would

be dismantled, leaving nothing behind, as if it too had never existed. It seemed that there was no permanence in anything. Nothing could be taken for granted any more. Nothing could be trusted.

He did not even trust himself.

Seeing no sign of Anne, Robert stepped outside and there she was, but so was Samuel Brown. He dare not approach her. The moment was lost.

The banquet concluded not a moment too soon for Robert who had forced himself to taste a little from each course so that he would not attract unwanted attention. So thankful was he that the meal was finally over, that he remained seated, almost oblivious to the scraping of chairs as everyone stood for the first of the toasts. Loud cheers resounded around the pavilion as the Queen's health was toasted, followed by silence as the orchestra played a rousing rendition of the National Anthem. After a succession of further tributes, Professor Leitner spoke movingly of the significance of Goethe and Shakespeare, but as soon as Patrick took his place to issue his reply, Robert became aware of a dry sensation in his mouth. Trying to clear his throat quietly behind his hand, he coughed and spluttered throughout Patrick's mayoral response whose volume increased significantly until it became a mighty oration to his audience's astonishment.

'The address from the German nation proves how thoroughly Shakespeare is appreciated and understood in Germany and shows that there is a sincere fellow-feeling between the two countries,' Patrick said, turning and bowing to Professor Leitner. 'I shall ensure that it is handed down through the agency of our Corporation from one generation to another. Each successive age which sees it, shall understand the sympathies between England and the Fatherland.'

And with this, Patrick thumped his fist on the table and everyone stood for the last time and it felt to Robert as if the applause for the mayor's speech would never end.

Finally, at half past seven, Robert watched his father help his mother into the carriage that would convey her to the Drew family home where the female guests had been invited to rest before the commencement of the firework display at nine o'clock that evening. Despite waiting a full ten minutes for the opportunity to speak to Anne, he could see no sign of her or of her family and he had to admit defeat. Cursing himself for wasting his only chance to apologise to her during the banquet, he turned to find Patrick's face inches from his. Recoiling as if a coal from the fire had spat out at him, he stumbled backwards. Patrick pointed to his carriage and they entered without a word passing between them.

Sitting next to Edmund, who was making light of something or other, Robert tried to avoid his father's inquiring gaze whilst his mind turned over and over the knowledge that he was harbouring a murderer. And all the time, the carriage conveyed them closer and closer to the White Lion Hotel where they would welcome England's foremost literary figure.

CHAPTER 36

The evening of Saturday the 23rd of April 1864

'Charles is bound to discern that something is amiss. You know how perceptive he is. Remember it was he who said that, *Scenes of Clerical Life* had been written by a woman before anyone else in the country had entertained such a thought,' Archibald observed, looking towards Patrick.

It vexed Robert that his father's statement neither supported nor dismissed the notion that Charles Dickens should be taken into their confidence with regard to Percy's death. A straightening of the contours of Patrick's mouth had silenced his father, whom Robert had hoped would go on to say that they ought to seek the great man's advice.

'Charles is a wily old fox, no doubt about it and he cannot help but play detective as we all know,' Edmund replied, eyeing Robert.

Patrick remained silent and motionless except for an almost imperceptible hardening of the line of his lips.

'Do you not think,' Robert ventured, determined not

to skirt around the subject, but to get directly to the heart of the matter, 'that if we were to tell Charles the truth, we should be spared the agonies of wondering whether or not he has guessed our secret? I, for one, would certainly value his counsel.'

Patrick turned his eyes to rest on Robert and the light from the oil lamp caught the rim of his spectacles making them look as if they were on fire, but still Patrick said nothing.

'If we were to tell Charles that we had lied about the death of young Percy, he would not be able to prevent himself from putting it into his next novel or one of his articles, so thinly disguised that we would be found out straight away!' Edmund replied and Robert knew that he alone believed that they should share their secret with Charles.

Since Percy's tragic death, they had all become guardians of their speech; he had not partaken of a single moment of honest or open discussion with either his father or Edmund since Wednesday night. Familial ties and friendships had been replaced by a new loyalty.

'Never forget that we each swore to keep our secret,' was all that Patrick needed to say to make it quite clear that Charles, a man whom he counted as an intimate, was to remain ignorant of their conspiracy.

Robert blinked. It was as if the walls of the sitting room of the White Lion Hotel had moved inwards, towards him, as if the room had somehow become smaller. Waiting next door to the private dining room into which George had burst on Wednesday night was the last place on earth that he desired to be, but the arrangement had been made in March when they were last in London. Charles had said that it would be fitting to meet in the hotel that was nearest to Shakespeare's Birthplace and they could not afford to offer him any ammunition for thinking that there was something wrong, Patrick had said. Charles had a way of sniffing out deception and as the door opened, the four men stared open-mouthed, giving the lie to their attempt at informal conviviality.

'My friends, your faces paint a picture of pain. I trust the Festival arrangements are proceeding according to plan.'

'Charles, welcome to our town. How was your journey?' Patrick asked, expertly steering the conversation away from any talk of a difficulty.

'The train was quiet, only about a dozen of us. I suppose most people arrived earlier. I dearly wish I had not stayed in London to see the tree planting ceremony on Primrose Hill for it was the dullest of affairs that our capital city could possibly have organised to celebrate England's most famous writer. You have nothing to worry about gentlemen, Stratford-upon-Avon's celebration will be written about throughout the world and I am delighted to be participating in one of the biggest events in your town's history. Let us drink a toast to the Festival's success.'

Charles's enthusiastic praise warmed Robert like malecotony soup and his fifth port warmed him still further.

'Charles, you may be able to assist us with a problem. You see...'

With dexterity surprising in a man of his years, Patrick flashed his pocket-watch from his waistcoat and announced, without even opening its case, that it was almost nine o'clock and time for the fireworks.

'Let us go out into Henley Street to watch them. We shall have a fine view from there if we hurry.'

Robert recognised Patrick's tone as that which he used when commanding any man below his station: direct and incontrovertible. As he waited his turn to descend the stairs, he felt the weight of Patrick's hand on his left shoulder; the hand stayed a little longer than a protective hand should have stayed and it dug a little deeper than a protective hand should have dug. But, Charles did not take issue with Robert's unfinished sentence asking for his assistance with a problem. Beaming and talking animatedly as they hurried down the hotel staircase, he was like a child who had arrived late to a party and could not wait to join in with the celebrations. Robert walked behind the others smarting from the knowledge that, in his desperation to share his secret, he had almost broken his vow to the group and, worst of all, he had committed the offence in Patrick's presence.

During his night walk in London with Charles, in his father's absence, Robert had forged a bond that made it all too easy for him to say more than he should. The sights and stories of tragedy and wrong-doing in the metropolis had shaken Robert to the core, but Charles had remained undaunted throughout, reassuring him that he had seen it all before. Almost as if reading his son's thoughts, Archibald turned to catch his eye and convey what words could not. Patrick had spoken. Charles Dickens was not to be confided in, no matter what the consequences.

In order to lessen the temptation to unburden his secret to the man whom he had come to think of as a friend, Robert determined that he must maintain a physical distance from Charles. And it was not only Charles from whom Robert would need to keep his distance this evening; he felt that if he were in close proximity to his father, or to Edmund, his school friend or even to Patrick, the family friend who had known him all of his life, they would in some way be able to discover the depths of his despair and his desperate desire to reveal the truth. These men, who dressed in similar looking heavy cloaks, stovepipe hats, scarves and gloves, stood a pace apart from one another with their hands behind their backs; there was nothing to suggest individuality from their outward bearing and for the first time, Robert saw them as others must see them: authoritarian and unapproachable. They looked like they owned the town because they did.

But, they were not alone in the street. A dense crowd bulged on the opposite side of the road, threatening to burst onto Patrick's freshly painted town. Seeping out from the alleys, the bodies squeezed against one another for warmth and now the swelling mass that had appeared from nowhere, it seemed, threatened to overwhelm his guests.

'Well, my friends, where are your famous fireworks?' chided Charles.

'We seem to have come out a little too hastily,' Patrick admitted.

'I am joking. It is a wonderful excuse to stand in Henley Street, yards from the birthplace of William Shakespeare and breathe in the April air. Just what I needed after the long train journey. It is why I asked you not to meet me at the station. A carriage ride would have been the death of me!'

Confident that Charles appeared not to have caught their infectious anxiety, the three men exhaled deeply. For the moment, they were content to believe that he had interpreted their unease as concern about the Festival and nothing more sinister. Robert, for whom the reverse was true, pulled his scarf more tightly around his neck almost as if he would strangle himself.

Then he saw them. The piercing blue eyes looked straight at him. His shock was so great that he did not even attempt to look away.

A shot rang out.

The imprint of light burned the inside of his eyelids as garish fires of red, blue and green erupted over Shakespeare's birthplace, spewing out sparks that wounded the sky. Insistent sheets of fire and a labyrinth of blazing wheels pierced the darkness as scores of rockets screeched overhead. An ancient army, they marched relentlessly, puncturing the night with their fiery arrows and roared in anger as they lit up their watching victims like phantoms in a ghostly nightmare. The concluding burst felt as if it would blow up the whole town.

Still dazed from the sight that not even a firework display of this magnitude could wipe from his memory, Robert reeled backwards, Samuel's face looming large in his mind's eye. When he had seen the boy at the banquet, he had thought it was a coincidence, but here he was again. Had Samuel followed him? Could a boy follow a carriage on foot? The streets had been choked with the Festival traffic and they had been held up, so perhaps it was possible. Attempting to blink away the bright scars left by the fireworks, Robert searched in the gloom, but the assault over, the startled mass had melted back into their surroundings. Robert shuddered as he looked over at his companions; the sudden return to silence and darkness was far more shocking than the noise and light of the fireworks.

'Mr Darby must certainly be the greatest pyrotechnician in this country,' enthused Charles. 'My friends, I congratulate you. I have never before seen such spectacular fireworks.'

'There is much more to come, commencing with the party at my house,' Patrick replied, gesturing towards his carriage in an attempt to hasten Charles who seemed loath to leave the street.

'Will you be in attendance at the Church of the Holy

Trinity tomorrow for the Shakespeare sermons?' Archibald asked.

'I shall attend every occasion associated with the Bard whilst I am in Stratford-upon-Avon. I intend to immerse myself in everything Shakespearean in the hope that I might gain inspiration and return to London ready to complete *Our Mutual Friend*.'

As the carriage rumbled over the cobbles on its way to Patrick's party, Robert pulled the curtain aside and squinted into the gloom. Flags fluttered, but not a soul could be seen in the street.

Away from the gas lamp, a pair of eyes fixed their look on the retreating carriage.

CHAPTER 37

The late evening of Saturday the 23rd of April 1864

Accompanied by her father and sisters, Anne followed Rachel as they all made their way past the large flaming torches that illuminated the generous lawn. The substantial garden had, as Rachel had promised, provided the ideal private viewing point for the spectacular firework display and the perfect commencement to the Drews' party. Anne's mother-in-law had assured her that her guests would be able to enjoy the fireworks happy in the knowledge that, although this was a public event, their experience would not have to be shared with the town. Rachel was at her regal best; cutting an imposing figure resplendent in an enormous red crinoline, she smiled at her guests as they moved aside to create a pathway to her house. Known for giving magnificent parties stuffed with the most distinguished guests, she had not disappointed her audience this evening. Waiting until not a sound could be heard, she paused on the steps to the drawing room. Giving her opening speech of welcome, she

286

concluded with an invitation to join her inside where the party would continue.

'Rachel, when do you expect Patrick to return with Mr Dickens?' the Reverend Dawson asked as they stopped for a moment to allow their eyes to become accustomed to the lighted pinpoints of what looked like hundreds of flames.

'At any time. I know that Patrick was keen to come straight to the party and did not mind missing part of the display, but he thought that Charles would probably want to watch it all.'

'Where did they plan to watch the fireworks?'

'I am not exactly sure. I know that Charles's train was due to arrive at about a quarter past eight. He insisted on walking to the White Lion Hotel, so I would think that they would have had to watch them in the public street outside. I do not think they would have had time to go anywhere else more suitable. It must have been awful...'

An eruption of applause interrupted Rachel. Unused to being upstaged, she turned her back on her audience to confront the interloper.

'Here is Mr Charles Dickens come to honour our party with his presence,' Patrick announced, unable to speak further due to the thunderous applause and cheers that filled the air.

The women turned as one with ready smiles to greet Charles and the men pushed forward to listen to him speak. He had this effect upon everyone; men and women were equally attracted to his vitality. They would forfeit their friends' company and even their family's to be associated with this man. Rachel eased her way into the drawing room, apparently admitting defeat, but only to herself, and only for the time being for it was plain to see that no one else wanted this master storyteller to stop. When Charles spoke, others listened and the bigger the audience, the more he talked.

Heated by a generous fire at each end, the warmth of the drawing room provided a welcome comfort to Anne. Unused to being outside at night for more than a few moments in the last two years, she had misjudged how cold it would be to remain standing for any length of time and had chosen a summer cloak when a winter one would have been more appropriate. Goodness, she really had lost all sense of the world beyond her own home during her time of mourning.

She would make the most of the freedom that had been thrust upon her with or without the approval of others. She would photograph whomsoever and whatever she wished, she announced to herself. In buoyant mood, Anne listened to Charles regale his audience with yet another of his humorous anecdotes. As much as she enjoyed his stories, she took an equal pleasure in watching the reaction of Charles's audience. One man, however, did not join in this spiral of good humour and kept glancing towards the door leading to the hallway and although she had told herself that she would remain angry with Robert Gastrell for his lack of interest in her street photography, she could not help but feel some measure of pity for him. He looked so terribly fatigued, as if he were agonising over an impossible problem. Following Robert's line of sight, Anne could see that Philip and George were about to join the throng, or more accurately, a pale imitation of the father and son. Talking in low whispers, they pressed their stony faces close together and George's blond hair curled a little around his father's sandy wisps of hair, obscuring their colour. Had Percy's condition worsened?

Charles's talk of his night walks and a nod to Robert elicited a thin smile, but Anne noticed that the moment its gaze landed on another's, even that joyless effort was wiped from Robert's face and the corners of his mouth adopted a downward slant. She could only surmise that the nervous exertion expended on the design and overseeing of the building of the pavilion must have sustained Robert up until now and that upon the scheme's completion, exhaustion had overwhelmed him, but it seemed an extreme reaction and she was not quite convinced by her explanation. In spite of her great disappointment at Robert's change of heart towards her photography, she yearned to know quite what anxiety it was that had dealt him such a severe blow in the space of a few days. Rachel was too busy in her role as hostess to ask what could be the matter with Robert, so she decided that she would approach him whilst the majority of Rachel's guests' attention was directed upon Charles.

'The Festival shall be a success because it offers entertainment to everyone, the poor included. I am delighted that the fireworks were seen by the townsfolk and the pageant will be seen by all who wish to include themselves. It was heart-warming to see the excited faces of the children in Henley Street,' she heard Charles say.

Anne excused herself from her father's company on the pretext of a desire to speak to Rachel, despite knowing full well that it was not her friend to whom she would speak, but Robert Gastrell. Praising the dimensions and acoustics of the pavilion, she would engage him in conversation about his future plans and thereby hope to discover the cause of his misery. He was talking quietly to Edmund with his back turned to Rachel, so she joined her friend on her right-hand side. Determined that she would be able to stand in close proximity to Robert without intruding upon his conversation, Anne positioned herself a step behind Rachel, near enough not to have told her father a complete untruth she hoped, but far enough away not to be noticed immediately by her mother-in-law.

Robert and Edmund were tucked into the corner of the room, but it was not difficult for Anne to stand close to them since they were engrossed in talking in low tones. Taking a half step, she leaned slightly backwards, misjudged the distance between them and the next moment, her shoulder came into contact with the material of his sleeve. Although her skin prickled at the touch of the harsh fabric, it was Robert who shuddered as if he had been attacked and before she knew what was happening, she found herself being escorted out of the drawing room.

'You must never tell anyone what you heard,' Robert whispered as he closed the door of the library. 'You must trust that we know best...we know the best way to proceed after this...this terrible accident. It will destroy the Wimlett family if you speak to anyone about Percy's death. They have suffered enough.'

She could not decide if Robert were issuing a threat or an appeal to her better nature. She had heard nothing. In any case, it made no sense. If Percy were dead, why were Philip and George in the drawing room in attendance at this party and not in London? Why were they not encased in the rituals that surrounded the mourning of the death of the closest of family members?

'Anne, how are you enjoying the party?' a man's voice asked as he entered the library to stand at Robert's side.

Taken aback at the mundane nature of the question, Anne could not even turn her head to face the speaker; she could only move her eyes, as if to turn her head would involve her body in too great an effort. Her mind was so full with the knowledge that she had just received that she felt that she could perform no more complicated a task than to keep still and remain silent. She wanted everything in the world to stop whilst she let the news seep in, until it was no longer a shock and she could pretend to herself that she had known all along that Percy was not in recovery. Only then did she think that she might be able to respond to the question.

'May I fetch you some refreshments or perhaps you would like to sit down?' Edmund enquired.

'Thank you,' Robert replied on her behalf, without taking his eyes off Anne.

'Thank you,' Anne heard herself repeat and when Rachel entered the room, enough of her strength had returned to allow her to rush forward to greet her mother-in-law.

'I have just enquired after Percy's health and I wanted to share the good news that Philip told me. He is getting better,' Rachel said, turning to include Robert in her happy observation.

Why Anne looked shocked at such good news and Robert immediately excused himself from the ladies' presence, Rachel could not fathom.

*

As soon as Robert regained the drawing room, he walked straight towards Patrick, paying no heed to the numerous mothers who were attempting to introduce their unmarried daughters.

'I should like a moment of your time.'

'Of course, if you insist.'

'Rachel has just told me that Percy's health is improving. Have you not told your own wife the truth?'

'Come...come over here,' Patrick said, drawing Robert away from his guests, all the time retaining a smile on his lips. 'How dare you talk about this subject here? Have you so soon forgotten your promise?'

Nodding and waving to his guests as they passed by, Patrick's smile never faltered.

'If I had a wife I would not keep secrets from her, not even this one. Does this mean that my father has not told my mother?' Robert asked, echoing Patrick's whisper, but unable to replicate his smile.

'You have no idea what it means to have a wife. Never forget what we all swore, Robert, what you...swore to uphold. We shall keep it between the six of us. We shall not involve anyone else, no matter what they mean to us. Do you understand?'

Swallowing, Robert tried to say, 'yes,' but no sound would come out of his mouth, so he nodded more times than was necessary as if to convince himself of his commitment to the affirmation. He was still nodding when he felt Patrick's heavy hand on his shoulder for the second time in as many hours and only stopped when the weight had been withdrawn.

'Patrick, what I meant to say was that I fear for George's sanity. The pretence that his brother is ill is surely too great a burden for him to bear. I believe he should be withdrawn from the Festival and, in his own interest, placed under the close supervision of a trusted physician.'

Patrick merely shook his head and turned on his heel, leaving Robert standing alone. He would not let it go, but for the moment he would continue to observe George's behaviour. In search of the young man, he could not decide whether he was relieved or concerned to see Rachel and

Anne looking towards him.

*

'Anne, I think that we should speak to Robert. He looks as if he would rather be anywhere else but here and it is my duty as hostess to convince him that he wishes to amuse himself!' Rachel observed.

It was hardly surprising that Robert wished to be somewhere else, Anne thought, as the shock of finding out that Percy was dead started to become displaced by feelings of puzzlement. Foremost of concern was Robert's phrase, 'we know best'. She knew that, 'we' must mean Philip because it was he who had lied to Rachel about Percy's death. His own son's death! Presumably, George was also included as he had not left his father's side. Rachel obviously did not know as she has been told Percy was getting better, so, did Patrick know? Would Robert, Philip and George keep such a secret from Patrick? From Archibald? Patrick and Archibald were intimates of Philip and it was unthinkable that they would not be aware of Percy's death. And lastly there was Edmund. He was Robert's closest friend and an invaluable member of the committee and the town and she had seen him in Patrick's company on an increasing number of occasions and so he must have been told. It was impossible to consider that they would not all know. So, six men must be involved in keeping Percy's death a secret. Why should silence surround the death of the young man? She could not bear to believe that Robert might in any small way be responsible for playing a part in Percy's death.

As Anne went over each detail of their distressing encounter in the library, irritation reared its head. How dare he treat her as if she were a child and issue her a warning to keep silent? She was not party to their plan or whatever it might be that they had decided and she certainly did not wish to be. She would make it clear in public that she was not to be intimidated by Robert Gastrell even if in private she would remain most concerned about his potential involvement in Percy's death. Somehow, she would discover the truth about the young man's death and why it was shrouded in silence, but she would be most careful not to add to the Wimletts' suffering.

Anne spoke before Rachel had time to address Robert.

'I wish to congratulate you on the design of the pavilion. It is a fitting tribute to Shakespeare and I am convinced that Stratford-upon-Avon will achieve its desire for a permanent theatre. I trust you will put forward a proposal.'

'...I...Thank you for your vote of confidence...I most certainly shall tender a design. I was wondering if I may include your photographs of the pavilion to support my proposition,' he said softly, so entirely at odds with the man of a few moments ago.

It was as if he were two different people.

'I should be delighted if my photographs were to play a small part in the proposal for a permanent theatre in the town.'

'I can think of no better evidence than the clarity of detail that you have elicited from the pavilion in your photographs.'

'That is very kind of you to say so.'

They had exchanged pleasantries and traded compliments as if they hoped to become more intimately acquainted in the near future. How easy it was to deceive, she thought. She would permit him to make use of her photographs if it would further her decision to become a professional photographer and for no other reason.

'I have taken more photographs of the streets of Stratford, especially of the poor, if you would care to see them. I remember that you lacked the time to consider the street scenes when we were at the pavilion last Thursday,' she said, pleased to be able to take a measure of control of the conversation.

'I apologise most heartily for my late arrival and hasty departure. Events overtook our arrangement I am afraid,' and here he looked into her eyes as if begging her to understand that his words carried more meaning than he was permitted to express in company.

When she nodded her head and gave the faintest of smiles, he continued.

'Excuse me for appearing a little taken aback, but I too have an interest in the poor of our town. In London, as you know, I accompanied Charles on a night walk and he challenged me to conduct a series of walks in my own town so that I could document Stratford's poor. I have written detailed observations of their plight.'

Anne watched the transformation of Robert's face when speaking of the townsfolk. His enthusiasm had reinvigorated his features and she saw the man who had first shown an interest in her photography.

'My photographs are here in Rachel's library,' she said, pausing after the last word, taking pleasure in the deep irony of her issue of an invitation to return to the room to which he had taken her against her will a matter of moments ago.

It was almost as if she had concocted the whole of the previous scene in her imagination.

'I asked Anne to bring them so that I may identify any children who attend my school,' Rachel added when Robert did not respond, but remained looking at Anne as if he wished to conduct a silent conversation.

'I have principally taken images of the children of the town. If it is convenient for you to look at them now, you are most welcome,' she added, keeping the measured tone to her voice.

'It would give me great pleasure,' he said and she was gratified to see that a sharp colouring of his cheeks was indeed confirmation of his embarrassment at the remembrance of his previous actions.

Before they were able to enter the library, however, Rachel received a message that Patrick was about to say a few words of thanks to the committee.

'He will offer his congratulations to the committee for its hard work and will look forward to tomorrow and the Shakespeare sermons at the Church of the Holy Trinity,' she announced with pride.

Unable and, truth be told, unwilling to contain her disappointment at once again being prevented from showing Robert her street photographs, Anne threw a look of exasperation at Robert which, to her satisfaction, was reflected in every detail of his face.

CHAPTER 38

Present day: Saturday 24 April early morning

Usually a bustling street choked with parked cars and vehicles dropping people off at the Shakespeare Hotel, Church Street was wonderfully traffic-free on the most important day in Stratford-upon-Avon's year: the Shakespeare Birthday Parade. Passing the temporary railings and traffic cones that had sprung up overnight, Christopher wondered where everyone could be. Everything was in place, from the officials in fluorescent tabards to the five Union Jacks flying from the District Council Offices, but it wasn't until they reached High Street at its junction with Sheep Street that they saw people gathered on the pavements and Christopher saw Nancy. Then he thought he saw the man who'd tried to grab his bag, but looking closely he could see it wasn't him. Was he going to see him everywhere he went now?

When Christopher had suggested that perhaps it wasn't safe for Nancy to walk in the parade, she'd nearly bitten his head off. She wasn't going to let anyone stop her doing what she wanted and anyway, she'd added, looking pointedly at Christopher's bag, 'it's the diary they're after and I won't be the one carrying it!'

As he patted the bag to ensure that it was still there, he looked at Nancy. It was the first time he'd seen her wearing anything other than jeans. Dressed in her academic robe and with her hair clipped up, she looked older, unfamiliar.

'There she is!' Bridget announced triumphantly, having scoured the crowd for several minutes longer than it had taken Christopher to spot her. 'Nancy! Nancy! Over here!'

'Mum, shush, she's with her friends and...lecturers.'

'The parade's not started yet. Let's go over.'

Bridget was not to be stopped. She was over the street before Christopher could tell her what an embarrassing idea he thought it was. Staying on the pavement until Nancy gave his mother a huge grin, he realised that it was he who looked an idiot for keeping his distance and he rushed over.

'Hey Christopher, good to see you,' Nancy said. 'Are you staying to watch the whole parade? I can meet you after,' but added, 'if you're free that is,' when she thought she saw Bridget's face drop a fraction.

'Text me when you're finished,' he managed to say, and mouthed, 'you okay?' before she was shepherded off by a marshal to stand with her group.

Officials and guests were leaving the Town Hall in dribs and drabs. Standing in the street, they greeted newcomers and formed the beginnings of what looked more like a disorderly queue of toddlers than a procession. Christopher didn't want to lose sight of Nancy, but unless he wanted to explain to his mother what had been going on, he'd have to 'put up or shut up' as she used to say when he and David were little. It seemed an age since Nancy had received the threatening text and the man had tried to steal his bag and he had to keep reminding himself it was only yesterday. He must still be in shock.

As the family walked towards Bridge Street to secure a vantage point, they found that barriers in High Street keeping the public off the main procession route had resulted in a crowd of spectators several feet deep. His height a distinct advantage, Christopher found a gap with only one woman in front that provided a good view from the corner of High Street and Bridge Street, until that is, she started waving a large bunch of daffodils and tulips with one hand and a yellow flag with Shakespeare's face on it with the other. Peter stood with his back to the parade and his earphones in and Madeleine jumped up and down until Christopher took her on his shoulders where she danced about, forgetting where she was and kicking him in the ribs. Music floated in the air. Something was happening.

To their right, a man was wrestling an enormous blue and white bag to the ground before tying it with some difficulty to a hefty metal weight placed in the gutter of what would usually have been a busy roundabout. Pillar-box red uniforms emerged from the deep shade of Bridge Street and the man dashed in front of the musicians, grappling the bag to an upright position to allow them to proceed without missing a beat of their march. Whilst many in the crowd continued to talk, Christopher watched his mother, father and uncle stand to attention as the rousing National Anthem was played, after which, polite clapping dwindled as the expectant crowd looked to see what would be next. His father and his uncle resumed their conversation, chatting happily together. It was as if his father had undergone some sort of transformation after all that banging on about Joanne's necklace. He hadn't mentioned it since. Goodness knows what all that nonsense was about.

Splashes of red at three of the first floor windows of Barclays Bank directly opposite, caught Christopher's eye. A flash of metal glinted and an image of assassins infiltrating the celebrations sprang into his mind. Three buglers sounded their call followed by a clash of cymbals that made Christopher jump and gave the signal for the opening of the straining bag in front of them. Christopher told himself that he really must find a way to chill, as hundreds of yellow balloons, one for each year since Shakespeare's birth, exploded against the bright blue of the sky like bubbles in a freshly poured drink. Cheers and delighted laughter erupted as the band struck up 'Happy Birthday', almost drowned out by the crowd's enthusiastic singing. Asking Madeleine to be still for just a few seconds, Christopher photographed the very last balloon until it had lost its yellow and turned to a single white dot against what had now become an uninterrupted deep blue April sky.

'Christopher, I can't quite see. What's happening?'

'Move this way a bit, Mum, you'll have a better view,' he said, gently guiding her to the other side of the now somewhat bedraggled bouquet of daffodils and tulips.

At first glance, Christopher thought he saw a young man in a suit give a Nazi salute, but when he looked again, he realised it was just a schoolboy with his left hand outstretched, holding a quill. When would these weird images stop? Surely he should be dealing with the shock by now.

'It's the Head Boy of King Edward VI School, the school Shakespeare went to,' he said as if to confirm to himself the normality of the situation, regretting it the moment it left his lips. His mother would correct his statement again, adding, 'probably' or 'most likely,' reminding him that there was no actual evidence that William Shakespeare had attended the school, simply that scholars were in agreement that references and language in his plays show he must have been a pupil. When she made no reference to his mistake, he saw that she too was caught up with looking for Nancy.

'Goodness only knows what state their flowers will be in when they arrive at the church,' was her only comment as they watched the young men dressed in their school uniforms holding posies of yellow flowers – some swinging them in an embarrassed manner and some who laughed and gesticulated with them, apparently having forgotten that they were carrying them at all.

The schoolchildren and local groups, together with representatives from various countries, passed by and then he saw her. And then he saw Dr Morrell. Holding Madeleine's trainers to stop her from fidgeting, he craned his neck to the right, wishing he could shove those bloody flowers down that woman's throat. She'd seen someone she knew in the procession and was shouting, 'Stephen, Stephen, over here,' flinging them around. Easing out his compact camera again, Christopher took multiple photos, hoping that one would capture Nancy. She seemed so far away, but when she looked into the crowd and saw him, she gave a thumbs up sign, despite Dr Morrell walking closely beside her.

As soon as she was out of sight, Christopher couldn't wait to move on, but, his mother wanted to see the whole of the parade and it was only when the procession dwindled, that he was able to bend down to let Madeleine climb off his shoulders. They walked down Bridge Street and along Waterside, past the tables outside the cafes all full of customers and the great expanse of grass outside the Royal

Shakespeare Theatre which was now covered in people. Following the path along the river's edge, as Nancy had advised this would be the quickest way to get through the crowds, they approached the steep steps leading to the back of the churchyard, only to find their way crammed full of the schoolboys whose hands, now devoid of flowers, were fooling around, pushing one another, filling the path. There was nothing for it, but to cut across the grass and turn into the main entrance to Holy Trinity Church and walk along the lime avenue. It was calmer here. There were fewer people.

'Be careful, Christopher,' his mother called as she tugged his arm to stop him treading on one of the many gravestones that made up the path.

He hadn't given it a second thought. He'd brought his parents to a graveyard, for goodness' sake! His mother and father though, didn't look upset, quite the reverse in fact, craning their necks to see who could spot Nancy first. Uncle Charles, Joanne and Madeleine had joined in the game of who would be the first to see her. Peter stood back from the crowds and leaned against a tree messaging someone, somewhere.

Christopher could see why Nancy had suggested they stand here to view the parade. The procession was forming a queue to enter the church, meaning that the participants were stationary and easy to photograph. He half-heartedly took some images, but he was only really waiting for one person and she was nowhere to be seen. It would have meant so much more if she'd been with them, pointing out everyone she knew. She'd talked about some of the fellows at the Shakespeare Institute and Stanley Wells, whom she called Mr Shakespeare as he was a former director of the Institute and a world expert who lived locally, but Christopher didn't recognise anybody.

Then he saw Nancy and Dr Morrell.

'Nancy! Nancy!'

His mother had spotted her.

'Who's that man who's always talking to her?'

Before Christopher could say anything, Nancy turned and beamed.

'Hi guys. Are you enjoying the parade? I'm so glad you came here. I saw you earlier, but there were so many people, I wasn't sure if you'd seen me.'

'Christopher, take a photo of us. Come on, let's all stand with Nancy. That's all right isn't it?' his mother added as an afterthought.

'Of course. It's meant to be fun.'

Christopher took several photographs and when Nancy suggested that she'd take one of him and his family, Dr Morrell offered to take it.

'Thank you very much,' Bridget replied before either of them could reply.

'You know you can join the end of the procession and come into the church if you want. I'll wait inside for you,' Nancy whispered out of earshot of Dr Morrell. 'Don't worry. He's off to the posh do in the marquee. He won't be free for hours.'

Joining the end of the procession, the family entered Holy Trinity Church to the sounds of a string trio and the scent of flowers. The smell was that of a florist's shop, but multiplied by a hundred if not a thousand. Bunches, wreaths, the occasional pink, white and blue, but overwhelmingly yellow – so much yellow it made Christopher squint. Nancy stepped out from beside a column and it was all Christopher could do to stop himself from hugging her right there and then in the solemnity of the church and in front of his entire family. A woman dressed in a white robe received their bouquets, struggling to find any space on the floor to add to the already dense floral carpet and Bridget craned her neck to see the plaque that marked the gravestone of William Shakespeare. Christopher couldn't wait to get outside and ask Nancy about Dr Morrell.

CHAPTER 39

Present day: Saturday 24 April 11:30am

Leaving the semi-darkness of the church, Christopher blinked as the bright sunlight assaulted his eyes, but Nancy walked straight ahead. Taking off her academic gown, she slung it over her arm before shaking her hair loose.

'Are you okay? I was so worried. What did Dr Morrell have to say for himself?'

'Nothing remotely controversial,' and she moved closer, brushing her lips on his cheek, leaning against him.

'There you are. Erm...'

Moving away from one another as if they were teenagers caught in a tentative first embrace, they shared a smile.

'Hey, it's good to see you all. Hi, Madeleine. Let's go on the chain ferry. They've got actors reading Shakespeare's sonnets,' and in answer to the little girl's scrunched up face, 'poems.'

A sizeable queue had formed, but Nancy reassured them that the River Avon crossing only took a few minutes each way so it would be their turn before they knew it. Christopher didn't care what the hell they did as long as they were together. The black and yellow balloons that decorated the approaching ferry were soon bobbing and diving towards them as the operator wound the crank towards the pontoon. An actress from the Royal Shakespeare Company was still speaking her sonnet when it reached the side and as one line of people started to disembark, she put up her hand to stop them for a moment so that she could finish reading. She received only a small ripple of applause from those at the back of the ferry who were still seated though and as Christopher and the family settled themselves facing one another along the two sides of the ferry, she got off.

'I don't believe it. We've missed the sonnet ferry! At least I heard the last few lines, I guess,' Nancy said, forcing a smile as no one else seemed in the least bit concerned.

As the clanking of the ferry chains announced their departure, Christopher noticed that Nancy turned towards the opposite side of the river to disguise her annoyance.

'I am expecting very rough weather. I've even laminated my sonnets,' declared a voice.

Another actor was standing on the ferry steps.

'I hope you've all taken your sea sickness pills. It will take at least two and a half hours!' he joked before launching into Sonnet Thirteen.

> *O! that you were your self; but, love, you are*
> *No longer yours, than you your self here live:*
> *Against this coming end you should prepare,*
> *And your sweet semblance to some other give:*
> *So should that beauty which you hold in lease*
> *Find no determination; then you were*

Yourself again, after yourself's decease,
When your sweet issue your sweet form should bear.
Who lets so fair a house fall to decay,
Which husbandry in honour might uphold,
Against the stormy gusts of winter's day
And barren rage of death's eternal cold?
> *O! none but unthrifts. Dear my love, you know,*
> *You had a father: let your son say so.*

Christopher was amazed at the physicality of the performance. The actor held the sonnet in his right hand and stretched his left out towards the audience, moving his hand to the rhythm of the iambic pentameter as if to the beat of music. The conductor of a silent orchestra, he motioned to each one of them, drawing them into his ensemble before tracing a wide arc overhead. When he pinched his finger and thumb as if it were the end of a note, there was a sudden silence and Christopher turned to Nancy, only to be shushed by her as the actor clicked his fingers and looked directly at him. Despite not having the faintest idea what the guy was going on about, Christopher responded instantly with his full attention. As the sonnet reached its final couplet, the actor switched hands and raised his palm to its highest extent before finishing with an extravagant bow to much applause.

'Now the difficult bit. What's the sonnet about?'

The question surprised them, but Nancy managed a quick, 'Procreation!'

And they all laughed.

'That's right. The poet asks why you would deny yourself the happiness that fatherhood brings!'

The word slapped Christopher around the face, wiping any sign of laughter from his lips and he shifted on the bench almost as if he needed to make a physical space for his child to sit between him and Nancy. As the actor continued to speak over the noise of the chains, Nancy brushed her hand against his, but he eased it away. He could still feel her touch minutes later – it felt like an invasion of his personal space, as if a work colleague had over-stepped the mark. He wasn't being fair to her. He needed to tell her.

'Look at the Royal Shakespeare Theatre,' his mother said. 'Don't you think that from this side of the river it looks like a huge cruise ship moored for the birthday celebrations?'

'I see what you mean,' Nancy replied. 'The tourists look like passengers standing on its deck leaning on the rail, gazing out over the water.'

Shit, it was all too ordinary. He must get Nancy alone and tell her.

'Let's go and listen to the steel band,' Joanne said, noting Peter's interest in the pounding sound that was reverberating from somewhere over the other side of the river.

'Can we take five?' Nancy asked and Christopher thought.

This is it.

But, the moment the family moved a few metres away, Nancy shut her eyes, allowing the sun to warm her eyelids and a huge yawn took over her face. She looked as if she'd had another bad night. As she ran her fingertips through her chestnut hair, red and orange strands danced in the sunlight and he wanted to photograph her. Rubbing her fingertips across her eyelids, she screwed up her face making the most of the yawn, which then set him off. How impossible it was to resist a yawn once someone else had started. Holding his face to the sun, he let the warmth trickle down his neck and across his shoulders where he relaxed into another enormous yawn that engulfed his features.

'What the hell!'

The weight had lifted from his shoulder. Literally! For a split second, he'd thought it was the relaxation of the yawn sinking through his body because he hadn't slept well last night either, but in the next moment he grasped the strap of his bag that was now dangling free of its burden. He thought he heard Nancy shout, 'Chris?' but there wasn't time to explain. To his left, there was a crush of visitors on the ancient stone bridge and easing his way between a pushchair and a couple of teenagers, he craned his neck to see ahead in case he could identify anyone who was running. Since everyone else was walking at a slow pace due to the press of people, any movement would single out the thief. The young man with the same curly, blond hair who'd tried to snatch his bag yesterday was barging through the crowd.

Heart racing, Christopher tore past the tourists to gain ground on the man whom he could see had the bag awkwardly cradled under his left arm, slowing his progress. Charging ahead onto the narrow bridge as fast as he could without actually knocking anybody over, Christopher kept the man in sight until the thief reached the end of the bridge and disappeared. As he arrived at the point where the man had vanished, Christopher glanced to the left towards a new-looking bridge that curved over the point where the canal joined the river. To the right, people were sitting outside at Cox's Yard, enjoying the river view, but there was no movement. He couldn't see the man at all.

Racing along the path ahead which was a lot less crowded, Christopher looked around the canal basin, but he was the only one running. The path joined the pavement by the side of the gyratory and he looked ahead towards the bottom of Bridge Street, but again he couldn't make out the man. Surely, if the thief had continued up Bridge Street, which followed quite a steep incline, he'd have been easy to spot. As Christopher looked to his left along Waterside and towards the theatre, he saw the top of the man's head disappearing underneath the road bridge. Making a three-quarter turn, Christopher found himself in an underpass that had a narrow path running alongside the canal. He hadn't noticed it before – he doubted if any tourists ever would. Ducking his head, he entered the underpass, splattered with graffiti and leading away from the theatre and all things Shakespearean.

Christopher hurtled towards an elderly couple who were huddled together. They were obviously in some distress and he felt horrible not stopping, but he was sure he was close.

As he passed them, he shouted, 'did a blond man come running this way?'

'Yes, he ran into the back of the pub car park here. Almost knocked us flying.'

Skidding to a halt on the dead fir needles that littered the canal path, Christopher peeped into the car park. There he was. The bastard! He had his back to Christopher and, having emptied the bag's contents onto the tarmac, was bending down to pick up the diary. Christopher pushed the man as hard as he could. He'd never actually been in a fight before, but he'd be damned if he'd let this git take the diary and wreck Nancy's plans for a book. Shouting out, the man lost his balance. Christopher let go and used his foot to push the man right over. He sprawled forwards onto the ground, but managed to kick out, landing his boot on the diary, digging into the leather cover. Christopher took hold of the side of the diary and wrestled it from underneath the toe of the boot.

And then something caught the side of his head. At this point, Christopher's legs went from under him. Putting his hands out behind him to stop himself from banging his head, which was by now thumping, he sat down heavily on the path. The diary cut into his left palm, fir tree needles and gravel pricked his right and the dust that he'd scuffed up, peppered his face. Keeping his mouth shut to stop the rising nausea, he took short, sharp breaths through his nose, but it made him feel lightheaded. He didn't dare open his eyes as the earth seemed to be turning.

A bony hand grasped his shoulder and shook it as if trying to wake him.

'Sonny, are you all right?'

'Mmm,' was all he could manage with his mouth closed.

'It's all right, Mavis, he's gone.'

'What shall we do?'

'You all right, son? What was all that about then? Did he hit you?'

Christopher peeped through a filter of eyelashes and the world seemed to have slowed down a little. Letting the white haze settle before he dared open them fully, he saw a wrinkled old face too close to his and he jerked his head away as if in disgust. His mouth didn't even seem able to form a smile, let alone words.

'Don't you worry, my dear, my husband will go into the pub and get them to call the police. They'll sort it out.'

'Please...don't.'

Christopher's sharp tone was not at all what he wished to use to this couple, but his jaw seemed set and it was all he could manage to say.

'I think he's hurt.'

At least he didn't have to speak this time. A slow shake of the head would do.

'Alf, you go and get someone from the pub to help him up.'

'No! Stay. Be all right in a minute... thank you.'

Using up all the breath he had left in him, Christopher's words came out in a rush through pursed lips. Easing his hand off the diary, he almost shouted out as his left shoulder dropped a few centimetres. He'd been so intent on keeping hold of the diary, that he'd not noticed the awkward position he'd been sitting in. Trying to move his hands to sit a little less stiffly, he found he could hardly move his left arm.

'Fine, fine,' was all he could mutter through gritted teeth before he managed a grimace to prove to the elderly couple that he wasn't seriously injured.

Gingerly rolling his shoulders, he moved onto his right side so that he could crouch on his hands and knees and raise one knee in a bizarre movement that looked as if he were about to propose to the couple. Pushing heavily on his knee, he straightened up, more to show the woman that he didn't need help than because he was ready to move. He hadn't even managed to keep the diary safe as he'd promised Nancy. The corner of the spine had separated a little from the cover, revealing the edges of the pages and there was a sharp indentation where the leather had given way under the heel of the man's boot.

'Here's your bag, son. You did well. He didn't even take your camera, but this doesn't look too clever I'm afraid,' the man said, showing Christopher the broken screen of his phone.

'Thanks.'

Jabbing at the glass, 'Nancy,' was all he managed to say

when she answered.

'Chris! Where the hell are you? Are you okay? God, Chris, I was so scared!'

Her concern shocked some life into him.

'Nancy, Nancy...it's okay...Listen. The man cut the strap of my bag, but, listen...it's okay, I've still got the diary.'

'I can't believe it. Where are you?'

'No. I'll come to you,' he said, wanting to distance himself from what had just happened.

An hour later, they were sitting in Nash's garden with a new bag he'd put on his credit card. Christopher hadn't quite told Nancy the truth about the attack. He'd not exactly lied – rather he'd left out the bit about being hit. Before he met her, he'd cleaned up the wound on the side of his head in the pub toilets and had smoothed his hair so it didn't show. He'd felt a bit of an idiot not being able to describe the man's face, but she'd been so glad he was okay that she didn't pursue it. She'd promised not to breathe a word of it to his family when they asked where on earth they'd been. But, no one mentioned it. Embarrassment had its place, after all.

Bridget had insisted they visit the mulberry tree that was said, she informed them, to be a descendant of the one that the Reverend Gastrell had cut down in the seventeen-fifties. Madeleine looked up.

'Is he a relative too?'

'I don't know. We haven't traced our family back that far yet.'

'Well, I don't want him to be my great-great whatever because he cut down the mulberry tree,' she shouted.

'I'm sure he's nothing to do with us,' Bridget added hurriedly as Madeleine pulled away from her great-aunt's hand and ran across the grass, singing at the top of her voice.

> *Here we go round the mulberry bush,*
> *The mulberry bush,*
> *The mulberry bush.*
> *Here we go round the mulberry bush*
> *Early in the morning.*
> *This is the way we wash our face,*
> *Wash our face,*
> *Wash our face.*
> *This is the way we wash our face*
> *Early in the morning.*

And on she went through three more verses.

'I didn't think she'd know the rhyme,' Bridget observed.

'They teach them all the old ones now Auntie, complete with actions,' Joanne replied as Madeleine came hurtling towards them.

'Mum, let's play hide and seek! I'm on.'

As they scattered to hide, Nancy and Christopher made for a bench that was positioned deep inside a hedge that had been pruned to afford only a narrow view of the garden.

'What I don't understand, is why they'd go to so much trouble to get the actual diary when they must have realised I've already photographed every page,' she said as soon as they were out of sight.

'What if it's not about stopping you using the diary? Perhaps they need to check something in it and there'd be no point stealing your laptop to read the diary because it's password protected. The diary itself is accessible to anyone once they've got hold of it.'

'You mean there might be something controversial in the

diary? But, it's so old. Everyone in the diary died a hundred years ago. What could be so important? And if they do find something? What then? Will they want to stop me using the diary?'

'I don't know.'

'Well they can think again. Nothing's going to stop me now. I've just completed the latest chapter of my thesis, thank goodness, so I can spare some time to continue my transcription. I got as far as Patrick Drew's party on April 23rd. It was so weird. Do you remember, I got to where Robert told Anne never to speak of Percy's death and yet according to the papers of the day, he didn't die until weeks later on May 9th?'

'Yeah...About the diary. I'm sorry, but it got damaged in the fight.'

As they leant forwards to look at the injured diary, he caught sight of Madeleine who ran towards them shouting, 'Mum, Mum, I've found them!'

Launching herself onto Christopher's lap, Madeleine threw her arms around his neck.

'Caught you!' she said, trying to pull him to his feet.

'We'll be with you in a moment,' he replied, seeing that Nancy hadn't moved.

'What do you think? Is this all linked to Dr Morrell's interest in the diary?' she asked.

'I think it could be. It's hard to believe a lecturer would get involved in such a thing though.'

'Don't fool yourself! Haven't you heard of intellectual property theft?'

CHAPTER 40

Present day: Saturday 24 April 7pm

That evening, the Royal Shakespeare Theatre had transformed itself from the cruise ship of the afternoon to a utilitarian building, almost a factory, Christopher thought. He wished he hadn't changed from jeans to trousers as the more formal clothing, together with his freshly shaved face, now made him look like he was about to conduct a business meeting. But, when he'd seen his mother emerge from the bedroom in a dress and his father in a suit, complete with a tie, it'd felt churlish not to.

Walking through the sliding glass doors of the entrance, they joined the crush in the foyer and he was happy to give in to Madeleine's pleas to pick her up. Nestling her face against his, she wrapped her arms so tightly around his neck that he could have done with loosening them a little, but he was enjoying it too much to want to disturb her.

Myriad voices criss-crossed in front of him and hands pointed in all directions, confusion written on the faces of their owners. But, it was the unexpected elbow in his back or accidental push that made him squirm. Looking at every blond male who even remotely resembled the slightly built young thief, Christopher stared at a man who'd crouched down to tie his shoelace. Catching Christopher unawares by standing up more quickly than he'd expected, the man reflected his stare before he turned to his companion, whispering furiously and darting irritated looks in his direction. Christopher seriously hoped there weren't any cameras in the foyer because if anything were to happen, his suspicious behaviour would surely warrant notice. But what could possibly happen here at a performance of *Romeo and Juliet* in the Royal Shakespeare Theatre in Stratford-upon-Avon?

Taking their seats in the front row of the stalls, Christopher turned around to scan the area at the back of the upper circle where Nancy had said she'd be standing with one of her friends. She'd come down to the front of the upper circle and was waving enthusiastically. He felt a little ridiculous, holding up his hand – as if he were a celebrity in the posh seats obliged to acknowledge a fan – and he was almost grateful to hear his mother's voice hissing his name. Wrapping the strap of his new bag around his ankle, he held it tightly between his feet. He wasn't going to let the diary go for anyone or anything.

Darkness silenced the audience who, moments ago, had been chatting, pointing, fidgeting in their seats and standing up for last minute arrivals and Christopher slouched in his seat, aware that the person directly behind him would be cursing their terrible luck to be sitting behind one of the tallest people in the auditorium. Every little detail of the actors' faces was clearly visible and he hoped he didn't sneeze or feel like yawning during the performance because they'd be able to see everything he did.

As the Capulet servants' threats and innuendo built in intensity, Tybalt ran onto the stage, posturing provocatively. His charismatic stage presence was obvious from the start. Dressed in a jet-black Elizabethan-style costume that matched his dark hair and goatee beard, he was looking for a fight. His short stature and youthful features belied a menacing command of the stage and, even when it was another character's turn to speak, Christopher found it difficult to tear his eyes away. There was something about him.

Christopher knew the plot of *Romeo and Juliet*, but he was thrown when Romeo arrived in trainers and a hoodie, playing the part of a tourist. Fire, candle flames and smoke were everywhere in the spectacular production. More young men dressed from head to toe in black costumes fought as if for real with swords flashing under the spots of light, but none exhibited Tybalt's powerful intensity and Christopher was almost relieved when the young Capulet wasn't on stage. Romeo and Juliet couldn't have provided a sharper contrast to Tybalt though. Juliet, who wore a simple charcoal-coloured nightdress, with arms and legs bare, looked young and vulnerable, sitting on the edge of the balcony, swinging her legs like a little girl – until she took control of the words, speaking with rising excitement in her voice. And Romeo was quite the comedian. He turned his back on Juliet and put up his hood, making him appear suitably weaker than his strong female counterpart as she set forth on her long and much-quoted speech and Christopher couldn't help but mouth the famous lines as she asked if a name was worth dying for.

What's in a name? That which we call a rose
By any other name would smell as sweet;

When the single note of a triangle signified that something wasn't quite as it should be in the play, Christopher couldn't help thinking how handy it would be in real life if you got a warning when impending danger was near. He could've done with that earlier, he reflected, touching the small lump on the side of his head. Then Romeo entered the stage on a bicycle giving Mercutio a backie and Christopher smiled at Madeleine's infectious giggle. She'd looked so concerned at the fighting that Joanne had had to whisper a reassurance that it was all pretend and Christopher had thought she might ask to leave. On the other hand, as soon as the fighting had stopped, Peter had slumped back in his seat, huffing and muttering about how boring it all was, only to sit back up when Romeo stepped in between his friend, Mercutio and his assailant, Tybalt. The latter's aggression crackled through the auditorium and Christopher thought, despite his height advantage, he wouldn't like to come up against Tybalt.

After Romeo had killed Tybalt, Peter slouched back in his seat and watched half-embarrassed, half-interested as the newly married Romeo and Juliet embraced passionately on the balcony. Madeleine snuggled against her mother's arm and Christopher wondered how long it would be before Peter stopped being embarrassed and Madeleine stopped wanting to hug everyone. Three years? One year? Christopher thought of his son. He'd be starting school next year and in eight years he'd be at secondary school. It all went too quickly – as if childhood were a stage to get through as quickly as possible. As if adulthood was better. If only children knew!

The house lights were extinguished and the audience started to clap. His mother was first to speak when the lights came back up.

'What did you think of the first half, Christopher?'

'Great, thanks. I'm really enjoying it. You?'

'Yes, but I do wish they had more scenery. It's a tiny bit modern and bare for me.'

'Let's see if we can find our interval drinks,' Thomas said, as the crowds started to gather.

Scanning the bar as he received his drink from his father, Christopher could see no sign of Nancy. She'd said she'd try to come down and see him, but couldn't promise as she didn't want to push it with her friend – since she was the one who'd persuaded her mate that it would be a good idea to stand for three hours.

'Tybalt's quite mesmerising isn't he?' Joanne observed.

'It's a shame he's dead. I liked him too.'

'Dead?' Madeleine pounced on her granddad's word.

'Pretending to be dead,' Charles said quickly, in an attempt to reassure his granddaughter who looked concerned.

'It makes you wonder what the actor does for the rest of the play, doesn't it? I mean, he only has to come on again at the end to take his bow,' Thomas added.

'Well, I don't mind that he's not in it anymore,' Bridget observed. 'He scared the life out of me!'

At the announcement that *Romeo and Juliet* would recommence in five minutes, Bridget started to walk back to her seat before the voice had even finished, chivvying the rest of the family to follow suit. The auditorium lights were dimmed until the stage disappeared into the dark to return with a single spotlight illuminating Juliet who was sitting at her window, desperate for Romeo's return.

Five minutes later, a bell sounded but didn't stop.

At first, Christopher thought that it was part of the production, but a stage manager dressed all in black and carrying a clipboard walked purposefully onto the stage, dodging the actors who were still in full flight. Juliet flinched and stared at the imposter, but didn't instantly stop. Then the Nurse hastened onto the stage and almost knocked into Juliet who was by now stationary. Looking from one to the other, the actors appeared a little uncomfortable to find themselves forced to stand silently in front of a full house.

'Ladies and gentlemen, we need you to evacuate the theatre. Would you please make your way to the nearest exit.'

From silence, there emerged a tremendous buzz of anxiety and excitement as the audience took up their belongings. Christopher unwrapped the strap of his bag, but kept his eye on it as he helped his mother, father and uncle to their coats. Joanne clutched Madeleine's hand and told Peter to get a move on. Wearing the bag across his body, Christopher made sure that he could feel the corner of the diary through the leather. Taking a moment to glance towards the upper circle for a glimpse of Nancy, he could see that everyone was now standing up and he gave up any hope of seeing her. At least she'd be one of the first to leave the theatre, he reasoned. He'd have to wait until he was outside though before he could phone her. It was way too noisy to hear anything.

A crush of people made their way out of the building. Standing on the grass in bemused huddles, the audience faced the theatre as if in attendance at an outdoor performance. Nobody wanted to take their eyes off it in case they missed the first flame. Christopher saw the actors coming out of a side door and thought how out of place they looked standing outside in their costumes. Two fire-engines screeched to a halt and Madeleine grabbed her mother's arm. Peter looked more interested. Perhaps there really was a fire. Christopher phoned Nancy for the third time, but there was still no reply. Why hadn't she taken her phone off mute? When he texted her again and heard nothing, he looked accusingly at the huddles of people nearest to him. Bastard! If he ever saw that little runt again, he'd beat the living daylights out of him. His mobile rang.

'Where are you?'

'On the grass in front of the theatre, not far from the swan fountain.'

'I'll come to you.'

'No! I'll come to you. Where are you?'

'At the fountain!'

'Stay put I'll be with you in a sec.'

Barging his way past the groups of people, Christopher clenched his right fist and drew it up as if rehearsing the movement of the first punch he'd throw if the little git tried anything again. Next time, he'd be ready. A light touch on his hand was all it took. He swung out to the side in an uncontrolled attack and a hand swiped his out of the way, but not before he'd caught the person under the jaw.

'You bloody idiot, it's me. What're you trying to do?'

'Shit, Nancy, I'm sorry.'

Nancy's friend looked shocked as Christopher started to snigger. Pulling his bottom lip under his top to try to stifle the laughter, he looked over at Nancy to find that she was doing exactly the same. Throwing his head back, he shut his eyes to blink out the tears of relief. Nancy's fingertips reached for his hand, but this time he stroked the back of her palm, whispering, 'sorry' as he eased her hand to his lips, kissing it gently.

'Just as well you're a rubbish fighter.'

'Let me have a look,' he said, using his mobile as a torch to examine the underside of her chin. 'I can't see anything yet. Do you feel okay? Have you got a headache?'

'No, you idiot. You only brushed my jaw. Thank goodness I've got quick reactions! With friends like you...'

'Sorry.'

'Next time, maybe check who it is first!'

Another fire engine screamed into view as Christopher, Nancy and her friend returned to the family who, as one, looked relieved to see Nancy. Christopher received a tight hug from Madeleine who whispered to him that she thought he'd got lost in the fire.

After what felt like ages in the cold night air, but was probably only around fifteen minutes, members of theatre staff walked down the steps in front of the building. A few seconds later they were almost chased back inside by the surge of the crowd towards the main door.

'I wonder if they'll tell us what it was,' Bridget said.

Walking onto the stage, the actors stood silently in position for a few moments, before restarting the play from the beginning of the scene in which they'd been interrupted. The fast-paced performance ended with a passionate death scene that was shrouded in smoke and eerie lighting before the stage was plunged into darkness for the last time. A trickle of claps signified that the play had finished and loud applause then reverberated around the theatre. The house lights brought Romeo and Juliet back to life and they were joined by the rest of the company. When Joanne stood up to clap Tybalt, Peter looked mortified, but Madeleine happily copied her mother. Christopher glanced at the actor, only to find that he was staring fixedly back. The company turned away to bow to the audience sitting to the left of the stage and Christopher didn't see him again, but his face stayed with him for some reason.

They rejoined Nancy, whose friend had just left, and Christopher asked if he could walk her home.

'Goodnight. It was so nice to see you. What an exciting evening!' Bridget smiled.

Their goodbyes concluded with a lingering hug from Madeleine, before Christopher and Nancy were able to leave.

'Am I safe to be walked home by you? You aren't going to use your right hook again are you?'

Christopher gave Nancy the gentlest of punches.

'Aagh. Help!'

'Seriously, Nancy, I was shit-scared when you didn't reply to my calls or texts. I hate to say this, but I think we've no choice. You're going to have to stop transcribing the diary and delete any reference to it in your thesis.'

'I'm damned if I'll give way to intimidation. I'll continue my research whatever happens. What're you going to do? Will you tell your family?'

'I won't involve my family. I don't mind for me, but you…'

'There's no way I'll give up on the diary!'

They'd reached the house and as she turned on her heel and ran towards the gate, something fell from her bag. Slamming the gate behind her, it kicked back, catching her ankle and as she hobbled along the broken concrete slabs, intent on not looking back at him. Christopher bent down and saw it was the programme for *Romeo and Juliet*. Flicking through to the cast list, he looked for Tybalt. And there he was. The thief with the curly blond hair. Elliott Wimlett. Christopher's jaw dropped.

Wimlett!

The text that Nancy had received yesterday had told her to stop researching George and Percy Wimlett and Anne's diary showed that she and Robert knew that there was something suspicious about the date of Percy's death. And what was it Nancy had said about Dr Morrell? Something about his friends whose relatives had been in Stratford in 1864 at the Festival to celebrate Shakespeare's three hundredth birthday. Could he have meant the Wimletts? And Dr Morrell had said he'd had dinner with their son who was working in Stratford for a few months. Elliott Wimlett! The costume Elliott was wearing must have been quite padded because it had made him look as if he was of average build when in fact he was slim. And the dark wig and goatee beard had completely changed his appearance. They'd been a couple of metres apart at the theatre and *he* wasn't in fancy bloody dress! Elliott must have recognised him.

The gate shut in Christopher's face and he could just about make out Nancy fumbling with the key before she slammed the front door. He was left looking up at the house as if he were a burglar casing the joint; as if he didn't belong in the street. Touching the handle, razor-sharp flakes of rust stabbed his palm. Glancing up at the arch, he could see that the whole thing looked as if it were about to collapse. The gate was a good couple of metres high, but the rusting iron had expanded, pulling it partly away from the brick archway. Patched with concrete and whitewashed many years ago, the bricks were now starting to show through where they'd crumbled to a fiery dust. Bollocks! Everything was falling apart.

CHAPTER 41

The afternoon of Sunday the 24th of April 1864

Inhaling deep breaths of fresh air before having to spend hours in the Church of the Holy Trinity in attendance at the Shakespeare sermon, Robert was thankful that he had decided to take an unusual course of action: he would leave his house on foot rather than take his carriage. He had used the pedestrian entrance to his house for his night walks in the town, but it was the first time that he had contemplated using it during the hours of daylight. When sallow skin and puffy eyes had greeted him upon peering into the looking glass this morning, he had told himself that the April breeze would bring some much needed colour to his face.

He had been unable to sleep, but this time Anne Drew had been the cause. As soon as Patrick's speech of thanks to the committee had concluded the previous evening, Robert had sought Anne's company. When she showed him several street photographs, he was amazed at the correlation between her images and his observations and they had spoken at length of a shared desire to assist the poor of the town. No further mention of Percy's death had passed his lips at Patrick's party except for his plea to her not to speak to her father or sisters at the moment. He dare not involve Anne any more than he already had. But, he could see in her eyes that she could not comprehend the need for silence. It was clear that, although she would not breathe a word of it to anyone, she did not agree that Percy's death should be kept secret. He should be mourned. And so Robert had promised Anne that he would speak to Patrick.

Turning the wrought iron handle of the gate, he thought of how differently he now felt about his house. The torment of keeping the manner of Percy's death a secret had stripped him of the pride that he had once taken in its every detail. From the design of the black and terracotta pavement tiles and the red bricks of the archway, to the scroll and leaf pattern of the wrought iron gate, it had all meant so very much to him. But the bricks and mortar offered no refuge from the terrible events of Wednesday evening.

Another yawn enveloped Robert's features as he neared the church and he thought with relief of his parents' decision to excuse themselves from attendance at the morning service due to the late hour of the previous night. Approaching the lime avenue, he was gratified to see that his father's carriage had just arrived, for he had no desire to enter the church unaccompanied. Patrick was standing in the ancient porch with Rachel and Charles at his side and now was not the time to speak to him. He would wait until the end of the service.

'How was the morning?' Archibald called to his friends.

'Long,' uttered an exhausted Rachel. 'The service did not finish until two o'clock and with the afternoon service due to commence at three o'clock we have hardly had time to draw breath, let alone eat.'

'What was the message?'

'I have no notion. It was virtually inaudible. All we could hear now and again was the word Shakespeare!' Charles answered, laughing.

Patrick ushered his wife and friend to his family pew at the very front of the church, leaving Robert and his parents to make their way to the row directly behind. Smiling at Anne, who was sitting with her sisters, Robert was delighted when she returned his smile two-fold and he felt relieved that in a couple of hours' time, he would tell Patrick the truth about Percy's death.

For the whole of the sermon on man's excellency, delivered by Dr Charles Wordsworth, Lord Bishop of St Andrews, Robert had Patrick in his view. There was no escape from the man. Thankfully, the nephew of William Wordsworth had inherited some of his uncle's way with words and Robert managed to stay awake, which was more than could be said of his father who snored gently during large tracts of the service, punctuated by occasional grunts. At its conclusion, Robert placed his hand gently on his father's arm and the latter awoke saying that he had heard every word and was merely resting his eyes.

Charles, who showed none of the fatigue that had overtaken everyone else, was the first to speak.

'It amuses me that the church, the institution that in Shakespeare's time and for so long after railed against all things theatrical, now embraces the playwright. Indeed, it uses Shakespeare's works to promote its own message no less,' he beamed.

If anyone else had spoken these words, great offence

would have been taken, but from his mouth anything could be said. Charles Dickens could do no wrong.

'Am I correct in my recollection that when you were a boy, you hated going to church?' Archibald asked.

'Your memory does you service,' Charles replied, dropping his voice to a whisper. 'It was four years ago when I wrote about how violently my body was scrubbed by my nursemaid and then, once inside the church, my mind was steamed out of me by the Boanerges Boiler and his congregation!'

'Boanerges?' queried Rachel.

'It was the surname Jesus gave to James and John. It means, 'the sons of thunder'.'

'But, surely you have friends who are preachers,' Patrick observed, looking a little concerned at his friend's words in his own parish church. 'You are not against the church as a whole,' he prompted.

'Of course not. I have many friends who are preachers, but they are unaffected and reverential Christians. It's the brimstone doctrine with which I disagree.'

'What do you think of our church in Stratford?' Rachel asked.

'The church of the Holy Trinity is so very different from many of the London churches that I have come upon. You know, I decided to visit as many churches as I could every Sunday for a year.'

'What did you discover?'

'That there are too many of them! Many have but twenty in their congregation. They are dusty and smell of mould and the churches are dilapidated as well!'

Charles's laugh flew out into the huge space of the church and circled the congregation who was happy to be within sight of the famous man. Turning to face him, everyone smiled silently despite a complete lack of knowledge of what had actually been said. All were present except Philip and George who, Robert assumed, were being kept out of the public gaze as much as was possible without provoking comment. He, however, needed to have the young man in his sights. Weighed down by an anxiety that George might commit another atrocity under the pressure of lying about the death of his brother, Robert could not bring himself to join in the banter and good humour that surrounded Charles.

'Patrick, I should like to speak to you about a matter of some importance regarding the pavilion.'

'Will it not wait?'

'No, Patrick, it will not.'

Moving apart from the happy group, Robert stood at the back of the church next to the font and waited for Patrick.

'What is it, Robert?'

'I cannot continue. I need to tell you the truth about George.'

'What do you mean?'

'It did not happen in the manner in which he told us.'

'What did not happen?'

'Percy's death. It was George...it was George who killed him.'

'What are you talking about?'

'I am ashamed to say that I lied to you and to my father.'

'How do you know that George killed Percy? You were not a witness. You were at the White Lion Hotel with us.'

'There...there was a witness.'

'Who could have witnessed such an event?'

'I cannot tell you.'

'Cannot or will not, Robert?'

Robert had never before heard Patrick direct this tone towards someone of his status. Tightening like a blacksmith's clamp, Robert's chest contracted and a tingling sensation enveloped his body, leaving him feeling unsteady. Fearing that his legs might give way beneath him, he put out his hand to touch the solidity of the font, leaning against it almost in the manner of a drunkard. Perhaps Patrick could see his difficulty or perhaps he wished to quieten him in this most public of places, Robert could not be sure, but his words now appeared to be more conciliatory.

'I suspected that George might have borne some small responsibility for Percy's death due to his indulgence in alcohol, but I thought that the best way in which to support Philip, who as you know has been a great friend to our town, was to accept George's story.'

'But George was not even drunk. I smelt alcohol on his clothing but nothing on his breath,' Robert replied.

'What do you mean?'

'That George killed Percy deliberately when he was sober.'

'That is not possible. They were inseparable.'

'But, the witness...'

'We need to protect Philip. What would it do to him if he suspected that one son killed another? Who is this witness?'

'He...'

'Yes.'

'A mere child.'

'Describe him.'

'It was black as pitch in the alley. I never saw his face.'

'No doubt he lives nearby. We will go this evening and you can point him out to me. He will be bound to be outside. They do not even care enough about their own to keep them safely inside.'

'I am sure I shall not be able to find him.'

'Well, you will try. You are as deeply involved in this matter as I am and as your own father is. Remember your family name. What would this do to your father if people knew that he was tangled up in Percy's death?'

Night prowled around Robert and Patrick as they entered Ely Court in search of the older man's prey. Robert had never expected to return to the alley, but here he was a scant four days later, and to his horror he saw Samuel Brown straight away amongst a group of children who were huddled together in the far corner of the alley. Tilting his hat deep over his forehead to shield his own face from the child, Robert took a step behind Patrick.

'Can you see the boy?'

'No, he is not here,' Robert answered a little too quickly.

'You there, approach,' Patrick commanded a tall, scruffy boy. 'Ask the others if any of them saw two young gentlemen four days ago on Wednesday evening. They were attacked here in this alley.'

*

Samuel was very frightened. He'd not told any of the other boys that he'd seen one toff kill another and he knew he'd receive a serious kicking for keeping such a lucrative secret from them. He peeped at the younger man when he raised his head. It was Mr Gastrell. Looking into his eyes, Samuel saw him put up his hand and shake his head behind the back of the older man, before crossing his mouth with his finger.

*

Robert could not be certain if Patrick had seen anything out of the corner of his eye. Had he noticed his gesticulation to the boy? If he were to give him a substantial amount of money to keep quiet, it would change the boy's life and that of his family, but, Patrick's tone, when he had mentioned a witness, betrayed a less benevolent attitude towards the child. What would he do?

CHAPTER 42

The morning of Monday the 25th of April 1864

The morning light pushed its way between Robert's lashes and prised open his eyes. The blessed relief of sleep vanished, jolting him back to full consciousness and he thought of last night in Ely Court. The older boy had returned to Patrick to report that no one had seen the two young gentlemen. Patrick had insisted that Robert should look through Rachel's school book of photographs in case he could identify the witness. Setting his features as if his face were carved out of stone in the hope that he would not betray a muscle of movement when Anne's image of Samuel presented itself, Robert looked steadily at each photograph. He had only ever considered that a photograph could serve as a reminder of a memorable moment in one's life, he had never before entertained the thought that it could be used in evidence against a person.

As soon as Patrick had returned him home last night, Robert recalled how he had rushed upstairs, thrown his clothes on the floor and changed into the disguise that

Charles had given him in London. He had to check that Patrick had not doubled back to the alley and...he did not know quite what he thought Patrick might do, only that he must keep watch over Samuel. Staying in the shadows of the alley last night until Samuel and the other children had been called into their houses to sleep, Robert had returned home where, to his great surprise and shame, he had fallen asleep as soon as his head sank into the pillow. The boy would surely be safe inside, he had reasoned. No one could remove him undetected from under the nose of his several brothers. Perhaps Patrick had been satisfied that the witness was too insignificant to be pursued after all, he had told himself.

But, it had been almost eight hours since he had seen Samuel and he needed proof that the boy had survived the night. Pulling his bedroom curtains roughly apart, he surveyed the street and saw the small figure and it was all he could do to stop himself from pushing up the sash window and declaring for everyone to hear how it gladdened his heart to know that the child was safe. He could not continue in this manner. He had brought danger to Samuel and there was no one else to protect him. Confining himself to holding up his hand in the hope that the boy would understand the mute instruction to stay where he was, Robert pulled on his crumpled clothes, tip-toed downstairs determined not to disturb Mrs Sellers and eased his hat and coat from the stand. Conscious that little passed the attention of his housekeeper, he closed the front door silently behind him. Although now master of his own home, he had to keep reminding himself that it was not his alone.

'It is imperative that you hide. Do you understand? You must hide.'

What a ridiculous sentiment he thought even as the words

tumbled out of his mouth. Where on earth did he expect the boy to hide? Samuel's face echoed Robert's thoughts and he found himself speaking.

'I shall hide you in my house. Wait here. I will return in ten minutes. I will give you money if you wait here. Do you understand?'

This time, Samuel nodded his head. Robert walked up the path without so much as a hint of a notion as to what he might say to Mrs Sellers to persuade her to leave the house so that he could smuggle the boy inside undetected. Smuggle. The word's connotations of wrong-doing, of breaking the law flew around in his head pecking at his resolve as he placed his hand half-heartedly on the front door. Giving way instantly, it resulted in an ungainly, rushed entrance into the middle of his hallway.

'Mr Gastrell, you gave me quite a start. I didn't hear you leave the house, sir. I was on my way out to the market, but I will serve your breakfast first. May I take your hat and coat?'

'Thank you Mrs Sellers, but please do not concern yourself with my breakfast. Please continue on your way out,' he said, unable to believe his good fortune, for he would not now have to put his deception into words.

Waiting a few long minutes after the door had closed behind his housekeeper, Robert rejoined Samuel, instructing him to walk around to the side of the house whilst he entered through the front door as if nothing unusual were in progress. The boy followed Robert upstairs and into the private sitting room that adjoined his bedroom. Looking around open-mouthed, he refused to sit when requested until Robert placed a coin on the table and gestured once more towards the chair. Telling the boy that he would return in a couple of minutes, Robert retraced his steps downstairs to leave a note on the hall table to inform Mrs Sellers that he had become unwell. He would remain in his private quarters undisturbed in order to recover sufficiently to attend that evening's performance of *The Comedy of Errors* and *Romeo and Juliet*. His meals were to be left outside his door at the times specified and he would eat in his sitting room.

Upon Robert's return upstairs, Samuel scrambled out of the chair as if he had been caught stealing and scurried into the far corner of the room where he squeezed himself down beside a chest of drawers in a space that did not seem big enough to accommodate a human. Robert had never before dealt with a small boy. Occasionally Benjamin had been presented to him during a party, but he had never actually spoken, as such, to Patrick and Rachel's son. As Robert stood over Samuel, the boy curled up into a tight ball, hiding his face and putting his hands over his head. Realising that he was towering over this small child as if he were about to hit him, Robert crouched down and whispered.

'Please do not be frightened. I will pay you.'

The moment the words left his mouth, Robert turned away in disgust at himself. Was this all that he could think of to say to the boy? A fly irritated the hairs on the back of his hand and he flicked it off in annoyance. The boy whimpered and he realised that Samuel's fingers had reached out to touch him. The boy trusted him. But how to keep Samuel safe this evening whilst he was in attendance at the pavilion?

CHAPTER 43

The evening of Monday the 25th of April 1864

Anne and Rachel were discussing Charles Dickens when the former noticed that her mother-in-law was finding it difficult to maintain her full attention. Casting a glance in the direction of Rachel's gaze, she saw that Robert had entered the pavilion and was making a beeline for them. She was desperate to know how Patrick had reacted to Robert's words at the church. He had not told her anything of what he would say to Patrick, only that he would talk to him about Percy and she longed to ask him the outcome of the discussion, but whilst they were in company, nothing of any significance could pass between them.

'Good evening ladies. Are you looking forward to the performances this evening?'

'Immensely…' Anne replied, thankful for even this small crumb of communication, but Rachel interrupted her before she could continue.

'We were discussing the conversation that I had with

Charles this morning, before Anne photographed him.'

'I should like to hear about the photograph,' Robert said, much to Rachel's irritation as she had been about to tell him every word that had passed between her and Charles in the five minutes that she had spent in his company.

'Charles told me that it was the first time that he had been photographed by a lady and he quite forgot that he had to remain motionless. I had to ask him more than once to keep still.'

The understatement of her words caused a faint smile to cross Anne's face. She had asked Charles more times than she cared to admit to refrain from moving, but he would not stop asking her questions about photography and telling her that he would be honoured if he were ever in a position to assist her in the future. They had talked for well over an hour about everything from theatre to foreign travel.

'I am not surprised that Charles wished to be photographed by you. Your skill, if I may say so, is obvious to all and I dearly look forward to viewing the result.'

Anne was about to thank Robert for his words of support when his features dropped as if he were a marionette whose string had been roughly pulled.

'Patrick, I wondered where you were,' Rachel chided.

'Do not worry, I am never far away,' he replied, his eyes resting on Robert.

Shivering despite the warmth of the pavilion, Anne turned to follow Patrick who seemed intent on ushering them with some haste to their box, but not before she had brushed the back of her gloved hand against Robert's. She watched as he ran his fingertips over his hand on the very spot that they had touched and imagined that it was her hand that was in receipt of such loving attention.

Frustration inhabited every nerve in her body at being in such close proximity to Robert without being able to speak to him. Due to Rachel's insistence that Anne should sit beside her, even though seating for the committee had been allocated on a strictly hierarchical basis for the evening's performances, she was seated directly in front of Robert. They were within two yards of one another and she could not even turn her head towards him without causing comment. How these silly rules of etiquette irritated her as they never had before. Why should a man and a woman not speak to one another whenever they wished?

But the brightly lit auditorium, that would remain so throughout the performance, would mean that the audience would be on display at least as much, if not more, than any actor upon the stage. Half of the audience would be watching the play, but she knew that the other half would be watching the audience; Philip, as the theatre manager and Robert, as the architect would both be subjected to particular scrutiny and any deviation from the normal rules of social interaction would be certain to be seen.

'I know that we are all grateful to Philip for allowing his company to perform *The Comedy of Errors* and *Romeo and Juliet* tonight in place of *Hamlet*, but I still find it difficult to accept that the comedy will be played before the tragedy. The audience should be laughing not crying when they leave the performance,' Rachel whispered.

'I agree that it is disconcerting, but we must keep in mind that there was no choice in the matter since some of the actors in *The Comedy of Errors* have to return early to London,' Anne replied.

'In London,' Patrick announced, cutting across his daughter-in-law's last words and silencing all conversations in the box as if he had waved Prospero's ancient staff, 'the first night of *The Comedy of Errors* was acted in the presence of the Prince and Princess of Wales. We are deeply honoured in Stratford-upon-Avon that our first night is to be graced by that very same play,' he concluded with a nod to Philip as proceedings began and Anne thought how odd it was that, on an occasion that should be entirely pleasurable, her father-in-law's tone was more suggestive of a command than an observation.

Before she had time to further consider Patrick's words, a cacophony of music burst forth and gaslight streamed onto the stage to reveal a symmetrical design in which colourful houses crowded the gallery. Two identical statues dominated the centre of the stage around which traders bustled as they made their purchases from market stalls crammed full of cloths of every hue. Anne joined in the delighted gasp of the audience that turned into a low chatter as people pointed to amusing disputes that were breaking out all over the stage. Mother- and daughter-in-law were so engaged in the commotion that they did not immediately notice that the orchestra, who had been playing a fast-moving piece of music, had stopped the moment that the Duke had set foot on the stage and their excited words were left to pierce the silence, much to the amusement of everyone else and their own acute embarrassment.

The Duke and Egeon, accompanied by several attendants, processed to the front of the stage where they paused for a moment to allow their eyes to become accustomed to the brightness of the footlights. Edging slightly backwards to avoid the smoke that rose steadily from the lights, the former began to speak, but the manner in which his features were lit up from below created a ghoulish shadow on his face and Anne could not, for some reason, help imagining the actor's face replaced by her father-in-law's. Forcing herself to dismiss this disagreeable image, she tried to recall Charles's enthusiastic praise for modern theatre now that it used gaslight. In the past, he had told her, it had taken an age before the dozens of flames on huge chandeliers could be extinguished or re-lit by performers dressed as servants and it had detracted from the performance. He had paused briefly and she had been about to take the photograph when he had leapt from his seat to demonstrate the exaggerated movements of the actors that had been the custom in the dimmer light of candles and oil and she had wondered if she would ever manage to photograph him.

When he had finally returned to his seat, he had explained that nowadays the gasman could regulate the whole lighting system from his gas table. By the turning of just one tap and the lighting of one taper, a flame, whose intensity could be increased or diminished at will, would spring immediately into life, allowing the stage to be flooded with light or plunged into darkness at a moment's notice. When the flames were dimmed to concentrate the audience's attention upon Egeon's rather lengthy exposition, Anne did not fidget and begin to talk as most did. Instead, she imagined the gasman operating from behind the scenes, the hidden master of all he surveyed.

Robert, however, unlike the gasman, would be on show for all to see throughout the entire performance and Anne could only guess at how disquieting an experience it must be. To settle her nerves, she recalled Charles's expression of complete confidence in Robert's skill as an architect. Praising Robert's attention to detail, Charles had been particularly impressed by the incorporation of vents into the ceiling and walls of the pavilion to counter the oppressively hot and dry air produced by the odourless gas that gathered in the upper boxes and galleries of all theatres. Due to this innovation, the pavilion performances would not be ruined, as others often were, by audience members who coughed and waved their fans frantically. When she had played devil's advocate and observed that gas seemed to be as much of a trial as a blessing, quoting the newspapers that all too often reported the instances of actors being set alight, Charles could not disagree more strongly in the case of the pavilion, telling her to look out for the thick wire mesh that Robert had insisted would encase the gas burners. Robert's theatre design would prove a success for both actors and audience, Charles had asserted. Throwing caution to the wind, she turned around to offer a confident smile to Robert and she was delighted to see it reflected back in every one of his features.

There was only one aspect of the production that undercut the perfection of the pavilion and made Anne wince at the thought of the embarrassment that it might be causing Robert. Every time that the under-stage equipment either opened the trap door or moved the free-standing scenery that was mounted on wheeled platforms, the noise it created was so disturbing that the orchestra compensated by playing extraordinarily loudly which in turn made the audience laugh well into the next scene, much to the annoyance of the actors whose voices could not be heard. She was relieved beyond measure when the Webb brothers, who were enacting the Dromios, appeared on stage and the audience was silenced. The intensity of the gas's glare rendered small differences in their features indistinguishable and gasps could be heard at their startling similarity. As the performance progressed, applause echoed throughout the auditorium culminating in the concluding scene of the shortened performance of *The Comedy of Errors* in which the audience was thrown into loud fits of laughter at the fun and drollery of the twins.

Upon her return from the private room in which a decadence of refreshments had been served during the interval, but during which she had not once been in Robert's company, Anne observed that the gallery had now become the balcony. Richly decorated shutters had been thrown open to reveal highly arched windows surrounded by climbing roses. Huge palms in enormous terracotta pots adorned the stage and the twinned statue had been replaced by a magnificent fountain. Expectation amongst the audience was high because Juliet was to be played by a young French actress. Having successfully played at the Princess's Theatre the previous summer, she had returned to London at the commencement of April to be met with a hearty reception and now she was in Stratford-upon-Avon.

For Anne, however, it was George's role as Romeo for which she waited with increasing impatience. The play's protracted build-up to Romeo's entrance was unbearable. Would George's portrayal of such powerful emotion in the play release his own personal anguish at Percy's death and, more to the point, at maintaining his silence? Keeping her eyes peeled for the moment of George's entrance, she registered not a single word of the speeches preceding him.

And then he appeared.

She was astonished to see how well George looked as Romeo. His gentle voice and slim figure fitted the part of the melancholic philosopher to perfection and his ability to transform from youthful folly to mature contemplation enthralled the entire audience. Only those who had witnessed the rehearsal of his stage fight with Percy would have noticed that, when he fought with the actor who now replaced his brother, all the malice and danger was lost. She noticed that he looked his father right in the eye and then each one of the other men whom she had identified as keeping Percy's death a secret and all, except Robert, registered their approval immediately, as if reading from a script, with a sudden burst of applause that surprised the rest of the audience.

Anne found it difficult to concentrate on Juliet because George took command of the stage, leaving little room for her to impress. Although beautiful and fascinating to look at, she did not elicit the expected reaction. It was difficult to hear Shakespeare's lines read with a foreign accent, Anne could hear people mutter, and the audience sniggered every time she exited the stage. Since the supporting roles had been reduced to provide more prominence for the main characters, it meant that the success of the play rested squarely on George's shoulders and he appeared to relish the challenge. Apart from the balcony scene, Juliet continued to receive scant regard from the audience and George took every opportunity to move towards the front of the stage, affording Anne the chance to look closely at the young man. His face showed no signs of what had happened and she could not believe how handsome the bereaved young man looked. There was nothing to suggest any sadness in his life. George was a most accomplished actor and not even his closest intimate would have guessed that there was anything amiss, she decided.

When Rachel had told her that Philip was to use a text for *Romeo and Juliet* that was based on David Garrick's eighteenth-century adaptation, Anne was most thankful that he had not adopted Garrick's view that much of the rhyme and any material that was considered indecent, such as bawdy jokes or sexual references, must be changed or deleted. They were not children, after all. Anne's concern, however, was reserved for the ending of the play; Philip had chosen to follow Garrick's version in which Juliet awakes before the poison kills Romeo, enabling the lovers to converse in the last act. It should have added intensity and passion to the scene because the lovers realise the irony of their situation and are allowed one last taste of their marriage and future together, but in Juliet's hands this deviation from Shakespeare's text prolonged the sentimentality of the lovers' final embraces and Anne was embarrassed to hear loud tittering from certain quarters. She was quite relieved when the performance was brought to a close. Despite the omission of many scenes, it was almost midnight and a glance at Robert showed nothing but fatigue on his face.

*

Robert could hardly bear to watch Archibald, Patrick and Edmund congratulate George after the performance. The three men, he noticed, heaped as much praise on Philip as they did his son and, as intended, the jubilant voices were heard by everyone. Philip had to play every bit as important a role off stage as his son did on stage. They all did. Philip seemed to have shaken some of his sadness off to join in their joyous delight, but Robert felt his flesh crawl as he in turn had to shake George's hand, all the time aware of Patrick's unremitting gaze. It was not that Robert regretted telling Patrick that George had murdered Percy; it was his need to add weight to his words by saying that there had been a witness when Patrick had questioned him. He had endangered a child's life and that child was at this moment waiting outside the pavilion for him, entirely at his mercy.

'Patrick, I must speak to you.'

'I must warn you to think before you speak this time, Robert.'

'I already have. I do not need to be told.'

'Say what you must.'

'Last night...'

'Let me stop you there. I know the name of the boy witness. I saw him staring at you and your gesture to him. It is Samuel Brown is it not?'

'I told you that the boy was not present last night. I do not know of any Samuel Brown.'

'When I had returned you home, last night, I looked again at the photographs Anne had taken of Rachel's school children and there he was. A lot less disgustingly grubby in the photograph, but his piercing eyes gave him away.'

'I reiterate that I did not see the witness last evening. This person of whom you speak is innocent of any connection to Percy's death and if you touch him, I shall have no choice but to inform a constable.'

'I will bear it in mind, Robert. Now, if you will excuse me, you are drawing unwanted attention to me. My wife and Anne have noticed that I am absent from their company and it is time for us to depart. It has been a very long day.'

CHAPTER 44

Friday the 29th of April 1864

The previous night, when Patrick had revealed that he knew Samuel Brown was the witness, Robert had waited until his father and mother, Edmund, Philip, George and Patrick had left the pavilion before he took his own carriage. Asking his groom to drive slowly, Robert had needed to make sure that Samuel would be able to follow him and that he could keep his eye on the boy. Back at his house, Robert had changed his clothes and had pointed out a spot to Samuel where he must present himself every morning. He had then shadowed Samuel until they had arrived at Ely Court where the boy had run indoors. Robert had determined that when the boy was not in his home, he would always make sure that he had either Patrick or Samuel in his sights and in this way he would ensure his safety. This system would work during the Festival, but, afterwards, Robert would not find himself very frequently in Patrick's company. Some other plan must be contrived.

For four long days, Robert kept Samuel under close surveillance. It was not an onerous task, however; Samuel was now present every time Robert left the house and would arrive hot on the heels of his carriage at each destination since the carriage took as long on the clogged Festival streets as the boy did on foot. Due to the closure of Rachel's school for the two weeks of the celebrations, Robert surmised that Samuel's parents must have sent him out to make money in whichever way he could and he had formed the habit of dropping coins whenever the boy was watching so that he could pick them up upon his departure. Every evening, Samuel waited at Robert's destination and every night Robert waited in Ely Court until Samuel was called inside to bed. The routine seemed to suit them both.

And betweentimes, Robert saw Anne, but not once did they find themselves alone. Sonnet readings, musical interpretations of Shakespeare's songs and performances of the plays filled their every waking hour, but all he longed for was a chance to talk to her without the constraints of others' expectations for he was certain that he would be able to share his anxieties regarding Samuel with her without compromising the boy's safety. The only thing preventing him from telling Anne everything was his concern that the knowledge might endanger her.

Today was different though. Robert had been parted from both Anne and Samuel all day. The committee and their esteemed guest, Charles Dickens, had been invited to visit Charlecote House from whose park Shakespeare, it was said, had poached deer. Although the date had loomed large in Robert's mind, he had forgotten to tell Samuel about the excursion that would take him out of Stratford-upon-Avon. It was not far for a carriage but too far for his young legs to follow. Robert found it impossible to keep up an appearance of jollity even in Charles's company as they returned to Stratford. Black thoughts crowded his mind like rain clouds piling in to whip up a storm. It took all of his mental strength to keep them at bay by telling himself that, since he had been in Patrick's company all day, Samuel must be safe. He could not imagine that Patrick would involve anybody else in the secret now that he knew the terrible truth that George had murdered Percy.

Feigning a slight headache in order to decline his invitation to the Drews' house for a drinks party before the grand fancy dress ball, Robert returned home. Samuel was nowhere to be seen. Damnation, he had put the boy in danger and there was no one to whom he dare turn for help. Everyone whom he knew was associated with Patrick. Even Charles, who did not hail from the town, was a great friend to Patrick. It had never mattered before that his life was inextricably linked to Patrick. Until that terrible Wednesday night, it had worked to his advantage to be associated with the most significant man in Stratford-upon-Avon.

The evening swarmed around Robert as he stood at the end of his garden peering through the gate. How much time he had spent designing this house to keep himself separate from everything outside his door, creating his version of perfection inside and now all he wanted in the world was to see that a small boy was safe. He would grant Samuel until seven o'clock to show his face before he would go out into the night to seek him.

Five minutes before the appointed time, the boy appeared and Robert almost threw his status into the wind by shouting and waving like a madman. Ripping the gate open, he rushed forwards to their agreed meeting place, stopping abruptly several yards short of Samuel when the boy did not reciprocate the movement. Holding out his upturned palm, Robert cradled several coins, ashamed to realise that he seemed to have adopted the pose of his groom when he was about to feed sugar-lumps to the horses. Still the boy did not come forward. Despite nodding encouragement, flattening his palm and tilting it towards Samuel, the child frowned even more and hugged his body tighter still, an angry look flashing from his eyes. Robert could not remain standing thus. He either had to approach the boy or put the money down on the pavement. He knew that he should follow their well-established routine, but he had so desperately missed the boy's presence that he wished for a greater connection and felt a physical need to place the coin in the boy's hand.

He took one more step towards Samuel and the boy stepped backwards, his hands now placed on his hips in a defiant posture as if they were engaged in a peculiar dance. Instantly defeated, Robert stooped to place the coins on the ground before retreating to the house. If he had not known better, Robert could have sworn that Samuel was deliberately withdrawing his contact with him, as if he, Robert Gastrell, had breached a contract between them. Then it dawned on Robert. Samuel had missed him too.

CHAPTER 45

Anne's sisters had bored her for months on the important question of, 'which character should I be?' Never was there an entertainment so eagerly anticipated as the fancy dress ball. The greatest social event in their young lives, they retorted whenever she tried to moderate their enthusiasm a touch for the sake of their father's nerves.

Dorothy had changed her mind about her chosen character at least twenty times, ranging from Rosalind to Miranda and all those in between. Shakespeare had given too much choice to young women she had complained, but she and Mary were both delighted in their final selections. Juliet's pure white flowing robe pinched in with a belt showed off her tiny waist to perfection, precisely as she had hoped, and Mary, dressed as Perdita, danced happily round and round with a ring of flowers in her hair and with her skirt, embroidered with daisies, violets and primroses, billowing out behind her. The two girls had decided that it would be amusing if their father would be the friar from *Romeo and Juliet*, but when he had refused, they had settled upon old John of Gaunt.

Anne, for her part, felt liberated as Cesario, Viola's male disguise in *Twelfth Night*, and was pleased that she had resisted Rachel's attempts to dissuade her in favour of a female costume. A fancy dress ball offered an opportunity to everyone, if they so desired, to deviate a little from their observance of the social code. For this one evening, they had been given permission to speak more freely with one another, she believed, and since the ball's theme was naturally that of Shakespeare's characters, a strong case could be made for a more equal meeting between men and women, for Shakespeare wrote such powerful lines for women. If he were basing them upon his observations of the women around him, Anne surmised, it would suggest that Elizabethan ladies enjoyed a greater freedom to express themselves than their counterparts now in present times and yet both eras were ruled over by a queen. Surely life should always be better for women when there was a queen on the throne, she had written in her diary.

As for the gentlemen's costumes, Anne was thankful that the invitation had specified that the voluminous cloaks called dominoes were not to be permitted; she could not wait to see Robert who, Rachel had disclosed, would be dressed as Prospero and she did not want his costume to be covered by an uninspiring domino. She had attended fancy dress balls in which the majority of men wore the domino that, when fastened, completely covered the wearer to the ankles obscuring whatever might be worn underneath. The spectacle and fantasy of the evening was always spoilt when the men dressed in this way, as they would inevitably revert to their usual dinner party conversation which would, more often than not, exclude female company.

Tonight would be different. The gentlemen too, so her mother-in-law had revealed, had wholeheartedly embraced the chance to dress differently from their normal habiliment and Anne decided that there would be no better occasion for her to speak to Robert alone. She would also take the opportunity to observe the five men who were intent on maintaining their silence with regard to Percy's death in the hope that one of them would lower their guard and provide an answer to the question that would not leave her. What was the cause of Percy's death?

Upon her entrance into the pavilion accompanied by her sisters, Anne was ushered into the ladies' dressing room. A scene from a fairy-tale greeted them, all looking glasses, apple blossom and bouquets of spring flowers to match the gay and glittering array of dresses and Anne was pleased to note that its femininity served only to emphasize how out of place her own man's costume looked. When Dorothy and Mary were finally satisfied with the precise draping of their gowns, they entered a side room in which Burton & Son's photographic studio had been set up and it took all of Anne's effort to convince her sisters to keep still and stifle their giggles or, she had explained to them, they would resemble blurred monsters which would lead to several distressing weeks of tears and recriminations.

Head held high, she adopted the pose of the male actors whom she had photographed at the Town Hall. Placing her right foot on a low stool to better display the periwinkle-blue breeches that were buttoned and finished at the knee with a leather strap and gleaming brass buckle, she drew the matching cloak aside so that the closely fitting tunic shot through with navy and red thread would stand out on the image. Her only regret was that she had not chosen a different hat; the turban with a plume of scarlet feathers was a touch more decorative than she would have liked, but it would have to suffice. At the last moment, she placed her gloved left hand on the hilt of the stage sword that Rachel had borrowed from Philip's theatre company and shuddered to think that its previous owner might have been George or Percy and that if she were to take it out of its scabbard, congealed blood would still be present from their stage fight as Romeo and Tybalt.

Having contained their giggles for the duration of the sitting, her sisters exploded into such fits of uncontrollable laughter as they approached Rachel and Patrick, who were gracing the head of the committee's welcoming line, that she felt obliged to give Dorothy a gentle prod.

'Anne, what do you think of our fancy dress ball?' her mother-in-law asked almost as if she and Patrick had organised the whole event between just the two of them.

'The pavilion looks breathtakingly beautiful and you look magnificent as Cleopatra. Of course, you do Antony justice as well,' she added to her father-in-law.

Of all of the ladies, Anne knew that her mother-in-law had taken the most trouble over her costume. The dressmakers had initially been commissioned to make it historically accurate, but this instruction had been entirely undermined to accord with her second, which was to make it as luxurious as possible, including her own additions of a starched lace ruff and enormous puffed sleeves. Rachel had confessed that Cleopatra's attire was neither regal enough nor respectable enough for such an occasion and therefore she had adapted the costume to more closely resemble that of Queen Elizabeth I than that of the Egyptian queen. Jewels and pearls covered every inch of the bodice of gold brocade and embroidery decorated the entirety of the full crinoline. To complete the costume, eight strands of necklaces were set off by a heavy headdress of ever more dazzling gems. Resplendent as the queen of all queens, Rachel displayed her power not only over her female social inferiors, but also over every man in the room who, even if he had chosen to dress as a king, was clearly outranked.

The costumes would be a source of discussion for weeks if not months to come and Rachel had ensured that hers would be the main topic of conversation of at least half of the three hundred and sixty-eight guests and over seven hundred spectators. Messrs Simmonds and Sons, the official costumiers, had received strict instructions to ensure that they did not make any outfit that remotely resembled hers. This they duly did, but had advised her that Messrs Nathan and May would take some of the business and they could not speak for them. Over the last few months, Rachel had attempted to discover the characters chosen by everyone she knew and had let it be known that she was to be the sole representation of either queen.

'Look at all of these young ladies in their gorgeous gowns. They had hundreds of characters from whom to choose and they have simply decided to display their figures rather than to play a part,' Rachel grumbled to Anne as they made a circuit of the pavilion.

Anne noted that her mother-in-law did not include her in this description of 'young'. As a widow of twenty-two, she found she was neither young nor old. It was a blessing in some respects, but now that she had re-entered society, Anne could not help wishing that Rachel would see her more as the former than the latter. Her mother-in-law had always been most conscious of her own age and this awareness had increased to an obsession when Harold had died. She had looked forward to a new stage in her life as a grandmother when her first-born son had married. It had given her fresh purpose and she could not stop talking about her expectations of an addition to her family and then in one fell swoop it had all been taken from her. Although she still had a son in Benjamin, who was only eight when his brother died, Harold's death had, in Rachel's words, made her feel old with nothing to show for her years. Patting her mother-in-law's gloved hand, Anne whispered that no one would give these young women a second glance when she was in the room.

When Rachel excused herself to greet two latecomers, Anne cast around for Charles whose Falstaff, she had been assured, would be unmistakeable due to his insistence upon a monstrous amount of padding. He was standing with Archibald, Constance and Robert, or more correctly, Oberon, Titania, and Prospero. What a peculiar play that would make, Anne thought and could not help wondering who would be charmed by whose spell first. Charles made a wonderful Falstaff, but Robert's choice of Prospero was more difficult to understand, for the ageing manipulator did not seem to match his personality or his years. Robert had either left it too late or had no interest whatsoever in the matter of his costume. Play-acting, she decided, was most definitely not for him and she was more glad of it than she could say.

Robert's anxious face showed every emotion. Since he had spoken to Patrick last Sunday at the Church of the Holy

Trinity and then again at the pavilion after they had watched the first two plays, she had noticed that his relationship with Patrick had become increasingly strained. On one occasion, Rachel had walked away to speak to a friend, leaving the two men facing one another and they had turned hastily away without the polite acknowledgement that ought to have accompanied such a situation. More worryingly, she was aware that her father-in-law was watching Robert's every move. It was at best disconcerting, if not a touch menacing. Why did Patrick need to keep such a close eye on Robert?

She could not stand aside as an observer any longer, certain that she was that Robert needed help. She was the only woman who knew about Percy's death and tonight, for these few magical hours when men and women could speak more freely on a more equal footing, would be her only chance. She dare not speak to Robert because of Patrick's watchful eye, but she could speak to Charles. He was not included in the group of six men who were keeping Percy's death a secret and when she had photographed him on Monday, he had talked with an ease of manner that had enabled her to share thoughts with him that she had told no other person.

She had been ready to dislike Charles because of his fame as a showman, but either he had moderated his behaviour or she had overcome her prejudice. Whatever it was, she trusted the man. Henry Fox Talbot had told her at one of Rachel's parties that when taking a photograph, a close bond should form between photographer and subject for a successful image, but that it would always vanish the moment the session had finished. This was certainly not the case for her and she was willing to stake her reputation that Charles felt the same as she did. He had talked with her so affectionately that she had taken him into her confidence and spoken of her desire to continue taking street photographs. When their conversation had drawn to an end, he had shaken her hand with both of his and she had felt perfectly happy. He knew more people than anyone else in England, yet she did not doubt for a moment that he would keep every one of his words of promise to her: to help her in any way that he could in the future.

She would tell Charles about Percy's death. It surely held the key to the difficulties between Robert and Patrick. She knew that this was not what Charles had in mind when he had spoken of assisting her, but he would be leaving Stratford-upon-Avon in the next day or so and this could be the last time that she would be in his company. As the conversations became louder and the laughter more extravagant around her, Anne edged towards Charles, waiting until Robert and his parents had moved to talk to someone else.

'Please excuse me. May I speak a word with you?'

'You may speak more than one at any time with me. I like your costume. It suits you to dress as a man, but I cannot decide which of the plays has inspired you.'

'Sir, I am Cesario.'

'*Twelfth Night*. My favourite comedy!'

'You look well as Falstaff.'

'Living in Gad's Hill, there was no contest. I even eat my lunch sometimes at the Falstaff Inn, which is opposite my house, and I have decided that I would like to be buried in my local churchyard of Shorne.'

'I wish a word in private, Charles, if you please.'

'I confess that I am intrigued,' Charles admitted. 'You may think I am a hypocrite for I have professed in writing that, at my age, I now hate parties,' he said as they moved to the nearest corner, 'but the moment I received my invitation to this Shakespearean fancy dress ball amongst my dearest old friends and my newest,' and here he bowed to his companion, 'I relished the chance to dress as Falstaff. I am not expected to dance in this costume and it has given me ample opportunity to observe the comings and goings of all manner of characters and I notice that you like to do the same. Have you noticed that there is something amiss between Patrick and Robert? I had hoped to ask Rachel but she is too busy in her role as hostess.'

'Something...' she echoed.

'The Festival seems to be going according to plan. Do you know whatever is the matter between them?' he asked.

'Charles, you are an intimate of Patrick. Has he not spoken to you?' Anne ventured, relieved beyond measure that she had not had to initiate the conversation.

'Ordinarily I would have asked him outright but I did not wish to cause him any anxiety during the tercentenary.'

'If I may, I will speak frankly, Charles. I have grave concerns, not only about the two men whom you mention, but also about, please excuse me, Philip and George. Have you heard about Percy's health?'

'I believe he is in recovery, but I can see from your eyes that that is not the case.'

'I need to know that you will keep my secret,' she said, immediately regretting her ownership of the secret that had after all been foisted upon her.

'My dear Anne, I know the importance of keeping a secret. I too have a secret that not even Philip and Patrick know.'

'I cannot keep it to myself a moment longer. Robert mistakenly thought that I had overheard a conversation he was having with Edmund about Percy's...Percy's death,' she whispered, the last word barely audible.

'Death?'

'Robert took me aside to tell me I must never speak about what I had heard. Even Rachel does not know. Help me. What is going on?'

'If Percy were dead, why would they pretend he is still alive and how would George have managed to act on the stage?'

'There is more. There is a boy called Samuel Brown who attends Rachel's poor school. She told me that both Patrick and Robert have asked about him and now they hardly look at one another. Why would they be interested in him?'

'I wonder to whom I should address our questions.'

Anne allowed herself the hint of a smile at Charles's choice of the plural pronoun. The secret was no longer hers to bear alone.

'All that I know, Charles, is that a woman's enquiries will not be taken seriously. Whatever the secret may be, it will be kept within the male purview. I beg you to speak to Patrick and discover the source of the problem between them.'

'I shall speak to Patrick, my dear friend and I shall be pleased to offer my full support.'

'Will you speak to him tonight?'

'I shall do nothing to spoil the occasion. I shall choose my moment to cause least upset to my friend, but do not worry, I shall address him tomorrow.'

Until then, she would watch and wait. Waiting would be difficult, but there was a lot to be said for watching, especially at a fancy dress ball when a character had been adopted and more and more alcohol was being imbibed. Patrick was nowhere to be seen, but Philip and George were close by. Philip was performing the same role that she had witnessed at the banquet; shoulder to shoulder with George, he kept his face close to his son's and whispered furiously. She wondered if Philip would allow his son to dance with Dorothy, for it would cause such a terrible upset to her sister if he were to decline and she had to miss the dance altogether. George certainly looked well enough to dance. After his great success on stage as Romeo, he had taken on an assured manner and, strange to say, looked better than he had before his brother's death. He would surely play many more such roles in the future on the grandest of stages. What she did not understand, though, was Philip's need to keep such a close guard on his son since George did not appear to require or to desire such consideration.

A trumpet sounded the signal for the assembly to take their positions on the floor for the commencement of the dancing to the accompaniment of Messrs Coote and Tinney's quadrille band. All eyes turned to scrutinise the participants and Anne breathed a sigh of relief that she had declined to enter this first dance; two years' absence from the dance floor was a very long time. Moving behind Philip and George, whose voices had risen to compete with the music, she took advantage of the excited pandemonium.

'Never trust Archibald's word.'

'But he is one of our group. Why do you say that?'

'He was the one who told your mother that we should take no notice of her dream. Against my better judgement, I agreed with him.'

'What was the dream?'

'I am sorry to say that it concerned the death of a child.'

'You mean Percy?'

'Your mother believed that her dream was a warning that one of you was in danger and Archibald persuaded me to dismiss my own wife's fears.'

'When did mother have this dream?'

'It was at Robert's party in his new house at the beginning of January. I stand here costumed as Julius Caesar who similarly trusted a man's word rather than his wife's premonition, but he merely paid the price with his own life not his dear son's. This is a far worse punishment. I resent the relationship that Archibald enjoys with his son when I cannot even mourn for mine.'

'Father...I do not know what to say...I had no notion of your sentiments towards Archibald. You have disguised it well this far.'

'I want you to know that I hold him responsible for your brother's death. He suits his character Oberon, the master manipulator who loves to play with the humans' emotions. I can no longer keep my feelings to myself. As soon as the last event of the Festival has passed, I will separate Archibald from Robert forever so that he can share my sorrow at the loss of a son.'

A sickening fear overwhelmed Anne. Had she heard correctly? How exactly was Philip going to separate Archibald and Robert at the end of the Festival? She must alert Charles. There could be no delay. He must speak to Patrick now and break this malicious silence. Before she had an opportunity, though, a face appeared, familiar in the extreme but she was so startled out of time and place that she found she could not immediately identify him.

'May I have the pleasure of this dance? My darling girl, whatever is the matter?' and the voice of her father lifted the veil of confusion.

'My dearest father,' was all she could say in response as he cradled her hands in his.

Both widowed, they had vowed to save her first dance, since Harold's passing, for one another. To refuse to participate in the dance would draw unwanted attention from her father-in-law: the last thing that she desired to do. She must continue as if nothing were amiss. Directly ahead of Anne stood Patrick, with Rachel to his right and diagonally opposite was George, who had, after all, been permitted to partner Dorothy. Standing side by side as Romeo and Juliet, they would have looked the perfect couple if only Anne did not know the terrible secret of his brother's death that George was keeping. Mary and Edmund made up the fourth corner of the quadrille, the latter standing in place of Percy.

The sinister square sent a shiver across Anne's shoulders, but before she quite knew what was happening, her feet were propelling her forward to exchange places with her mother-in-law to stand at Patrick's side with George now to her right. Her scabbard swung against her leg and pointed first towards her father-in-law and then towards George as if it was singling out its next target. Knowing from experience the injury that the sword's blade could inflict, she moved her gloved hand, wishing that her fingers did not have to be clothed in the kid leather, imagining how powerful would be the feeling of the hilt on her bare skin. How she would love to demand an answer to her question then and there, but the moment passed all too quickly as she was obliged to change places with Mary and partner Edmund, her beloved father now to her right.

She had felt faintly ridiculous curtseying in her man's costume at the beginning of the dance, but now she embraced the ease of movement that the breeches allowed in comparison to the costumes of the other ladies. The repeated movement continued in a whirl of noise and swishing of dresses until every lady had partnered every gentleman and Anne had returned to the haven of her father's side. This brief respite lasted only a moment, however, as she once again had to take her place beside her father-in-law. Glimpsing Falstaff's bulk in one turn, she put up her hand but he was not looking in her direction and it was not until the end of the quadrille when she and her father had dispensed with the official bow of the other dancers and clasped one another in an unusual demonstration of emotion for a ball, that Anne was able to look properly for Charles. How annoyed she was with him that he would not join in the dancing. With such frequent changes of partner they would surely have come face to face and been able to exchange a few words, enough to convey the new danger that the silence surrounding Percy's death had bubbled to the surface.

As she headed towards the refreshments' room in search of Charles, Robert presented himself and only then did she remember that she had committed his name to her dance card all of those months ago. She would not tell him of Philip's threat because it might precipitate events. Instead, she would bide her time and tell Charles as she had planned. If anyone could resolve such a terrible situation, it was Charles. And only Charles. Until she could speak to him, she would pretend that nothing was wrong. At the very least, with Robert in her sights, she knew that he was safe from Philip.

With her thoughts thus entangled, Anne found herself out of position for the dance. She had had half a mind to perform a bow instead of a curtsey at the beginning, but managed to mangle the two and overbalanced, taking a couple of ungainly steps into the centre. A hand grabbed her left arm and she flung it off, remembering when her arm had been clasped in a similar manner and she had been escorted into the library at Rachel's house as if she were a criminal. She turned to see Robert remove his hand from his face where a slight red mark was visible. Ignoring the faintest of giggles that she thought she could detect from two young ladies who were standing behind them, she placed her left hand firmly on his shoulder and raised his left hand with her right to join the couples who were about to start the evening's first valse. Without the layered skirt of a crinoline to provide a physical barrier between them, they found themselves dancing closer and closer, their faces almost touching.

Despite knowing all of the steps off by heart, she felt entirely different in her man's costume, as if she should lead the dance, contrary to every lesson in which she had been carefully schooled on how to follow the man's lead. But she knew that Robert would have received the opposite instruction and to set oneself against this order would destroy the fine balance of the dance. Leaning slightly forward, Robert held his arm and shoulder rigidly, cupping his right hand firmly under her shoulder blade. She responded whenever she felt a gentle pull towards him or a subtle movement that propelled her a little away from him, to his left or right so that they moved as one. Was her role as follower less important than his? Were they equal but merely opposite? Did it matter who lead and who followed as long as they took one role each? In her breeches and tunic, she knew that she would prefer to lead and so, on the next turn, she took the lead and to her delight, he followed.

With indefatigable vigour, the lively and agile moves of the dancers became more and more exaggerated. The brilliant, gay whirl of rainbow-hued costumes and gaudy figures danced in the glow of hundreds of jets that burned inside the pavilion's zinc lantern, spilling onto the faces and costumes: a brilliant stoke of design they had all congratulated Robert upon. Having started somewhat sedately, Cesario and Prospero too now span around. The faces of Othello and Desdemona, Hamlet and Ophelia, King Lear and Macbeth passed in a blur, but Anne could see no sign of Charles's Falstaff.

CHAPTER 46

The evening of Friday the 29th of April 1864

As they swung one another around the dance floor, Robert found that the off-putting experience of dancing with a partner who was wearing a sword had entirely dissipated and he enjoyed the closeness that Anne's costume allowed. He was at first concerned when Anne pushed him away, but delighted when she pulled him towards her, all performed most delicately, but determinedly. The next time, he took the lead and so they took it in turns and somehow it worked. As the valse progressed, they did not take their eyes off one another and had even shared a smile when she commented that the red mark had disappeared from his cheek.

A shared spiral of their combined confidence led to evermore exaggerated moves and when the dance finished, they bowed to one another with great reluctance. He watched Anne look around as if searching for someone, before hurrying towards Rachel. Striding off in the opposite direction in search of Charles, he knew what he must do.

He would no longer keep the secret within the group of six. Charles was the man in whom he would entrust the truth. A moment later and Charles appeared before him. Robert could not believe his luck.

'I wish to speak to you, Charles.'

'And I to you, Robert.'

'I am sorry to say, Charles, that it is a matter of the utmost urgency.'

'Let us talk outside,' he said, taking Robert's arm.

As the cold April night blasted his face, Robert thought of Samuel. In Anne's company, he had forgotten all about the boy whom he had left outside the pavilion for the duration of the fancy dress ball. Heart beating, Robert peered into the dreary darkness, his eyes not yet accustomed to the gloom after the burning brilliance of the pavilion's lights. A pair of piercing eyes fixed themselves upon him. He held his breath, but not for fear. Samuel was safe.

'Charles, I need to speak to you about Percy.'

'And I to you about Patrick. I shall speak to Patrick tomorrow, but my close observation of him and of certain of his intimates, has led me to believe that I need to speak to you now.'

Robert was so taken aback at Charles's mention of Patrick that for a moment he did not speak, but he would not be silenced again.

'Percy is not ill...He is dead.'

The words were uttered in a monotone.

'I am very sorry to hear of the young man's death.'

'No, you do not understand. He was killed.'

He could not quite bring himself to say the word murder.

'How did he die?'

'He...he...'

Opening his mouth to form what might have been a word, Robert closed it without making a sound. Determined not to be silenced again, his second attempt crept out in a whisper.

'He was killed by George.'

'How terrible, but especially for George.'

'No...no...you do not understand. He did it on purpose. He pretended to be drunk when he was sober. I think it was because of an argument over a sweetheart. I fear for George's sanity. I strongly believe that he should be confined under the orders of a doctor.'

'My dear fellow, have you told anyone else that George killed Percy deliberately?'

'A witness to the...the murder told me and I disclosed it to Patrick. But I regret it. The truth is dangerous.'

'Why do you say that?'

'Because I believe that Patrick may harm the witness and he is only a child.'

Robert could not believe what he had just said. He, Robert Gastrell, was accusing Patrick Drew, the most prominent man in Stratford-upon-Avon of threatening to harm a child. Not only that, but he was telling one of Patrick's most trusted friends.

'I am saddened to hear that Patrick would contemplate such an action.'

'I had to threaten to involve a constable if he were to touch the child.'

'And would you actually speak to the police if he were to harm the child?'

'Yes, without a shadow of a doubt, but I believe that with your influence, you may be able to make Patrick see reason. Far from threatening a child, he should be helping the vulnerable of the town. As the largest employer, Patrick is in a position to do much to alleviate their poverty.'

'Young man, I admire your courage. I shall speak to Patrick this very evening.'

'Thank you, Charles. I shall await his response.'

*

Samuel remained amidst the sodden apple blossom that had been viciously whipped from the trees. He'd watched their carriages arrive at the pavilion hours ago: Mr Gastrell, Mrs Drew, who ran his school and her husband, his father's boss. He didn't know the other gentlemen or ladies, but he knew that the guests must all be very important. And now Mr Gastrell was talking in a most serious manner to a very fat ancient gentleman. He'd seen this old man before in Henley Street when the fireworks had half scared him to death. Moving from side to side, Samuel looked into the two men's faces, trying to work out what they were discussing from the way their lips moved and the manner of their gestures, but all that he could tell was that whatever it was, it was very serious. All of a sudden, they turned on their heels and re-entered the pavilion, but not before Mr Gastrell had nodded his head in his direction. How it warmed Samuel's heart to know that he hadn't been forgotten.

CHAPTER 47

The morning of Saturday the 30th of April 1864

Stratford-upon-Avon had reached the last day of its holiday. Like a tourist, it had enjoyed itself, stayed up late and risen early so as not to miss anything, but now it was fatigued. The flags and banners had coiled themselves around their staves as if weary of the fluttering and flapping that they had embraced so wholeheartedly throughout the Festival. The town's energy had been consumed and drained after the sustained effort of the last few months. In equal measure, it both craved a return to and feared the restoration of its quotidian routine.

His ears still ringing from the repeated applause of the committee members and invited guests at this very last meeting in the pavilion, Robert heard a call for three cheers for Patrick. Relieved to return to his seat, Robert found that his name again rang through the air followed by a further hearty cheer for Patrick. Their two names, it seemed, would forever be linked. As Patrick held up his hand so that he could begin his final speech from the pavilion, Robert wondered at the man's ability to conceal the truth; his voice, his features betrayed not a moment of doubt and more disturbingly, he looked Robert straight in the eyes as he spoke his warm words of congratulation. There was not even a hint of an outward sign of what must have been a singularly shocking exchange with Charles. Since Robert had not had the opportunity to speak to Charles, all he could do was wait to hear Patrick's true reaction. And waiting was unbearable.

*

Weighed down by the anxiety of waiting to hear from Charles, Anne recalled how, finally, last night at the ball, she had managed to speak to him regarding Philip's terrible threat against Robert's life. Charles had taken her shocking words in his stride, but had set forth immediately to find Patrick. Anne, for her part, had kept her eye on Robert the entire evening and to her great relief, Philip had shown no interest in him. Today was different though. It was the last event in the pavilion and the day which Philip had appointed as Robert's last, but the former was nowhere to be seen and neither was George. Her father-in-law had kept Charles by his side throughout the morning's festivities and Anne was sitting at some remove from the two men. The moment the speeches ended, she had determined that she would approach Charles and ask him if her father-in-law had agreed to her proposal that Philip must be detained under the supervision of a doctor.

Meanwhile, she had to listen to Patrick who was speaking of the dismantling of the pavilion, the materials and fittings of which would be sold at the auction that was booked for the next month. Although the pavilion had been a resounding success, he announced, the Festival had unbelievably lost money, mainly due to the excessive amount spent on advertising, but he, as mayor, would underwrite the deficit so that the townsfolk would not bear its burden. As all around her cheered, all Anne could think was that the town would be forever in debt to her father-in-law and all talk of a permanent theatre would stop in its tracks. What would happen to Robert whom everyone had spoken of as the man who would design the permanent theatre for the town?

Patrick had barely finished speaking when Charles left his seat with such haste that Anne found her plan to immediately engage his attention, in danger of certain failure.

*

'May I congratulate you on the magnificent success of your theatre, Robert,' Charles said, shaking his hand warmly. 'Would you mind if we take a short walk? I have something I would like to discuss.'

Robert followed silently in Charles's footsteps, but they did not leave the building. Instead, they walked a few yards before stopping.

Anne could not believe her eyes. Charles and Robert had stopped in front of her. She was expecting to speak to Charles, but not to Robert.

'Anne, would you mind joining us outside?'

Charles, Robert and Anne left the pavilion without a word passing between them.

'I have spoken to you both separately and now it is time to talk to you together.'

They listened as Charles told them about his discussions with Patrick and confirmed that Patrick would benefit the poor of Stratford-upon-Avon using some of the vast profit he made from the brewery. He would resign as mayor as soon as the improvement plan, that Robert had devised, had been set in motion. When he reassured them that Philip and George would be kept in London under the strict guidance of an expert who worked in the field of mental diseases, they shared a sigh of relief. To their surprise, he finished with a proposal of his own.

'My great fondness for France occasions me to cross the Channel perpetually. If you would both agree to accompany me to France, I would like to ask for your assistance with a secret of my own that I have felt unable to share with anyone. I believe that with your help in this most personal of matters, I should then be able to charge at *Our Mutual Friend* with new vigour.'

Opening their mouths, Robert and Anne only managed a joint, 'I...' as Charles continued.

'And as for your own professions, the time has come for you both to put your talent for photography and architecture to good use. What do you say, Robert, Anne?'

CHAPTER 48

Present day: Sunday 25 April

Christopher and Nancy had talked and talked into the night and the house, so incomplete without her, now felt as if it could be a home. When Christopher had told Nancy that it was Elliott Wimlett who'd tried to steal the diary and that Dr Morrell must have supplied him with personal information about her, she'd said they should go to the police. Arguing against it, Christopher had said that it would delay her thesis and her book and when she'd looked unconvinced, he'd said it would also upset his parents. He'd told her about David's death and of course she'd relented. It felt so good to tell her.

Together, they worded the email to Dr Morrell to say that they knew about Elliott Wimlett and that Christopher had photographic evidence of his identity. It was true up to a point – Christopher did have a snap of the back of Elliott Wimlett's head. It was hardly the conclusive evidence they made it out to be, but Dr Morrell didn't know that. If Elliott Wimlett kept away from them, they wouldn't go to the police.

As for Dr Morrell himself – Nancy would ask for a different thesis supervisor and would not mention his involvement with Elliott Wimlett if he left her to complete her thesis as she saw fit. She'd recorded all of their conversations on her cell, she'd said – that one was a complete lie. She'd finish the transcription of the diary and would use it in her thesis and they wouldn't be intimidated by Dr Morrell or Elliott Wimlett or anyone else. There was one thing they were sure of. Nobody would get their grubby little hands on the diary.

At ten fifteen, they rushed to join the rest of the family at the Town Hall where there was an exhibition of photographs from past Festivals.

'Where have you been?' Madeleine asked, running up to them.

'Well...'

'Madeleine, come over here and look at this photo,' Joanne said, smiling at Christopher and Nancy.

'Thanks,' they said together before collapsing into fits of laughter which puzzled Madeleine even more.

'While you were asleep, I transcribed the last few pages of Anne's diary,' Nancy said when Madeleine was out of earshot. 'Anne writes about their *unrelated family*.'

> *April 30th 1864 – Charles, Robert and I talked for hours today. The most shocking of news is that Percy was murdered by his brother, George. But, even as I write these words, I think that perhaps I had guessed that something along these lines had occurred.*
> *May 7th 1864 – As we had discussed with Charles, he will arrange for our houses to be used as schools until our return to Stratford-upon-Avon: mine for the instruction*

of girls and Robert's for boys.

May 11ᵗʰ 1864 – I told Paul Brook today that he may take charge of the photographic equipment that I am leaving as long as he displays my Stratford photographs under my name.

May 12ᵗʰ 1864 – We four arrived in northern France today to live for a short while as guests of Nellie and Amandine. Robert, Samuel and I are the only people who have been entrusted with the knowledge that Amandine is Charles's child and we are honoured to keep them company whenever Charles is in England. When the time comes, we will help them move to London where we will join them until our return home.

Nellie greeted us with open arms. Her delightful little girl, Amandine, who is just above three years of age, was timid at first, but after half an hour, she was running around with Samuel. Samuel – I cannot imagine what words Charles used to persuade Samuel's parents to allow us to bring their child to France, but with regular letters between them and Charles's boundless enthusiasm, I think it is the best for all. I never thought that I would write this, but perhaps it is a blessing that Samuel witnessed George's murder of Percy for now he has an opportunity of a new life. Charles insists that he will sponsor Samuel to become a doctor! He has such ideas – truly, he does not see the barriers to progress that others do.

For the time being, Charles will post our letters to our parents in England so that it will be impossible for us to be traced to France. As far as we know, Patrick, Charles and George are the only people, apart from the three of us, who know the truth that George murdered Percy. We are certain that Patrick will never breathe a word of it to anyone, but we wonder if George may feel the need to confess – I have heard of many a deathbed confession, but we will face that difficulty if it arises. Samuel's safety and happiness is our main concern, so we have decided to adopt new names and live as a family.

Meanwhile, Charles will present the finer details of our proposal to Patrick. For years, Robert's dream has been to design a permanent theatre for Stratford-upon-Avon, but now all he can think about is to design new housing for the poor of the town, starting with Ely Court – Samuel's home. We both still support, with all our hearts, the building of a theatre in the town, but it will be for someone else to design. When Charles presented my photographs and Robert's written observations to Patrick as proof of the unacceptable conditions in the town and threatened to release them to the newspapers alongside the accounts of the vast amount of money spent on the improvement of the areas visible to the dignitaries who visited the town during the Festival, Patrick agreed to set up a poor fund. He will contribute an enormous initial donation of one thousand pounds and then he will resign as Mayor.

May 15th 1864 – Charles already has workmen starting to turn one of the outbuildings into a darkroom for me whilst I reside in France.

May 18th 1864 – Alicia Dunster, Alicia Dunster, Alicia Dunster. It will take me some time to become accustomed to my new name. Each day that I write it, it becomes a little more natural to my hand, but it will take many a day for my mind to come to terms with this transformation. Robert writes Raymond Dunster as often as I write my name. Even Samuel writes Stanley now with ease.

May 31ˢᵗ 1864 – I am determined that this will be a fresh start for me. I have taken my first photograph and developed it in my new darkroom.

We are a strange, unrelated family – Alicia, Raymond and Stanley Dunster, together with Nelly and Amandine, not forgetting our perpetual visitor, Charles, but we are a family and I have never been happier.

'I made a very quick search of their adopted names and Raymond and Alicia Dunster were buried in the graveyard at Holy Trinity Church! They had several books published under these names documenting the living conditions of the poor. Christopher, there's something I need to tell you and it involves your whole family.'

'Mum, Dad, everyone, come over here. Nancy has some news about the diary that she wants to share with us all.'

'Hi. Sorry I just rushed in and didn't say anything to you. I was so excited, I needed to tell Christopher something that we've been puzzling over in the diary.'

'Hello Nancy, you've found something interesting?' Bridget asked.

'You could say that! I don't know how to tell you now. I guess I'd just better come out with it. Robert Gastrell, your relative and Anne Drew, the woman who wrote the diary, registered the birth of a son, Francis Robert Dunster in France, where they were living at the time.'

'Dunster? Not Gastrell?' Thomas queried.

'Francis reinstated the name of Gastrell.'

'Is this the Francis Robert Gastrell whom we have on the family tree as Robert's son?' Thomas wanted to confirm.

Before Nancy could reply that it was, Bridget spoke.

'So, Anne, the lady who wrote the diary, is Francis

Robert Gastrell's mother. She's your great-great-great-great-grandmother, Christopher! And Peter, come here, and Madeleine, Nancy has found your great-great-great-great-great-grandma. You've filled in one of the gaps on the family tree, Nancy. Thank you so much!' she said, touching Nancy's arm.

Thomas and Charles patted one another on the back and Peter took out one of his earphones, shrugged, but left it out. He needed to keep an eye on them all. They were behaving very strangely – all laughing and hugging one another. Disgusting!

'Where is she?' Madeleine wanted to know.

When they smiled, instead of answering her quite reasonable question, she stood in the middle of them all, folded her arms and put on her best cross face.

'Sweetie, she's the lady who wrote the very old diary. She's not still alive now, but isn't it great that she's your relative?' Joanne said, choosing her words carefully.

Madeleine, not in the least interested in someone who died ages and ages ago even if she was a great whatever grandma, blew out her cheeks and wondered why her great-Auntie Bridget was rubbing her eye and putting her arm around Nancy and smiling at Christopher.

'There's more. Francis became a successful photographer and registered a studio in London under the name Francis Robert Gastrell.'

'We know that Francis Robert Gastrell was buried in Stratford, so he must have lived here, but, wouldn't it have been difficult for Robert's son to return to the scene of George's murder of Percy?' Christopher asked to the surprise of the rest of his family.

'Murder! Who was murdered?' Peter wanted to know.

It was the first interesting thing anyone had said about the old diary.

'Well, a man called George Wimlett murdered his brother Percy and he and five other men covered up the murder,' Nancy said, not wanting to reveal that Robert Gastrell had been one of them. 'But, to return to your question, Christopher, I looked up the dates when Patrick Drew died. Guess what? Robert and Anne, or should I say, Raymond and Alicia Dunster, returned to Stratford a year after Patrick died. Francis Robert Dunster was definitely Francis Robert Gastrell.'

'So the family tree is correct?' Charles wanted to confirm.

'As far as Archibald, Robert and Francis go. There's more. I looked up Stanley Dunster. He did practise medicine in London, but I don't know if he came back to Stratford,' she said, rubbing her eyes. 'Sorry, I only caught a couple of hours' sleep.'

'Look here. There's a photo of a Dr Dunster in the exhibition. Could it be the same family? It's an unusual enough name.'

Before Christopher had a chance to reply, Nancy nudged him and they walked towards a display from the 1864 Festival.

'No way! Those are Anne's photos not Paul Brook's. She describes the actors' costumes to the very last detail in her diary. I want to rip his name off and write Anne's in its place,' she whispered to Christopher.

'Or should it be Alicia Dunster?' Christopher asked.

'No, she was Anne Drew when she took these photos in Stratford.'

'That reminds me, there's a photo in the theatre tower of George Wimlett as Romeo which has Paul Brook's name on it. I wonder if Anne took that as well.'

'I remember her describing in great detail the photos she took of all of the actors who played at the 1864 Festival, so it's definitely one of hers.'

'There's another one at the Garrick Inn with his name on. I wonder how many photos there are in the town with Paul Brook's name that were actually taken by Anne. I'm going to find them all and get them officially re-attributed. After all, we have the evidence,' he said, touching the diary through his bag. 'While you're finishing your PhD, I'm going to get a book together of Anne's photos with her descriptions of how she took them and then I'll take the same one of modern Stratford using my camera. I love the detail she gets though and I've decided to get a reproduction made of Anne's 1864 wet-plate camera, so I can experience what she describes in the diary.'

'Photos taken one hundred and fifty years apart by two members of the same family. It's a gift of an idea for a book and it sounds like you're going to be living in the house for quite some time.'

'About the house. I want you to stay living in it. That's if you want to, of course!'

Holding hands, they stood in front of the photograph that Anne Drew had described in her diary. Samuel Brown and three other boys stared back at them.

'No matter how hard you stare at their faces, they remain a mystery. It's no more than a record of a split-second in time of a whole life,' Nancy said.

'Even if you took a picture every second of every day of someone's life, you wouldn't capture any more of them,' Christopher acknowledged.

'I think the mystery of the photo is the point.'

'Could we find Amandine, do you think, now that we have a name, albeit only a first name for Charles's child?' Christopher asked.

'I don't know, but it's worth pursuing as this must be the child that everyone has assumed died in infancy. She was three years old in 1864. Has everybody got it wrong and she survived and there are descendants who have no idea who their famous relative is?'

'It makes you wonder how many people think they know their bloodlines when actually they're completely wrong. So much money and property changes hands because of it and yet how many must be unrelated. How ridiculous it seems to place so much importance on blood inheritance. For all anyone knew, your grandfather might not be your grandfather and did it matter, anyway?'

'I think it's important to be able to say where you come from, to trace your line if it's at all possible.'

'Even if it may not be one hundred per cent accurate?'

'Absolutely! We all need to belong to something don't we?' Nancy said resolutely.

Christopher sent the email he'd been keeping in draft from the moment he'd received the news.

I want to see my son.

'Nancy, there's something I need to tell you,' he said, brushing his lips against her ear.

'Christopher, that's great. You're a dad!'

'You don't mind?'

'Idiot! Of course not. It's what it's all about isn't it?'

'Mum, Dad, Uncle Charles, Joanne, Peter, Madeleine, I've got something I want to tell you all.'